Charity Shumway's *Bountiful* is as bountiful as the title suggests: A warm, compassionate look at a Mormon mother and daughter who are both navigating their way through their faith and their community. Though the general push-and-pull of the mother–daughter relationship will be familiar to most readers, Shumway's genius is the specific Mormon spin she adds. She brilliantly illuminates the ways this particular (and sometimes peculiar) faith both strengthens and strains family bonds.

Without shying away from the challenges faced by women in a male-led religion and in a conservative state like Utah, Shumway manages to excavate the inexplicable wonder of the two women's different experiences of their shared faith.

—Rosalyn Collings Eves
Author of the *Blood Rose Rebellion* trilogy
and the forthcoming *Beyond the Mapped Stars*

BOUNTIFUL

BY COMMON CONSENT PRESS is a non-profit publisher dedicated to producing affordable, high-quality books that help define and shape the Latter-day Saint experience. BCC Press publishes books that address all aspects of Mormon life. Our mission includes finding manuscripts that will contribute to the lives of thoughtful Latter-day Saints, mentoring authors and nurturing projects to completion, and distributing important books to the Mormon audience at the lowest possible cost.

BOUNTIFUL

Charity Shumway

BCC PRESS

For information contact
By Common Consent Press
4062 S. Evelyn Dr.
Salt Lake City, UT 84124-2250

Cover design: D Christian Harrison with Jon Forsyth
Book design: Andrew Heiss

www.bccpress.org
ISBN-13: 978-1-948218-31-3

10 9 8 7 6 5 4 3 2 1

For Flora Shumway,
and Larry and Mary Shumway,
with love and gratitude

Chapter 1

December 2013

Heather locked herself in the bathroom, as if she were 15 again, but she had to do something to stop herself from yelling at her mother and wait for her cheeks to stop quivering, so there you have it. Those quivering cheeks were a genetic malady. Of the five Walker children, Heather and everyone else except always-lucky Aaron suffered from it. When they were nervous, when they were angry, when the spotlight turned on them, the muscles of their cheeks twitched. It was a terrible giveaway. Sometimes you wanted to be towering with rage, but when your cheeks shook, all anyone had to do was take one look to see that far from towering, you were crumbling. Heather's mother, Nedra Walker, was the one who passed this blessed trait along, and so there they'd been, Heather and Nedra, facing off with matching wet eyes, raised voices, and cheeks atremble.

Heather had plenty of excuses. The first was a bit of righteous flint. Her mom deserved it. Heather had started off gently. She was simply sharing. Well, sharing with an agenda, but sharing nonetheless.

"So did I tell you Jerry started a blog?" Heather said. She was tearing chunks of bread for the Christmas stuffing into a giant bowl, pretending absorption in the task.

Although she tried to say Jerry's name casually, she knew her mother would perk right up at the mention. Heather and Jerry had dated their freshman year at BYU, more than a decade ago now, but her mother had always hoped they'd get back together after Jerry's mission. They hadn't. Jerry had come home from his mission, fallen into an abyss of despair, and dropped out of school. Heather thought she knew why, but it wasn't until later that a friend confirmed he'd finally come out of the closet. Jerry had eventually transferred to the University of Minnesota back home, and Heather had kept up with him a tiny bit on Facebook, but in the last few months he'd been much easier to track thanks to his new blog, chronicling his life with his new husband and their son.

"Jerry! How is he?" her mother asked enthusiastically, lifting her head from the celery she was chopping.

Her mother knew Jerry was gay. Heather wasn't going to be breaking any news there. But earlier that month a judge had struck down Utah's ban on gay marriage, triggering many an anguished letter-to-the-editor about the demise of the family, so Heather knew she was getting into it.

"He's good! He got married!" Heather said. And just to clarify before her mother could ask any confused questions, Heather added, "He and his husband are doing great!"

Silence from Nedra, but Heather thought she detected deep breaths.

Heather knew this next tidbit would really get her mother. "They're adopting a little boy. He's so cute!"

2

Nedra was back to chopping, chopping quite vigorously.

Heather and her mother weren't alone in the kitchen during this *pas de deux*. Heather's older sister Audrey was perched on a stool at the kitchen bar, supposedly doing something with green beans, but in fact answering lawyer-y emails on her phone with micro-movements of her thumbs. Audrey hovered over her screen, discreetly listening to them. Heather's younger sister Caroline was spread out at the kitchen table, rolling out pie crusts and snapping pictures of the pastry dough for her own blog. Caroline, too, kept at her labor as if the temperature in the room were not rising around her but was also obviously half-listening. The final person in the room, their oldest brother Brian, was not so subtle with his attention. Brian had been peeling a bag of potatoes over the sink, but he'd stopped peeling and fully turned to watch Heather and Nedra.

Nedra was still silent, but it was a silence growing more taut by the second.

"What's the blog called?" Caroline finally piped up, perhaps trying to be helpful, perhaps just being professionally curious.

"Mos in Love," Heather said.

Finally Nedra put her chopping knife down and looked up, frowning.

"Like Mos, for Mormons, but also Homos . . .," Heather explained with an encouraging little laugh. No one echoed her giggle, and the sudden ramrod straightness in her mother's spine piqued Heather like a scratch on the side of a matchbox. A single swipe doesn't necessarily light anything, but who ever stops at one? Heather was going to keep going and going until she got the whoosh of a flame.

3

"Well, you know Jerry had a hard time after he came out," Heather rushed on. "And he stopped going to church and all that. But I guess his husband was raised Mormon too, and after their son came into their lives they realized how much they missed church. So they went back."

Heather watched as her mother grew stiffer and stiffer, as if she were willing herself into stone.

"And they're clearly not celibate so they can't have callings or go to the temple or anything like that, but they still go to church every week, and the big thing Jerry says is that he's finally realized that God loves him exactly as he is and that his gayness is a gift, like a fundamental part of his soul." Heather's voice quavered at the end because she fully agreed with him. She loved Jerry much more now than she ever had when they'd been freshman kissing in a dormitory stair well. His blog entries were so genuine and generous, full of patience and obvious spiritual tenderness, which was amazing because Mormonism wasn't a faith that was easy on oddballs. Most people who didn't fit in found it too painful to keep that level of vulnerability.

The point of everything in Mormonism was family, family, family, a heteronormative drumbeat under every Sunday School lesson and ward barbecue and temple session. At the end of every young person's mission their Mission President sat them down for a final meeting and told them their next mission was to return home and find a worthy companion. If you passed the age of twenty-four or so and hadn't yet found your husband or wife, no one knew what to do with you. And as still-single Heather could tell you, you didn't know what to do with yourself either. Except cry, maybe? Or desperately flail about in the ice cream socials and snow-fort-making parties that virginity and culture relegated you to, all of which were fun enough when you were nineteen but which wore thin as you matured and as progressive coupling winnowed the group to leftovers and then leftovers of leftovers. And if you were (unthinkable) gay? Then you were really in trouble.

But Jerry found a way! He went to church every week and heard that he didn't fit and kept going anyway. Heather wasn't gay, but she needed to find a way to be like Jerry, to just keep going anyway.

Silence. More silence. Even though her cheeks had started their trembling, Heather just couldn't let it go. "I think he's so inspiring," she said, further goading her mother's non-responsiveness.

Nedra didn't answer for a few more seconds, and then finally, with a quiet intensity that should have been exactly what Heather predicted but that nonetheless took her aback, Nedra said, "I feel very sorry for him."

Heather's voice eked louder and skewed sharper as water sprang to her eyes. "Why? He's amazing."

Jerry, she knew, would not have approved of her tone. In fact, this whole exchange was exactly the opposite of what "Mos in Love" was all about. Jerry chronicled plenty of "hard conversations," but almost all of them ended in hugging. *This* was not headed for hugging.

Alas. Mothers, daughters—it happens. But Heather had to admit there was more to it than that. Audrey and Caroline were still discreetly ignoring the unfolding events, albeit with appalled, nervous smirks, but Brian looked at Heather with a direct and wide-eyed entreaty for her to stop. Heather looked back at Brian and saw that he was right, and all it made her want to do was push right past.

Brian, Brian, Brian. Maybe he was the one Heather was actually angry with. Only a few months out of a divorce, and he had a new girlfriend here at the house for Christmas, a new, *22-year-old* girlfriend. As in, 16 years his junior. Also, his ex-wife's human opposite. His ex-wife, Danica, a woman Brian's own age, had been (still was) tall and buxom and brusque. You looked at her and thought: community theater. She brayed when she laughed. She and Heather had never been best friends, but you had to give it to Danica, she had opinions, very loud opinions. And now the new girlfriend—some lithe little dancer child, was upstairs napping. Not even a pitch-in type. *Napping!* Every part of this girl was like a whisper, including her actual voice, which had thus far said practically nothing. (If this girl was the type of woman even her most beloved brother preferred, what chance did Heather have in the world?) With Danica's Junior Miss replacement around, Heather wanted to smash things just to prove that women were allowed to smash things.

And so she looked away from Brian and back to her mother and said, "When you say things like that, Mom, you sound like a bigot. I'm just telling you because I really don't think you're a bigot, but you should know that's how it comes across."

At this, her sister Audrey put down her phone and gave Heather a solid look of reproach. Heather registered it, but it was too late for looks of any sort to stop her.

Her mother still held the knife, the blade floating limp in mid-air, forgotten but dangerous. The pink of Nedra's lipstick pulled into a grim line and her voice quavered. "So I'm not allowed to believe things?"

"No, you're allowed to believe things," she said. "It's just that some of the things you believe might be considered offensive." Heather's face and neck had gone pale as her emotions rose, but now a splotch of red climbed from her collar and streaked up the side of her neck.

"Let me ask you, Heather, what is your big dream here?" Nedra's voice broke on the final words. She paused and gathered herself back up to continue. "For any marriage to be accepted as equal to any other marriage?"

"Yes, exactly!" Heather said, her cheeks shaking.

"I don't know how I failed to teach you about the sacredness of marriage and family," Nedra said, her cheeks shaking in return, the pretense of holding back useless at this point. "I think you'd feel differently if you were married," she said.

When you are a single, 30-year-old Mormon woman and your mother makes a reference to the sacredness of marriage and your failure to achieve it, especially when she does so with a precision mix of disappointment and accusation in her voice, you feel, quite naturally, provoked. Nedra was not trying to end this. The tilt of her chin practically begged for Heather's best shot.

Heather hadn't been prepared for so personal an assault. She looked to her sister Caroline for some relief, but found no help, only bemused alarm. Audrey gave her nothing either.

Finally Heather angrily trembled out her retort. "Maybe you should have spent a little more time teaching Brian about the sacredness of marriage and family," she said.

In the periphery of her vision, she saw Brian turn away, his whole body pivoting back toward the kitchen sink. Angry? Wounded? Hard to read from the blunt turned back, but either way Heather winced. She shouldn't have said it. She could feel everyone in the room gaping, appalled at her. Poor divorced Brian. She should have apologized that very instant. Instead, she squared her shoulders and walked out of the room, tears already dripping off her chin.

Hours later, before they all sat down to dinner, Heather found Brian and apologized.

"Back in the kitchen, I shouldn't have said what I said. I'm sorry." She said it with humble sincerity, sure of pardon to come.

Brian snorted and gave a sort of jocular, doubtful smirk.

"Really, I'm sorry," Heather repeated, a tug first of surprise and then anger. She was practically groveling. What more did he want?

"I forgive you," he said, a blurry outline of irony bracketing the words.

Did he have to sneer at her? Heather seethed through the rest of the evening, picking absently at Christmas dinner and staring out the window at the falling snow, not fluffy and beautiful, but slushy, steady and bleak.

Chapter 2

What Heather's mother didn't know was that, in fact, there was a new someone in her daughter's life, the first maybe-I-don't-have-to-be-single-forever someone in a million years.

Mormons have created a utilitarian and some might venture to say perverse institution: the singles ward. Rather than attending church with teenagers and old people and parents and babies, if you were between the ages of eighteen and thirty-one and not yet married, you had the privilege of attending church with all the other unmarried Mormons for miles around, the lot of you corralled together for find-a-mate mingling. (After thirty-one, the cut off for young single adults, good luck to you. Maybe you could go to a "mid" singles ward, for even older unmarried Mormons, but those wards were few and far between, and inevitably even stranger and sadder than your usual singles ward. Poor Brian.) Naturally, there were those who found worship mixed with sexual scanning to be a disconcerting combination, and if you were among them you could always opt out and go to a family ward, but woe unto you then, because what were your odds of meeting your eternal companion there?

In a singles ward, the chapel thrummed with need and the anxious effort to mask that need, the masking of need, after all, being essential for the functioning of polite society. But despite the effort, sometimes you felt a spike of nerves and hilarity, the room bristling like a cattle yard threatening stampede, all head tosses and nickers. Like the time a man in one of Heather's singles wards got up during Fast and Testimony Meeting and rather than bearing his testimony asked all the girls without boyfriends to raise their hands because a lot of girls he'd asked out lately had been telling him they had boyfriends, so he just wanted to see. The bishop gently tapped his elbow and whispered him down from the podium.

In moments like that, your eyes bugged out of your head, and you felt a wash of pity and embarrassment, and you laughed like crazy later, but still, you were in the congregation with the offending party, for all the same reasons he or she was there, so you had to stop laughing eventually.

Heather had gone to a singles ward at BYU, and after she graduated and moved to Salt Lake she went to a singles ward there too, and a few years later, when she moved to Baltimore for Public Health grad school, she figured she'd go to a singles ward yet again. But in Baltimore she'd showed up and taken a look around and decided she just couldn't.

The problem was math. There were always more women than men. It got worse as you aged. And more than that, Heather wanted someone she was at least mildly attracted to, someone who laughed at her jokes and vice versa. The true death knell was that she also wanted someone who was progressive. Add it all together and you had a Mormon unicorn. Oh, and of course she wanted this imaginary person to return her interest, that little problem too.

The singles ward in Baltimore was small. There were a handful of Johns Hopkins undergrads, all of them too young for her. There were a few grad students, obvious oddballs, and a couple of unremittingly earnest recent converts.

"I should try to date them," Heather had said to her sister Audrey on the phone. "I don't know why I'm so judgmental. Jesus would date them!"

"Haha," Audrey had said. "Remarks like that are probably why *they* don't want to date *you*." Audrey was a lawyer in New York and at that point had only just graduated from the singles ward scene herself. Her new husband Mike was inarguably ugly, stocky and pale with tiny eyes, a Neanderthal-ish jaw, and hair that seemed to cover half his forehead and connect directly to his caterpillar eyebrows. But he was funny and smart and Audrey had gratefully snapped him up. Heather liked him very much.

"You know what the best thing about going to a family ward is?" Audrey had said with a laugh. "Now I can go to church without curling my hair and not worry that I am putting my eternal future at risk."

Audrey wasn't the only one Heather discussed singles ward defection with. "I think I need a break, Mom," Heather had said to Nedra during one of their regular Sunday evening calls. "You don't know. Singles wards are exhausting."

"I just want you to remember there are opportunities for service wherever you are," Nedra had replied. What an exactly typical Nedra response that had been. Not exactly harsh or unsympathetic, but boy, the woman never missed a chance to remind you to stand up straight.

"Noted," Heather had drily replied.

Despite her mother's encouragement to serve where she was, Heather went ahead and ditched the singles ward and spent the next two years in a family ward. There, her calling was to play the piano for Primary music time, an adorable delight of kids singing about pioneers and Book of Mormon stories and head, shoulders, knees, and toes mixed with occasional pull-your-hair-out child wrangling. Far superior to boring adult Sunday School teacher or activity coordinator or whatever they would have called her to in the sad-sack singles ward.

Midway through her first year, revived by her time away from praying while prowling, she'd said to her mother, "I think I might have gone apostate without this." They'd laughed, her mother somewhat warily, but Heather wasn't entirely kidding. Singles wards could wear you down. Sometimes you thought, *what if I just stop?* Not even just the singles ward. All of it. That was something you could really actually think. But not really, because what then?

Growing up, Heather remembered watching movies and being baffled that all these people kept meeting and kissing and falling in love and never once did anyone of them ask the other what religion they were. Like it wouldn't come up. Which made absolutely no sense, because religion came up all the time in her life, every single day. Family prayer in the morning. Family prayer at night. Family scripture study. And that was just the unofficial stuff. Then there was the actual church activity.

There was of course church itself, a full three-hour affair every Sunday—Sacrament Meeting, Sunday School, and then

Primary for children, Young Men or Young Women for teen-agers, or Relief Society or Priesthood Meeting for adults. And you went every week. Not some occasional Easter-Christmas-summers-off laissez-faire thing. Every week. But there was the rest of the week as well.

Monday night was Family Home Evening, the official night for families to gather for their own song and prayer and lesson and treat. Tuesday or Wednesday evenings were youth activity nights. You might go as a group to an old person's house and weed their yard, or to Temple Square to look at the Christmas lights, or to your leader's house to learn embroidery. Other nights were for church sports, volleyball or basketball in the church gym. Every once in a while there were Friday dances, affairs that took place in the same gym, transformed with streamers and tables of punch and cookies.

That still wasn't the end of it. There were firesides, where you reconvened at the church on Sunday evenings to listen to a special speaker. There were ward choirs and youth choirs and regional choirs and stake choirs. There were ward temple nights, ward service projects, ward Christmas parties and summer bar-becues. There were summer camps—a week away for girls and many more trips for boys who were all part of church-sponsored Boy Scout troops. And there was Home Teaching and Visiting Teaching, once-a-month appointments where the men visited families and shared a short gospel lesson and generally checked in (Home Teaching) and where women visited women and did the same (Visiting Teaching). And there was having the mis-sionaries over for dinner. And there was making casseroles for sick people. And Relief Society Enrichment Nights and Primary Activity Days. And taking turns cleaning the church. And setting up and putting away chairs and tables for all of the above. This was not just for the zealous. This was every-Mormon-on-the-block kind of engagement. Nothing special. Just average.

Once you hit 9th grade, you also went to seminary, an hour of scripture study every morning before school if you lived outside of Utah, or an hour of "released time" during the school day if you lived in Utah, the seminary building always just across the street or the parking lot from the school, ready for you to cross over out of school property and into the church-owned mini-chapel. In college there was Institute, a similar set-up.

After you were an adult, if you were married you went to a family ward full of children and teenagers, and since Mormons had no professional clergy that meant that instead of just participating you were the one running all those activities. If you were married, you'd plan a sleigh-ride caroling party for the youth. If you were single, there was still going to be a sleigh-ride caroling party for your ward, but now it was just for you. And you had to both organize it and show up to sing.

Given all this, a partner outside the faith wasn't really an option, because what non-Mormon would want anything to do with that whole shebang? Not to mention the actual beliefs, the chastity before marriage, the ban on coffee and alcohol, the Joseph Smith story, the ongoing revelation thing. And if the faith was your family, your people, everyone you loved, what was the real alternative? Walk away into oblivion? Being back with families had made it all make sense again, or sense enough.

But there was more to Heather's time off from the singles ward than just a reconnection to generational diversity. Back in high school and college and after, when Heather was fat, she had always projected forward: *If I lose two pounds a week, then in forty weeks. . . .* Or *If I lose five pounds a week, then by the end of the summer . . .* But all the projecting had always been for naught. Until Baltimore. It was her adolescent fantasy but in real life—she'd go away and come back transformed. And she'd actually managed it.

All through the change, a misery of deprivation, she stared into mirrors for what felt like hours a day, the same way she had when she'd gone through puberty, trying to get a fix on what she actually looked like. Near the end, as her hip bones began to emerge from their covering of fat, she couldn't stop touching them, like someone nervously patting their pocket for keys. There? Check. Thin? Check. Two years of rigorous dieting, a police state of stricture, no magic whatsoever, but it seemed like it to people who hadn't seen her.

When she came home for Christmas the first year of grad school twenty pounds lighter than when she'd left, her mother said nothing, keeping to her longstanding charade that she didn't notice or care about her daughter's weight. Heather lost another thirty before her summer visit, and Nedra had commented exuberantly on what cute clothes Heather was wearing.

"It's not cute clothes, Mom. I lost fifty pounds."

"Oh!" Nedra said, as if her eyes were broken and she'd truly discerned no difference in her daughter's physical form. "Well, good for you! I just always think you're beautiful."

What a colossal eye roll Heather had given that one. Did she appreciate that her mother wanted to instill in her a positive self-regard that had nothing to do with weight? Sure. Bully for you, protofeminist Nedra! But it wasn't like Heather was actually fooled into believing her mother didn't care how she looked.

Finally, by graduation, Heather was even thinner than her goal weight, eighty-two pounds down. Nedra's only comment was to pull her aside and say, "I'm so proud of all your hard work," with a heavy emphasis on *all* that Heather inferred was meant to congratulate her on both her master's degree and her new physical form. No further discussion. A bizarre pretense in some respects. Irritating. Infuriating even. The sort of thing she could trot out as a story for friends. "I lost like a hundred pounds and my mom pretended she didn't notice." And yet, ultimately, Heather was relieved by her mother's act. It was her body, her business. A little circumspection on her mother's part was in some ways an oasis amidst the "Oh my gosh! Look at you!" exclamations of the rest of the world.

Thin Heather said goodbye to her family ward, and back in Salt Lake it was with considerable anticipation that she approached the chapel for her first day in her new singles ward. New degree, new job, new apartment, new wardrobe, new self. (Was it really possible to have a new self? She had a new shape, certainly, but hadn't all that hunger done something to her? Hunger which wasn't going anywhere because to keep her weight down she had to maintain a near constant state of emptiness?) But anticipation, yes! Because math was still an issue, certainly, but the odds just had to be better now.

Mormon churches, at least in Utah, are comfortably, remarkably interchangeable. The same Kawai grand pianos, the same oak pews, the same green hymnals, the same beige grasscloth walls, the same little plastic sacrament cups from the same silver trays. But the hot August day Heather had arrived at her new singles ward was not interchangeable with every other Sunday because there, that day, like clouds parting and a ray of light beaming down on the valley floor, was a man named Devin McIntyre, and because she was the new Heather, he looked right at her.

During the opening prayer of Sunday School, everyone else's heads bowed and eyes closed, Heather had kept her head tipped down but had opened her eyes to peek around. Across the room, Devin's head was up and his eyes wide open. He gazed at her with a wry half smile, mocking his own irreverence. Heather tried to but couldn't keep from smiling back.

He'd introduced himself over pink lemonade and cookies at the "linger longer" after church. Heather didn't actually eat her cookie; she just broke it into pieces, a way to participate in social eating without actually ingesting junk calories. In a similar vein, she took a scant two sips of her lemonade during the whole hour—another trick: keep the cup full and people won't offer you refills.

Devin had hair like a messy golden retriever's and a wild number of freckles, so many that his skin was almost more brown than white. He hunched his shoulders in a permanent stoop that undermined his lanky height, and he gave a slow, sarcastic edge to almost every statement and gesture. He was a third year med student from Fruit Heights, Utah, about fifteen minutes north of Heather's family in Bountiful.

They cracked a few weak jokes about Davis County. Our diversity is shades of blonde. Haha. They talked all about her new job at the Utah Department Of Health. She was just getting caught up on the latest possible cancer cluster in a town built on top of a defunct vanadium mine in southeastern Utah. And then they talked about his hospital rotations; he planned to go into psychiatry, but just then he was on surgery, and he'd watched a fascinating hand reconstruction that week. He took her hand in his and turned her palm face up, then named every muscle, trailing his finger around to each mound.

His touch made her eyes grow wide and her hand grow hot. The refined tickle of it, the sudden intimacy of skin on skin. Would Devin have touched the fat Heather in this way? She doubted it.

"Opponens pollicis," he said. "Flexor digiti minimi brevis."

She felt weirdly, suddenly faint. She liked him.

The week after that, Heather arrived late for church and claimed a seat in the back of the chapel, which gave her a perfect view of Devin on the fifth row, sitting next to a 19-year-old cosmetology student, a glossy brunette named Kenzlee. Devin and Kenzlee sat together every week after that, and soon enough, Kenzlee was using her acrylic nails to scratch sensual circles all over Devin's back for most of the hour-plus sacrament meeting.

That went on for a few months, until he broke up with Kenzlee (or at least that's what the ward gossip chain reported. For all Heather really knew, Kenzlee could have broken up with him). A mere two weeks later, Kenzlee's replacement, a 20-year-old personal trainer named Brecklyn, took up residence twirling the back of Devin's hair.

Heather's reaction to all of this was manifold. She felt foolish. Hadn't she and Devin hit it off? Had she been wrong about the tiny frisson of recognition? She felt unattractive. Was losing all that weight truly not enough? Why had she thought that would be some magic bullet? Fat people got married all the time, so maybe it was her face, her pores, her hair, her laugh, something about her, unchanged and unchangeable. And she felt mad. How was it that smart, funny, ambitious Mormon men like

Devin did not seem to mind dating and marrying women who were no match for them? What did they talk about? Didn't it even matter? And there was always a new crop of Kenzlees and Brecklyns, adoration sparkling in their every gaze and giggle.

"I'm such an un-Christlike snob," Heather said to Audrey. "I shouldn't think mean things about these girls. Did Jesus care about graduate degrees? Was He snide about yoga instructors? He loved yoga instructors!"

"You know I'm really into yoga, right?" Audrey said. "But anyway, I know what you mean. You don't want to judge because who says you can't be smart and still wear glitter, and maybe those girls are secret geniuses, and why does it matter anyway? But the trouble is, you're not going to date their male equivalents, so where does that leave you?"

"I'll tell you where it leaves me. Alone forever!" Heather said, pretend sobbing. At least it was good to laugh about it, or half-laugh. But then Heather's voice caught for real. "I guess I just thought it would be different now," she said.

She didn't have to explain. Audrey knew exactly what she meant. "I know, Heath. I'm sorry."

But then the miraculous occurred. On December 15th, at 8:11 p.m. Devin McIntrye called her on the telephone.

She didn't recognize the number. She let the call go to voicemail. When she heard Devin's voice in the message, her stomach plinked and churned, a surge of hormones and nerves.

She called him back, and he asked her to a play. She said sure.

It was a strange production of Medea, the doomed children played by paper plates tied to the hands of an affectless woman dressed in black. They'd snickered about it over ice cream afterward (lower calorie sorbet for her) and he hugged her on her doorstep at the end of the night.

Devin sat alone at church that week. No Brecklyn anywhere near his hair. Heather and Devin chatted after church, and later he texted and asked her to dinner. She kissed him on the cheek at the end of that date. He'd looked at her as if she were an odd-bod—*Cheek kissing? What a weirdo.* And yet he'd texted her again that very evening.

They'd given each other a little space the week of Christmas, just a couple of texts here and there. But now it was back to work and life, and this weekend Devin was coming over to her place and cooking for her. Their third date.

Heather thought about telling Nedra, but her mother's attempt to feign nonchalance was exactly the sort of thing that would stoke her anxiety, not lessen it. Instead, she texted her brother Aaron.

Two years younger than her, Aaron had trailed her through school, and yet as soon as he arrived on the scene he always instantly outpaced her socially. "You're Aaron Walker's sister, right?" she remembered people asking her. His popularity could have been irritating, but he always wore it so lightly, as if he barely noticed and as if he would have gone about his business exactly as he did regardless of the approval it garnered. Heather scrupulously labored over school projects. Aaron finished his in the hallways outside class and still earned As. Heather effort-fully memorized piano pieces. Aaron had perfect pitch and could improvise anything—name a song and he could play it. Maybe not the pinnacle of cool at every school, but among choir-loving Mormons? Tippy top of the trees. And maybe it was strange, maybe it wasn't, but Devin reminded her of Aaron. A sort of shrugging ease to both of them. You could call it entitlement, or confidence. Either way, it was an attractive quality, a tiny part of what made Devin the sort of person Heather might always have wanted to go for but never had until now.

"I need advice for being cool on a third date," she texted Aaron.

"Is this your third date ever, or your third date with this particular person?" he texted back.

"Very funny, jerkface. So no advice?"

"Don't do anything weird like cry or propose. And don't tell any stories about your exes. Oh wait, not a problem."

"Har har. How are you seriously the rudest person ever."

"You mean funniest?"

"You're uninvited to the wedding."

"Don't talk about weddings! Did I say that already?"

Aaron hadn't made jokes like this back when she was fat. At least not to her face. It felt good, a welcome to a new club.

"Okay, well, I'll tell you how it goes."

"Gross. No details. Good luck."

They had a sign-off, invented before emojis, and as far as Heather knew neither of them shared it with anyone else: ". Just one side of a quotation mark. It was supposed to be two hands giving a high five. Not cool, but they'd been doing it forever, and it carried with it the same shorthand for affection that's contained in every secret handshake. She typed it. Aaron sent it right back.

Devin, it turned out, was not the only new person in Heather's life.

Back in August, just before Heather first laid eyes on Devin, she'd spent way too much money on a Dutch Style commuter bike. Her new job as a "Health Program Specialist, Grade III," was in a building out on the west side of Salt Lake City, past the state fairgrounds, where the pioneers hadn't built much that lasted and where gas stations, fast food places, and cheap cinder block buildings like her new office building were scattered in the dry scrub like day-old confetti along a parade route. She had imagined riding her lovely bike to work every day. From the leafy streets of the Avenues on the East Side where she'd rented an apartment, she'd cruise down through the center of the city, saluting Temple Square and the orderly downtown office buildings before coasting in a lazy blur out to what she cast as the rural edge of town.

But in the months since then she'd ridden the bike to work a grand total of once. Her one ride included no sprinting, not much effort at all, and yet after she'd locked her bike up the sweat at her hairline wouldn't stop streaming. Droplets kept blooming on her upper lip. She strolled toward her office, waiting for the morning breeze to whisk away the moisture. She pressed a handkerchief to her face as if she were applying pressure to a wound. Finally, she stopped in a spot of shade where she hoped no one would see her, one scraggly tree climbing out of a weedy patch of gravel next to a twelve-foot chain link fence. She waited and waited. Four minutes passed, then eight. Still sweating. She could have gone inside, passed a few colleagues in her sweaty state, and let the air-conditioning work its magic, but she *would never.*

Back when she was fat, Heather did everything possible to avoid overheating in public. No coat on freezing winter days, workouts only in the privacy of her apartment. She imagined the things people would think if they saw her sweating, far beyond "ew, sweaty fat girl." She had hair so blonde and skin so white that she felt like a walking, talking overexposed photograph most of the time, and she conjured the meanest slurs for her sweaty self. People would think she looked like a greasy German Weisswurst or a glistening albino larva. It didn't matter that she was thin now. She did not sweat in public.

This was something Heather thought about regularly: being fat and then being thin warped you. It wasn't just that you had horribly embarrassing extra skin, like a sagging old lady before your time. It wasn't just that you knew you could be fat again if you let up even the tiniest bit. It was that you developed certain overwhelming ways of thinking. Everyone was either skinny or fat. First thought, above all else. When she walked into meetings at work, she looked around the table and thought, *fat, fat, skinny, fat*.

Most of all, though, being fat and then being thin gave you disturbing insights. You had the awful, eye-opening experience of being two different people. Heather's mother used to proclaim loudly for all the siblings to hear that "it's what's inside that counts," a bromide made all the more mortifying because it was clearly intended for Heather and no one else. Now that Heather was thin, had she wanted to endure the agony she could have sat her mother down and explained exactly how wrong she had been.

Everyone was so nice to thin you. They were happy when you walked into their stores. They smiled when they saw you strolling with an ice cream cone. They flirted with you. They complimented you. It was easy, as a thin person, to believe the world was full of nice people, that strangers were kind, that doors were always held and that geniality reigned throughout the land. But because you had also been the heavy you, you knew it wasn't so. Back then people didn't smile when you entered a room. Then, no one thought of carefree summer days when they saw you licking gelato. Flirting, when there was flirting, was rough, like dry hunks of bread torn off and flung, as if you'd ravenously gobble up these scraps. Compliments were always safe, hair or shoes or, for a daring soul, the color of a shirt or jacket. Even those were sometimes poisoned with encouragement. *You take such good care of your hair.* As if you'd get the hint and start *taking care* of the rest of yourself.

Now whenever someone told Heather she looked pretty, it created a strange echo. She couldn't help but imagine how the interaction would have gone, or wouldn't have gone, with the other version of herself. These days a sweaty Heather might make people think of fresh air and cheery athleticism, but no way did she want to find out.

And so in lieu of her dream of biking for exercise, she'd taken up walking, not all the way to work but around her neighborhood, a few miles most evenings. That was how, not long after she first met Devin, she also met Ted and Linda.

Heather noticed Linda first. Linda walked around the neighborhood every evening with a fiercely alert Doberman Pinscher, the sharp points of the dog's ears twitching and turning like satellite dishes in a frenzied search for signal. The dog's paws never seemed to settle into the sidewalk. Its whole stride was a taut tiptoe, a lunge at the ready.

The woman holding the leash was just as notable. Her slim profile matched the Doberman's, and she was a tip-toe walker too—a ha-ha owners-match-their-dogs observation—but instead of fierce, the woman looked fragile, like the dried, ribbon-tied sheaf of wheat Heather's mother hung on the front door at home every fall. After the slightest of run-ins—strong breezes, shoulder bumps—wheat-wreckage dotted the doorstep. You got the sense the woman was the same: one jostle and you'd have to sweep her up. The fact that she dressed like a scarecrow didn't help, trailing the dog up and down the Avenues in paint-spattered overalls, her long gray hair in braids. Maybe some people would see this as the epitome of graceful aging, the woman's sharp elbows and pale, un-mascaraed eyelashes exuding a praying mantis elegance, but Heather gave her makeovers in her head every time she saw her.

Heather's apartment was the front half of the first floor of a subdivided '20s era bungalow, tidy enough, but with all the signs of a rental—no flowers, multiple mailboxes, cobwebs in the porch beams, and a line of residents' semi-battered vehicles parked on the street out front.

Just down the block was a similar bungalow, though one that was clearly owned and loved. Flowering shrubs lined the broad porch, annuals bloomed in vast flowerbeds, wind chimes tinkled near the glossy purple front door. One evening the doberman woman knelt on a pad digging with a small spade at the border of the flowerbeds in front of the house, a man beside her with a shovel. The man's back was turned, but even from behind Heather noted the incongruity. With the woman's stick arms, you could almost believe a spade-full of soil was all she could lift. The man, on the other hand, was broad, not necessarily muscular but solid underneath his flannel shirt. When he turned she saw that he had a beard the color of maple syrup and perfectly round tortoiseshell glasses. The woman was alfalfa sprouts; the man was Lumber Jack breakfasts.

As Heather neared the house the man stepped and lifted a shovel of soil. Before repeating the motion he paused to say something to the woman. Heather was passing on the sidewalk directly in front of the house just then, and instead of saying whatever he'd planned to say, the man saw Heather and raised a hand in a contained but neighborly wave. Heather quickly waved back, then looked straight ahead and walked on without breaking stride.

A few nights later, the couple's garage door was open, and the roar of a tablesaw and the smell of sawdust rushed out into the golden evening. Heather strode by at a clip, glancing at the garage out of the corner of her eye. She was not surprised to see that it was the man, not the woman, at work.

Carpentry, or at least carpentry at a distance, is undeniably sexy. There's the rough, earthy wood, the hoisting of lumber, the precise and steady pressuring of boards through the saw, the planning, the measuring, the delight in building and beauty, the gentle fitting of joints, of tongues and grooves, the lavish attention to sanding, to smoothing, to finishing. The shades of Jesus do nothing to diminish this appeal. If anything they enhance it. What craft is more soulful, more manly than carpentry?

Heather looked just long enough to see broad-shouldered flannel and plastic work goggles. Not exactly eroticism incarnate. Not that she was searching for eroticism in any form! But nonetheless, she imagined the man wiping the wood clean with his hand, leaning in close, blowing the final dust away with a gentle puff of breath. She thought about it again and again.

The next week at work, Heather, who rarely strayed from her first floor desk, had a meeting upstairs. Walking down the hall toward the conference room she saw the man, her neighbor, across a bank of cubicles. At first she wasn't sure it was him at all, just a trick of imagination, but as she got closer the face behind his glasses and beard came into focus. He was standing with a forearm resting on top of the cubicle wall as he chatted with the person seated below. His brown corduroy jacket had leather elbow patches.

Heather didn't march over and put out her hand in a jolly howdy neighbor. She just slipped into her meeting. But then, a few days later, they turned up in the parking lot together at the same time, his Lexus just one spot over from her dented Civic.

He smiled, without recognition.

"I think we're neighbors," she said. "Not here in the parking lot. On 5th Ave between I and J street."

"Oh really, how funny," he said. His voice was deep and engulfing, like molasses. He put out his hand. "I'm Ted Glenner."

"Heather Walker."

They shook.

"Pleased to meet you," he said.

"Likewise."

In all this he was courteous but without real enthusiasm. You got the sense his enthusiasm was something precious he saved.

After they got into their cars, Heather followed him out of the lot, but at the corner, she turned the opposite way, as if she had some other destination, some errand, although she had nothing of the sort. She just didn't want to tail him home.

Avoid awkwardness. How did you say that in Latin? Whatever it was Heather should have had it inscribed above her door, on her flesh, on her tombstone. She was well aware of the regular and often profound inconvenience this invited into her life and the fact that most well-adjusted people would advise bucking up and braving such moments, but what trouble was it really driving out of your way a few blocks, or a few miles?

She searched the online office directory that night until she found him. Ted Glenner, Director of the Utah Department Of Health Mental Health Division. This amused her to no end. He was a perfect Paul Bunyan Freud. This was before Devin had ever asked her out, back when she was jealously pining, but she still noted: Devin, Future Psychiatrist; Ted, Mr. Mental Health. What did these attractions say about her?

She ran into Ted in the parking lot regularly after that, fall days when it was warm once the sun came up but still chilly in the morning, purple light just barely spilling over the mountains. She always parked in a far corner of the lot. This was a fat-person-turned-thin-person trick. Always park far away. The extra walking burns calories. She'd refrain from pulling her sweater tight around herself—shivering burns calories too—and take quick steps across the asphalt, and if she ran into Ted getting out of his car as she reached the near rows, she'd say hello. The interactions elicited an embarrassing adolescent flutter in her.

She exchanged pleasantries with Linda too. Evenings on the street, if they passed each other walking she and Heather would wave, say hi, and Heather would try not to look the dog too squarely in the eyes, but that was all.

Until December, the morning after Heather's first date with Devin. There'd been a snow storm overnight, two feet of accumulation on the ground and still more lightly falling at daybreak. In some cities, this would stop the world, but not Salt

Lake. Salt Lake had enough salt and plows to last through the millennium. Heather woke with her alarm, showered, dressed, didn't eat, and then, just before walking out the door, she thrust her hands into her purse to fish for her car keys. They weren't there. She checked the counters, her nightstand, her other bags. She checked her purse again. She looked in strange places like the fridge and under the bathroom sink. She checked yesterday's pants. Devin had picked her up and dropped her off for their date, so she hadn't driven since coming home from work yesterday. Had she somehow kicked her purse over and lost her keys in the weird Medea theater? She pulled the cushions off the couch, upending them with limp anger, one final effort. Nothing.

Finally, she took another key off the hook: she could at least unlock her bike. The streets had been cleared before dawn, and with that as at least a small encouragement Heather pulled on her gloves and boots and began pedaling.

She flipped slush the whole way. By the end of the first block she had a solid stripe of muck up the back of her coat, like a second spine. Cars passing, even at graciously low speeds, lobbed half-frozen gray chunks at her. Her nose ran. She sniffed, tried to wipe it with her bulky glove, and finally let it drip.

She braked down the hills of the Avenues and turned cautiously onto North Temple, worried that her tires would get away from her. But they didn't get away from her. She was wet and cold and dirty, but she was fine. Fine, that is, until she'd gone up and back down the highway overpass to the west side of town. At the bottom of the overpass, she reached a long stretch of interconnected strip mall parking lots, and thinking she'd avoid the car-tire splashes, she veered into the first lot. Maybe the pavement was uneven, maybe her tires were finally fully caked with snow, the treads completely buried. Whatever it was, this was when her wheels finally slipped. A quick and fluid descent, and then her hip and shoulder hit the pavement and she continued her slide, like a baseball player stealing into home. The bike followed her down, sliding along with her and then on top of her.

At least she hadn't crashed in front of any cars. She thought this even as she was sliding, the abrasions, or sprains, or whatever her injuries were going to be yet to be made clear. The hurt shriveled before it struck. With a dazed feeling, she pushed the bike away and sat up. She took her glove off, and her hand floated to her cheek. She wasn't sure whether she was touching slush or blood. The answer, when she pulled her fingers away, was both.

She stood up slowly and checked the rest of herself. Her whole left side was a wet skid of brown, sleety gravel. Her hip and shoulder throbbed, and they were probably good and scraped under her clothing, but her coat hadn't torn. The road burn on her cheek seemed to be her gravest injury.

Heather was still about a mile from work. She could have called someone. Not an ambulance. Her face was bleeding, hardly 911 material, so maybe her mother? But if she called her mom, what would she do? Just sit out in the cold waiting for Nedra to drive down from Davis County? The thing that probably made the most sense was at least stopping by a gas station or a fast food place and cleaning herself up, but she was almost more embarrassed to limp into a store full of strangers looking like this than she was to limp into work where at least they knew she wasn't a crazy person.

Finally, she gave her bike a check, kicked the slush and snow off the tires, and got back on. She gingerly rode the rest of the way to the office.

Faces bleed more than they should, and she spent ten minutes in the office bathroom, a wet paper towel pressed into her cheek, before it finally stopped seeping. She had a couple of Band-Aids in her purse, but the scrape was large, and she'd have to pull the adhesive off raw skin later if she tried to cover it now, so she patted her face dry and sat down at her desk, wound open to the air.

Ted passed by her cubicle that afternoon, something he almost never did.

"Good Lord!" he said.

By then, Heather's face had swollen darkly beneath the abrasion, giving her not quite a black eye, but a bruised plum of a cheek, so puffed that it squeezed her lower lid half shut.

"I'm fine," Heather said. "Really! It looks worse than it feels!"

He eyed her with real concern.

"It was a bike accident."

"You're not planning to bike home again tonight, I hope. I can give you a ride."

He said it as if it were nothing, but Heather knew it wasn't nothing. The two of them, in his car, together—that was different from saying hello in the parking lot, different from waving on the street. She could have said she had a ride. She could have made some other plan—her mom, her sister Caroline, Devin even—but she didn't.

"That's so kind of you, really. Sure, yes, thank you," she said. Whatever something this was, she said yes. That was something she'd think about later.

The sky was heavy and gray all that day, and by the time Ted stopped by Heather's cubicle to collect her, precipitation had returned, now in the form of heavy sleet. Under the awning just outside the building, Ted opened a hefty umbrella with a fine wood handle and a mechanism that whooshed and clicked loudly and satisfyingly into place. All Heather's umbrellas were rickety affairs that twisted and inverted with even moderate gusts. Ted's umbrella seemed like an extension of himself: manly, mature. Heather joined him under its protection, and together they walked to his car.

He could have thumbed the unlock button from a few feet away and let Heather let herself into the passenger side, but he walked her over and opened the door for her. The tan leather interior was spotlessly clean. Devin's car was a collection of wrappers. Her own was tidier, but certainly could have used a vacuuming. Ted's car seemed a manifestation of personal mastery and self-possession. Uptight? That might be someone's word for it. Alluring, that was Heather's.

The radio turned on with the ignition, but Ted reached over and flipped the knob off. She glanced quickly at his left hand on the wheel. Not that she was looking for a wedding ring—she'd already assumed he was married—but there one was, definitively.

There was also a travel coffee mug in his cup holder. So, he wasn't Mormon. She'd already assumed as much—the beard for one; the lack of children too, and certainly the way he'd said "Good Lord" that morning. Mormons were scrupulous

32

avoiders of taking the Lord's name in vain. Maybe you'd get a jokey "damn" or an angry "shit" but never an OMG, except typed, and that was for oh my gosh, sometimes even spelled out OMGosh. Most of the time, you knew right away when you moved someplace new who was Mormon and who wasn't. You went to church the first week, and you saw who from your street was there, or you saw someone mowing his lawn in a tank top on Sunday, or smoking. Easy giveaways. But the singles ward meant Heather didn't go to church with the families on her street, and so she'd kept open the possibility in her mind that Ted and Linda were just the sort of off-beat Mormons who really loved NPR. But no, non-members it was. Coffee was definitive.

"That's the button for the seat heaters, if you're cold," Ted said, gesturing to the console.

The windshield wipers droned a soothing rhythm. The defrost fans huffed gently at the windows. The whole car felt to Heather like a remarkable cocoon.

They made their way through all the normal chit-chat. He'd been at the UDOH for seven years. Before that he'd been a therapist in private practice. He and Linda had lived in their house for twelve years. They were originally from Washington state. Their dog's name was Hoover.

Heather told him she'd been working at the UDOH for five months, that she was new to the Avenues but grew up just north in Bountiful. Her parents were still there, her grandfather too. She was one of five children. Her younger sister lived in Salt Lake, but everyone else was spread out—Moab, Los Angeles, New York.

"I'm going to need to hear more about these characters in the future," Ted said with warm interest.

The implication of future conversation put a fizz into her.

Ted pulled up in front of her house without her telling him which one it was, so apparently he had observed at least something of her comings and goings around the neighborhood as well. This set off another tiny burst of feeling.

She thanked him profusely for the ride.

"I recommend an ice pack and staying off your bike till spring," he said. "Actually, if you have any interest in carpooling, we could probably do the earth a favor and use one car instead of two."

"That could be good," she said, as if the idea of riding with him did nothing to her.

They'd carpooled every workday since, always his car, Heather walking to his driveway at 7:30 a.m. on the dot to find him already sitting in the driver's seat, answering emails on his phone, frost scraped from the windows, engine and heaters on. In the evenings, he always stopped at her curb, let her out, then pulled down the block to his own driveway again.

On her second date with Devin, when Heather told him the story of her black eye, she left Ted out of it. The next morning when Ted asked about her evening, she didn't say anything about Devin. She so easily could have told them about each other. Made it simple and clear from the start. And yet something in her resisted.

And now here it was, the New Year, a Friday, the day before Heather's big third date with Devin. As they drove home from work Ted told Heather that he and Linda were going snow camping that weekend.

She and Ted arrived at the curb outside her house, but Ted went on talking. He explained how you constructed your quinzhee, piling snow high and then digging it out, just like you did as a kid in the yard, building an igloo. But then you cut a few holes for ventilation, and inside you lit candles, the flickering light of the flames glistening on the walls and ceiling all around you. It made a warm sparkle, like being inside an enchanted ice palace, albeit a humble one, he said.

"And of course you're in there together, so that keeps you warm too," he said, though he pronounced this last statement with a trailing, delicate distance. Whose feelings would be affected by a mention of marital coziness? Surely not his. Did he think Heather's would be? Were they? Or was it just the general mention of intimacy? As if "you're in there together" implicated the two of them, sitting in a similarly enclosed space together?

There were several long moments of silence.

Finally, just before Heather began to say her goodbye, he asked about her weekend.

"Oh, not much," she said. "Probably just hanging out with some friends." Why was she failing to mention Devin? He wasn't her boyfriend yet, really. So maybe that was part of it. But did she also have to admit it was because if she had a boyfriend something might shift between her and Ted in a way she didn't want it to? That even though there was nothing happening here, the "nothing" would be different if she were unavailable?

"Well, my girl," Ted reached over and placed his hand briefly on top of hers, "I look forward to Monday."

He had never touched her before. It might have been a grandfatherly affection. It was not wholly inappropriate. And yet it was a touch, and for Heather the sensation of it lingered and lingered, a phantom warmth that wouldn't go away.

Chapter 3

It irked Nedra to no end when Heather tried to cast her as an arch conservative, as if she were some fundamentalist fruitcake. There was Christmas of course, that lovely episode. And bringing Brian into it like that. Just awful. Nedra had done her best to move along, but Heather seemed determined to maintain her battle stance. Was is that Heather thought a couple of years of living on the East Coast had turned her into an all-knowing cosmopolitan? Or that she somehow misconstrued the new confidence that came with losing all that weight as a right to be rude?

She and Heather had been cleaning together, barely a week after Christmas, when the latest outburst occurred. Nedra had started doing the heavy cleaning at her parents' house years ago, when her mother's strength first began failing and hiring a service would have seemed both an imposition on her parents' privacy and a dereliction of daughterly duty. Now that her mother was gone and it was just her father living in the house he probably wouldn't have minded professional cleaners, and yet the precedent had been set. Saturday was vacuum and visit day. Heather, always devoted to her grandfather, usually joined.

They were in the kitchen together, Nedra mopping, Heather cleaning the appliance fronts, her father napping in the bedroom. She and Heather were talking about Audrey, who'd flown straight back to New York after barely three days in Utah for the holidays. Audrey had spent the last six years in a little room with one small window on the 24th floor of a Manhattan law firm. Nedra had only visited the office once, but the idea of it got to her. She wished Audrey would put some family photos on her shelves. She wished Audrey wouldn't eat at her desk. She wished Audrey didn't have to crane her head to see anything other than the mausoleum-black office building across the street. All those years of study and the endless days and nights at work—Doug had had a couch and plants and windows and a parking space in half as many years with half as much effort.

"Do you know what she told me?" Heather said. "That the dinner she had with us the night she got in was the first dinner she'd eaten away from her desk since November. Literally every single night, weekends included, she's been at her desk."

Nedra sighed and said to Heather, "Do you think it's harder for her, because she's a woman?"

It was a reasonable question! There were plenty of reasons being a woman at a big law firm could be a challenge. But Heather had made a rude p-shaw sound and said, "What, like she shouldn't really be there? She should be home taking care of kids, so that's why it's hard for her?"

"That's not what I meant at all!" Nedra stiffened.

Oh, that tone of Heather's. As if taking care of kids were a miserable occupation, unworthy of anyone with any smarts. And clearly, Audrey and Michael didn't have kids yet, so was Heather implying that Nedra was some backwater bumpkin who thought that the second a woman got married she should quit her job to stay home to embroider pillowcases for her husband? Hardly.

"I meant do you think they treat her differently than they treat the men," Nedra said, a hard edge to every word.

"No, I think being a lawyer sucks for everyone," Heather answered, unrepentant.

That had closed the conversation. They'd reached the point where Nedra no longer chastised her children for using words like "sucks."

What really got to Nedra in all this was the presumption that she was a fool, brainwashed by "the patriarchy." Absolutely not! How was it possible that Heather could fail to see that she was self-determined, a woman who made her own choices and held her own convictions? The way Nedra saw it, she was half-way to a rebel.

Her first clear choice: Doug. All those years ago when Nedra met Douglas Walker, future husband and father of five little Walkers, she was exactly the sort of working woman Heather seemed to think she had no ability to understand. She'd been a secretary at Zion's Bank in Salt Lake for going on three years by then. At first, she'd lived with roommates downtown, but then she'd moved back home to Bountiful to live with her parents. Another decision most certainly not forced upon her. She liked her parents, she liked Davis County. She'd even taken on half-a-dozen Saturday piano students, not the move of a woman planning to break camp at any moment. She felt herself, at twenty-four, placidly unspooling into spinsterhood.

And yet she'd made a point of getting out and meeting people. Another bit of self-determination. On the fateful day she'd met Doug she'd driven her little green Chevy to a football party at the house of a friend's cousin in Salt Lake. BYU versus the U of U, the rivalry game (she herself was a BYU grad). It seemed a poor choice from the moment she arrived. Everyone gathered around the TV, jammed on ratty couches, splayed on the questionable carpet. The coffee table covered with bags of chips, two-liter bottles of soda, and plastic cups. No plates or bowls in sight, certainly no napkins. People barely talking and then with no notice jumping to their feet, howling and flailing at the screen. She stayed fifteen minutes and didn't sit down once, but just before she left a boy emerged from the mass of bodies on the sofas and introduced himself. His name was Doug Walker.

Nedra could tell he was too young for her, but he made his move with his eyes never once flitting back to the game, and when he asked for her phone number it was without either flustered embarrassment or stagey machismo, just a straightforward request, the way Nedra asked people to spell their names at the bank.

And so she thought: yes, he will do.

She gave him her number. It didn't hurt that he was good looking.

Thirty-six years later, Doug's good looks were still something Nedra appreciated in her husband. She was amazed by how many pretty women settled for unattractive men, but not her. She'd found a man with good bone structure, a long angular jaw, a nice straight nose, heavy brows that hooded his long-lashed eyes with mystery. He'd been a high school track and baseball star, and like her, he'd always stayed trim. Now, nearing sixty, his athleticism was less something you noticed in his muscles and more something you noticed in his focus. He seemed perpetually coiled, ready to spring. She could sometimes feel pinned by his narrow attention, accused, over-examined, but more often when he fixed his eyes on her she still fluttered, even all these years later, a blushing *who me?* coupled with a solid sense of deserving.

Within six months of the football party they were married, which made Nedra forever dismissive of young women—first her oldest daughter Audrey, and now Heather—who worried they'd end up alone. (Caroline, the youngest, seemed unconcerned, and fair enough, she was hardly lacking for suitors).

"You'll see. When it happens, it'll happen like that," Nedra said to her daughters, snapping her fingers. They always rolled their eyes.

That first year after their wedding, Nedra had found the age difference between her and Doug embarrassing. Doug was home from a mission in Portugal so recently that he still referenced it all the time, like a college freshman still talking about high school. Because he was smart and a hard worker, he'd crammed three years of civil engineering courses into two years of college, but still, he had a year of his bachelor's left. He carried a ratty backpack. She bought him a nice leather satchel.

The hint of scandal in the words *the older woman* occasionally appealed to Nedra, all knowledge and sophistication, as if she'd plotted and seduced him, but she also blanched at the idea, a deep discomfort in even pretend wantonness. For a time the two-and-a-half years between her and Doug had made her tiptoe around her natural inclinations.

"You like having things your own way," her mother had said the night before the wedding, sitting on the foot of Nedra's childhood bed and patting her hand. "Just remember, marriage is about compromise." Nedra had considered this both a dour bit of advice and a delicately-worded insult, but she also recognized the truth in it, which is what made the criticism sting. Yes, she could be bossy, and so she let Doug decide whenever possible in those early years. They bought the pickup he wanted, even though Nedra knew it was impractical for kids (true enough, they had to sell it less than two years later). They went on the camping trips he suggested, despite Nedra's hesitance (Nedra's family did not "sleep in the dirt," as her father referred to it. To her surprise, she found she loved it). The fact that she was the one earning all the money made deferring to Doug feel doubly important to her back then.

Only after she was finally pregnant (she'd expected it instantly; it had taken over a year) and after the girls at the bank held a going away party for her, and only after Doug framed and hung his diploma on the wall of their apartment and started going to work at the construction firm every day in a suit, and really really only after Brian was born, did the age gap between herself and her husband seem to fade. Fade, but not disappear. When Doug's brown hair went gray, heavy streaks along his temples by thirty, while hers at thirty-three remained unsilvered chestnut, she was still sensitive enough to be grateful for the trick.

Whatever age-related nervousness remained, Nedra found that her opinions returned in force with motherhood. By the time she and Doug had saved enough for a down payment, Brian was almost in school and Audrey was two, and Nedra steered them straight to where she wanted to live: Bountiful. Heather and the rest of the children grew up there because she, Nedra, had decided it for them.

The town was still surrounded by farms when Nedra was a girl, the houses including her parents' clustered around the pioneer-settled blocks of the small downtown, mountains above, grids of fields below. But over the last decades Bountiful had spread and spread, up the hillside in a rush toward the cougars and the rattlesnakes and the shrubby trees, each new development higher up and grander than the last, and down, first the flatland farms subdivided, and then further, almost to the sulfur-scented marshes of the Great Salt Lake, neighborhoods filled in and laid out in tight cul-de-sacs, houses built right up against the freeway sound wall. When they were looking to buy, Nedra and Doug's house was at the top of town on the edge of hiking trail wilderness. Their address seemed fancy. It didn't anymore. Now there was a half mile of lawns between them and anything untamed.

In most of the developments these days all the houses coordinated, one builder, one architect, variations on a standard floor plan and choices relegated to more or less vinyl siding, but back when Nedra and Doug bought their house the designs were more experimental. Their neighborhood tended toward low-slung seventies-era ranches and split-levels, but here and there you got an oddity: a Scandinavian A-frame, a timbered Tudor, a few houses built during a short-lived gingerbread fad, putty-colored mortar between the bricks not scraped away but left to dry in droops, like frosting. And, of course, the Walker's house, a white federalist with tidy black shutters, Connecticut picked up and dropped on the Wasatch Front.

Nedra had loved its formality immediately. Doug liked it too, just one of the many pleasing moments in their marriage when they surprised themselves with their steadfast agreement. Besides which, the house actually had less square footage than the finished-basement ranches and had been on the market for long enough that the price had dropped into their range. Or close to their range. To help make up the difference, Nedra went back to teaching piano in the afternoons while her mother watched the kids. She'd been teaching piano ever since.

It had not been uncomplicated. Doug had gone along with her piano teaching—they needed the money, and he knew it—but her father had been unsparing in his disapproval.

"You have responsibilities to your children," he'd said gruffly.

"I'm not planning on neglecting my children," Nedra had answered, matching her father's tone with some snip of her own. "It's a few hours a week, and Mom is happy to watch them."

"There's no substitute for a mother," her father had said, a rebuke Nedra thought was more insulting to the grandmother than the mother, as if their grandmother's care would somehow be lacking.

Nedra had turned to her mother for defense but had faced a blank retreat. She should have realized that disagreeing aloud with her husband was not in her mother's playbook. In spite of this, Nedra dismissed her father's bluster and went ahead with her plan. After a tense start, everyone settled in and seemed perfectly happy.

But over the years Doug had advanced at work; the money she earned became less important. And then President Benson gave his famous talk to Mothers in Zion.

The head of the Mormon Church has a thoroughly American title: President. President McKay, President Kimball, President Hinckley, President Benson. It is a title befitting the leader of a large bureaucracy, which the church most certainly is. It's also a title easy to pronounce in public. Harder to pronounce in public (or at least non-Mormon public) would be the other, more important descriptions of the head of the church: Prophet, Seer, and Revelator.

Joseph Smith, founder of the church, was always called the Prophet. God the Father and his son Jesus Christ appeared to Joseph. Joseph regularly received angelic visitations. God spoke to him, and Joseph dictated the words into scripture, a book known as The Doctrine and Covenants, as holy to Mormons as the Bible or the Book of Mormon. So: Prophet. When Brigham Young took over after Joseph's murder, he assumed the mantle of leadership but went by a new title: President. Not exactly a timid appellation, and yet one chosen in deference to Joseph, a way of emphasizing allegiance to the prophet and his legacy, a flag to say *no usurpation or apostasy here, thank you very much*.

The President title stuck, but the Joseph Smith-ness of the position also stuck. Modern-day revelation is a central tenet of the faith. Now and forever, the President of the church is also the Prophet. The church is the Church of Jesus Christ of Latter-day Saints, and when Jesus Christ wants to speak to the saints He does it through the prophet. The prophet's words are inspired revelation, as powerful as scripture. Especially when delivered from the pulpit.

And so when President Ezra Taft Benson, former Secretary of Agriculture, fervent anti-communist, and 87-year old leader of the church took to the pulpit in 1987 to share his thoughts on the proper roles of parents, he was not simply sharing opinions. His words had a godly bite. *Fathers are to provide, to love, to teach, and to direct. Mothers are to conceive, to nourish, to love, and to train. Come home, wives, to your husbands. Come home, wives, to your children. The Lord's way is not the world's way. A mother's calling is in the home, not in the marketplace. A child needs a mother more than all the things money can buy. Magnify the noblest calling of all—a mother in Zion.*

Nedra was hardly flouting President Benson's holy utterances at the time. She wholeheartedly agreed with them! Mother of four with a fifth on the way, she believed raising children was a sacred calling, the highest and best use she could possibly think of for her time. It could be exhausting and occasionally thankless, and her heart burned with gratitude for President Benson's recognition of her value. And yet, even as Nedra embraced the prophet's words, she felt the tiny barb of chastisement inside them. Those two and half hours of piano teaching Monday through Thursday. It wasn't as if she was abandoning her children to pursue godless Mammon. It was piano lessons! Music! A community service! *Raise a song of praise to the Lord*, etc. etc. A mere two and a half hours a day! And yet after President Benson's talk she and Doug discussed her teaching in strained, quiet voices. He could provide everything they needed. What reason was there for her to go on working?

She might have given in. She certainly felt guilty. She prayed and pondered it. She played out the phone calls she would make to her students' parents, informing them of the change. And yet there was an undeniable fact: she liked teaching. She liked the music. She liked the students. And something more inexplicable and more compelling than those easy explanations—she liked the way teaching piano lessons transformed her. As soon as she took up her chair next to the piano bench it was almost as if she'd never left, one lesson connected to the next on a timeless, satiny ribbon. Whatever had happened outside the piano room—squabbling children, dirty laundry—turned to air, not forever, but for a moment. She could have been teaching a lesson for two minutes or two hours and yet the feeling was the same. Eyes on the keys and fingers, ears alert, green pencil poised to mark the page.

It's not the same as really working. I teach lessons at home, she'd said to Doug and to herself. *It's good for the kids to spend time with their grandparents.* When it became clear she wasn't changing her mind, Doug finally stopped pushing, and Nedra had searched her own heart and found her compliance with the Word of the Lord to be perfectly adequate. The issue had come up again here and there over the years whenever Doug encountered a new stress at work or in his church calling, whenever they were especially worried about one of the kids, but Nedra had remained firm.

Not that choosing to be a piano teacher was some marker of wild liberality. She knew Heather would roll her eyes if she tried to claim that one. But it signified something; Nedra was a person with experience finding her own way. She wasn't a person who had never struggled or questioned or thought her own thoughts. She'd made her own choices, and the fact that Heather couldn't see this, that Heather seemed to think she needed to open her mother's sheltered little brain to the big wide world? It brought out all of Nedra's slapping impulses.

Heather was lucky she'd been out of arm's reach for their most recent altercation. Over the phone Heather had mentioned that she'd started carpooling to work with a neighbor.

"Oh, that's great. Tell me about her," Nedra said.

"It's a man, actually."

"Is he in your ward?" Nedra asked.

"No," Heather answered with a prickle.

"Is he married?" Nedra asked. She didn't bother to suppress her worried, prying tone. If anything she played it up. Sometimes all Heather's resistance did was urge her on.

"Uh . . . yes?" Heather said. "Why does it matter?"

"Riding in a car every day with someone. I just think you should be careful." Nedra said.

"Yeah, thanks. I'll watch out." Heather replied sarcastically.

Could Nedra's comments be construed as overly protective? Sure. But were they completely off base? Nedra could have told Heather a story or two—like the time when she was a secretary and a middle-aged banker from Nebraska sweatily pressed a note with his hotel room number scrawled on it into her hand. Revolting. So no, the ridicule was quite unnecessary.

Frankly, she worried about Heather in the world these days more than she had before, not that she could say so aloud without incurring Heather's wrath. But Nedra saw the way Heather seemed to alternate between fear and excitement over her new body, flaunting it in fitted clothes one day and hiding it in oversize pants and sweaters the next. Shuffle then swagger, like a surly, tentative teenager.

Back when they were actual teenagers, puberty had greeted each of Nedra's daughters differently. Audrey's nose and chin had stretched like fun house mirror versions of themselves. Her hips had come on suddenly and then almost as swiftly disappeared, an alarming reprimand of near starvation that took a terrifying year to pull her out of. Heather had expanded like the bubble letters she used to trace around her name—H-E-A . . .— each iteration bigger than the next until the word became unrecognizable. Caroline alone had remained unbattered. Her skin should have been speckled with pimples but instead stayed smooth, with adorable freckles across her nose and the tops of her cheeks. She'd grown too evenly, nothing awkwardly out of proportion, all of her stretched to a charming ribbon of girl. Maybe Nedra should have been grateful—one darling daughter, spared—but instead, she had been wary and patrolling of Caroline. With her other girls, their struggles felt contained, terrible but bounded: they were like snow globes, teenage turmoil swirling but enclosed within their own minds and bodies. The world seemed to step gingerly around them, eyes sliding over, ignoring, dismissing. But Caroline drew attention. Boys noticed her, adults noticed her, and Caroline herself hadn't seemed to mind this one bit. The glass around her was permeable. Nedra had kept a constant, uneasy eye out for incursions.

But that was years ago. Caroline had long since learned to guard herself. Audrey too, had settled into her body and developed the reflexes that came with experience parrying advances. But Heather. Heather had been encased in all those obscuring layers until so recently. She had developed defenses, but of a different, angrier sort. Nedra's great worry was that newly thin Heather would be grateful for attention instead of wary of it, as a woman always should be. It made her want to keep Heather close, which at the moment seemed the exact opposite of Heather's desires.

These worries and imagined counterarguments with Heather all swirled about in Nedra's head as she folded laundry then ironed and ironed and ironed, liberally applying spray starch to collars, cuffs, and t-shirts alike.

Once upon a time ironing in a quiet house would have been a great pleasure to her. A rare respite. But Nedra's relationship with time had changed. It was almost sacrilege to say you had too much time. Borderline un-American. Certainly Nedra had never experienced even a moment's surfeit of time when she had children at home, and she understood that there were women who would have loved nothing more than to luxuriate in the space and time of an empty evening, women who dreamed of one long bubble bath after all their harried years of mothering. But Nedra was not one of them. She could barely comprehend them, frankly. After living for so long in a boisterous home full of children demanding her attention, what she felt now that they were grown and gone was not relief at the silence. Instead, she felt lost in the loneliness of it. The few hours of piano lessons that had once been such an effort to steal away from the rest of her life were now the tiniest blips. Ridiculous to feel anything but gratitude for a wealth of time, wasn't it? And yet she could hardly stand the hours!

Not that this was a problem one could really discuss. There were so many obvious solutions. TV. Reading. Volunteering. If Doug were retired, they would go on a mission. Young people went on proselytizing missions, but senior couples could go on missions too. You didn't door knock, but there was always service to perform somewhere, staffing a family history library or managing some facet of the church's welfare system or following up with investigators that young missionaries introduced you to. Some couples went on back-to-back missions, year after year. But Doug wasn't retired yet. He wouldn't be for ages. And a mission wasn't the real solution anyway. What she needed was grandchildren.

She had been ready for them for a good ten years now. She had expected them from Brian and Danica. For years, every time Brian called she had prepared herself for the exciting news. It had never come. She'd been that way with Audrey right after she got married, but now she knew there was something going on, fertility issues she inferred from the way Audrey clammed up when she so much as hinted at the subject of babies. And the other children, well, they were all certainly taking their sweet time to find partners, weren't they. Had she done something that scared them away from marriage?

Grandchildren, oh grandchildren! That was exactly what was missing from Nedra's life. Children gave shape to each day, to each month, each year, to a whole sweep of years. While the constant attention they required could be exhausting it was far better than the formless void. More than just giving shape and meaning to your days, children were fun! Of course you had seen daffodils and sprinklers and pumpkins and snowflakes, a blur of experience, but children hadn't, and showing them renewed those pleasures for you too. Children took regular days and spilled joy into them. Yes, look at the clouds. Yes, hear the ice cream truck. Let me show you how to cross your fingers over to play a scale. Let me show you how to fold your arms and bow your head to pray. And teenagers! Thinking about the grave issues of life for the first time, sorting out the ethics of everything. Testing out personas. Such vital matters! Such high stakes!

You couldn't walk around talking about joy without sounding like a nutter, or a braggart, or methinks thou dost protest too much Prozac Nation. As a Mormon you had more space than the average person for the declarations of happiness. You could, in fact *should,* get up in monthly Fast and Testimony meetings and talk about the joy the gospel brought into your life, the beautiful burning in your heart that came with the promise that your family would be together throughout the eternities. You could make similar declarations, often through heartfelt tears, at the end of the talks you were assigned to give in Sacrament meeting, at the end of Sunday School lessons you taught, throughout Relief Society or Priesthood meetings. Much of church each week centered on such shared emotion surrounding the sweet fruits of the gospel. And yet outside these public forums, to say to your friends not just that you looked forward to the eternities but that you found your time with your family right this very minute to be a real delight, that you were—hear the boldness in so ordinary a word—*satisfied*? This did not come off well. Say those words too often above a whisper and see how many friends you have left.

But by and large, that was how Nedra had felt. Raising children had taken all her love and energy, all her strength and creativity, and it had given her joy in return. And remembering the burden and pleasure of it was how she knew just how sorely she was lacking now.

She had once been the ruler of an impressive and well-or-dered kingdom. When her children were young they woke when she told them, ate what she cooked them, wore what she bought or sewed them. She set the calendar. She made the rules. She'd been so good at it. She'd been so useful. At church, she'd looked down her pew and seen five heads of nicely combed hair, and sure they'd fidgeted and sometimes an unruly child had had to be hauled out to the foyer, but they'd been right there, an arm's length away, for her to love and protect and discipline. And then they grew up, and all that was left was the loving, not the pro-tecting and shaping, and you couldn't count on quite the same success rate with that, now could you?

How irrelevant she had become.

She finished ironing the shirts and then moved on to the sheets and pillowcases for good measure. Not entirely unsatisfying, and yet instead of feeling soothed and tidy, Nedra's hours playing fastidious laundress left her restless. No grandchildren, and so this was what she was putting her love and energy into these days? P-shaw, as Heather would say.

A better outlet for Nedra's energy: her father. It had been three years since her mother died, and although he had grown undeniably slower and more stooped, although he now shuffled and made her heart freeze with his occasional losses of balance, he was still managing, still sufficient. All told, Nedra thought her father had adjusted to living alone better than many men would have after sixty years of matrimonial cohabitation and care-taking. Nedra made him two casseroles a week, enough for most of his dinners, and for the rest she took him grocery shopping, and he made do. He ate oatmeal and sandwiches day after day without complaint. He consumed a shocking amount of salsa.

She took a lasagna over to him at lunch, then stayed to wipe down the kitchen and bathrooms (a little spruce up was always in order), and after that she stayed even longer to settle in on the couch with him and look through mail-order seed catalogs (not that her father gardened anymore, but he liked to imagine).

An afternoon spent with her father meant it wasn't strange that he appeared in her dream that night. But it was strange that she woke, startled and a little panicky, just before three a.m. not sure what was dream and what was real.

In the dream, her father wanted to drive. He'd given up his license years earlier, but now here she was handing him her keys, and getting into the car with him. In the dream she'd been afraid, troubled, but still hurtling forward, with him behind the steering wheel.

Finally fully awake, sitting up in bed in the dark of her bedroom, she couldn't shake the feeling that something was wrong. Three a.m. is an hour for anxiety, for concerns to pirouette maniacally in the dark before collapsing at dawn. But this wasn't that. This was more precise.

Nedra nudged Doug awake. "Honey, I'm so sorry to wake you. I just have this feeling. I think we should check on my dad."

Doug opened his eyes, groggy but attentive.

"You want to call him? What time is it?" he said.

"No, I think we should just go down to his house." She stopped herself. "No, you're right, I'll call first."

Doug watched her drowsily as she dialed, not caring for the hour.

No answer. She tried again. Still no answer.

"Okay, so now I'm really worried," she said.

She expected a protest, for Doug to say it was the middle of the night and of course her father was just sleeping, as people do. She keyed herself up for the small drama of it. But Doug didn't argue.

"Okay, let's go," he said, instantly erasing the blurriness of sleep.

She loved him for it, although she might have felt better if he had protested. It might have convinced her that she was being silly. But no. They dressed with hurried efficiency.

The drive to her father's took five minutes, less with rolling stops, and when they arrived Nedra didn't knock. She used her key and walked in and straight to her father's bedroom, Doug following behind. She knocked gently on the open door of the room and called out, "Dad?" Even in the dim light she saw immediately that he wasn't in bed.

"Dad?" she called again more urgently.

"Here," came a strained voice from the bathroom.

She hurried to the bathroom and turned on the light. Her father was crumpled on the floor, his shoulders hunched against the wall. He had clearly dragged himself to his half-upright position, a smear of wet, yellowish fecal material across the tile.

"I fell. And I was sick. I'm afraid I'm a terrible mess," he said. His lips looked blue.

"It's okay, Dad. It's all okay. Are you hurt? Do you think you can stand?"

"Yes. I just couldn't get up myself."

Together, she and Doug each took one of her father's arms and straining, lifted him to his feet. The smell was sharp, urine and excrement together.

"How long have you been on the floor?" Nedra asked. She was crying now. She was unable to pretend she wasn't.

"It's okay, honey. An hour maybe. Not long. I tried to get up. I was just sick. That's all."

His blue cotton pajama bottoms were soaked through with diarrhea, a stain of it that ran down his leg.

"Let's get you out of this," she said. "Doug, turn on the shower, will you? Do you think you can step into the shower, Dad?"

He said yes.

Wordlessly, she and Doug divided duties. Her father was still unsteady on his feet, and Nedra held his weight and looked away as best she could while Doug undressed him. Doug unbuttoned her father's pajama shirt and then Nedra held her father around the waist as Doug lifted his garment top up and over his head. Her father put his bare arm around her shoulder for support as Doug gently pulled the soiled pants and garment bottoms from him. The bare flesh of his side, his stomach and hips, pressed against Nedra as he struggled to lift one foot and then the next.

"I'll help you in the shower," Doug said, stepping quickly out of his own clothes until he was in just his garments.

They each took an arm and helped her father step into the shower, Doug stepping in with him. Nedra's eyes fell on her father's white puckered skin, gooseflesh everywhere, varicose veins improbably dark and winding, explosions of spider veins like lines of falling fireworks, his body hair sparse but still shot through with pigment. On his flank, she could not help but see the already darkened bruise from where he'd fallen, like a flattened spoiled plum with juices that had spread and run, the reach of it under his skin alarming.

"Keep a hand on him, Nedra," Doug said.

She did, tightly. She suspected he'd have bruises from her grip later, but there was no helping it.

Her husband soaped her father, a soft efficiency in his manner, his gentle hands the opposite of Nedra's harpy grasp. She'd stopped crying, and once her father was out of the shower Nedra's nerves eased. They dried him and got him into new garments and new pajamas. They helped him back to bed. She brought him water.

Doug borrowed dry garments. She borrowed a shirt to replace her soiled one. She cleaned the bathroom. She texted her friend Barbara to cancel their morning walk. Doug took the clothes and towels to the basement and turned on the washing machine. Once her father was clearly resting, they closed his bedroom door and she and Doug sat on the living room sofa next to each other, waiting for dawn. He took her hand and knit his fingers through hers, a tight clasp of togetherness.

The fact that Nedra had woken, that she and Doug had come and found her father, it felt like a miracle. She should have been so glad for that strange blessing. But something else was bothering her.

"I brought him a casserole today," Nedra said to Doug. Was it the lasagna that had made him sick? She didn't announce this theory, but Doug could extrapolate.

"Oh, I'm sure it wasn't that," Doug said reassuringly, but there was a tutting to his dismissal. Nedra knew she shouldn't hear it as a rebuke for bringing up something so silly, and yet she did.

She'd cooked the meat well. She hadn't left the sauce sitting out. It wasn't her fault, and it didn't really matter if it was her fault. It had happened. It was over. And yet it did matter to her.

"You should go home and get some sleep," Nedra said to Doug, trying to cover over her irritation. "You have to go to work in a couple of hours."

"How long are you going to stay?" he asked, rubbing his hands over his face, as if he could wipe away the fatigue.

"He'll need help again, if he's still feeling sick. I don't think I should leave him. I'll call his doctor first thing and see if he thinks I should bring him in. Just to make sure nothing is broken and that nothing else happened. Like a stroke, or I don't know."

"I'll call in today," Doug said. "I'll stay with you."

Nedra didn't argue. She nodded, grateful. Finally she said, "I'm just so thankful I had that prompting."

The Holy Ghost usually whispered but the Spirit could shake you awake just as well. You could say it was some other sort of intuition—she'd noticed something amiss during her visit or part of her knew there was something wrong with the lasagna. But that's not what Nedra truly believed. She felt certain she'd been woken by a prompting. That was exactly the point of the Holy Ghost, that out of nowhere the Spirit spoke to you and gave you thoughts and impressions, helped you to act in ways you never would have otherwise. That was the miracle of it all.

"I'm glad you listened to it," Doug said.

"I think you should give him a blessing when he wakes up," Nedra said.

"I will," Doug said. "I'll call his home teachers in a couple of hours and see if they can come join me."

"I think we're in a new era," Nedra said.

Still holding hands, they leaned back into the couch and closed their eyes.

Nedra didn't know how other Christians thought about the Holy Ghost. Maybe the Virgin Mary was their thing or they were praying to saints or what have you and the Holy Ghost didn't really register, but for Mormons the Holy Ghost was an essential, daily companion. Just as the prophet was entitled to revelation for the church and the world, individuals were entitled to revelation for themselves and their families, and the Holy Ghost was the one who delivered the message.

Ask and ye shall receive, knock and it shall be opened unto you: you prayed, and the Spirit bore witness, for spiritual matters like confirming the truth of scripture, or comforting your troubled heart, but for more worldly matters too. You didn't want to become the sort of person who prayed about which way to turn at a traffic light, but if you were trying to decide where to move, which job to take, how to help someone, you prayed and the Spirit would guide you. But it wasn't just when you prayed. Sometimes the Holy Ghost would come to you as you were going about your business. Promptings, like call your neighbor, skip that trip, or check on Dad. Dreams. Feelings. The more humble you were, the more obedient, the more in tune, the clearer the whisperings.

That didn't mean people said things like "The Holy Ghost told me to XYZ," or "I had a personal revelation that PDQ," in regular everyday conversation, but they did say things like "I had the distinct impression," or "I had a strong feeling," or "I had a prompting," and you knew exactly what they meant—The Still Small Voice—and you couldn't argue with that.

Nedra's phone rang that afternoon: Heather.

"Caroline says Grandpa isn't doing well?" Heather said. "He had a fall?" She sounded concerned but also aggrieved, the sharpened voice of a person who believes they've been wronged.

Nedra had texted Caroline that morning. She knew that Heather would be irritated that she'd told Caroline first. Typical Heather-Caroline nonsense, Heather perpetually on the lookout for favoritism. Heather was the one who helped clean her grandfather's house, the one who stopped by for visits most frequently, the one who'd always had the closest relationship with him, so she felt a special claim. Nedra knew this. But she had been scheduled to help Caroline set up for a blog photo shoot that morning and had obviously needed to cancel. Thus the text. No favoritism whatsoever. She could have explained it all, but defensiveness was a waste, and she'd long ago decided to forgo it whenever possible.

Instead Nedra ignored Heather's tone and simply told her about the visit to the doctor that morning. Other than the stomach bug and the bruising, Grandpa was in surprisingly good health for a ninety-one-year-old. (The doctor had clearly said stomach bug, not food poisoning, though how he could say for sure was something of a mystery). Nothing broken, no underlying stroke or other disturbing explanation for Grandpa's loss of balance. He just needed the same rest that anyone needs when they've been under the weather, with maybe a little more TLC.

"So you're just going to leave him living alone?" Heather said. Her voice wasn't all accusation, but it was strident enough.

"Would you like to move in?" Nedra parried tartly. But when did sniping ever help? Nedra softened and explained that for at least the next few days she would be staying at Grandpa's.

"What about piano lessons?" Heather asked.

"I'm canceling them for a few days."

"Wow," Heather said. She seemed almost more stunned by this than anything.

Nedra knew it was notable. All the kids had at one point or another begged her to cancel lessons. Audrey when she had her tonsils out and wanted motherly rather than grandmotherly ministrations, Brian when his basketball team was in the finals and he wanted her to come to the game, ditto Aaron with baseball, Caroline on a regular basis when she'd desperately needed a ride to the mall. Nedra had never conceded. But this was indeed a new era.

"You can come over if you want," Nedra said. "I'm sure Grandpa would like your company more than mine."

Heather didn't argue, which rankled Nedra a bit. Wasn't that the sort of remark you were supposed to good-naturedly rebuff? All Heather said was that she'd head right up after work. Fine.

That afternoon Nedra's father sat up in bed while she tidied his room. Doug had been on duty all day as the upset stomach ran its course, a supportive arm to help her father out of bed, standing just outside the bathroom door ready to help if needed. He was finally asleep on the couch in the living room. Her father had been asleep too, off and on, but now he'd woken again. Nedra turned on the lamp on her father's dresser. He looked thinner. Just a day in, and the bones of his eye sockets had become more pronounced. But his color looked better, so that seemed promising.

As she was gathering mail and half-drunk water glasses she noted something stranger.

"What are these, Dad?" Nedra asked. She held out little pieces of paper to him, scraps she'd found, one tucked into the rim of the lampshade, a few others on the dresser. "A Talk on Witnesses," one of them said. "Dice and Cards," another one said.

"Oh, well, I guess you could say those are . . . well, night litter, I guess I'd call them," he said, trying to laugh.

Her father seemed to speak more slowly every day now. He still had his memory. Words were not failing him. Both were enormous blessings. But there was a thickness to the pace of everything now.

"I never know when something I think of while I'm half-asleep is a good idea," he smiled effortfully. "So I just have to write it down and stick it someplace where I'll be sure to see it later."

The penmanship on the scraps looked shaky, like the handwriting a ghost would leave behind. Nedra had a sudden picture of herself cleaning up the house after her father was gone, finding ragged indecipherable scraps everywhere, the mystery of each one pricking her with longing for him. Here he was in front of her, and yet she already felt him gone, his missing self almost as much of a presence as his real self.

She sat down beside him on the bed. Strangely enough, she couldn't remember ever sitting on the bed with him like this before. As a girl, she'd never been allowed in her parents' room. That had been her father's rule, she was certain, but one her mother deferred to, her mother being a great deferrer.

Mormon children sang a song in Primary, "I'm so glad when daddy comes home, glad as I can be; Clap my hands and shout for joy, then climb upon his knee." This hadn't been the homecoming scenario when Nedra was growing up. She and her brother Roger were much more likely to make themselves scarce when their father arrived home from the office. When they had to emerge for dinner, it was with dread for the etiquette chastisements and general admonishments that would dominate the meal.

Doug, on the other hand, had turned out to be the embodiment of the song. All the children sprang forth from wherever they'd been playing to surround him when he arrived home each night. Whenever they wanted special permissions, easy discipline, or horseplay and general frivolity, Doug was the clear parent of choice. She preferred this to her father's parenting, most definitely, but she had the lurking sense that the children might have turned to her more regularly for tenderness, might still turn to her more regularly, had Doug not been so tender himself.

Nedra's children didn't believe her stories about growing up—her father kicking her and Roger out of the car when they were maybe five and seven, leaving them curbside to walk the miles home because of their tussling in the backseat. Or his pulling switches from the willow tree out back. Or his regularly locking them outside until they'd finished their yard chores, no exceptions for rain or bathroom breaks. Her father had been a farm boy, and hated the idea of his children growing up soft. These stories were all laughable to Nedra's children because by the time they knew him, Grandpa had mellowed into an armchair advice giver and hand-patter who often closed his eyes as if overtaken by a dream when he pontificated on matters great and small. He was no threat to them; her children were free to heed or ignore him. Nedra's feeling toward him had grown milder as she saw him through their eyes—why had his opinions ever seemed so all-important to her anyway?—and yet it wasn't as if she forgot how it had been for all those years.

Sitting beside her father on the bed now created an unsettling yet curious intimacy. She didn't want her father to be sick, to be frail, and yet she saw how a person could come to rely on providing this sort of care, the sense of closeness and indispensability it gave you. She felt a power over him she never had before.

Nedra thought he was going to tell her about "dice and cards," or maybe that he was going to tell her to stop tidying and leave him be, but instead he reached for her hand and patted it. Then she thought he was going to say something about missing her mother, or about wanting to stay in his house whatever it took, or maybe he was going to thank her. Instead, he said, "I wish I were sixty again. You should enjoy it!"

He was trying to be light, but the way he had to plod through the words turned the sentiment melancholy.

She had thirty years till she would be the age he was now. Thirty years till this scene played out with her as the one in bed. Thirty years, practically her whole adult life, to fill again. She thought she'd gotten away from the thought, but here it was again: what was she going to do with herself?

Chapter 4

Nedra's father let her stay for four days. After that, he insisted he was just fine; she needed to go home.

So it was back to normal, supposedly. When Doug pulled into the driveway after work that evening Nedra was sitting next to Kelsey Richter, age thirteen, braced of face and splayed of foot, an awkward girl in most every way when not on the piano bench. Yet now she was playing Claire de Lune with an eerie dancer's grace, as if inhabited by another being, her hands crossing in subtly elegant, arcing waves with each lilting treble third. But Nedra noted all of this at best peripherally. She should have been focused—wasn't that what she counted on piano lessons for?—but the magic of lessons wasn't overtaking her.

As always, Doug came through the garage door so he wouldn't disturb the proceedings. A few minutes later, Nedra could smell the beginnings of dinner—butter, garlic, maybe mushrooms. She ought to have felt grateful for a helpful husband and all that. Instead she felt accused. Reprimanded, even. As if he were cooking up dinner to wave a spotlight over her failure to have made something earlier in the day, to have put it in the oven on low, a beautiful meal, ready for her family. Because why hadn't she? It wasn't as if she didn't have the time. The only thing worse would have been for him to come home and start vacuuming. Not that Doug meant to be critical. Nedra knew he didn't. And yet she couldn't help feeling stung.

She sat there listening to Debussy and imagining the argument she and Doug might have. She'd say *really, you shouldn't have*. And he'd say *don't be silly,* and *is my cooking really that bad?* And she'd say, *I know you don't mean it to, but your help makes me feel bad* and he'd say *don't be silly* and she'd say *don't tell me I'm silly,* and it would unravel unpleasantly from there. But no. She couldn't help feeling put out, but she could certainly help what she said aloud. Bite your tongue: that was Nedra's best advice for marriage. It wasn't passivity. It was called self-mastery, and if you asked her, a lot more people should look into it.

When she finished the lesson she bid Kelsey a fond farewell and made an attempt to come cheerfully into the kitchen. Doug served the pasta, and they sat down at the kitchen table together. After the blessing on the food, she was still doing her best to come into herself when Doug raised his head and with a glimmer announced, "I got an interesting call today."

"Yes?" Nedra said.

"From Verna Smith."

Verna Smith was a Davis County political fixture. Nedra had been a delegate to the county convention a number of times over the years, Doug too, and Verna was always there in some capacity, telling people where to set up chairs, introducing speakers, or standing politely among the dark jackets at the front of the room with her bubble of white hair and her cotton candy skirt suits, looking like a china doll grandmother to them all. Verna had been the state party vice-chair at some point, Nedra was certain, but that was the end of her certainty.

"She said she just wanted to let me know that Gary Swenson has decided not to run for reelection," Doug said.

Nedra gave him a surprised look. Gary Swenson was their dentist as well as their representative in the State Legislature. He'd seen her and Doug and every one of the kids since baby teeth, and he was good at taking his hands out of your mouth before he asked you questions, so whenever Nedra went in they did a fair bit of chatting. Nedra door-knocked for his first campaign eight years ago. After that, it seemed he needed little in the way of reelection assistance—the Republican hadn't lost in Davis County in at least two decades. But at her last appointment he hadn't said a thing about not running again. Had Gary known then and just not mentioned it to her?

"That's all Verna said?" Nedra asked.

"Yes, she told me and then just waited silently, and then I finally said, 'Well, that's very interesting Verna. What do you think of that?' and she said, 'I'm more interested in what *you* think of that." Doug smiled with amused pleasure as he recounted the exchange.

It was easy for Nedra to imagine Verna as she'd been on the other end of the line, her lips puckered and her eyebrows urgently raised, her tiny eyes glimmering in her wrinkled face, a tart flirtation in her aged voice. Nedra dreaded exchanges like that, all innuendo, the other person trying to flush you into the desired position. They always left you feeling foolish, either presumptuous or dense, depending on the hinted meaning you chose to favor. But after a brief moment Nedra found she was barely thinking about Verna. A sudden flush stole over her entire body.

Gary Swenson wasn't running again. Apparently no one else had declared themselves yet. There was an open seat. And she, Nedra Walker, had feelings about all this. What was this sudden heat? Was it the Holy Ghost, nudging her forward?

"What a funny conversation," Nedra finally replied, half-choking on the words.

Nobody was asking *her* to run, they were asking Doug! And he seemed to be interested. And yet the bright wave of feeling surged again.

"So anyhow," Doug continued, oblivious to the stirring across the table, "I said I didn't have any real thoughts about it at the moment, but I'd be sure to let her know if anything occurred to me down the line." He gave a satisfied half-snicker.

The walls and furniture around Nedra seemed to lose their substance for a moment, the edges of everything wavy as if she were looking through a Jell-o mold. Within the blur, came a voice. *You should run*, it pronounced. The Holy Ghost? Or just projection? But the voice was so distinct!

"So what do you think?" Doug said, calling Nedra back to herself.

The lines of the room began to straighten again.

She shook her head in noncommittal confusion and managed at last to say, "I wonder who put Verna up to calling, or if she put herself up to it." As she said it, Nedra realized how sincerely she hoped the answer was Verna alone, no further apparatus at work in support of Doug.

"Hard to know," Doug shrugged.

"And, what do you think?" Nedra asked, trying to keep her voice even.

"Hah," Doug said, waving his hand as if he were swatting a fly away, a gesture of dismissal too sharp and dramatic to be genuine. He sat back in his chair and at last seemed to fully turn his attention to Nedra.

"The real question is what do *you* think?" he said with a sly smile. It seemed he wanted her declaration of support. Wanted it without having to ask for it. Ordinarily she would have given it to him. When had she not supported Doug? Work projects that took him away for days at a time, church callings that took him away for weekends and evenings for *years* at a time. She was a wife who said yes. And yet, the voice. *You should run.*

But it wasn't enough. Not yet. Maybe it was the Holy Ghost but maybe it was a flash impulse, a prideful, grandchild-less grab for meaning. Whatever it was, it needed much more attending to before it could be articulated.

Instead of a fumbling revelation of resistance, Nedra did her best to assume a jokey, imitative tone.

"I'll be sure to let you know what occurs to me down the line," she said.

Doug took this well enough. End of discussion.

She needed to think, and to pray.

That night before bed, she and Doug knelt at their bedside for their usual prayers, and although one or both of them often stayed on their knees for a silent prayer alone after their prayer as a couple, tonight Nedra rose quickly from the floor. She needed greater privacy for this prayer. She'd sleep on it. She hoped for revelatory dreams.

Unconscious revelation did not come, and the microwave clock glowed 5:24 the next morning as Nedra pulled on her cap and coat and walked out the door, still waiting for the right moment for her prayer. The stars had faded but not even a hint of green appeared behind the mountains yet. She took off down the driveway at a clip, her body shuddering at the initial shock of cold. Some mornings this time of year you had to keep a lookout for black ice, but not especially today. Snow-plowed piles lined Orchard Drive, but the snow was all old, the past week's temperatures too low for any melting and slick refreezing.

Two blocks from her house, a familiar shadowy figure waited by the curb, marching in place like an aerobics video instructor, the pom pom on top of her hat bobbing in time. Nedra didn't even have to slow her pace; as she approached, Barbara fell right in with wide strides and pumping elbows, matching Nedra's exactly. The two of them had been walking together for nine years.

When Nedra's kids were growing up, she'd walked in the mornings alone. For one thing, most of the women she'd tried walking with were too slow. For another, she walked so early—4:45 on the dot every single day—that no one else was ever interested in joining her for long. These days she didn't start her workout until 5:25, the time she used to head home to rouse whatever sluggish teenager she'd assigned the earliest piano practice slot that week.

Brian and Heather in particular had loved to snooze through their alarms. It should have driven her crazy, but it didn't. She'd open their bedroom doors and waves of cozy sleep would waft toward her, warm and comfortingly stale. She'd crouch down and turn on their bedside lamps and reach under their covers to gently nudge their shoulders. No matter how big they were, they were still so young when they first opened their eyes, their gazes soft and dopey and alarmed, like startled milk drunk babies. "Rise and shine," she always said in a quiet sing-song. Sometimes they groaned and threw pillows over their faces, but one of them was always on the bench by 5:30, followed by another at 6, and another at 6:30 and another at 7:00, with Caroline, the youngest, at 7:30.

She'd started walking with Barbara when it was just Caroline and Aaron left at home and she didn't have to leave the house quite so early anymore. She and Barbara had been in the same ward for a few years by then, seeing each other at church week after week, but they hadn't been naturally drawn to one another. Not that it was really a conscious thought; they just didn't seem like women who would be friends. Nedra never left the house without matching earrings and necklace. Barbara, on the other hand, appeared perpetually frazzled, her clothing overlarge, her hair short and frizzy with gray roots half-grown out. Her round cheeks and owlish eyes gave her the look of a panicky, aging kewpie doll, this regardless of her actual weight, which fluctuated noticeably.

And then there was the fact that Barbara was divorced. Not that Nedra thought, "She's divorced, I won't be friends with her," but it did create a distance. Being divorced also meant that Barbara worked. Not that Nedra didn't work, but Barbara worked full-time, as a high school history teacher at the school a few towns north, and so she wasn't around during the day. And while Nedra was still busy with her last few kids at home, Barbara's were grown. The one 20-something daughter was still occasionally around, all hard-edged eyeliner, piercings, and bleached hair.

None of these were real impediments. They were just things Nedra thought about later, when she wondered how she had gone so long without discovering her friend.

What finally brought them together was Visiting Teaching. She and Barbara were assigned to be companions, the papers handed out at the end of Relief Society one Sunday morning, her name next to Barbara's at the top of the slip, the names and contact info for three women in the ward listed beneath. Each month, the two of them were supposed to stop by and visit the others, share a brief inspirational message and generally provide a bit of friendship and support.

Nedra immediately imagined that she would be the one setting up the appointments, the one following up with calls and cards. But Barbara had surprised her. She'd called Nedra that very night to talk about their visiting teachees, and then she'd called and set up the appointments with each of them. And every time they went, Barbara did something above and beyond. "I just had a feeling you could use this," she'd say, handing one of the women a frozen casserole. Or, "I was just cleaning off some shelves, and I thought some of these might be up your alley," she'd say, presenting a stack of novels.

Most impressive, Barbara had a particular way of talking to people, an attention that didn't wander so much as occasionally flit away. Those surprising dashes elsewhere were the magic. You could be speaking about the most serious things—infertility, marital disagreements, childhood traumas—and at just the right moment Barbara would crack a joke. Otherwise, Nedra had found, these womanly confessional conversations could be like weights, dragging everyone under together. You could stay calm for a while, the intimacy mesmerizing, like looking up at the sun from below the water, but eventually you drifted so deep that a thrum of panic began. You just wanted to get away. Sometimes it was hard to look at people after talks like that. You smoothed over your shame with clumsy smiles. But not with Barbara. She was a buoy. You were in the water, but always safe, always splashing.

After their third month of visiting teaching together—their brief message that month had been about the power of fasting and prayer—Nedra was dropping Barbara off after an evening appointment, the two of them idling in the dark in front of Barbara's house, like teenagers in a car after a night out, not quite ready to go home.

"Would you like to go walking with me sometime?" Nedra asked, apropos of nothing. Almost blushing, she stammered a further explanation. "I go every morning, just a few miles around the neighborhood, and maybe it'd be too early for you, or not your idea of a good time, and it does get cold, but it might be fun."

"What time?" Barbara asked.

"5:30?" Nedra said, as if it were a question.

"Make it 5:25 and I'm in."

In all the years since, they'd never faltered.

"How was the birthday party?" Nedra asked now, the words a billow of white breath in the morning air, trailing over their shoulders like the puffs behind a steam engine. In the end, Barbara's frighteningly bleached daughter had grown into a gentle brunette, happily married, with three little boys. The youngest was just now two. Barbara relayed all the details. The unsuccessful piñata, finally pulled apart by grown-ups. The blue teddy bear cake. All the boys taking turns blowing out candles after the birthday boy.

Once they finished that topic, they moved on to Nedra's father.

"I called Oak Haven," Nedra said.

Oak Haven was an assisted living place down near the freeway, not the fancy sort of assisted living community with golf courses and pools, the more necessary and serviceable sort, with lots of oxygen tanks on hand. Barbara's mother lived there. She'd moved in after a hip fracture. She liked it. "I don't ever have to cook!" she said regularly, with airy, undirected cheer.

Nedra could see the advantages. The meals were a plus, as Barbara's mother said, but there was also the regular and reliable company, the classes and activities right there at every hour of the day, housekeeping staff that stopped by and cleaned your rooms for you, even church services, conveniently held in the dining room on Sunday mornings after breakfast, a nice abbreviated thirty-minute Sacrament Meeting. And of course the on-hand medical care, if need be. It seemed like a happy place, none of the aggressive tang of industrial cleaners or the troubling human smells that came with some nursing homes, the whiff of urine and hidden bodily crevices, sweet, acrid, and repellant. If anything, Oak Haven smelled like popcorn, an old-timey machine that left a fine mist of butter behind wheeled out for movie nights. But Nedra's circumstances and Barbara's circumstances were different. She had Doug. Together surely they could take care of her father. Nedra didn't say this to Barbara, of course.

They talked for a few minutes about the options, then walked on in the silence of footfalls and breathing. Walking was like driving, the graceful and just-obscuring-enough way it allowed you to talk without looking, and even when the words stopped you were still moving along together in the same direction.

Finally, Nedra ventured to bring up the matter that was truly on her mind. "A strange thing happened to Doug yesterday," she said. "Someone from the state party called him about running for the legislature."

"Interesting," Barbara said. "Gary Swenson isn't running again?"

"No, apparently not."

"And? Do you think Doug should run?" Barbara asked.

Exactly how much did she plan to say?

"Well, a funny thing happened," Nedra ventured. "We were talking about it yesterday, and I just got this feeling. I think *I* might be interested in running."

She half-expected her friend to laugh. Nedra Walker, house-wife and piano teacher, putting herself up for office.

But no. In fact, Barbara smacked her hands together, a muf-fled crack because of the gloves, but a crack nonetheless.

"Nedra! Really?" Barbara's excitement was clear and genuine.

Nedra laughed. "I mean, I think so," she said, a shyness overtaking her.

"I think you'd be great. And it's not like you don't have experience. You've been a voting judge for like twenty years, and a precinct chair, and a delegate to all those conventions and caucuses, and on the library board. You loved the library board."

"Doug was the bishop, and he's in the stake presidency now," Nedra said. "I think that makes a difference."

Being the bishop of a Mormon ward was like being a country doctor (albeit an unpaid one). People in the ward called on you for more or less anything. Crises of faith, heart-to-hearts over wayward children, job advice, confessions, marital counseling, help from the church welfare program. Doug had served as their ward's bishop for five years. This was back when Caroline was in high school, but people still called him Bishop Walker. A few years after he was released as bishop, he'd been called to the Stake Presidency, the group that oversaw all the wards in the area. He wasn't the president, just the first counselor, but he still got the honorific—President Walker. Bishop or President, either way, people knew and respected Doug.

"Yeah, and you're his wife, so people know you just as well because of that," Barbara said. "And also you've been a Relief Society President and you were in the Stake Young Women's Presidency and a gazillion other things." Barbara's walk was taking on an extra bop.

"He knows so many government people from all his building projects too," Nedra said, as if she were trying to change Barbara's mind.

"People know you too," Barbara countered. "You've lived in Bountiful your whole life. And think of all your piano students!"

Nedra had made all these points to herself, but hearing Barbara articulate them boosted her considerably.

"I mean, there is of course the fact that they called Doug, not me," Nedra said.

"Well, it's not your fault if they weren't clever enough to begin with," Barbara smiled.

"I think Doug might have been excited about running . . ." Nedra said.

"Well," Barbara shrugged, "that's one point where I really can't help you."

They walked quietly along, the sound of gravel beneath their shoes.

"Pray about it! I'm just sayin'," Barbara said, gleeful goading in her voice. The words trailed behind them along with two laughing clouds of breath.

From there, Nedra's morning moved along without interruption—shower, breakfast with Doug, organizing for a day at her father's house—and she arrived at her father's doorstep still not having found what felt like the right moment for a significant request for personal revelation. She circled aimlessly about her father's kitchen while he read the newspaper. She picked up and put down a sponge without wiping anything. She opened and closed a few cupboards, her intentions unclear even to herself. Finally, she blurted, "I'm thinking of running for office, Dad. For the legislature."

"Oh, is that so?" her father answered with surprise, but also with a sort of cautious amusement, the way he might have replied had one of his grandchildren announced plans to become a professional hot air balloonist.

Nedra picked up the sponge again and started wiping here and there as if she were only casually interested in what she was reporting. "Gary Swenson isn't running again, so there's an opening. And the caucus president approached me about running, so . . ." Had she really just said that? Both inventing a title for Verna and fabricating an entire interaction? But somehow given her father's tone she just couldn't bear to tell him they'd in fact approached Doug, not her.

"That's very flattering," her father said. In another person's mouth this might have been an exclamation of support, but from her father it sounded a clear note of caution: do not be ensnared by flattering tongues. (Even if the tongues had never flattered her, since she'd lied about the call, it still stung).

"Do you think I shouldn't run?" Nedra said. She put the wet sponge down and faced him directly. The question was more argumentative than she'd intended.

"No, I wouldn't say that!" her father said. "I'd just say it's important to remember your priorities."

Remember your priorities. Remember who you are. Remember what you stand for. The maxims of Mormon parents everywhere. *Remember* was not a gentle word. It was freighted with the implication that you might forget, and Nedra had hardly forgotten her priorities! Of course her family came first. But her children were grown, and it wasn't as if Doug and her father needed her full-time. Was her father insinuating that she had been neglecting him? That she would forget him in his hour of need? As if she didn't *remember* her priorities every day when she cooked and cleaned and shopped for him, when she rushed to him in the middle of the night. Did he think she should be doing more? Not that she was looking for gratitude exactly! He was her father. Of course she'd take care of him, but to act as if she were somehow deficient or looking for some excuse to be. Or as if serving in the state legislature would be some silly hobby. As if she would be the sort of daughter who would say *Dad, I'm sorry, I can't take you to the hospital. I have Scrabble Club.* How insulting it all was.

Her brain practically writhed with responses, but she tamped them down. School thy feelings, as the hymn said.

"I'll keep that in mind, Dad," she said, calmly. Despite her victory over herself, in the end she couldn't help but turn her head away and roll her eyes like an irritated adolescent.

Back at home that afternoon, Nedra finally found the moment for prayer. Her first piano student wouldn't arrive for an hour. Her house was tidy. What else was there to do? She could have knelt beside her bed, but instead she found a place in the piano room, beside the settee.

In any other house, this room would have been called the living room, but in their house it was the piano room, a room that belonged to her. She'd chosen the grand piano, black but not glossy (she hated the fingerprints you could always see on a glossy piano), and while the furniture in the rest of the house had all been purchased with family comfort in mind, the furniture she had chosen for this room inspired good posture, a room of pale fabrics and straight lines that testified to the enforced absence of grimy hands.

The sun shone through the piano room's windows in bright white blocks. She knelt in one of the warm rectangles and bowed her head. She began the prayer with an apology. She felt selfish and foolish and her mind should have been elsewhere—with her father, with her children, on matters of the spirit—but, she said, her thoughts had returned and returned to the idea of running for office. Was this her own vanity or was this an enlivening of her mind, the Spirit speaking to her? Showing her a path for service? She said these words aloud, in a quiet murmur, and waited, and in the quiet of the piano room she felt a growing spirit of calm, a gentle warmth, a little flush of tearfulness. No blaze of glory, no fireworks of confirmation, but not a confounding no. She waited for more. Perhaps the voice would come again. But the room stayed quiet. And yet serenity was its own confirmation, was it not? So call it a yes.

She got up from the floor and played a Chopin waltz.

That evening Doug offered their bedside prayer, a prayer full of concern for her father, for their children, for their own peace and strength, and when he was done, before they rose from their knees, Nedra turned to him.

"I want to talk to you about something. It's not about my dad," she said, hoping to allay what she imagined would be his immediate concern.

He looked at her with all his taut attention, and she felt a flip of nerves.

"Sure," Doug said, "What is it?"

She ran her hands along the blue coverlet, as if it needed smoothing.

"Verna Smith," she said. "I think you should call her back and tell her you've thought about it, and you've decided to support your wife's candidacy."

There was a blank moment before Doug's mouth fell into a smile, a moment of processing, a moment when it could have gone either way, and in that moment all her arguments marshaled themselves behind her teeth. She was surprised to find she'd created quite a list of them. She'd be good at it. The issues at stake were important. They didn't have any grandchildren. She wasn't old yet. There were thirty years between her and her father. Thirty years, think of that. It would be a good experience for their family. Doug was too busy to add another thing to his own schedule. It needed to be her. She could win. And of course, she'd prayed about it and gotten an answer. That was the most important reason, the irrefutable one.

"You?" Doug asked. "Why didn't you tell me you were interested?"

She shrugged girlishly and pursed her lips, as if these affectations could hide her intensity of feeling. "I didn't really know until we were talking about it the other night. I'm sorry if you were feeling excited about maybe running yourself."

He put his arm around her waist. "I was thinking about it, but I certainly wouldn't stand a chance if I tried to run against you," he said, making a joke of it.

"Of course I wouldn't run against you either!" she said.

He shook his head, as if trying to clear away his dismay. "You're sure about this?" he said. There was something amused and indulgent in his manner, a shade of her father's tone. But what right did she have to be so prickly and particular—he was saying yes, wasn't he? Did he really have to say it in the perfect way to please her?

"I know it might seem out of the blue," she said, "but I actually think it's a really good idea. I think I'd be good at it."

"You'd be good at anything you put your mind to," Doug said, and he pulled her to him and kissed her, a showy peck.

"It's not like I have no experience," she said.

"Experience is overrated," he replied, which Nedra noted was clearly not a refutation of her statement.

But yes, she'd declared herself and he'd said yes. And it was done. All that was left was to call Verna, a call for the morning. She wondered what her father would say, and her children. She had half a mind to text Heather the news that very minute.

Chapter 5

Ice cream: the quintessential Mormon date. When you don't drink alcohol or coffee, what else is there for you? But ice cream is not mere settling. No, no. Anywhere you go, ask the Mormons where the best ice cream place is, and they'll give you the goods. But Zion itself is the real promised land of dairy. Utah, a place where the descendants of Danes and Swedes and the panoply of the British Isles, as lactose tolerant as they come, eat thick-as-soft-serve milkshakes with spoons. "Minis" are the size of Big Gulps. Toppings, when deemed necessary, are the richest of hot fudges, the heapingest dollops of fresh whipped cream. If you are thin, you devour all this with showy shoveling. *Look at me! Where does it all go!* If you are fat, you do the opposite, calm, what-do-I-care bites, cool as the cream sliding over your lips. Either way, you leave no ice cream behind.

For their third date, Devin brought ice cream over to Heather's, homemade. That it was winter was no impediment. Ice cream is an all season comestible for Mormons. His was chocolate cherry almond. His family had an orchard, Devin explained. His mother provisioned each of his seven siblings with many gallon bags of cherries for freezing each summer, and he always used his up throughout the year making ice cream.

When Devin kissed Heather for the first time, his mouth was still cold with it. A hint of chewed almonds, not disgusting, just barely noticeable, came to her with his tongue.

They were sitting on her sofa, and after that first gentle exchange, he pulled her to him, a firm hand on her back, then a few moments later his body pressed hers against the cushions. They kissed and kissed until his scruffy chin scratched hers raw, and even after, the discomfort of it pleasing in its way.

Heather had been kissed before, and despite Aaron's remarks, for a time after college she even had a boyfriend of sorts. They were boys who had walked her home from ice cream parlor and laser tag dates. There had been no urgency to their kisses. Their mouths hadn't been cold. They'd waited till there was nothing left to do but lean in. Surely they'd felt the same disappointment she had. But what she was feeling now was deeply un-disappointed.

Even after Devin's hands left her waist or the soft skin of her neck, she felt the pressure of his fingers, like an afterimage from a bright light. The arcing of their forms forward and back, her hands kneading at his shoulder, the twist of the muscles in his back as he moved against her. By the time she closed the door behind him at the end of the night her lips were puffy and tingling, wonderfully tender from overuse.

The next day at church he was clean-shaven, no sign of the stubble that had reddened her chin. They didn't sit together, but she looked at him during the Sunday School opening prayer, as she had the first day they'd met, and once again his eyes met hers. This time his look wasn't wry. Instead it was the barest hint of a smile, a look of collusion, a look that clearly conveyed desire.

Being wanted made her delirious. Heather had feared humiliation all her days, the scorn that could come to her if she presumed interest when there was none, the snicker of mean movie fat girl jokes, a whole world of cruelty opening like a fissure. But Devin wanted her! She boldly returned his look, and with a jolt, previously unused machinery began to whir inside of her, a marvelous churning. She felt slinky walking out of church, as if not just Devin but everyone might be noticing her.

He came over to her house again that afternoon. He traced his fingers around the freckles on the back of her hand and trailed kisses up her arms and neck, all of it shocking from moment to moment. They went to the kitchen together, and he took a cold Diet Coke from her fridge. He pulled her toward him and bent her head gently down to his chest. Then he rolled the can sensually up and down the back of her neck like a massage ball. She laughed and shuddered. He opened the can with a waggle of his eyebrows, and then took a sip and handed it to her for a sip, his eyes locked languidly on hers the whole time. She laughed again. The whole ridiculous Diet-Coke-rolling-thing was a joke. But it was also not a joke. She took the sip, and then he set the can aside, sat back on the kitchen table and pulled her roughly to him, her body between his legs. They kissed and kissed for what felt like hours.

After Devin left, Heather sat perfectly still on her couch and tried to make a level-headed assessment of her feelings. Was this jangly feeling a rush of excitement or was it a manifestation of anxiety? Did she really like Devin or did she just like that he liked her?

People were smug about love. *If you have to ask, you're not in love.* Or *you just know when the right one comes along.* Blah blah. Easy for people with dozens of boyfriends behind them to say. But here she was at this late age, as experienced as your average adolescent, and after a not insignificant period of time trying to plumb her pubescent stirrings for meaning, she decided to turn instead to a thoughtful pragmatism.

She didn't have enough data points. It was bad statistics. The most basic of her bio-stats courses in grad school would have pointed this out immediately. But Heather concluded something. She and Devin were alike. A good pair. They were Diet Coke Mormons.

It was a crucial distinction. Official church policy said no coffee or tea, and yet you had above-and-beyonders who said no caffeine at all. They were the same Mormons who didn't just shy away from R-rated movies; they said no to PG-13s just to be safe. Mormons who didn't just shun fornication and heavy petting, who said no to premarital French kissing too. They were often very nice, but often too smiley, and definitely too zealous. But Diet Coke meant Devin would get that she wanted a family and a life and a career. It meant she could make fun of the Glenn Beck protégés at church who loved to talk about the constitution hanging by a thread. It meant it was dangerous and yet okay for Devin to lift her shirt just enough to trace his fingers over the small of her back, to kiss her spine, to lie on a bed beside her, limbs here and there, lips craned to necks and fingers pushing gently into collar bones. It meant potential and the exciting and awful effort required to maintain hope—*just enough, not too much, please don't wreck this all*—every muscle straining with the balance. The fact that she had to regularly stop herself from thinking of Ted's hand on hers? Meaningless. He had nothing real to offer her, and Devin had everything.

Two days later, she and Devin were back on her sofa, leaning into each other, her knee draped over his. Both wearing long pants, no skin contact whatsoever, and yet it seemed a bold and intimate entanglement. Telling stories about their families. His grandparents had all passed. Her mother's father was her last one left. He asked if she and her grandfather were close. She said yes. They'd lived just a few minutes from her grandparents her whole life, and before Brian and Audrey were old enough to watch the younger kids they'd all spent their afternoons at their grandparents' house while their mother taught piano lessons.

"My grandmother always loved my sister Caroline the most. But my grandpa has always been secretly rooting for me," Heather said, dropping her voice to a jokey whisper at the end, as if it were a funny minor family drama and not a longstanding source of personal pain.

Devin asked what her grandfather was like, and a story came to her. She'd brought a project home from school, a stegosaurus-shaped pillow she'd painstakingly hand-stitched and stuffed. Her grandpa gave her a big talk about how people said dinosaur fossils were millions of years old and that their age proved that the world wasn't created when the bible said it was, but had they never considered the fact that Heavenly Father might have constructed this earth from pieces of other planets? And maybe those dinosaur fossils were from those other planets?

"Not the craziest theory I've ever heard," Devin said with a pleased smirk.

"At the time I thought it was, like, so smart," Heather said. "I went to school the next day and raised my hand and presented this great new information to my teacher. I still remember the way she looked at me. It was this sort of panic mixed with disapproval, and she said something like 'scriptures are a really good thing to talk about at home, but here at school we need to stick to science.' I was so embarrassed. I still have dreams that are variations on that scenario, me raising my hand and getting chastised by whoever is at the front of the room."

He laughed. He took her hand and twined his fingers through hers.

What was the exact point of this story? She wasn't sure, and yet the exchange had gone just as she'd hoped, Devin laughing sympathetically at the Mormon impulse toward biblical literalism, just as she did, amused by her family, by her, Devin knowing one more thing about her, their hands clasped more tightly than before. A tiny comfort, a small moment of unity, a test run and a data point that said she could trust his reactions. She liked him, there was no doubt about it.

Her grandfather came up in conversation with Ted a few days later, a parallel to her conversation with Devin that then veered. A warm, wet winter evening, winds from the west and the smell of the sulfur from the Great Salt Lake thickening the air, appealingly familiar in its unpleasantness. In the car, Ted asked about her weekend plans. She was heading up to Bountiful to visit her grandfather and spend the day with her mother while they cleaned her grandfather's house. He asked about her grandfather's age, his health. The same basic conversation.

But then Ted adjusted his spectacles and said, "It always amazed me, when I was in private practice, how comfortable with death Mormons seem to be."

He looked to her, and when she didn't immediately reply, he said, "You have such certainty about an afterlife."

She hesitated because she hadn't really planned on having a Mormon conversation with Ted. Not right then. Not really ever. But if he wanted to, well, she didn't quite know how to resist.

"Well, it's a very well organized after-life, that's for sure," Heather finally said with a laugh. Because, indeed it was. There were degrees of glory, all carefully spelled out, and all the degrees, even the least, were supposed to be happier heavens than you could even imagine.

Ted didn't say anything, and she continued on. "Joseph Smith said something along the lines of, like, if we could even glimpse the lowest degree of glory we'd all rush to kill ourselves to get there. I mean, not those words exactly and what self-respecting Mormon would settle for the lowest degree, so no mass suicides for us! But still . . . glorious futures await!"

He smiled and she kept talking.

"Maybe it helps that we don't really have hell," Heather said. "I mean, there's 'outer darkness,' but that's just for the devil, and maybe Judas. It's pretty much impossible to get there as a regular person."

"I appreciate that leniency," Ted said, lifting his travel coffee mug and tipping it slightly towards her in an imaginary toast. They both laughed.

"Though it also always seemed to me that there was potentially some denial there," he said, a hint of provocation in his voice.

"Denial? Us? Never."

They both laughed.

And they drove on in companionable silence until Heather felt compelled to say something more.

"I guess it's true. You know how no one wears black to Mormon funerals? Or maybe they do, but at least not in Davis County."

"I'm not sure I knew that."

"Well yeah, it's a thing. Everyone wears like lilac and florals and khakis. Or you can wear black, but it's usually like a black floral pattern. I think it's because you're not really supposed to be mourning. They're in a better place, you'll be with them soon, et cetera. But I was so sad when my grandma died, and I didn't want to wear lilac, so I sort of rebelled and wore a very dark navy dress."

He gave her a look of such warmth—amused, as she meant him to be, but also liquid with sympathy.

She had not intended to discuss anything of this sort with him, and although she'd been casual enough in her tone, it felt like an intimate revelation. A revelation that cast her as someone straining at the boundaries. She was trying to build a relationship with Devin. Sharing stories was straightforward. Comfortable. But what was she trying to do with Ted? And how was it that he always seemed to pull them somewhere laced with risk? It reminded her of high school experiments with electrophoresis. A little dish of augur, molecules lined up in a well on one side of the dish, and then you ran an electric current through the gel and, oh, how those particles moved, slowly but steadily traveling across the expanse of the dish. Being with Ted felt like that. Whenever they were in the car together there was a charge, and with all the fluid movement of a dream she migrated toward him. Which, she reminded herself, she should not do.

Another evening entangled on the sofa with Devin, they talked about the piano. Like most kids in Utah, Devin and his many siblings had all taken piano lessons at some point. "I was supposed to keep a practice journal, where I wrote down my practice times every day," he said. "But I totally made it up every week in the car on the way to lessons."

"Didn't your mom see what you were doing?" Heather said, laughing and incredulous.

"Are you kidding? I'm kid six. I could have asked her to sign and initial the bottom of every fraudulent page, and she would have happily whipped out a pen."

"So opposite-world at my house," Heather laughed. She told him about their enforced practice regimes, alarms starting at 5:30 a.m. so they could all get in their practice sessions before school.

"And you never thought about just, like, hitting snooze and skipping it?" Devin said.

"Clearly, you haven't met my mother yet," she answered, a nip of pleasure in the "yet."

Heather made it sound like a complaint, but in fact it was a bit of braggadocio. Nedra Walker was not trifling. Was this not something to be admired? And Devin's response to that little "yet" was to lean in and kiss her again, a physical affirmation of the future to come.

The very next day Heather and Ted came around to the topic of piano and her mother as well. He'd asked if her parents were retired. She said not yet, but her dad would probably leave his engineering firm in a few years. And her mother, well, she was the piano teacher in town you transferred to if you showed real promise. She'd been teaching every afternoon from three to five-thirty for Heather's entire life. "I think the day she quits is the day the stars fall from the firmament," Heather said, attempting a humorous grandiosity.

"She sounds serious," Ted said with a laugh.

"Oh, you wouldn't want to cross her," Heather laughed back.

"So that's where the moxie comes from," Ted said with a sly glimmer.

"Moxie?" Heather said, putting her hand to her heart. "My my!" No one had ever used that word to describe her before. She wasn't sure it was at all accurate. It made her sound like a flapper from Chicago or something. But she liked it, and she was acutely aware of how much that had to do with it coming from Ted. Worldly-seeming Ted, nudging her into that category too.

When her mother's big announcement text arrived, Heather was home alone scrolling through a miserable website dedicated to lambasting blogs like her sister Caroline's.

Caroline had started out as a wedding photographer. She still shot a few weddings a month, but now thanks to an army of sponsors she spent almost all her time on DinnerForEight.com. The site was all about entertaining and was full of beautiful photos of vintage mismatched dinner plates, wildflowers tied with string, and, of course, Caroline herself, in a seemingly endless array of aprons and party dresses. It was outrageously popular, always dozens and often hundreds of comments on posts. Naturally, it had also drawn its detractors, all of whom seemed to have found their way to the particular string of comments Heather was reading on YouRuinTheInternet.com.

"Has anybody ever seen a single non-white person on dinnerforeight?"

"Her chin is so pointy. I can't stand looking at it."

"I bet she pukes up every cake she bakes."

"Great, another fabric banner. Perfect for hanging myself with. Boooooring."

Heather was five years older than Caroline, so they were too far apart for there to have been a real rivalry growing up. Or at least that was what Heather always said aloud. It was true enough in some ways. When they were little Heather had always referred to Caroline not as "the baby" but as "my baby," all the adoration and care-taking that went along with that never really dissipating. But Caroline also had a way of making Heather quiver at the injustice of the world. It wasn't Caroline herself who outraged Heather, to be fair. It was everyone else and the way they treated her. No one would ever acknowledge favoring Caroline, or at least Nedra and Doug wouldn't, but everyone did.

Had they ever asked, Heather could have instantly offered dozens of examples. Here was an easy one: the time Caroline was seven and Heather was twelve and their grandmother gave Caroline an adorable red wool coat with a hood and a huge bow at the neck. It was a fairy tale coat, the stuff little girl dreams are made of. Not a birthday or Christmas gift, just a present on a random fall day, and Caroline had opened the box with a huge grin, and put on the coat and spun and spun around the room, a swirl of scarlet that delighted everyone. Everyone except Heather, who had retreated to her room in fury and tears. It was a perfectly distilled moment of adolescent agony—Heather wanted to be a darling little girl, she still *felt* like a child, and yet she looked like a fully grown woman, an unappealing one to boot (mature,

91

that was the horrid word her mother liked to employ). In fact, she seemed so far from a little girl that her grandmother hadn't even considered getting a coat for her too. There was only one adorable child on the scene, Caroline, end of story. A few days later, most likely prompted by a watchful Nedra, their grandmother had presented Heather with a coat of her own (Nedra at least tried to balance out the favoritism, even if she wouldn't admit to it). A terrible plus size rain coat in an olive drab with an unflattering and stylistically confusing bit of ruffling at both the sleeves and hem. Afterthought incarnate.

How ridiculous that Heather held onto these things! And yet she could call up the disappointment of that raincoat and all that it stood for in an instant.

So not exactly a rivalry, but a nagging awareness of difference. As the years pushed on, Heather sinking into adolescent body shame and Caroline deftly dodging it, Heather's protectiveness of Caroline grew stronger even amidst the jealousy. She worried that all the favoritism shown Caroline made her too trusting. She worried that her sister was too ready to be a good-time gal, certain that the world would be kind to her when really it might not. Nowadays, Heather had to constantly fight to keep from pestering Caroline with judgment-laced questions. *Have you considered graduate school? Aren't all those fancy dresses a little expensive? Are you sure that guy's not a player?*

Caroline's internet fame seemed to trouble Heather far more than it did her sister. A great *yeah yeah, you love her, eye roll,* came over Heather in the face of the outpourings of adoration for Caroline in the comments on her blog. It seemed so superficial. What made people think they really knew Caroline? When they said they loved her, didn't they just mean they liked her pictures?

But it wasn't as if this online hate forum made Heather feel good either. A desolate dread settled into her when she looked at these threads. No satisfaction in it, but still a sort of irresistible draw, as if she were somehow vigilantly patrolling her sister's safety when she knew in fact it was something more perverse that drew her there.

In the guilty silence of Heather's scrolling, the ding of the arriving message on her phone rang out like a doorbell, catching her in the act. She exed out of the window with a hard click and grabbed her phone to see who it was.

The screen read, "NEWS FLASH: I am running for state legislature. I am serious. Haha. Love, MOM."

Heather sat up straight and widened her eyes cartoonishly. Her hand went to her mouth in a pantomime of shock. And yet she couldn't help these gestures and the genuine surprise they indicated. She shook her head and looked at her phone again. Her mother was running for office? It seemed both out of the blue and like something that made total sense, all at once.

Before she could reply to the text, or even really begin to formulate a response, the ping of a gchat message pulled her eyes back to her laptop.

Did you see Mom's text? Audrey asked on the screen.

I don't know whether to be excited or afraid for America, Heather typed back.

Audrey: **Ha. Well, I think it's great. Over Christmas she seemed kind of depressed. I think this'll be good for her.**

Heather: **Depressed? Really?**

Audrey: **Okay, maybe not really. But I think the last few years with her parents have been hard on her. She took care of all of us, and then them, and what about after Grandpa's gone?**

Heather: **Naturally, she will now care for the people of Davis County!**

Audrey: **I am serious. Haha. But seriously, I think this is going to be good for her. Or maybe what I mean is good for me, since she'll be otherwise occupied. Did I tell you she sent me a picture of one of her visiting teachee's daughter-in-law's sonograms? She was like "look, twins!!!!" and what am I supposed to say to that?**

Heather: **You should have sent her the picture from your ultrasound where they put the glowing dye in your ovaries. :(Sorry. That was sad. Not funny.**

Heather knew something her mother didn't. Audrey was hardly holding back on having children for hard-driving lawyer reasons. She and Mike had been trying and failing for more than two years. They'd entered the medical testing phase, with nothing to show for it yet either.

Audrey replied with a jokey emoji of waterfall tears.

Just then Heather's phone rang. A call interrupting a chat interrupting a text? Her apartment had turned into a sudden millennial joke of buzzing, chirping, and ringing. She ran her fingers through her hair, the exact sort of social preening she would have done had all these visitors shown up in real life.

Gotta go. Mom calling! Heather typed.

Okay, Good luck, love you, Audrey signed off.

"Hi!" Heather said, answering the phone energetically.

"Hi!" Nedra said, with matching enthusiasm. "Did you see my text?"

The sarcastic tone Heather had taken with Audrey hadn't quite lifted, and Heather said, "I don't know if anyone has ever explained textual communication to you, Mom, but typically the idea is that you send a text and then wait for a reply. Calling immediately after sort of defeats the purpose."

"Thank you for that important lesson," her mom replied drily. "But I have something serious I need to talk to you about. So you saw the message?"

"Yes," Heather said, shaking off any shades of irony. "It's really exciting, Mom!"

"Thank you!" Nedra said.

"So how did this happen? I mean, I think it's great. It's just a surprise."

"Oh, well. Gary Swenson isn't running again, so there's an open seat, and they asked Dad if he'd run. We talked about it a little, and the more I thought about it the more I thought why not me instead?"

"Really?" Heather said. "Wow!" She wondered how her father actually felt about this development. At the very least this was going to lead to some interesting discussion amongst the siblings.

Heather fumbled for what to say next and finally asked, "So you're running as a Republican?" She regretted the words the instant she said them. Of course her mother was running as a Republican. What else was there in Davis County?

"Mm-hm," her mother said, a long-suffering fatigue drawn out in the hum. Heather winced. Was this going to tilt into another argument?

"So listen," her mother finally continued, "I want to talk to you about my campaign."

Still unsure of whether they had climbed out of the quicksand she had pushed them into, Heather tried a more business-like tone. "Yeah, so when does everything start happening?"

"Well that's the thing, Heather. It doesn't just start happening," Nedra replied, flashing an edge. "I have to make it happen, which is what I wanted to talk to you about."

The sharpness in her mother's voice made Heather retreat even further. "Sure, no, of course. So tell me, how can I help?"

Nedra took a deep breath. "I want you to be my campaign manager."

Heather screwed her face up, pulled the phone away from her ear, and gave it a look, as if the device were malfunctioning. "Really?" she finally said.

"Are you surprised?" her mother asked with another little half-laugh.

Surprised was a word for it. Apparently Nedra wasn't holding the Christmas Crying and Yelling against her. That was good. But this was maybe stretching things a bit too far in the other direction?

"I mean, I don't have any experience," Heather said, grabbing at the first easy excuse.

"Me neither!" Nedra laughed. "Listen, I know there's a lot we don't agree on. But I need help, and there are a lot of things you know about that I don't. Like designing a website, and social media."

"Caroline would be much better at social media than me," Heather said.

Her mother sighed. "Listen, sweetie, I need you. Caroline can help. I already talked to her, and she's happy to help with the web stuff. But I need someone who can help me manage everything. There's campaign finance stuff, and meetings with donors and delegates and all sorts of other people, and you have a lot of professional experience that would really help me."

Her mother had said a lot there—complimenting her professional experience, sincerely asking for her help—and yet what Heather heard loudest and clearest was that she had already talked to Caroline. Had she already asked Caroline to be the campaign manager and only after Caroline pleaded off moved on to calling her next daughter? Why did it matter? Pettiness over who got called first was just that—pettiness. Heather recognized it as such, and yet she couldn't deny the sting.

Later, she wondered if overzealously attempting to overcome her small feelings led to her reply, but whatever it was Heather took a moment and then said, "Okay. I'll do it."

"You will?" her mother sounded genuinely surprised. "Oh, terrific!"

A long silence followed.

"Uh, so what do we do now?" Heather asked.

"Well, we're having some people from the party over for dinner tomorrow night."

"The party?" Heather snorted. "Is this the USSR?" She couldn't help herself.

"Yes, thank you, the Davis County Republican party, okay? It's the county caucus president and her husband and Gary Swenson and his wife."

If Heather didn't learn to bite her tongue this was going to be a real slog.

"What time are they coming over?" Heather said repentantly. "I could try to leave work a little early and come up and help with everything."

"No, no need to come early. Caroline is taking care of dinner. Just come up after work."

"Uh huh," Heather said, humming with the same degree of restrained emotion her mother had earlier. It didn't really bother her that Caroline was in charge of the dinner. Caroline had a blog about being in charge of dinners, for crying out loud. It was just the nagging sense of being second pick. But bright side: if she had to attend a Republic Party get-together, at least she'd have Caroline there to carbonate the mood.

After she said goodbye to her mother, Heather put her face down in a pillow on her bed and let the conversation sink in. She was managing a Utah Republican legislative campaign. Hilarious. And troubling.

She pulled up Brian's number on her phone. Heather could go months without talking to her oldest brother. It wasn't indicative of any strain (although she'd been irritated enough with him at Christmas). He lived in L.A., so there was that. And he'd been busy being married for the seven years before he'd been busy getting divorced. But really, if anything, Heather thought their ability to go ages without talking was an indication of their steadiness, a long-standing, deep connection that didn't require silly "what's up?" texts to validate it.

When they were kids, Heather had puppy-dogged after Brian, sitting on the side of the driveway while he played basketball, following him around the house from room to room. She hadn't thought this at the time, but looking back she thought part of it was that she had seen herself in him. Like her, he was somehow lonely amidst the throng, somehow different, ill at ease. He had plenty of acquaintances, and maybe he'd had best friends when he was little, but by the time he was the teenager she remembered he was a loner, no best buds, never a girlfriend, just her brother, reading, or dribbling a ball by himself.

Even though she was a teenager herself by then, Heather sobbed when Brian left on his mission. But he wrote her at least once a week for the entire two years, and she still had all the letters in a shoe box. "I think Mom and Dad think the only reason I'm liberal or whatever you want to call it is because I'm heavy," she wrote in one, which was at the time a grand baring of her soul. "You're progressive because you're smart," he wrote back. Then he went on about how their parents didn't necessarily see them as they really were, but as who they wanted them to be. It made Heather feel grown-up, getting a letter like that.

She'd called Brian in college the first time she'd been dumped. He was the first person she called when she got into grad school. A tiny bit of her hadn't forgiven him for his rudeness at Christmas, but she'd been plenty rude herself. So, she dialed.

Voicemail.

Heyoo. So did Mom text you? She's running for state legislature. What what. Oh, and I'm helping? As campaign manager? Now that's something that demands a call back. Call me when you have a chance. Love you.

She thought about calling Devin next. This was certainly a development worth discussing, and they'd gotten to the point where on nights they weren't seeing each other they usually called to talk. But she didn't. She composed a few text messages to him but deleted them one after the next. Instead, she saved up the news and told Ted in the morning. It felt like a strange, small betrayal—Devin should be the one she called for just about everything nowadays, should he not? And yet she was somehow more curious about what Ted's reaction would be.

"Big news," Heather announced when she climbed into the car. "My mother is running for state legislature." She said it with outsize skepticism, the way you might say *my mother is setting up an alpaca farm in our backyard.*

"That's very exciting," Ted said. "Has she ever held public office before?"

The question struck Heather as a polite way of asking about her mother's qualifications, presumably inadequate, though she realized it might also have been genuine, no presumption of inadequacy whatsoever.

"Nope. 100% housewife till now," she said. A moment later she backtracked, feeling guilty. "That's not quite fair," she said. "I think I told you before—she's taught piano lessons for years and years. She's very good. And she's held plenty of leadership positions. Church things and civic stuff too. She's the sort of person you call if you need a parade organized."

He smiled. And then gently, as if he were inquiring about frail health, he asked, "Is she running as a Republican?"

"Is there anything else?" Heather laughed. "My mother is a devout conservative."

"And you?" asked again with great delicacy.

"Am I a Republican? Hahah, no."

"So how did you happen?"

"I'm sure my mother asks herself that question all the time."

"Well, it takes real chutzpah to run for office. She's got to be quite a lady. Can't say I'm surprised."

Heather smiled. "Chutzpah! I'll have to tell her that. I bet she's never heard that word before. Wait, I didn't tell you the best part. I'm her campaign manager."

Ted gave her a wide-eyed look and stroked his beard. "Well, well. I suspect I'm really going to enjoy this."

Heather stored this reaction away with pleasure.

Devin called her that day at work. It was the first time he'd done that.

"I'm just grabbing lunch, and I was thinking about you," he said.

She liked this. But still, what she said was, "I can't really talk." Then she stage-whispered the word, "*Cubicle.*"

"I mean, I wasn't really planning on having that kind of a conversation, but okay," Devin said.

"Haha," Heather said. Though it was in fact a fairly racy joke for a Mormon. She was surprised.

"So you'll never guess what," she said. She told him about her mother.

"That's great," Devin said. "Seems like she's kind of getting to have it all."

"What do you mean?" Heather asked, even though she was pretty sure she knew exactly what he meant.

"Well, she got to stay home with kids, and now that you're all grown up she's getting to do this new, interesting thing."

It wasn't a bad thing to say, really. It shouldn't have irritated her. She was overreacting and she knew it, but the assumption that staying home with kids was the right thing to do, the desirable thing to do, was so obvious in his remark, so unquestioningly Mormon and male, that Heather bristled.

"I wish I didn't have to go, but I have to run into a meeting," she said, not bothering to tell him the news about being campaign manager. She hung up and didn't go anywhere, no meetings scheduled for hours and hours.

The fastest route from her apartment in Salt Lake to her parents' house in Bountiful took only twelve minutes, but after work on her way up to the dinner with the people from *the party* Heather drove far out of her way, up to the newly poured curbs and large empty lots at the very top of the developed part of the mountainside in Bountiful. From there you had a view of the whole valley, the Great Salt Lake stretching far and wide, its dim winter gray set shimmering by the evening sun.

All of it, the snowy hill, the dark stripe of freeway, the houses, the schools, the churches with their steeples every few blocks, everything she could see down below was once underwater, an ancient freshwater lake. Every kid in Utah learned all about it in school. Formed in the last ice age, Lake Bonneville had covered the whole valley, almost all of northern Utah, in fact. It had been more than a thousand feet deep, a hundred stories down, down, down. High on the mountains you could see the lines where the water used to be, benches that had once been beaches, freshwater trilobites embedded in the rocks.

All those thousands of years ago Lake Bonneville had risen and risen until it finally breached its natural dam, the Red Rock Pass in Idaho, unleashing a cataclysmic flood. One day silence, the next, three thousand times as much water as pours over Victoria Falls every second bursting through rock. In its rush across Idaho to Oregon, the Columbia River, and finally the Pacific, the roaring floodwaters carved canyons, widened gorges, and deposited hundreds of miles of sediment. Within weeks, The Great Salt Lake was all that was left, dregs of the once mammoth body of water growing saltier and saltier.

Heather and Ted had talked about Lake Bonneville on the way home from work that day.

"I'm going to my parents' for dinner tonight," she'd said. "A campaign thing. I'll have good stories tomorrow, I'm sure. Anyway, have you ever really spent any time in Bountiful?"

Ted said he hadn't, and if he had been someone from Utah, someone Mormon, she would have simply made fun of Bountiful—where sandals with socks still reign supreme—but somehow, with Ted, she wanted to burnish the place.

"You know about Lake Bonneville, right?" she said. "How you can see the benches it formed all along the mountains in Bountiful?" He didn't, and she told him everything she knew. She said she liked to drive up and look down at the lake. The sunsets there were the prettiest she'd ever seen. He and Linda should drive up there sometime. "It's especially beautiful right by the Bountiful Temple. I am not trying to convert you! Just saying that's a great place to watch the sunset."

All of this he had greeted with easy enthusiasm, and Heather had responded by unspooling more and more of her thoughts for him.

"I had an interesting conversation with a friend today," Heather said. "He said it seemed like my mom was really getting to have it all, raising kids first and running for office now, and it's so weird, but I kind of freaked out on him."

"Why do you think that was?" Ted said, his eyes on the road but his face angled toward her, interest in his voice.

"I think it was, like, a Mormon freakout. There's so much *stuff* about gender roles. I mean, it's cultural, but it's also explicitly religious. You know about The Proclamation on the Family? The First Presidency published it in the 90s?"

"I'm familiar," he said. She supposed he hadn't been in private therapy practice in Utah for all those years without coming across it.

"Well, you know how it's framed and hung on practically every Mormon's wall? And you know the part about fathers presiding and providing and mothers nurturing children?"

"That part bothers you?"

"Yes! I mean, saying that aloud is like torching the flag, so don't tell my mom I said that. But yes."

"I am not appalled," he said, laughing.

"I mean it's not like I don't want a family. And it's not like I'm hoping to have kids and then neglect them or anything, but it's just, it's just so frustrating. It's this idea that if you just go ahead and say roles are equal then poof like magic they're equal when that's not really how things work. And especially acting like you can talk your way around a word like 'presiding.' And if you even so much as consider anything different you're probably motivated by vanity and pride and woe unto you and what nice Mormon man would ever want to marry you, and yeesh."

He smiled, his eyes owlish and amused at her rant but clearly sympathetic as well. "Clearly this is something you've thought a lot about," he said.

"It's this whole argument that the rest of the world settled in like 1972 and that Mormons are still wringing their hands over. It's exhausting! It's like trying to argue with someone who came in a time machine from the 1800s, and you say, hey, kids should go to school, and they say, but their families need them to work in the mines! Or hey, women should vote, and they're like, what? How unseemly!"

He laughed. "I sense you're not done yet," he said.

"No, I'm not! I have this terrible vision," Heather said. "My grandmother spent her whole life in the kitchen. We'd be over there after school, and she was always preparing a meal, setting the table for a meal, cleaning up from a meal, whatever, the kitchen, always the kitchen. And she was obsessive about her faucet. She wiped it down and kept it shiny, like one hundred percent spot free, all the time. You didn't want to get a drink of water for fear of messing up the faucet. It was serious. And I can just see myself being exactly like that. The world's smallest dominion. At home, kids in bed, husband reading, me just wiping and wiping the faucet over and over. It terrifies me."

"And your friend doesn't share any of your feelings?"

"Nope. At least I don't think so. It seems like most everyone is perfectly comfortable with all of it except me. And some of the other old maid Mormon spinsters and maybe some weirdo liberal Mormon bloggers."

He laughed.

"Am I treating you like a therapist?" she said. "Sorry. I don't know why I suddenly unloaded all of that on you."

"I believe this is called friendship," Ted said. "If this were therapy, there probably would have been more crying."

They had both laughed.

What she hadn't said to Ted but could have was that more than fearing the faucet, she feared being alone, no family of whatever difficulty materializing. She'd spent infinity more time festering over whether she'd ever find a husband, ever have children, than she had about the details of how she and this imaginary husband would share bread-winning and child-raising responsibilities. As much as it galled to be told the way she'd likely want to work that out was wrong, it galled even more to

105

hear that if she failed to marry and have children nothing else she could ever do would measure up. Her life would be a hopeless wasteland of squandered womanhood. And let's be honest, wasn't that the most likely outcome? Here she was a full decade into the singles ward experience and Devin was the first real hope she'd ever had.

Whenever any well-meaning bishop or stake president or general authority got up and talked about the dear sweet single sisters, the righteous desire of their hearts for children sadly not to be fulfilled in this life but surely to be met in the life to come, Heather could barely cope with the condescension, and rather than draw any comfort she splintered with anger. But the trouble was that it was only half indignation, because deep down she knew she felt a sorrowful agreement with them.

She could run the World Health Organization someday, she could be the Secretary of Health and Human Services, she could be the Intergalactic Commander of Everything, but it still wouldn't make up for not having children, at least not for her. And that was what really killed her. You could work really hard and do well at your job. That you could control. You could keep all the commandments and be a good and righteous soul. That you could control. You could even lose a hundred pounds! But you couldn't make someone fall in love with you and want to have children with you and raise them beautifully with you. That you could not control. Try as you might, you couldn't make yourself not care either, at least if you were Heather. And it was all bad enough without godly opprobrium coming into the picture. That made it practically intolerable.

Up above Bountiful now, Heather looked out over the lake, the winter evening fading all the way from its brief glow to a dark smokey purple. She probably wouldn't have driven up here if she hadn't told Ted about it, but it somehow seemed necessary to prove that she hadn't been lying, she really did come up here and enjoy the view. Five, then ten, then fifteen minutes ticked by in her parked car. She wondered if Ted recounted their conversations to Linda.

She shouldn't have hung up so quickly on Devin. This was the sort of behavior that led to *alone forever*. She liked him. He seemed to like her. They were Diet Coke Mormons. There was real hope for them! So she really ought not to sink it over some little hangnail of a nothing that she was worrying into a grave injury. *Don't be stupid,* she half-whispered aloud to herself.

She texted Devin: "**Having dinner with fam now, but talk later? XO**". She thought about trying to be flirtier, but how exactly? Call him hot stuff or something? What a horrible idea.

Within a few moments Devin had texted her back. "**Even better, how about I swing by on my way home from the hospital. 9:30/10ish? Too late?**"

"**Not too late at all, sounds good,**" she wrote.

She felt a whir of anticipation in her body and relief that she hadn't scared him away, more than just relief, the charged and nervy gratitude that comes with the burden of hope, still alive.

When Heather finally came through the kitchen door at her parents' house, the sound of her mom finishing a piano lesson drifted from the front room. A student was playing a Goldberg variation, one of Nedra's favorites to assign, the runs too slow and plenty of notes flubbed for now, but with sure improvement to come. Caroline and Doug were working away in the kitchen. Heather had dressed with some care that morning. She'd blow-dried her hair and worn eyeliner, and she'd swept on some lipstick in the car. But as always, Caroline made Heather's efforts seem inadequate, embarrassing even, a sad why-even-try. Caroline's long honey-colored hair was perfectly waved. Her lilac floral dress made Heather's office-appropriate black skirt and cardigan look tragically drab. Heather would have felt ridiculous with fuchsia lips, but Caroline looked like the coolest girl in school. Why did it matter? No one was planning a style contest for the two of them that evening, and yet Heather always felt the comparison being made. In some ways it had been easier when she was fat, a clear no-contest.

"Can I help set the table?" Heather asked after giving hello hugs.

"Nah, we're eating in the dining room, and it's already set," Caroline answered, thankfully unfazed by Heather's tardiness.

Heather peeked her head around the corner. The dining room was fully propped. A dozen white candles in brass candle holders in the middle of the table, bright green boxwood bows and pomegranates laid artfully among them, all atop a deep indigo tablecloth, with eight white plates on eight gold chargers.

Nedra finished her lesson and joined them, hugs and kisses all around. The dinner guests arrived not much later. An elderly woman who was apparently the county caucus chair, her similarly aged husband, their dentist Dr. Swenson, the current incumbent, and his wife. Nedra introduced everyone, taking special care to mention Heather as her campaign manager. Heather was gratified by their momentary attention to her, but she noted that the ooh-ing and ah-ing over the beautiful table and the attendant attention to Caroline soon outpaced their interest in her. Per usual.

Everyone bowed their heads for a blessing on the food, and then they got into it. Dr. Swenson said that he didn't think there could be a better candidate than Nedra. The elderly woman, Verna Smith, said that all Nedra really had to do was officially file, and then with the support of the party things could go quite smoothly. But then Verna Smith's husband piped up with a voice as shaky as his hands. "What these two aren't telling you is it can get dirty. If you have a primary challenger, that's when I've seen it go badly."

Everyone rushed to reassure Nedra. "I haven't heard any rumblings from anyone else thinking of running," Dr. Swenson said.

"You've got our endorsement and that's what counts," Verna Smith said.

From there it was all talk of fundraising and neighborhood caucuses and strategies for recruiting delegates, no real contributions from Heather necessary. She kept tidy notes in a notebook she pulled from her purse and didn't say a word.

Once the guests were gone, the family cleared the table and retired to the kitchen. Caroline cracked open a Diet Coke and flopped down on a stool at the kitchen bar.

"I have a million ideas, Mom," she said, "We need to make your campaign website incredible. I'll take a bunch of pictures of you and make sure we get some gorgeous ones. And not just boring studio pictures. Pictures up in the mountains that really show you and Bountiful and make people feel all woozy with scenic beauty. And then I think we need to get a ton of testimonials from your piano students and neighbors and people like that. We should run one a day. I can do photos for those too. That'll be awesome for Facebook. People love seeing themselves. I mean, right, Heather?"

Heather had been nodding along as Caroline spoke, but before she or Nedra had a chance to properly reply Doug jumped in.

"Slow down there, kiddo," he said. "Let's start with the basics."

"So are you going to quit teaching piano after you're elected?" Caroline asked, disregarding him.

"That's the spirit. Already assuming I've won," Nedra laughed.

"You wouldn't really quit teaching, would you?" Heather said, breaking her silence.

Growing up, the stream of kids through the house had been both a burden and a delight. Older girls, popular girls Heather watched around school, would take their place on the piano bench, and she'd hear their voices and their musical strivings, all with the tawdry prickle known to young eavesdroppers everywhere. Boy piano students were even more fraught. But that had been when she was young. Now she wasn't around for comings and goings and she wouldn't have cared anyway. It was just that her mom was Nedra Walker, the famous piano teacher of Bountiful. People knew Doug—Bishop Walker, President Walker—but people knew Nedra too. Saying she was your teacher earned you a certain regard. Heather remembered in high school the way her students had carefully dropped her name, expecting to impress and doing so! Her reputation aside, her mother seemed genuinely to like it. Maybe the money was an important part of it too, but Heather assumed that Nedra also taught because she found teaching rewarding. Heather was proud of her for it.

Nedra answered Caroline and Heather with a laugh. "The legislature only meets for six-weeks a year. I'd just give my students a vacation."

"I think you'll need to cut back during the campaign, if things get heated," Doug said.

Nedra raised her eyebrows, a quizzical expression, and it was hard to tell whether she was appreciating this insight or dismissing it as hogwash, or whether she was just imagining for the first time what heated might look like.

"So, Heather, what did you think of the evening?" Doug asked, turning the conversation.

Heather looked around at everyone's eyes on her and searched for the right reply. "I think everyone was very enthusiastic about your candidacy, Mom, which is great," she finally said.

"And?" Doug asked.

"And what?"

Heather weighed her options and decided for honesty. "I guess I was surprised that they didn't want to talk about any policy issues. You know, feel out your positions on things."

No one answered and finally Heather pressed ahead again, even though she knew she probably shouldn't have. "Like insane land use stuff. Did you know that last legislative session Dr. Swenson voted to turn all of Utah's federal lands over to the state, so they could put them up for mining permits or whatever. I mean, who needs arches when you can have gravel pits. Crazy, am I right?"

Nedra took a considered breath, like a person play-acting staying cool. After Christmas, Heather supposed she deserved that.

"I think I'm flattered that they didn't ask me to make decisions on all those matters right now," Nedra said. "How could I without hearing all the facts and arguments? I think it means they trust that I am a person who'll think carefully about the issues."

Heather nodded, half-heartedly.

"Should we get back to the campaign website?" Caroline said.

Eventually, Caroline found her way to a computer to edit photos, as she was wont to do, Doug found his way to his study, as he was wont to do, and Heather and Nedra were left finishing the dishes, Nedra handing Heather dishes and platters to dry.

"I hope you know I really am excited for you, Mom," Heather said. "I think it's great that you're running. I'm proud of you."

"Thank you," her mother said.

"It's taking a real risk! It's a nice feminist move!" Heather said.

Nedra rolled her eyes.

With a laugh, the mood still light enough, Heather said, "Mom, I don't know why you think you're not a feminist."

And just like that, the feeling between them shifted.

"Seriously," Heather said, still smiling but with misgivings. Why couldn't she seem to stop herself from pushing things like this!

"You really want to know?" Nedra said with a sudden ruff of anger.

"Sure, of course," Heather said, though she didn't mean it. She wanted to take it back, to leave it at being proud of her mother. Because she was. Couldn't she just say that?

Nedra paused. For a second it seemed like she might just shrug, laugh it off, but Heather saw her tilt over the edge.

"Well, I'll tell you. There are a lot of reasons. For one, feminists are all angry about something, and I'm not angry. But mostly, it's because feminists think that what I do and what I care about is worthless. I think raising you kids is the best and most important thing I ever could have done, and the feminists I know certainly don't agree with me. They think my life has been small and wasted, and I certainly don't agree with *them*."

"But that's not true, Mom! The whole point is that women should have choices," Heather said, her voice feeble.

"You say that, but the feminists I know don't think my choices are valid, like I'm brainwashed or something. But I wanted to be a mother. I wanted my family to be the focus of my life. I think motherhood is the highest calling, and I don't appreciate the way feminists dismiss women who stay at home."

"Mom, I don't know who these 'feminists you know' are. Who are you talking about?"

"You really want me to answer that?"

"Sure."

"Well, you, for one."

Heather stammered. In the moment, she had no answer for that. She felt herself tearing up. This again? Were they really back to making each other cry already?

"So why are you running for office?" Heather finally asked, an edge to the question.

"Well, it's not like I have children anymore, now do I?" Nedra said.

The words sounded like a disownment, and even though Heather knew that's not what her mother meant she'd spoken them sharply enough. And then of course there was the underlying dismissal of Heather herself. Childless as she was, Heather could work away in her un-divinely ordained job for as long as she liked, she could get promoted a dozen times, and all she'd ever earn, aside from her thrilling government salary, was her mother's pity.

She kept it together admirably while standing in the kitchen, but a few minutes later, as Heather drove down the hill and out of Bountiful, her chin trembled, and as she passed the oil refinery, gravel quarry, and freeway interchanges of North Salt Lake, she wiped uselessly at her eyes. By the time she reached Victory Road and drove up the hill past the Capital Building and into the Avenues, she'd collected herself, but in her visor mirror she saw that it was a splotchy collection, her face patchy and red, as if she'd suffered an allergic reaction. Devin would be at her door in twenty minutes or so. She didn't know if there was enough ice water and concealer in the world to remedy the situation in time.

At a red light she took out her phone and texted her mother. "Are you sure you want me to be your campaign manager?"

Before the light had even changed a reply arrived. "YES."

Heather sniffed and wiped her eyes again. Part of her had hoped for a release from duty, conflict resolved by simple avoidance, but there was the other part too. Her mother still wanted her help, exasperation and all. That reassurance was a surprisingly strong balm for her spirit.

Chapter 6

Barbara was the one who'd suggested Heather.

"I'm going to need a campaign manager," Nedra had pronounced as soon as Barbara's gloved applause at her announcement had ended. Nedra said it with an enticing arc, a hint of request. Barbara ignored this, either willfully or obliviously.

"What about one of your kids?" Barbara said, returning their walk to its brisk pace. "Heather would be a great campaign manager."

"Not Caroline?" Nedra puffed. "I feel like half of a campaign is just social media stuff these days, and she clearly knows what she's doing there."

"That's true, and you should definitely rope her into that stuff," Barbara said. "But there's lots of other stuff too. All the finance stuff, all the meetings with donors and delegates and, I think Heather might be better there."

Not that she disagreed, but Barbara's implied criticism of Caroline raised Nedra's hackles a bit, as outside criticism of one's child always does. She smoothed her own feelings and said, "I think you're probably right. Although Heather is pretty much a socialist so I don't know if she'll go for managing a Republican campaign."

"Oh come on, you're her mother!"

"You never know," Nedra said.

Even though Nedra suspected Barbara was right about asking Heather, she still wanted Caroline to be the easy answer. No arguments about politics constantly threatening, just some fun work designing yard signs together. She'd gotten home from her walk that morning and managed to hold out all the way till 8 a.m. before ringing her youngest daughter.

Caroline had answered groggily.

"Did I wake you, sweetheart?" Nedra said.

"Uh, yeah," Caroline said.

"Well, I'm sorry. But I have some news. I'm running for state legislature!"

"Woah, cool," Caroline said, still sounding half-asleep.

Nedra repeated what she'd said to Barbara, her inflection exactly the same. "I'm going to need a campaign manager." The hint hung there.

Caroline yawned audibly into the phone. "I can help you with web stuff," she finally replied. So, no volunteering for chief duties there either.

"That'd be great, honey," Nedra answered, trying not to feel perturbed. "I can use all the help I can get." After a further silence Nedra continued, "I think I might need to have a dinner for some of the important county people, to get started planning."

This Caroline jumped on. "Oh, cool! I can do dinner and shoot it for my site and like even totally announce your candidacy in a post. That'd be awesome."

"Great, but maybe just pictures of the table," Nedra said. "I'm not sure the guests would be up for being featured."

Caroline never seemed to understand why anyone would object to appearing online, but thankfully she accepted these terms without protest. Maybe because she realized Davis County Republican grandees were unlikely to be photogenic darlings. Either way, Nedra had gotten her answer. Caroline was in for fun but out for work.

She could have called Heather right after that, but instead she'd spent the day thinking on it. If she asked Heather to be her campaign manager it would be an opportunity to let her middle daughter witness her competence and savvy, a little *see here, I'm quite well-respected.* And sure, maybe there would be some tussling, but it would also be a chance for Nedra to keep tabs on Heather without seeming to do so. Was her daughter finally dating? Was she carpooling with a sexual predator? Not to be ridiculous, but Nedra wouldn't mind a little more information, and Heather wasn't exactly forthcoming.

Nedra had said a little prayer, asking for guidance. She hadn't gotten back either a fervent burning or a muddle of thought, and she interpreted this general blank to mean: *up to you.* So she'd sent her text and made the call to Heather, and it was all working out despite a few flare-ups here and there. At least until the flyers appeared.

The air was thick with gloom the morning Nedra spotted them. The high pressure inversion happened every winter, a lid of heavy air that trapped a murk of fog and pollution in the valley. People wrote endless letters to the editor about it, but nothing ever changed—you dreamed of spring and endured. Nedra had hoped they were past all this by now, late in the season as it was, but apparently not. When Nedra and Barbara met on their usual corner, all the porch lights left on overnight glowed with smudgy haloes, and the women's breath disappeared into smog.

Barbara immediately asked Nedra how she was doing, her voice syruped with concern.

"What do you mean?" Nedra asked.

"The flyers?" Barbara said tentatively. "They were up and down the street yesterday? The campaign flyers?"

"Campaign flyers?" Nedra replied with surprise.

Whoever had tucked the blue half-slips of paper into front door jambs and under windshield wipers had apparently known enough to skip the Walker's house.

Barbara didn't say anything for a couple of steps. "I'm glad you didn't see them," she finally replied.

"Why? Were they bad?"

"I didn't even know anyone else was in the race until yesterday," Barbara said.

"I didn't know anyone else was in the race until right now!" Nedra said. She'd filed at the courthouse the day after she'd announced the news to the family. She was the only one on record at that point. She thought someone would have called—she wasn't sure who, but someone, Verna maybe—if there had been a subsequent filer.

Nedra put on a strange, droll accent for Barbara. "Whatever did the flyers say?"

"I don't remember exactly," Barbara said.

"Oh, sure you do."

"Well, they were just silly. But I guess there's someone named Holly Rasmussen who must be running for the same seat."

"Is she a Republican?" Nedra said, unable to tamp down a strident note of incredulity.

"I googled her last night and couldn't find a thing on her."

"What did the flyers look like?" Nedra asked. "I mean, were they professional or . . ."

"Oh, definitely not professional. Just a run-off-at-the-copy-shop kind of thing. From their tone, I'd say I really don't think she is a person you need to worry about."

"Is that one of them?" Nedra said, pointing at a piece of blue paper on the frosty windshield of a minivan, half-way up a sloping driveway.

"How can you see anything at all in this haze?" Barbara asked. But she obviously saw what Nedra saw because she swiftly trotted up the driveway and snatched the paper from under the windshield wiper, then shoved it in her coat pocket.

"You're actually going to hide it from me?" Nedra said.

"I just don't know if you should see it," Barbara said.

"Now you're really being silly! Look, I'm going to see it eventually."

They walked another few paces and finally Nedra stopped under a corner street lamp and put out her hand.

Barbara sighed. "Fine."

Nedra pulled off one of her mittens so she could unfold the paper.

In Comic Sans font, words bolded here and there, the flyer read:

Who do you want to represent you in the state legislature? Shouldn't it be someone who shares your **values**?

- As PTA President, Nedra Walker pushed to extend the **government's reach** on sex education, putting bureaucrats between parents and their children and pushing an **immoral agenda**.
- Her family directly benefits from **tax increases** through lucrative **government contracts** given to her husband's business.
- As a parent of school-age children, including a son with special needs, **HOLLY RASMUSSEN** understands the **issues facing families in Davis Country today**.
- As a taxpayer who receives NO benefit from higher taxes, **HOLLY RASMUSSEN** has **uncorrupted financial values**.

Does Nedra Walker stand for **your beliefs**?

"Well! That certainly is negative!" Nedra said. "I must be doing something right to get this kind of attention." She tried to hit a cynical, world-weary note, but in truth every word stung, leavening her stunned and shaken.

"You don't have to pretend it doesn't bother you," Barbara said.

"Well of course it bothers me! I mean, everything on there is nonsense! I'm pushing an immoral agenda? I'm corrupt?" She could hear her voice shaking and tried to even it out. Barbara had certainly seen her cry before, but she didn't want to fall apart over this. What kind of politician was she going to be if she cried at everything?

"Like I said, I looked up Holly Rasmussen online and didn't find anything about her," Barbara said, "but I'll ask around at school today. Someone has to know her. Especially if she has school-age kids."

"She obviously thinks she knows a lot about me," Nedra said, trying and failing to avoid sounding petulant.

The rest of their walk was faster than usual, a heart-pumping, heavy-breathing pace that might have been unwise given the smog but which neither woman could seem to help.

Doug was already up and in the shower when Nedra got home. She made their bed, yanking and smoothing the sheets and comforter with urgent sweeps of her arms, then sat on the bench at the foot of the bed, still in her coat, waiting for him to come out of the bathroom.

He emerged in a towel and a cloud of soapy steam and looked at her questioningly. Nedra thrust the flyer at him. "Have you seen these?"

What she really wanted to be was stony and furious, but now that she'd come in from the cold she could feel tears rising again, like an irrepressible spring thaw.

Doug took the sheet of paper.

"Who is Holly Rasmussen and what's she even talking about?"

"What really makes me mad," Nedra's voice shook, "is that there's no point to this at all. The precinct meetings are coming right up, and barely anyone shows up for those. What's the point of blanketing the whole street with this garbage when it won't even make a difference to her campaign? It's just mean."

All the angles of Doug's face sharpened. "My business benefiting from tax increases? That's a joke. And what is this sex ed nonsense? Did you ever even have anything to do with sex ed?"

She took these as rhetorical questions and plowed ahead. "The best thing to do is ignore it, I think," Nedra said, nodding, as if trying to cue Doug to agree. "I mean, at least in terms of public response. But I also think I should call all the precinct chairs from previous years and the other people I know who are likely to show up to the precinct meetings and make sure they know this is a bunch of hogwash."

"I'm sure they already know it," Doug said, "but I bet they're also itching to discuss it, so calling them is smart." He was half-dressed by then, efficient as ever. "You know how people are. They'll want to talk about the nerve of this woman and how it must have hurt your feelings, and the sooner you get that conversation over with the better. Otherwise, they'll be thinking about it and talking about it behind your back, and the more time it sits in their brains the more it muddies things up, even if they don't really believe a word of it."

"Good. Agreed," Nedra nodded. She took off her coat and sneakers and headed for her turn in the shower.

By the time she was dressed and downstairs Doug had eggs, toast, and grapefruit on the table. He'd even used cloth napkins, the blue floral ones Brian and Danica had given her for her birthday a few years back. The scene rankled her even as it pleased her. It was thoughtful, undoubtedly, but it was also as if Doug presumed she couldn't have made them breakfast in her weepy condition. They ate without any further mention of the flyers.

After Doug kissed her goodbye, she listened to his car pull out of the garage and sat staring at the wall instead of getting up to do the dishes. The wall clock ticked audibly in the quiet.

She needed to call Heather—wasn't addressing this situation exactly what campaign managers were for?—but this development certainly undermined her hopes of showing off for her daughter. It was going to take some swallowing of pride to bring Heather into this one. Besides which, Holly Rasmussen's attack dredged up her irritation at the way Heather had prodded her about her reasons for running. As if caring about the community weren't a good reason. As if she needed to justify it.

Way to take a risk, mom! How could Heather say things like that? As if her life had been risk-free. Nedra had bitten her tongue in the moment, but she'd spent quite a while after vividly imagining how she could have answered back. Nothing in life was riskier than having children. Nothing could ever destroy you like harm befalling them, and each new child exponentially increased your exposure to potential tragedy. That was *real* risk, Heather! Every bit of your heart pulled taut, perfectly primed for breaking. This silly election business was nothing. And yet there she sat, immobilized in her kitchen by this Holly Rasmussen person. Nedra Walker, a corrupt immoral money grubber? Ridiculous! Sure, maybe political campaigns were nasty in someplace like, say, Las Vegas. But this was Bountiful. If it was going to be like this, why indeed was she running?

Finally, far too many ticks of the clock later, Nedra shook herself out of it and grabbed a pad of paper off the kitchen counter. "To Do" she wrote. But she didn't write anything more. She stared at the paper just like she'd stared at the wall.

The previous weeks had gone so well. The money had come in, just as Gary Swenson had said it would. Five hundred dollars from the Bountiful Chamber of Commerce; five hundred dollars from the Bountiful Rifle Club; three hundred dollars from "Your Friends at Carlisle Construction." And plenty of smaller checks from friends and neighbors too. "Go get 'em!" one of her former piano students had written in a card, along with a check for $50, "Elect Nedra Walker!" in the memo line. She planned to use it all for yard signs and mailers, still in the works, maybe for some signs and decorations for a float in the Pioneer Day parade this summer.

Beyond the cash, word had gotten around and there had been such an outpouring of good will—in the halls at church, when she bumped into friends and acquaintances in the aisles at the grocery store, parents of piano students who took the time to get out of their cars and knock on the door to pick up their kids instead of just waiting in the driveway as usual. It reminded her of occasions when her family was younger. When she was pregnant with each of the children and for weeks had the news to share with everyone, or when the kids had gotten their mission calls, Brian to Taiwan, Audrey to the Ukraine, Aaron to Chile. *How are you? What's new?* How wonderful to have something exciting to say. And now? *What's new? Hate flyers, but you've probably already seen them.* "How are you?" asked with a wince.

"Call Caroline?" she wrote on her notepad. Caroline had been pitching in. She thought Nedra needed to start with the right image, so they'd gone shopping together, and Caroline had rated every outfit Nedra tried on for attractiveness, authoritativeness, and likability. On a clear day, after a snow storm temporarily blew off the inversion and covered the mountains and valley in a layer of perfect, glittering white, they'd driven up to Lakeview Cemetery high on the hill, and Caroline had taken dozens of pictures of Nedra looking out over Bountiful and the lake.

"Won't the gravestones be a problem?" Nedra had wondered.

"Ever heard of Photoshop?" Caroline said.

When Caroline sent her the photos a few days later, Nedra noticed that the lines between her eyebrows looked as smooth as the cemetery's edited hill, a tweak she didn't mind one bit but couldn't help remarking on anyway.

"That's the secret to being a successful wedding photographer," Caroline said. "Everyone thinks they're better looking than they actually are. You have to edit photos to match the vision they have of themselves in their heads. It takes forever."

"So you're saying I took forever to edit?" Nedra said with mock outrage.

"You are a notable exception," Caroline said. Flattery, but she'd take it.

Caroline had then created a Facebook page and a Twitter account, all using the chosen photo.

But that was all fun, and this flyer development was decidedly un-fun. Nedra scribbled out "Call Caroline?"

"Call Heather," she wrote on the pad next, no question mark, a command to herself, but even as she wrote it Nedra felt her resistance flare up again. Heather had done the un-fun work of opening a campaign bank account and starting to compile mailing lists, and she was finishing up the full website. Aside from all her ulterior motives, in the end Nedra had asked Heather to be her campaign manager because she knew Heather was a genuinely helpful work-horse, dutiful and scrupulous. She'd probably even make all the calls to precinct-chairs-past if Nedra asked. And yet, showing her this flyer? Oh, the shame.

Instead of writing anything more on the "To Do" list, Nedra decided action was the answer. She grabbed her keys and her purse and headed to the car. Had a flyer been delivered to her father's house? She certainly hoped not.

Driving along, Nedra felt like a bed sheet flapping on a laundry line, a billow of anger every time a gust of Holly Rasmussen blew through her head. What kind of person puts out flyers like that? And yet, as much as she wanted to furiously dismiss the whole thing, she couldn't help but probe the insults. Wasn't it impossible for remarks like that to hurt your feelings if there wasn't some tiny, cutting shard of truth wrapped up in them? And even if not, it still seemed impossible to rebuff them as a whole. You had to pull them apart, comb through them, dismiss them strand by strand.

She knew exactly what Holly Rasmussen was referring to with that sex education jab. So long ago, but such a dramatic episode that she could call it up immediately. It was a "maturation clinic" at the elementary school when Heather was in 5th grade, the boys and girls divided into separate classrooms and shown gender-specific videos about adolescence and body changes. After that they all went home with small bags of goodies, a travel size unscented deodorant and a pack of cheap disposable razors for the boys, the same deodorant and a small pack of sanitary napkins for the girls.

It had always been an afterschool opt-in session, but that year the school had decided to make it part of the regular school day. They'd also decided to use new videos. The old ones had been laughably 80s, all feathered hair and grainy production quality. The school informed the PTA of the changes months before the day of the session. They'd offered to share the new video with any parent who wanted to see it. They'd sent home slips of paper informing the parents of the day and time of the session and letting them know they could choose to keep their children out of the session if they preferred and that they were also invited to attend the session themselves if they wanted to be present for the discussion with their children.

Nedra had been president of the PTA at the time. She'd watched the video and found nothing objectionable. In fact, if anything, the videos were a little vague. In the one for girls a mother drew a picture of the female reproductive organs on a griddle with pancake batter. The one for boys had a father and son chatting after a baseball game. Thankfully, rather than deal with any drawings in the dirt around home plate, it flashed sterile health book line drawings for its discussion of seminal vesicles and hormones. Neither video directly addressed sex. They were focused on individual changes, nothing more. Still, to be thorough, Nedra put the maturation clinic on the agenda for two different PTA meetings leading up to the day. No one raised any objections at any of those meetings either. Nedra showed up the day of the clinic with oatmeal cookies for the whole class and sat by Heather, who strenuously doodled throughout the video.

But when Nedra asked if there were further items to discuss at the end of the next PTA meeting, a mother Nedra had never met before, a pale, pinched woman with limp blonde hair, red-rimmed eyes and cracked lips had raised her hands and gotten to her feet. Although every bit of her seemed rumpled and down-trodden, she'd raised her voice in pointed outrage. She couldn't believe her child had been shown a sexually explicit video in school. The session never should have taken place during the school day. In fact, it shouldn't have taken place in a school classroom or on school grounds at all. At the very least permission slips should have been required, and she blamed both the school and the PTA for their failure. Her words were brief, but explosive. She shook as she spoke, which if anything made her all the more frightening.

Everyone else in the meeting had looked to Nedra, their startled expressions begging her to defuse the situation. She had only managed a vague response, something along the lines of a stilted apology for any offense the video had caused and assurances that the PTA would communicate her feelings to the school. Then she'd quickly ended the meeting. As soon as Nedra said "adjourned," the woman rose and walked straight for the door, without another word to anyone. Nedra had never seen her again. Was that woman Holly Rasmussen? Some friend of Holly Rasmussen's?

Nedra was not the sort of person who came up with snappy retorts in the moment. She built responses in the aftermath, layer upon layer, imagining what she could have said, might have said, might yet say in some new context; she even labored over the terms she might use to describe whatever slight it was to Barbara or Doug. But thankfully, most of these internal flare-ups went no further than her own mind, fires that ran out of fuel before any unfortunate airings.

But now she wished desperately that she had something to say to that woman at the PTA meeting all those years ago. It had been a decade and a half since then, and still with just those few words of reminder on the flyer, Nedra's body immediately called up the sting of that day in her chest, in her limbs. She was not used to being rebuked, publicly or otherwise. The whole thing had been so needlessly *dramatic*. She remembered the way all the other women had looked at each other after the irate mother walked out of the room, with the sort of shock you have after a truck barrels past you on the street, just missing you as you step off the curb. You know nothing has really happened to you, and yet you feel the need to check yourself for injuries. That day all those years ago she'd felt flustered, stammering, exposed, yet indignant. She'd wanted to protest, had protested endlessly in her own head later—surely simply acknowledging the reality of puberty wasn't improper—but all she'd been able to do in the moment was hold herself upright and retain the mild dignity of composure.

Immoral agenda was ridiculous. The whole thing was ridiculous. It was fanatics like that who gave reasonably conservative people like herself a bad name.

She pulled into her father's driveway and immediately spotted a blue flyer, its corner tucked under his front door mat. She snatched it up and crumpled it into her pocket before knocking. She imagined that if he saw the paper her father would gently take her hand and ask if she might not reconsider this whimsical recreational political engagement of hers, probably with suggestions that she needed to think of Doug's business and the harm this could cause him. Or maybe her father would be upset on her behalf, riled up, ready for a fight. That wouldn't be good either. Thank goodness she'd gotten there in time for an interception.

Although she always knocked, she didn't usually make her father trek all the way to the door. "Dad? Hello! It's Nedra!" she called as she stepped into the living room. She couldn't open his door now without an expectant trepidation. She looked for his body. She prepared for him not to answer her call.

"Hello!" her father called from the kitchen, his voice muffled despite the effort behind it.

Whenever he answered now, whenever she saw him upright and well, she found she'd conjured the alternative so thoroughly that she didn't quite trust her eyes and ears. It was almost a let down—relief was a better word, surely—but a lowering nonetheless, and even a small sense of wasted effort. She'd have to prepare again.

There was a scrap of paper with his scrawl on top of the sideboard near the kitchen. "Gunshots and apple tree," it said.

"What's this one, Dad?" she asked, holding the paper out to him when she joined him in the kitchen.

"It was the strangest dream!" he said. "Someone was shooting at me, and I floated up to the top of the tallest and most beautiful apple tree to escape. Yellow-pink apples the size of your head. Sounds like a bad dream, but it was really quite pleasant."

Maybe that was what old age felt like. Being pursued, but with the surprise that you didn't fear your exit as much as you thought you might.

Before piano lessons that afternoon, Nedra sat down to make the calls Doug had suggested. And yet somehow again she just couldn't bring herself to do it. She'd have to look up numbers. She'd have to practice what she was going to say. She'd have to muster an easy cheer when that wasn't at all what she was feeling. Instead of doing any of those things, she sat with the same blankness that had fallen over her that morning. This was unhelpful procrastination. She tried to buck herself up repeatedly with half-hearted pep talks, but her self-mastery failed her.

Call Heather. At least she could cross that off her to-do list. She held the phone in her hand and dialed half of Heather's number before hanging up. And then on impulse she quickly dialed another number—her son Aaron.

Aaron: he was guaranteed to buoy her spirits. Nedra worried about all of her children. Brian, who'd fumbled through relationships for so long before he'd gone and chosen someone as strangely incompatible as Danica, and his divorce—she'd fasted and prayed endless Sundays over that one. Audrey, finally married but with no children forthcoming. Heather, who found an antagonist in her own body and hardly stopped there in her search for antagonists. And Caroline, who seemed to flutter through life without ever taking anything seriously. Somehow, though, of all her children, cheerful and good-natured Aaron was the only one who rarely tripped her alarms. There had been a teenage incident with pornography, but that had been dealt with and tucked away long ago in her memory. Nowadays, he had found his way to a sort of dream life. Doug had fretted when he'd moved to Moab to work as a rock-climbing instructor (not the height of long-term stability), but she'd remained unconcerned. Aaron didn't always have a plan, and yet plans seemed to form around him. Now, just a few years later, he was a part owner of his own tour company.

"Hi Mom," Aaron's voice sounded in the receiver.

"Sweetie, you answered!"

"I know. It's pretty shocking."

She wasn't necessarily planning on bringing it up, but when Aaron asked how the campaign was going the words just came out. "Someone put out hate flyers yesterday. I'm feeling pretty terrible today, if truth be told."

"Hate flyers?"

She told him the gist.

"I wouldn't mind if this were some sort of big election. You know, if strangers were reading those words. But these are our friends and neighbors. It just feels so . . . embarrassing."

Once she said it she realized how true it was. She wasn't really angry, or she was, but that wasn't the primary emotion. It was more that she shuddered thinking of everyone in every house for who knows how many blocks seeing her name and those words and thinking anything about her, whether it was anger or pity or even believing the flyer. The attention beyond her control, that was the issue. Most of the time, she believed she knew how she came across. She collected herself and went out into the world and she gauged reactions and adjusted accordingly. Discreet and composed. That was the Nedra Walker she wanted to be. But this? This was her scattered and ricocheting. This was a mess. She was *embarrassed* by it.

Aaron didn't have much in the way of solutions, but within a minute he was telling her about rival white water rafting companies on the Green River and the spoof video battle they'd gotten into on YouTube. Friend to all, Aaron had featured as an actor in both company's videos, with increasingly elaborate faked injuries as the duel went on. Ketchup running from his head. Fake arms, twisted to improbable angles, and then missing altogether.

As they laughed, Nedra had a sudden vision. She'd find Holly Rasmussen's address, and when Aaron was in town she'd send him over with a pie. The retraction flyers would be printed in no time. From there she couldn't keep from imagining more and more scenarios of revenge kindness—shoveling this Rasmussen woman's sidewalks, leaving flowers on her doorstep every day.

"Mom," Aaron said with a change in his tone. "Next time I come home I think I'm going to bring someone with me."

"Someone?"

"A girl, as in a girlfriend."

"Well well!"

"She's from Mesa and she runs a camp outside Moab for *wayward* teens." He pronounced the final words with a stagey overemphasis. "You'll like her. Her name is Jennifer."

Aaron had a lot of girlfriends. But he didn't bring them home very often, or even bother to mention them. Nedra only knew about most of them because they appeared in Facebook photos beside him for a time and then vanished. She'd see about this Jennifer.

"Don't tell her about the hate flyer," Nedra said.

Maybe this Jennifer would matter. Maybe she wouldn't. But either way, no need for her to start off her acquaintance with a tarnished Nedra.

After hanging up, Nedra sat with the phone in her hands, trying to work herself up to calling Heather. But she failed again.

In the end, she made a new plan. Heather never needed to know about the flyer. She'd mention Holly Rasmussen in some other context, and they'd move right along.

Chapter 7

Devin's roommate Kevin was never home. "Devin and Kevin, I know," Devin had said when he told Heather they were roommates. Devin hadn't really introduced Heather to Kevin. It hadn't been necessary. Kevin was in their ward, and she'd met him already. Kevin's dad was a lawyer who specialized in gun law and ran seminars all over the country on gun laws in each state. If you wanted to compare and contrast the particulars of concealed weapon laws in Nevada, Minnesota, or Arkansas, or you wanted to know exactly who you could shoot and when in Delaware versus Arizona, he was your man. Kevin booked all the hotel conference rooms for the seminars, sold his dad's books and CDs at tables in the back and was a general right-hand man, which meant he was in exciting locations like Peoria or Jacksonville a few days every week.

"Don't be freaked out if you open a drawer and there's a gun in there," Devin said to Heather one evening as she hunted for a can-opener in the kitchen. "He has like seven, and he moves them."

"Are they loaded?" Heather asked, taking her hands off the drawer pull slowly, as if hoping not to alarm its contents.

"I've never checked, but I think they probably are."

Devin seemed remarkably unfazed by this. Were guns really not a problem for him? Heather could have gone on about the horrors of guns for ages—anyone in public health could. The data was inarguable. It was one among the many outrages in Utah politics that drove her crazy. You had your general western range and ranch libertarian streak among Utahns, but you also had the early church history of mob attacks and U.S. military marches on the saints that left a lingering best-be-armed mindset in some corners of Mormondom. But really, it was more important to people to be armed against some imaginary invasion than to keep real people here and now from shooting themselves? And especially kids! The way she figured it Jesus always sided with kids. So Mormons, unite around gun control, how about it? But nope. What was wrong with people! Still, she bit her tongue—at least they weren't Devin's guns, and who knew, he was in med school, he probably agreed with her. In fact, she was almost certain he did. She couldn't really imagine that Devin had no problem with loaded guns in the utensil drawers. But she'd save that for another day. (What day? Unclear. Just not today). She closed the drawer and didn't poke around in the kitchen or anywhere else after that.

She and Devin were how many dates in? Eleven? Twelve? It was a good sign that she'd lost count! There had been movies where they whispered amusing things to each other and held hands, dinners at hole-in-the-wall Mexican and Thai restaurants where they ate off each other's plates, a snow-shoeing adventure, glittering and exhausting, a sense of well-being atop the snow drifts that seemed to bless their togetherness. She'd learned that as a kid he'd been obsessed with whales, that in high school

135

he'd been voted Most Likely to Win a Nobel Prize, that his big rebellion as a teenager was listening to early '90s rap. She had seen again and again that he tipped well in restaurants.

Tonight, roommate Kevin was gone as usual, and she and Devin were watching a movie together, a change from their more typical jaunts about town. The apartment was outfitted with an overstuffed, slippery leather sectional, the sort of couch that Mormon families with six kids chose for their basements, and Heather, a lifetime frequenter of such basements, tucked a blanket under herself with practiced efficiency to keep from sliding toward the edge of the cushions. Devin held her hand, drawing circles over and over with his thumb on her palm. It was affectionate, maybe it was even supposed to be arousing, the soft, repeated caressing of it, but the unending attention to such a small patch of skin irritated her. She wanted to move his hand away, but she didn't want to seem spurning. The irritation was minor though. What thrummed above every other feeling for her with Devin nowadays was the desire to keep her audience wanting more. It felt like an incredible power—the wielding of her physical self to capture attention. And yet she could already sense just how powerless it truly left her. Love me, want me, I stand at the pinnacle. Turn away, and I fall.

Finally, halfway through the movie, Devin put his arm around her and left her hand alone, and then a short time later he tilted her head so he could kiss her neck, and soon they weren't watching the movie at all. His hands found their way under her shirt. Not the front of her shirt, the back, his fingers kneading the muscles around her spine. His hands traced around the back clasp of her bra, a dangerous place for them to be, and she worried that she'd have to twist herself to reposition them to safety.

She worried also that he'd feel the skin that sagged around her lower back, leftover from vanished fat rolls. But Devin stopped without her doing anything. His hands came out of her shirt and with his face hot against her ear, he said, "I love you, Heather Walker."

The words jolted her. It was almost as if he'd said them to justify where his hands had been, or as a way to stop himself. But the words were rougher and more sincere than that too. Heather pulled back to look Devin square in the face and make sure she'd heard him right.

"You do?" she said.

He half-laughed and moved his face back to her neck, then nibbled her earlobe with his lips. "Uh huh," he said.

She paused for a long moment and finally whispered back, "I love you too." *I love you*—it felt reckless and daring and possibly true. Her head was a sudden muddle of middle-aged pragmatism and teenage impulse. Did she really love Devin?

Not much later they said goodbye for the evening, and she began a frenzied mental pacing. It was hard for her to hear her own heart when every moment she'd been busy listening for the next still-devoted beat of his. But yes! He was funny. He was smart. He was nice. What more did a person want?

The fact that she had to search her feelings, was, she knew, damning in the eyes of women's magazines across the land. It was supposed to be obvious, and if it wasn't it meant you were kidding yourself. But those were the same magazines that offered tips on fellatio, so what did they have to say to her really?

She wanted Devin to want her. (Maybe she also wanted Ted to want her, but that was a rogue data point). She didn't want every man on the street to want her, nor even every nice

Mormon man. Especially not every nice Mormon man. If she'd gone down the roster in her singles ward she wouldn't have been able to find another single suitable candidate. So she noticed him, he noticed her. Was this not the beginning of love? And she could see a happy life for them. Was this not the end of love? In between, yes, she bucked and kicked with nerves, but she suspected that had more to do with discomfort with settling into the role of a romantic partner to anyone rather than anything particular to Devin.

"Romance" required her to see herself in a new way. She wanted to be a woman a man could love and marry without anyone raising their eyebrows, without any surprise or discounting or working out of why and how. Maybe people weren't actually awful enough to think this way, but Heather had always imagined speculation when a couple didn't physically match. *She's so fat, and he's so thin, but maybe she's very nice, and maybe he's not very confident?* Maybe no one would have been surprised if she'd found someone whose weight matched hers back when she was heavy, but that had never happened either. And now? Maybe no one was surprised at her pairing off with Devin, and yet she felt that someone might call fraud at any moment. This two-sided affection—she was a grown woman, and yet it was completely new to her.

Heather had been infatuated before. There had been a piano student of her mother's, a boy a couple of years ahead of her in school. Years, *years*, she'd fixated on him, infatuation frankly far too delicate a word for the way he'd consumed her thoughts. It was so horribly *typical.* He was one of the most popular boys in school. What girl didn't have a crush on him? It was all so mortifying that Heather never told a soul, never so much as wrote about it in her journal, an incredibly shameful secret, the very idea that she might imagine he would ever look at *her* so embarrassing to her, and yet the yearning! The fantasies! And it had gone on long past high school. Home on college breaks she'd still looked for him in every parking lot, down every store aisle. John Culver. Even thinking his name now made her cringe.

When she was a teenager and she saw him unexpectedly at school, her entire body tried to flip itself inside out, like the jolt of a funhouse ride every single time. The times she expected to see him weren't much better, her every physical fiber stretched taut with anticipation. When he arrived for piano lessons every week she hid in her room, but she could hear him playing, and if she sat in a certain spot she could feel the reverberations of the piano traveling through the wall, a remote yet stunning physical intimacy. She had loved him with a completely one-sided devotion that occupied her brain and heart for more than half a decade.

Did she feel that way about Devin? Thankfully not! (Though she did sometimes feel a little that way about Ted, but forget about that). After all, she was an adult now, not a juvenile obsessive, and that was, in her final assessment, how she felt about the whole business with Devin—mature, rational, considered, and appropriately emotionally engaged. She yearned, but it was for something far beyond Devin. It was for a family, a future, a life. And who was going to make that possible if not Devin? (Certainly not Ted). She may have had roughly the same amount of actual romantic experience as an adolescent, but gosh darn it, she had a fully developed frontal lobe nowadays, and that was worth something.

For her entire adult life so far Heather had been cramped in a particular pose. And that pose was: just fine! Not bothered to be single at all! After all, nothing is more off-putting than desperation. Mormon singledom might have been tough on men—certainly perpetual virginity wasn't an ideal state—but for women? Even worse. There were always more women than men and social custom cast you as the passive party, which meant direct action was not quite impossible, but vastly more likely to repel than attract. Your choices were to enter a losers' competition, all the unchosen alternately mewling and scratching for the ever-diminishing available male attention, or to try to retain some dignity by staying aloof, silent but for your white flag flapping pathetically in the wind: *mercy, a miracle, someone, please.* That had been Heather. But here she was, finally, a rescue vessel pulling up alongside her.

She could see a life with Devin. She tried not to spend too much time conjuring it—you don't spend your whole life being disappointed in love without learning some lessons in self-preservation—but it was right there, a future. She loved Devin the way you love a life preserver. Gratefully, most definitely, but did that mean the love wasn't real? No, it did not.

She went over all of this again and again, a swirl of nerves and ardor and self-reassurance. Heather hadn't mentioned Devin to her parents yet. She feared they'd be too enthusiastic: at last, a chance for our poor fat daughter! But the moment had come, had it not?

The very day after the exchange of I-Love-Yous, Heather headed up to her parents' house. The ostensible reason was to debut the campaign website she and Caroline had designed for Nedra. But of course she could have just sent her mom the link and called her on the phone. But no. If Heather was going to talk about Devin, she wanted to do it in person.

Heather and Nedra settled in at the dining room table, with Heather's laptop lighting their faces. The website featured plenty of red, obviously, but the fonts Heather had chosen were delicate yet stately, not overbearing. Caroline had come through with photos of Nedra that were, as promised, beautiful. Woozy with scenic beauty, was that what she'd said? Whatever it was, Nedra looked pretty yet plausibly authoritative, and they'd taken the shots up on the hill by Lakeview Cemetery, the valley and the lake laid out below Nedra in a perfect background bouquet. The actual language Heather and her mother had come up with managed to be general enough that she wasn't horrified either. *Supporting local businesses and keeping our community strong. Neighbors helping neighbors. I love Bountiful. I grew up here. I raised my family here.* Nothing too right wing there.

Nedra oohed and ahhed, thanking Heather again and again. Sailing on the good cheer, Heather nonchalantly said, "So, I'm sort of seeing someone. It might be getting kind of serious."

Nedra sat up straight in her chair and cocked her head excitedly, like a sheepdog suddenly alert at the sound of the round-them-up whistle. "Tell me all about him!" she said.

Agh. The overexcitement, so troubling because it so closely mirrored Heather's own feelings—*Yes, alert, alert! A suitor at last!* Heather wanted to be cool, but of course she wasn't. Her face flushed. Her hands descended into dampness.

She gave Nedra the outline. A guy, from her ward. In medical school. Grew up in Fruit Heights.

Her mother turned practically phosphorescent with delight.

"How old is he?" Nedra asked.

"Uh, twenty-eight, twenty-nine?" Heather said.

"You don't know?" Nedra said.

"Yeah, okay, he's twenty-eight."

"We should have him over for dinner!" Nedra said. "Or have Caroline invite us all for one of her dinners!"

Caroline. It was immature and lacking in self regard to even worry about it, but Devin had clearly shown a weakness for a certain form of fizzy female before—wouldn't it be just perfect if Caroline tap-danced onto the scene and Devin tapped off after her?

"We'll see," Heather said.

But still, she'd done it. She'd told her mom. That was an official check mark of relationship progress.

Later that week, she and Devin were out to dinner together when he said to her, "If we were going to live someplace totally different, where would it be?"

That "we" was the first of its kind, and it sang out, the tones and undertones carrying long past the end of the sentence.

"In the world?" Heather said. "Morocco. Or a lake in Italy."

"I'm being more serious. U.S. only. You might not have thought of this, but I have to match with residency programs next year, and I think we should think of places we might like to live."

This was more than fantasy. This was presumption. This was declaration. This "we" was sudden and sweeping in its inclusion. She was at once lit up and slightly deadened by its reach. The way he just pronounced it surprised and put her off. It was wonderful and yet seemed to cut her out of something crucial, some trepidation on his part missing. Should he have been so sure of her affection? Of her delighted participation in this *we?* Should he so easily presume that she would follow him? She masked her confusion of feelings and tried to be game with a light and easy reply.

"No California," she said. "It's crowded and full of itself. How about Boston?"

"Ambitious. Just go and pick the town with the hardest programs to get into why don't you." He pushed his hair off his forehead and smiled at her with narrowed eyes, a look of warmth and desire.

She put her hand out across the table, and he met hers with his, and she threaded their fingers together. There, all better.

Later in the chilly parking lot he pulled her tightly to him and Heather could smell the skin of his neck and his scalp and the faint spicy clean of his aftershave.

She hesitated, rehearsing the words, but then she lifted the gates and let them free. "I love you, Devin McIntyre," she said.

It was her first time saying it first, not in response, and it felt like an act of freedom and fancy, like swinging out over the edge of a cliff on a rope. Maybe, she was finally a person who got to say such things.

After he'd kissed her, she buried her face in the space between his neck and shoulder and breathed in and out, calmly, as if she weren't giddy and stunned all at once.

Chapter 8

Nedra stopped by her father's house every morning these days. Her father's house—that was how she thought of it now, and yet, it was the same house that she'd thought of as her parents' house until just a few years ago and as "my house" for an entire childhood before that. It wasn't as if the house had never changed. Her parents had repainted. They had installed new carpet several times over. The kitchen flooring had been replaced. Her once-bedroom certainly didn't still contain the white wicker of her girlhood. But it was still the same house. The same spaces, the same corners, the bay window the Christmas tree had been placed in every year, the narrow hallway where as a girl she'd spread her feet and arms between the walls and scaled to the ceiling. That was fifty years ago, and yet it was the same hall.

Coming through the front door now, the same scent as always greeted her. Wood paneling and paperbacks, linoleum and nubby wool drapes, Ivory Soap and Lemon Pledge, a smell suburban and outdated that tugged at her heart, the very definition of familiar.

"Hellooo," she called out.

"Just in here reading the paper," her father's voice came from the kitchen.

He looked well, his face less sallow than it had been. She saw dishes drying in the rack beside the sink. Good, he'd had breakfast and cleaned up. Good signs all around.

"Big day today, isn't it?" he said as she leaned down to give him a hello hug.

"Oh yes indeed, the neighborhood caucus meetings!" she said with showy enthusiasm.

Nedra had been waiting weeks for this day to arrive. Tonight at the junior high, the thirty-seven precincts that made up her legislative district would each elect a delegate for the County Convention. If she could get 25 of those 37 delegates to vote for her at the Convention in three weeks time, that would be it: Republican candidate officially selected, no open primary, and Holly Rasmussen would disappear like the Wicked Witch of the East, legs rolling back up under the house that smashed her. (The Democrats of course had their caucus meetings tonight as well, but somewhere else, certainly not somewhere as spacious as the junior high; Nedra didn't know where. It didn't matter).

"Are you still up for coming tonight?" Nedra asked her dad. Heather, Caroline, Doug, Barbara—they were all coming. The way Nedra figured it, the more presence the better.

"Oh, well," her father shrugged. "I think I might stay in tonight after all."

"Oh no, are you feeling okay?" she said, worried.

"Oh fine, fine. I'm just less and less interested in politics these days," he said.

Less and less interested in politics? Even though his own daughter was the one running for office? A shot of rage rushed from her spine to her extremities, leaving her fingers suddenly tingling.

He motioned to the *Deseret News* open in front of him. "The sports section, that's about all I have the stomach for now."

"Mm hm," Nedra answered, suppressing a more vigorous reply. She turned to put away the breakfast dishes so she could scowl without consequence.

That evening, Nedra dressed carefully. Perfectly pressed slacks, a lovely peach silk blouse, a soft grey cardigan. Nothing too showy. Just a competent and friendly neighbor, running for office. Doug looked just as he would any Sunday: navy suit, white shirt. He'd asked her if he should take off his tie. Nope, she'd said. The Bishop Walker look serves you well. Serves me well too.

He took her hand as they walked through the parking lot toward the school. Nedra had spent at least a decade with one or another of her children enrolled at the junior high, and so she walked through the front door feeling calm and in control. She had this. She waved hello here and there, gave quick hugs. Doug gave handshakes and his own hellos. Caroline and Heather trailed them just as they had as children. Was Holly Rasmussen here? Nedra looked for glaring unfriendliness, a strange rude woman lurking, saw nothing but smiles coming her way.

"This is so weird," Heather said. "I feel like I am 13 again, and I do not like it."

"Are you kidding me?" Caroline said, jumping up on one of the carpet blocks that dotted the commons area. "I love it!"

"Please do not make a spectacle of yourself," Nedra said, calmly.

Caroline climbed down without further comment and they all walked toward the gym door where room assignments were posted.

"Okay, Mom and I are in the gym," Doug said. "You two, pick any other room and go do your duty."

"Yes, sir," Heather saluted.

Doug took Nedra's hand. "Ready?" he said.

"Yes, sir," Nedra said with a bit of sarcasm in her voice.

Nedra had been in this very gym for an election that felt like ages ago and just yesterday at the same time. None of Nedra's daughters had ever run for school office, but both Brian and Aaron had, Brian for class president in eighth grade, and Aaron for sophomore class president and then student body vice president. Aaron was a natural, but Brian had surprised them when he said he wanted to run. He wasn't shy exactly, but he was always more of an observer. Tall already at thirteen, he was good at basketball—he'd end up starting all throughout high school—and Nedra supposed that gave him a sort of popularity, but he was not a gregarious teenager.

"It's a great opportunity to practice public speaking," Doug had said, hopefully.

No harm in running, Nedra had decided, or only the sort of harm that taught good lessons, though of course she hadn't said anything so discouraging aloud to Brian.

She'd bought him all the posters and poster paint he'd asked for. She'd helped him tape little "Air Heads" taffy candies to quarter sheets of paper that said "Don't be an airhead, vote Brian Walker, 8th Grade Prez." The entire eighth grade class had gathered on bleachers in the cafeteria to hear the speeches. She'd sat on the same side of the room she was now making her way toward, a row of chairs set up for teachers and parents, her

147

armpits trickling with sweaty anticipation. Brian had worn a tie, though a sort of humorous one, with a picture of Snoopy playing the piano on it, and he'd delivered his remarks from memory, his large, soft boy hands sweetly, nervously twiddling with the side of the podium while he spoke. His cheeks shook. She was sure she'd mouthed half the words along with him.

The boy up after him did a running handspring and some sort of flip on his way to the microphone.

Brian hadn't won. Aaron had won both times.

At the very least Nedra could take comfort in the fact that there would be no gymnastics in this room tonight.

She and Doug took their places at a cafeteria table and waited. One by one, familiar faces joined. More handshakes. More hugs. No Holly Rasmussen. Of course she wouldn't be in their precinct, but still, Nedra kept an eye out around the room.

Barbara took her place at another cafeteria table across the room and gave Nedra a wink and a discreet thumbs up.

At last, Nedra and Doug's group of nine got started. A quick prayer, then the pledge of allegiance, a reading of the State Republican Party Platform, and then down to business. They needed to elect new precinct officers and new county and state delegates.

"These are such important civic functions," the precinct chair, their longtime neighbor Bonnie Clayton, said. But then her bright smile fell, and she shook her head and frowned dramatically. "You know, I look at America today, and I'm just sad. It's just horrible, the corruption and decay in Washington and all around us. The immoral majority. But, I'm always full of hope," here her smile returned and she turned her eyes to Nedra. "If people like us, right here in this room, raise our voices in support of good people with strong values, I think we can make a difference."

Nedra felt a bloom in her chest and smiled demurely.

"Now," Bonnie clapped her hands together. "Let's get to nominations!"

When it came time for county delegate, Doug raised his hand. No one else did. One quick vote of acclamation, and Nedra had herself a delegate.

After their precinct meeting disbanded, Doug and Nedra headed back to the commons to wait for the girls. Caroline emerged first.

"Wait till we're in the car," Caroline said, sidling up. "Boy have I got a story for you."

"Any sign of 'the opponent'?" Nedra said. She didn't want to say Holly Rasmussen's name aloud in case she were somehow within earshot.

"Nope," Caroline said. "Coast was clear."

When Heather joined them Nedra silently mouthed the words "Holly Rasmussen?" to which Heather shook her head no.

So maybe she just hadn't shown. Bizarre, and yet somehow unsurprising.

Barbara buzzed by on her way out. "Done and done!" she said, which Nedra knew meant she'd gotten herself elected as the county delegate in her precinct as well. So, two delegates in her corner. Nice work for one evening!

Once the car doors safely closed around the family, Caroline launched right in. "Okay, oh my gosh you guys," she said. "This guy in my group, he had a bunch of emails he'd printed off and brought to pass around. They were all about how the first thing the Nazis did in Germany was take guns from the people and about how public schools are just like the Soviets' centralized government evil. By the way, he kept calling them 'government schools' not public schools. And whatever, nothing that hugely surprising, but the best part was that he also had all these flyers he was handing out for his bunker business."

"A bunker business?" Doug said incredulously.

"Fine, not exactly a bunker business. I guess he called it 'Emergency Preparedness,' but this wasn't like a little 72-hour food supply. This was like machetes and MREs for the Obama apocalypse."

"You know, emergency preparedness is not a bad thing," Nedra said.

"Yeah, whatever. This guy was nuts. And I haven't even gotten to the best part yet. He nominated himself to be a county delegate, and everyone voted for him, so he's all yours, Mom!"

"I look forward to talking with him and hearing his concerns," Nedra said with only the slightest hint of humor.

"Oh boy. And concerns he has aplenty!" Caroline said.

"I don't know how you put up with crazy people so well," Heather said.

"Oh, as if I could head over to the Democrats and everyone would be sane," Nedra replied testily.

She could feel Heather squirming, clamping down her own retort. Good. Exactly right. Clamp it down.

"You know what might be a total Instagram hit?" Caroline said. "Pictures of pretty bunkers. I should ask that guy. I'm sure there's someone around here with underground shelves lined with gorgeous Mason jars of fruit."

At least you could always count on Caroline for excellent diversion.

Once they were home Nedra laid out her plan. The party would pass along the contact information for all the delegates in the morning, and from there Nedra would make appointments to meet with each and every one of them.

"I'd love companions for the meetings," Nedra said to all of them. Companions—the Mormon way. Missionaries were paired with companions; visiting teachers and home teachers too. You could think of it as someone to check up on you (and vice versa) or you could think of it as helpful backup. Either way, it was a mode they were all comfortable with. They all said sure. Nedra just hoped Heather would be able to buckle down and behave herself well enough to be of some service.

The next morning, Nedra was back at her father's house. He greeted her from his armchair in the living room, the TV turned to a cable news channel, volume low, closed captioning large. A political talk show. So much for being "less and less interested in politics these days." He was wearing the same shirt he'd worn yesterday. His prerogative, after all it probably hadn't really gotten dirty, and yet Nedra blanched to see it. He never would have done that when her mother was alive.

She waited for him to ask about the neighborhood caucus meetings, her balloon of excitement bobbing around, waiting to be seen. Of course she could have brought the evening's events up herself. She'd imagined discussing it all with him. That would have been the mature thing to do. And yet she waited and waited, and her balloon sank lower and lower, and when an hour later her father hugged her goodbye without so much as asking a single question about her "big night," she felt fully deflated. Here she was, sixty years old and still a child.

Chapter 9

The days were getting longer again, and after some bleak-of-winter time off Heather had gotten back to walking in the evenings. Wool socks in her sneakers, the sound of her feet and her breath and the swing of her arms and a pleasure in the cold that pinked up her legs beneath her leggings and in the warmth that seeped back into them when she returned home. She understood why her mom liked walking so much.

The inversion had finally cleared, and in the hour before dark a glow took over the whole valley. The snow far up on the mountains blushed a rosy lilac, a soft, human color. Heather felt a romance in the Avenues then, all the cozy charms of sweet historic homes called forth. Dinners cooking, firewood burning, lamps glowing.

She hadn't thought much about winter in Utah till she moved to Maryland for grad school. It was just winter, like winter everywhere she imagined. But her Baltimore winters were damp and depressing, days that felt like wet wool coats, the sky low and suffocating, and now that she was back she appreciated how different Utah was. In Salt Lake, the cold air carried a brittle current of energy, cracking like kindling. You could imagine a bell singing out for miles, nothing in the dry air stopping it till it echoed off the mountains.

It was a whole world, this valley, the curve of the valley floor up to the foothills and then the mountains all around like the sides of a globe. In Maryland, you got on a train and you were in DC in an hour, or Delaware, or Pennsylvania, cities and states all right there, scrunched in close. In Utah, once you left Salt Lake it was nothing for hours. To the west past the lake and the Oquirrh Mountains you hit desert prairie and then the salt flats, an epic emptiness all the way to Nevada, and what then? More of the same till Reno, hours and hours away. If you passed through Emigration Canyon or Parley's Pass up and through the Wasatch peaks and ski resorts to the east, you came to the grassy hilltop plains of Summit County, and then it was open scrub, distant hills, and spartan ranches all the way to Wyoming where the same endless vista stretched on to the Tetons and Nebraska. Head north and past the suburbs of Davis County and the final outpost of Ogden, and it was the same barely speckled range all the way to Idaho and beyond. South, around the point of the mountain, you had Utah Valley, Provo and BYU, a flourishing like a droplet of civilization, a final drink before the hours of grassland desert, and then just vast hills and range where cloud shadows moved across the face of the land in giant heavenly drama. You could see the dots of towns along the interstate coming for miles and miles before you reached them, gas stations near the freeway exit, a smattering of houses and a church, not much more, then receding, receding, leaving just you and clouds and range all the way to the red rock monuments of the south.

For all the epic towering, the ring of mountains around the Salt Lake Valley was a cozy embrace, a steady compass circling the bustle of life. In Salt Lake you always knew which way was north, south, east, and west. You could always find your peak: the crazy vertical granite of the Devil's Slide to the east, sharp and straight above Cottonwood Canyon; the gentle rise of Ensign Peak to the north, where Brigham Young first stood to survey the valley below, curving round the north side of Salt Lake; the little notches and pavilions of Antelope Island out in the lake, the last dark outline against the fading western light in every sunset.

Heather had taken in the full blush one evening, feeling good, feeling, she imagined, like a woman in love. She trooped the whole loop around Memory Grove and City Creek Canyon, from the Avenues over to the Capitol Building and back—a good hour—and was only a few blocks from home when she spotted Linda and Hoover coming from the other direction. Even in boots and a hugely oversize barn coat, Linda's walk was still ginger, as if she were a puppet, her feet only gesturing to the ground before springing up again.

Heather put her hand up in a friendly hello. In all the time Heather had been carpooling with Ted, she and Linda still had yet to have a real conversation. Their communication was limited to waves from curbs and cars.

"Hello there!" Linda called, her voice carrying down the block like a carol.

After her hour of quiet walking, Heather's own voice didn't come to her easily, but she cleared her throat and hallooed back.

"I thought that was you!" Linda said excitedly when they were finally face to face.

Heather tried not to let the giant toothy dog make her nervous. Or was it Linda, the wife, who in fact made her jittery?

Hard to tell, but either way she felt pulled from her evening reverie toward a sudden nervy edge.

Linda rushed past Heather's nervousness with a bright, presumptuous friendliness. "We're just heading home!" she said. "Are you walking that way too?"

"I am," Heather said.

"Great!" Linda trilled, with tra la la energy. "We'll walk with you!"

Heather noted that Linda took care to shorten the dog's leash and keep him on her other side rather than between them, simply because she was polite or because he might actually be dangerous was unclear. He had a new contraption around his snout, thin tan leather, like a pretty bridle.

"You know," Linda said after barely a pause, "I've been hoping to run into you for ages! Ted speaks so highly of you, and I'm always wishing I knew our neighbors better! Could we get you to come over to dinner sometime? I was going to ask Ted to ask you, but now that I'm seeing you I can ask you myself. Will you come? It'll be so fun! I'm a great cook, I promise!"

Linda's eagerness was like a great trembling of wings, a pleading before you'd even had the chance to demur. Heather could probably have said no, somehow, someway, but looking into Linda's fervent, twitchy eyes that sort of reply seemed impossible.

"Oh! Well, that's so kind of you," Heather said. "Thank you. Of course. Dinner. Sure."

"So you'll really come?" Linda said, as if she needed to verify the affirmative.

"Yes, for sure," Heather said.

Linda still looked skeptical.

"Yes!" Heather nodded vigorously.

Linda reached out and gave her a quick, grabby hug. "Great!" she said. "Oh, I'm so excited!"

They arrived at their block and Heather said, "Well, this is me," gesturing toward her house.

"Have such a good night!" Linda said. "I'll talk to Ted and we'll get a date for that dinner set!"

From across the street Linda spangled her hand in the air, a wild and fervent farewell.

Heather felt windblown. It was hard to imagine a person with atmospherics more different from smooth and mellow Ted.

She wanted to rush inside and send Devin a funny text about it. But no. Too much explanation required. Devin did not know Ted's name, certainly not Linda's. She had conveniently failed to mention her platonic old man crush. (Though if it were really so platonic, might she not have mentioned it?)

The next morning Heather walked over to Ted's waiting car with her head up, scanning for Linda's waving fingers in a window. Nothing.

She opened the door and climbed into the passenger seat as usual, trying not to feel conspicuous.

"I hear you're coming to dinner," Ted said with a tilted smile.

"It seems I am," Heather said, a sly gravel to her voice.

It wasn't exactly clear what private amusement they were sharing, but the car took on a conspiratorial atmosphere.

It took a week to set a date and another week for the night in question to arrive, but at last it did, and a mere hour after Ted dropped her at her apartment after work, Heather headed back out and crossed the street to Ted and Linda's. She would have told Devin she was having dinner with neighbors, had he asked, but he was busy at the hospital, no spare thoughts for even asking about Heather's whereabouts that evening.

After knocking, Heather heard a bark and a slight scuffle, and then Linda flung the door open, a fierce grin on her clean-scrubbed face. Her hair was braided around her head like a princess crown, coarse hairs springing from her head like live wires.

"Come in, come in!" she said to Heather.

Ted joined Linda in the entryway and air-kissed Heather's cheek.

"We meet again," he said, his beard brushing her skin.

He'd never kissed her cheek like that before, but they'd never gotten together socially before either. It was a normal thing to do, really it was, and yet the softness of his beard beckoned in a way that alarmed her.

On the wall just behind Ted and Linda there was a line drawing of a nude woman—a beautiful drawing, pencil shadings and bending curves, nothing objectionable, just something you'd be incredibly unlikely to see in a Mormon household. There was a faint smell of incense in the air. Again, not bad, just remarkably unfamiliar. The houses Heather was used to did not smell like patchouli; they smelled like sugar cookies. She felt like she'd stepped into a different world, a more sophisticated world.

Heather pulled the berry pie she'd made out of its bag and presented it to Linda.

"What! Oh, you shouldn't have!" Linda said, clutching her heart. And before Heather could hand the pie over, Linda grabbed Heather's shoulders and gave her a shake. "So sweet!" she said with a kind of growl.

Heather let out a bewildered giggle.

Ted took the pie from her hands, and Linda hooked her arm through Heather's and led her to the table. Their dining room was red, with a thick craftsman style table and hand thrown mud-colored ceramics on the table, all so different from her mother's wedding china or the floral fiestas Caroline put together. Again, it just seemed so . . . not Mormon. Which did not make it better! And yet Heather could not stop herself from making a comparison that ranked the taste on display here above her people's.

"Let's sit!" Linda said. "Ted can ferry everything in," Linda said, waving dismissively toward the kitchen, a gesture that seemed to assert her rule over the household. Ah, so perhaps that was how they worked?

"This is such a funny thing," Linda said, "but we've lived in Salt Lake for almost twelve years, and I still feel like we don't really have any Mormon friends. I'm so excited to get to know you better!"

"Oh, well," Heather stumbled. She didn't know quite how to react to these overtures. Linda was so much so fast. "I'm sorry if people haven't been friendly," Heather finally stammered.

"It's not that!" Linda said. "People are very friendly. It's just that it usually feels like there's a little something they're holding back. Does that make sense? Like you're always still on the outside if you're not part of the fold. But I'm so glad you and Ted have really been becoming close!"

Heather was sure her pale skin turned pink. There was of course the flush of all this attention. She felt like an anthropology subject, *Mormon young person*, or like an ambassador here to make up for long years of her people's failure to truly welcome this woman. Either was a bit much. But "becoming close"? Were those Ted's words or Linda's? She was embarrassed by how much they pleased her. And also had to admit her own excitement at being invited into the Glenners' world. If she was honest, she was exactly the sort of "friendly" Linda was describing. Sure, she knew people who weren't Mormon. But could she count a single one of them among her inner circle? She could not. But maybe that could change, starting now?

When Ted joined them again and they were all in their places, a tagine shaped like an alien chimney in the center of the table, Linda stood, lifted the lid, and said "voila!" A cloud of steam rushed into her face. Heather doubted her parents even knew the word tagine.

"It's Morrocan couscous," Linda said. "Vegetarian. I didn't know if you ate meat."

"It smells amazing!" Heather said, noting with relief that it was the sort of food you could eat in small amounts without anyone being the wiser—she could take her time, push it around her plate, no set portion like a giant pork chop or something she'd have to forcibly consume or risk commentary. Linda handed her the serving spoon and she took enough to lightly cover her plate, pine nuts, and golden raisins, and parsley like beautiful edible confetti. It really did smell amazing.

"So Ted has told me so many interesting things about you. Your mom is running for office and you're working on her campaign? I want to hear about everything!" Linda said with a manic teenage fan euphoria. Did she say anything any other way?

"Oh, well, yes, my mom is running for state legislature. In Bountiful. It's really just getting started. But I went with her to the Republican caucus meetings the other night. And wow, fascinating!"

"Do tell," Ted said.

"I mean, there was this formal reading of the Utah Republican Party Platform, and it basically made my brain explode. 'Government regulation is an impediment to productivity. Market forces forever!'" Heather said in a mocking voice. "I just wanted to pipe up and ask if anyone remembered what life was like before the EPA. Market forces, yeah, great stuff. They should see the cancer cluster data! And then there was a bullet point about opposing government benefits to illegal immigrants that really made me lose my mind. Like what, ban kids from schools and check government IDs before you let people board buses? Ugh. It makes me crazy."

It felt so good to say all of this out loud! This was exactly the sort of stuff Heather had spent the last 15 years learning not to say. Mormons should have been socialists, as far as she could tell. She'd thought it as a teenager, and she still thought it now. Back in the early church there had been something called The United Order. Everyone gave everything they had to the bishop and he meted it back out to each family according to their needs. Sharing! Communal utopianism! *Yeah, and it didn't work for very long,* Mormon Republicans would say. *Yeah, but it's still in the scriptures,* Heather would say, *and a goal to strive for last I checked.* The trouble with starting that argument was that it ended with Heather yelling *Jesus would have been a Democrat!* And while she actually truly thought so, and had as an adolescent yelled those very words, she was well aware that invoking Jesus was as outrageous as invoking Hitler, and so she'd learned to still herself, even as all the steam inside her head turned her brain to popcorn. But here she was with Ted and Linda, the two of them nodding along. Ah, the comfort of kindred spirits!

"And your mom lines up with all of that?" Linda asked, owl-eyed.

"I mean, not really. There are all these Republicans who seem to think any government at all is a malevolent force, and they're, like, running for office in hopes of shutting down the whole operation, but she's definitely not one of those."

"So what is she really like, politically?" Linda said.

A sudden protectiveness pinged in Heather—in plenty of contexts she might have made all sorts of sarcastic remarks about Mormon conservatives like her mother, but sitting here with non-Mormon Ted and Linda? No. No way. She was entirely ready to circle the wagons.

But Linda's question came without a smirk, her face open, genuinely curious. Heather waited a moment, and then another moment, weighing her answer, and finally tamped down her defenses.

"Well, I think there are a couple of things," she said. "The first one is that, in terms of party, there's nothing else to be in Davis County. I mean, there are like two Democrats, so if you want to be relevant at all you have to be a Republican. And then, I think, when you get down to it, my mom's politics are pretty much just her religion. Basically, I think she thinks everyone should be Mormon, or if not Mormon, they should act like they're Mormon. Which I guess sort of makes sense if you think about her life and the people she knows. If you're a good, nice, church-going Mormon in Bountiful you don't really need the government for that much and how bad can your life really be? I mean, it can be bad like cancer or terrible-accident-could-happen-to-anyone bad, but it's not going to be bad like rehab and jail and kids you can't support. If you hit some hard times, the church and the people in your ward take care of you, and no sex and no drugs and no alcohol certainly takes care of a lot all on its own. So I guess I see where she's coming from. She just thinks everyone would be better off if they were more like her. And I guess she thinks public policy should encourage people in that direction? You know what I mean?"

Linda nodded uncertainly, and after some time she just shrugged and said "Hm."

So it seemed Linda had no real reply to that. Heather wasn't really sure she had a reply to it either. That was half the reason her mother flustered her so often. It was hard to say "you can't expect people to be like that," because in her mother's experience you certainly could.

As they'd been talking, Ted had been quietly eating and drinking. Linda, though, had barely touched her plate. Heather noted, however, that she was refilling her wine glass for the second time.

After a slight lull, Linda jumped in with a subject change. "So Ted tells me you and your mother are both gifted pianists?" she said.

"Oh, I mean . . .," Heather flushed, flattered by the description. In her family, the musical ones were Audrey and Aaron. "My mom for sure," she said. "I think I'm probably kind of a hack?"

"I am sure that's not true!" Linda said, sounding personally offended by Heather's light disparagement of herself.

"Listen," Linda went on. "It sounds like you could use a break from politics, and I know you're very musical, and so this is why I am asking you. Do you like opera?" she leaned heavily on her hand, as if waiting for Heather to weigh in on one of the great questions of the ages.

Heather couldn't quite tell where this was headed. Her eyes flashed to Ted, who was leaning back and taking in the scene, giving no real direction.

"Um, opera? Yes. I don't know that I'm a real aficionado or anything. But I enjoy the music . . ."

"Good then!" Linda said. "It turns out I made a bit of a miscalculation. I bought us season tickets for the Utah Opera, and now I just can't make it to all the performances. Hoover doesn't do well if we're out all day and then all night, and I haven't been able to work from home much lately. So if you'd like tickets, they're yours. They're good seats too!"

Her mother would probably like a night out at the opera. So would her dad, actually. She could take turns, taking them to performances. Or let them go together. Or she could take Caroline, though Caroline would probably want to arrange some sort of opera-themed dinner party and invite a whole crew of chirpy twenty-three-year-olds to accompany them.

"That's so sweet of you." Heather said. "You sure you and Ted don't mind?" She glanced to him again.

"I think Ted would love to go with someone who doesn't fall asleep before intermission!" Linda said, looking to him as well. Their exchange seemed well-practiced, her mild self-disparagement, his bemused deferral.

Oh. Heather had misunderstood. She would be accompanying Ted? Suddenly, weirdly, it was as if Linda were sending her out on a pseudo-date with her husband.

Ted raised his eyebrows to Heather, a half-cocked why-not expression. A look that clearly implied he had no objections to this pseudo-date, if anything, that he was quite pleased by this development.

"And if Ted wants to stay home with Hoover now and again, maybe you and I could go together!" Linda said. "I'll email you the performance schedule, and you can just pick any of them that interest you. Really, you'll be doing us a huge favor!"

Heather said thank you and how sweet and hoped her dismay stayed well hidden. What was she doing? The delirium of being wanted was one thing with Devin, but it was foolish, more than that, *wrong*, to let it wash over into her relationship with Ted. But the way he had looked at her. The way he had been looking at her for a long while, if she admitted it. And did she not feel a thrum of anticipation every day as she walked across the street to his car, to their little chamber of intimacy? She was greedy for the flattery of it. Had she not been enjoying this game all along? She should have said no. She knew it. And still she said yes.

A few mornings later at work, Ted appeared in her office email inbox. He'd never emailed her before, a new incursion.

"Conference room lunch rendezvous? Your floor?"

She typed a few different responses, deleted them, and finally replied with the shortest assent she could come up with. "Sure. 12:30?"

At the appointed hour he appeared with a brown bag in hand. She grabbed her own lunch from the fridge in the kitchen and joined him. It would have felt strange or perhaps seemed strange to others in the office, she imagined, if she and Ted went out together. But plenty of people ate in the conference room, and the room itself was lined with windows onto a busy interior hallway, so it wasn't as if they'd be alone, even if they were alone.

Ted's sandwich was hearty—dark brown bread with seeds and grains jutting out and thick layers of turkey and toppings—but the little bag of chips and the orange he brought out of the bag were the exact sort of accompaniments her mother used to pack for her in elementary school. Heather remembered the large "variety pack" of assorted chips coming home from the store. Cheetos were always the first pick and they were gone by the end of day one. She had always raided the box first thing and snuck a bag of Cheetos up to her room, and after she'd eaten them all and licked her fingers thoroughly, she'd always turned the package inside out and licked every last bit of orange powder from its inner corners. Cool Ranch was second in line, though the powder wasn't worth turning the wrapper inside out for. Ted's chips were some sort of organic salt and pepper potato chips, but Heather knew what awaited him—a bag that seemed full and then turned out to be half air. She hadn't eaten a chip in three years.

"Linda read an article the other day about how all the biggest bloggers are Mormons, and it mentioned your sister's blog, and she and I looked it up," Ted said. "I had no idea the Walkers were famous."

"Oh, not really famous. And just Caroline. And just famous on the internet."

"You make quite a few appearances," he said, smiling.

She didn't really, unless he'd combed through page after page of the archives, and the thought of him searching for her did what to her exactly? Gratified her? Excited her? She could feel the heat of a blush rising, and she vigorously attended to her salad and he didn't say anything more about Caroline's site. He asked her about work. They talked about his spring gardening plans.

It was a nice lunch. On the surface entirely appropriate. And yet there was a feeling in the room.

Lunch started to happen regularly after that. Always that same conference room. Some days Ted brought treats for Heather in his lunch. A cookie or a brownie. She always said she'd save it for an afternoon snack. She never actually ate the sweets. And yet he always brought them, little gifts, *gestures.* And was there not something to those gestures? A sort of winking sugary courtship? Wholly deniable! Probably nonsense, and yet the gestures continued. What would her mother think if Heather told her what was going on? She'd probably react as if passing along a cookie were one step removed from passing along Chlamydia, so really a topic best avoided.

One day during lunch, Ted was telling her a story about a mental health conference where he'd been on a panel with a guy who'd gone off script and started crying about his crumbling marriage up on stage in front of everyone. Rather than cutting the guy off and steering him back to public dignity, Ted described how he and the other panelists had all started acting like therapists instead, sympathetically probing his sobs.

"A total clusterfuck," Ted said.

At the word Heather gasped, and Ted laughed and seemed delighted to have made her gasp. They both laughed together. People swore! It wasn't that Heather was so sheltered that she had never heard people swear. But it had been a while since she'd lived in Baltimore, and when you weren't used to it, it could be jarring. But it also seemed to her something Ted would have been more careful about earlier and wasn't being careful about now. That it was maybe a little test.

As they were gathering up their things to leave the room, Ted said casually, "ah, remember the opera? We have one of those extra tickets this Friday. Would you like to go with me?"

It felt exactly like being asked on a date. The quick surge of nerves. But she'd already said yes to this opera outing back on the night of dinner, hadn't she? And it wasn't a date really, just an evening of music with a friend and neighbor.

"Oh Friday, yeah, let me think if I have anything," she stalled.

He gazed at her warmly, none of Linda's flustered begging, just the magnet of his eyes, waiting.

"I think I'm free," she said, finally.

"Great then," he said, just a hint of a smile.

They both walked toward the conference room door. He opened it for her and then briefly placed his hand on the small of her back to guide her through. Nothing, gentlemanly, and yet a particular touch that declared both intimacy and possession.

"A friend from work had an extra ticket," Heather told Devin when she mentioned her opera plans. There was nothing untoward going on here, and what she said was completely true. Devin had exams and not a moment to spare and certainly didn't mind. And yet she felt furtive curling her hair and putting on eyeliner the evening of the performance.

Once she was ready, rather than walk across the street and join Ted already sitting in his car as she did every morning for carpool, she waited for him in her living room. She'd settled on a kelly green dress, nothing too formal—no silk or glitz, just gabardine, but fitted in a pencil skirt that came down just past her knees with darts in the bust and hips and three quarter length sleeves—a vintage slimness to its fit that she knew was sexy despite its simplicity. She'd considered red lipstick, but that seemed too brash, too purposeful. She limited herself to chapstick.

Ted knocked and she answered. "Are you ready for an evening of operatic adventure?" he said at the door. He'd changed from the blazer and slacks he'd worn to work into a full suit, navy blue and handsome. It also looked as though he'd trimmed his beard since she'd last seen him. The warm brown whiskers still soft, but the line of his jaw clearer, even more appealing than usual.

"You bet," she said.

She followed him out to the car, which he'd driven across the street and parked in front of her house.

"Wow. What service!"

"I didn't put my seatbelt on to pull across the street. Hilda Cross would be horrified." Hilda was the director of the Utah Department of Health's Traffic Safety Initiative.

"I'll never tell," Heather said

The drive was short, five minutes at most, and Ted turned the radio off before he pulled away from the curb. "Some quiet—it's like a palate cleanser," he said. She nodded and tried not to fiddle with her fingernails.

Once they arrived, he offered her his arm outside the car, and they walked toward the Capitol Theater with her hand slipped through the crook of his elbow. Did people think she was his daughter? His inappropriately youthful girlfriend? Without meaning to, she found herself playacting a certain slinkiness, a stretching of gestures, half-way to pretending she had a long cigarette holder in her hand and a stole around her shoulders.

Two tickets for Glenner, he said at Will Call. Something about that felt as scandalous as anything to Heather. Here she was, under his name. The seats were good ones. Center orchestra. For music lovers, her parents were stingy about such things. Concerts at Temple Square were free and good enough for them, and if you were going to splurge for the symphony or orchestra, things sounded just as good in the top balcony, even better actually, her mother always said. Heather had always stuck to the same philosophy herself. She'd never really considered the alternative, and stepping into it felt to her like stepping into a glamorous movie, handsome couple at opera.

At their row Ted gestured for her to go ahead of him, and she sucked in and moved with even more awareness of her form than she'd felt in the parking lot and lobby. She thought of something she'd heard her mother say a hundred times to piano students: "Posture, but with ease." She made her way forward with tiny sideways steps, like fingers running up a scale, a self-conscious but undeniable pleasure in this performance.

Once they'd settled in she and Ted both leafed through their programs, occasionally looking up and smiling at each other. When she put her arm on the armrest he leaned his shoulder into hers.

"I've been reading up on all the operas this season," he said in a low voice, his lips just beside her ear. "Rossini wrote this one when he was twenty-two, and he wrote it in a grand total of about three weeks. Isn't that astonishing?" His breath was conspicuously minty.

"Three weeks? Sounds like my college thesis, though perhaps this is of a more enduring quality. Ha ha." The flirtation in her voice clear for anyone to hear.

169

The lights dimmed, the overture began. Ted shifted his legs and his knee fell against hers. She moved hers gently away. It happened again a few minutes later. She adjusted again, but only slightly. When she shifted again, not much later, her knee ever so slightly grazed his thigh, and she left it there. He didn't move away. They stayed like that, touching just so, for most of Act One. When her eyes were on the digital translation in the back of the seat in front of her she couldn't help but look at their legs in the dim light, green touching blue. You pressed much more of your body against strangers on a bus, and yet her leg tingled, like a neuron center all its own, half her consciousness relocated there. The low stirring this contact created was not altogether pleasant, and at last she crossed her knees, moving them away from Ted. Without quite realizing it, she also crossed her ankles, a comforting hug of limbs.

After the opera was over, Ted didn't offer her his arm, but they stood close among the shuffling crowd. He asked what she thought of the performance, and she said that of course the performers were impressive, but what had amazed her most had been the set. The production that evening had featured a town square that whisked around to reveal a gloriously rendered villa interior. She didn't say this, but somehow the well-crafted set seemed to reflect well on Ted, as if it had something to do with him. It didn't! All he'd done was buy the tickets, and yet Heather could feel her sense of the splendor of the evening expanding to encompass him.

Ted agreed. The set was quite a feat.

Outside her house, Ted put the car in park, and then he turned the engine off. "Let me walk you to the door," he said.

"Oh, you don't have to," she said.

"It's the only gentlemanly thing to do," he said.

She hadn't turned her porch light on before leaving, and so they stood in the dark.

"Thank you for a lovely evening, Heather," he said.

"No, thank you! Thank you to Linda really." She fumbled in her bag for her keys.

"You're an incredibly beautiful girl, Heather," he said smoothly.

"What?" she laughed nervously. "That's sweet of you to say."

"You're ethereal, really."

"You mean super glow white."

"No, I mean ethereal."

Devin had never really said anything like that. The way he sighed, his low moans and exhalations, all of that had felt like proof enough, but the words were like an incantation, dazzling Heather into a sort of befuddlement.

It wasn't cheating on your wife to compliment another woman. It wasn't cheating on your boyfriend to be complimented.

A calm descended on her, the way small creatures sometimes go still when you lay a hand on them, somewhere between peace and frozen panic.

Ted took her arm and slowly leaned toward her.

He touched his lips to her cheek. They lingered there for a soft moment.

It wasn't cheating on your wife to kiss someone on the cheek. It wasn't cheating on your boyfriend to be kissed on the cheek.

"Good night," she said, her voice sounding rushed and overloud.

"See you tomorrow," he said, not rushed or overloud at all.

Chapter 10

"We really appreciate you making the time to come by," Brother Marsden said, easing himself into his recliner. He was fifteen years older than Nedra, fifteen years younger than her father, and yet the way he gingerly maneuvered around the possibility of pain with every cautious bend seemed much closer to her father than to her.

"Not at all! Thank you for making time!" Nedra said brightly. Neil Marsden—delegate number eight on her list. She believed most of the delegates she'd talked to so far would probably vote for her. It was just that if they didn't readily offer up their voting plans, straight out asking them felt rude. Doug thought she should press more.

"No one likes to feel cornered," she said.

"Yes, but if they tell you they'll vote for you, it makes it more likely that they actually will," he said. "It's called a commitment pattern. Just ask the missionaries."

"Probably so," was all she said in reply, which was exactly the sort of evasive reply she herself would have offered had anyone tried to pin her down in a little delegate chit-chat. They'd left it at that.

Now, she and Doug sat beside each other on a stiff powder blue sofa in the Marsdens' living room, lace medallions draped over each sofa arm. The whole room was a pastel affair, pink carpet and a sort of suburban Rococo, replete with collectibles. One curio cabinet featured shells, conchs and nautiluses but also smaller, spindlier finds. Another cabinet was lined with an array of delicate floral china cups and saucers. Around the rest of the room on every shelf and table and embroidered footstool sat dolls—porcelain babies with rosy cheeks, plastic dolls in elaborate national costumes, little figurines posed together in conversation. Across from Nedra, two marionettes sat side by side on a doll-sized rocking chair, a boy and a girl in lederhosen and dirndl, their strings and cross bars tucked tidily in their laps.

Sister Marsden had disappeared into the kitchen and returned now taking tiny, nervous steps as she balanced teacups full of hot chocolate on a tray.

"Let me get those," Doug said, jumping up from his seat beside Nedra on the couch.

"Oh, thank you President Walker," she said. "I hope I didn't make them too hot."

"I'm sure they're perfect," Doug said gently.

His manners always went over well with older women. Older women—maybe Nedra was in that category herself now?

They all settled in with sips and smiles.

Nedra cleared her throat. "I'm so glad we have this chance to get together before the county convention. I just wanted to sit down with you and give you the opportunity to ask any questions you might have about my positions on issues. And I also just wanted the chance to visit with you and hear about any concerns you might have."

"That's awfully kind of you," Brother Marsden said. His voice was airy and dry, a breeze rattling a screen door.

"We didn't know your mother very well," Sister Marsden interjected, "but we always knew she was as faithful a saint as they come."

Nedra nodded gratefully.

"Your father gave most of our grandchildren their patriarchal blessings," Brother Marsden added.

"Did he?" Nedra said. Her father had been the Stake Patriarch for ten years or so, a priesthood position that carried a special spiritual distinction. "He was always grateful for that calling," she said, striking a note of humility.

"Shall we get to the matter at hand?" Brother Marsden said.

"Of course," said Nedra.

"I'll tell you right now. You already have my vote at the county convention," Brother Marsden said. "I don't know Holly Rasmussen or her family, and I don't approve of the way she has handled this campaign at all so far."

"I am so grateful for your support," Nedra said. Almost no one brought up the flyers directly, but Brother Marsden was far from the first delegate to have expressed oblique disapproval of them.

Brother Marsden's gaze shifted to the ceiling. His eyes fluttered closed. "We need people who can send a strong message to Washington" he said, still with his eyes closed. Sister Marsden nodded at him, even though he couldn't see her. "We do things differently here, and we're not afraid of them. That's what we need them to know."

He opened his eyes again, but he didn't fix his look on anyone. Was he looking at the wall, perhaps? Though he may well have been looking beyond it, to the kitchen, to the yard, to the mountains, his speech made for all who had ears to hear.

"The people of God are always going to be under threat from the forces of evil," he said. "That's the way it will always be. Just like the scriptures say. There has to be opposition in all things. But that just means we have to fight all the harder. No more of this compromise. Once you start compromising with people like that, you start to lose your way. You can't trust them. You have to hold to the rod and stick to the straight and narrow."

Nedra didn't exactly nod, but the tilt of her head and the softness of her expression showed no objection. Heather was exactly right about her—she was quite skilled at tolerantly listening. Frankly, she thought Heather could be just as skilled if she'd adopt the right spirit. They both had plenty of opportunities for practice. Every Mormon did, since you didn't have sermons at church, just talks given by members of the congregation. The same was true for lessons in Sunday School and Relief Society. No official clergy, just your neighbors. Everyone was well-intentioned, and anything truly improper would probably get an interruption from the bishop, but quality control was light.

Some people argued a moral obligation to loudly state your contradicting beliefs or at least subtly correct those who held what you saw as errant points of view, but to Nedra that seemed like an awful lot of beholding the mote in your brother's eye while ignoring the beam in your own. "Hm" sounded an awful lot like "uh huh," and she'd found that with a gentle usage of both, you could almost always stay friends. The not-quite smile: it got you through. It was like something she told her piano students—when you're performing don't react to mistakes. Just glide right over them.

"I always liked Bob Bennet," Brother Marsden continued. "I did, but you know, I think we needed new blood there."

Bob Bennet had been their Senator for years, until the last election when an uprising among delegates at the state convention made sure he didn't even make it onto the primary ballot.

"He spent too long in Washington getting too comfortable with the dirty players," Brother Marsden said. "Harry Reid, now there's a man I will never understand. That man was a bishop, and yet he consorts with all the worst criminals and crooks you can imagine. I wonder what he says in his temple recommend interviews."

"Fortunately for Nedra, things at the state level aren't quite so turbulent," Doug said, good-naturedly.

At last, Brother Marsden returned his gaze to the people in the room. "I don't know about that!" he replied. "I think the battle here is as fierce as anywhere. There's an agenda. They push atheism. They push promiscuity. They push dependence. And they're smart. The adversary always has a way of making evil appear good and good evil." He inhaled deeply. "Vigilance, that is what's required. Vigilance."

"What I can promise you, Brother Marsden, is that I'll always let my values be my guide," Nedra said.

He closed his eyes again. "I know you will. I know you will."

"We'll keep you in our prayers," said Sister Marsden, rapidly blinking with a sweet and practiced bewilderment.

In the car, Nedra put her hand on Doug's knee. "Well, I'll tell you one thing. Sometimes I feel old, but after that, I am feeling quite young. Doug, we are very young."

"I couldn't agree more. Though I'm younger."

Nedra gave his knee a little shove.

Aging. When you were a child you changed so quickly that the adults around you gasped at your growth and development. And then adolescence, goodness! And the shifts of early adulthood, those were remarkable too. But then you reached a grand middle place, and once you were there you could go thirty years as the same person. The same abilities, the same interests, even looking more or less the same for years on end, but then there came another shift. Somewhere around fifty, or sixty if you were lucky, you became the *older* version of yourself. It could have been happening for quite some time, slowly, but then something shifted all at once. A settledness to the sag.

Nedra was there. She knew it. Politeness demanded that anyone she discussed aging with would cluck and compliment and assure her that absolutely not, she looked forty-five if a day, but she knew better. She saw the way her jawline had squared, the way her upper arms had begun to droop. The wrinkles that once might have disappeared with a good moisturizing could not be rubbed away now. There were new ones, not the horizontal lines that had appeared decades ago, but new vertical fissures connecting them. Her eye cream did wonders for that poof beneath her eyes, but even wonders were limited.

But now that she'd reached this place, she could stay here for another twenty years. Older, but not elderly. Until another great shift. True old age. When true old age came it came with a speed that was like a return to childhood, developments that left others gasping—no delighted joy at this end of the spectrum, but the same shocking, visible rendering of the passage of time. You don't see a child for a few months, and lo and behold he can walk! You don't see Grandma for a few months, and see here, she can't climb stairs.

She and Doug would get there. She hoped so at least—they should be so lucky—but that was twenty years away. Thirty maybe. Enough time for what felt like a whole other life.

Nedra's next delegate appointment was in one of the new townhouse developments, down by the freeway.

"I know Kerri Peterson" Caroline had said, looking over the list of delegates. "She used to be Kerri Spinaker, before she married Ryan Peterson. They were in my prom group. She was a sophomore when we were seniors. They got married like one minute after he got back from his mission."

"Do you mind if I take Caroline to this one instead of you?" Nedra had asked Heather.

"Be my guest!" Heather said all too willingly.

"I'm not sure if you remember my daughter, Caroline Walker," Nedra had said in the voicemail she'd left for Kerri, trying to set up an appointment, "but she remembers you, and she thought it would be fun if she came along on the visit so she could say hi."

Kerri had called back moments later, her voice trilling with chirpy enthusiasm. "Sorry I didn't answer," she said to Nedra. "I just never do if I don't recognize the number! But I'm so glad you called! I totally remember Caroline! Are you kidding? I mean, of course. I would love to see her! I read her blog like every day."

They'd set a date. Unfortunately, from there Kerri had proceeded to text last minute cancellations time after time.

"Sorry. baby boo has an ear infection!!!!! Later this week?"

"Oh my gosh, today has gotten totally crazy!!!! Next wk?"

Children were unpredictable, Nedra could definitely cut some slack for that, but this was nearing the zone of inexcusable.

Finally, Kerri confirmed. Tuesday morning, ten o'clock. "babes should be napping! should be perfect" she texted.

"Oh, I'm so sorry! I can't make it!" Caroline texted back. "I have a wedding photo shoot!"

Wedding photos on a Tuesday at 10 a.m. might be implausible in many circles, but in Utah it was perfectly ordinary. You got married when the temple could schedule you into a sealing room, whether that was a Tuesday at ten or a Friday at five.

Nedra called Heather. "I know it's a huge imposition, but is there any way you could take a few hours off work for a delegate meeting? It's just that I think this girl would really respond better with someone else young in the room," she explained.

Heather sounded reluctant but in the end agreed.

On the appointed day she came by the house to pick up Nedra, and when Nedra got in the car she sniffed the air.

"Is that banana bread?" Nedra asked.

"Mini banana muffins." Heather said. "Is it weird to bring a treat?"

"No, it's fine. You just don't bake much . . . anymore." The words were out before Nedra felt the awkwardness they'd create.

"Right. Since I lost a hundred pounds. Mom, I don't know why you pretend you don't notice."

Nedra pulled a face and looked out the window. What was she supposed to do? Bring up Heather's personal shape all the time?

When Nedra was a girl and had herself "bloomed," her mother's horrid word, her mother had taken to regularly plucking at the shoulders and waists of the blouses Nedra wore, trying to loosen the fit. "I wish there were something we could do about that bosom," she'd once said with the same sigh she used when discussing impossible stain removal. It had engendered such shame in Nedra that she vowed never to subject her daughters to anything like it. When Heather, always chubby, had begun her significant spread in adolescence, Nedra was, accordingly, not about to say a word. No one was ever more aware of her physical self than a teenage girl. Heather had taken to spending at least an hour a day in the bathroom, and Nedra imagined her behind the closed door, grabbing at and examining her flesh from every angle, a torturous interrogation. Clearly "how about we lighten up on the pizza?" type remarks from her mother weren't going to be a lightning bolt of help.

Still, Nedra had stopped buying soda and put cookie baking on hiatus in an attempt to offer some assistance, but the boys had complained and when Nedra had made a speech about "a family health kick," Aaron, eleven at the time had said, "Can't we just send Heather to fat camp and eat what we want?" Nedra had slapped him, the spring of her hand seemingly outside her control. Heather and Aaron had both run off crying. She had visited each in their rooms hoping for redemption, but had only been granted shrugging silence. She suspected that episode was one of the childhood moments that leapt from their memories, all the gentleness in between lost in the gloss.

"So let me tell you about Kerri," Nedra said now, avoiding engagement on the weight issue. "She was in Caroline's prom group, I guess?"

They parked the car in an open space in the townhouse development's lot, next to a snow pile half-melted and miserable with grit and litter.

Moments after they knocked on Kerri's door, a jarring bang rang out from the other side.

"Tucker! Back it up!" said a muffled voice, and then Kerri whisked the door open with a big smile, a toddler on a riding fire truck at her feet, a maybe one-year-old baby on her hip, and the swell of another pregnancy under her tight, striped t-shirt. Despite her pregnancy, she had a teenager's willowy slimness in her arms and legs. Two years younger than Caroline. That made her twenty-two? Impressive.

"Hi you guys! I'm so glad we're finally getting together! I'm so sorry I've been so crazy. These guys!" she gestured at the boy on the truck and kissed the head of the baby girl. She wore rings on almost every finger, and her nails were painted a dark matte navy, a stylish edge that contradicted her pert, freckled features. "Come in, come in! As you can see, nap time didn't exactly work out."

Nedra imagined that her daughters thought this girl, Kerri, was what she wanted them to be. And they weren't entirely wrong, because here is what you could say for her: married at nineteen to a nice return missionary and a gaggle of kids right out of the gate meant she was safe. Kerri was going to live in Bountiful and serve in the Young Women's or Primary Presidency at church and shop at Target and drop her kids off every morning at the same schools she'd gone to not that many years before, and she and her husband would have the company of friends and family and ward members whose lives were just like theirs. They'd have good peers and examples for their children, and a steady path laid out for decades to come.

You could say it was boring or provincial, and where was the adventure and ambition? She could just hear Heather: The divine role of motherhood made you a mere vehicle. Your only hope for glory was that your child (let's be clear, your son), would achieve something remarkable. But boo to that, Heather would say. She wanted to be the one. What about *her* great destiny? *Her* calling! *Me, me, meee!!!*

And Nedra heard her. It wasn't like she didn't see what Heather meant. But really? Stuck in an office churning out reams of paperwork was a greater destiny? Nedra found that hard to believe. What really mattered in life was family. Even if you were an Amazon adventurer instead of a wife and mother, your days were still made up of moments, and it was up to you to find the divinity in them, and sweating with mosquitos or sitting in a board room seemed significantly less meaningful to her than helping a child learn to read. Backpacking companies wanted you to believe that the Himalayas were the joy in life, but that wasn't true. Love, family, service, faith. That was where you found lasting happiness.

So did she wish her daughters had dropped out of college and birthed a dozen grandchildren between them by now? Not exactly. But did she think their thinly veiled hostility toward such choices was most definitely misplaced? Yes, she did.

"We brought you some . . . .muffins!" Heather bent down to the little boy and whipped the prettily wrapped box of muffins from behind her back to show him.

The boy looked at her blankly.

"That's so sweet of you!" Kerri said, crouching down to the boy's level and taking the box. "What do you say, Tucker? Do you say thank you?"

"Thank you." he said then buried his head against his mother's chest before lifting it up again and smiling flirtatiously.

Kerri motioned them to the oversized sectional. She set the box of muffins, unopened, on the cushion beside her. Behind the sofa on the wall hung a giant photo of Kerri and her husband on their wedding day, his lips pressed to her cheek, her eyes dreamily staring into the camera, the soaring spire of the Bountiful temple behind them. Right beside it was a framed "Proclamation on the Family." The other walls were adorned with wooden plaques covered with flowing script: "Live well, laugh often, love much"; "Bless this home"; "We are a forever family." Swap the photo, and it could have been the home of a dozen other young Mormon couples.

Kerri took her dark hair with its broad artificial caramel streaks out of its ponytail, ran her hands through it while she held the rubber band in her teeth, and whipped it back up into a bun on top of her head.

"So can I tell you, this political stuff is just so fun!" she grinned. "I've been getting calls from everyone! All the county commissioner candidates, the county treasurer people, the state senate people. I actually told everyone else I didn't have time to meet in person, but of course I had to make time to see you guys. I'm so excited for the convention. I've heard it's tons of fun. Ryan is going to babysit. Whenever I leave Ryan with the kids his friend Mike Shirtliff comes over and they play video games all night." Kerri rolled her eyes with a laugh. Then she kept talking. "I'm so sad Caroline couldn't come! She knows Ryan and Mike and everyone. Anyway, I didn't know she had a pretty older sister! I swear I would have remembered you!"

"Oh, I'm a lot older," Heather said. After the flare-up in the car Nedra was glad Heather didn't embarrass Kerri by saying, *oh, you wouldn't have noticed me. I was really fat back then.*

Though Nedra winced inside because wasn't it true that Kerri would have been aware of Heather had she looked this way back then?

During all of this Nedra smiled at the baby in Kerri's lap, who gave great gaping drooly smiles in return.

"Did you know Misty Porter?" Kerri went on, not waiting for a real answer. "She was friends with Caroline. She married Michael Shirtliff. Video game Mike."

"Oh, interesting," Heather said.

"I always thought your sister should have married Keith Hooper." Kerri laughed. "They were like the cutest prom dates."

Heather nodded genially enough.

"Well, I just have to say your sister shouldn't worry at all," Kerri said to Heather. "It'll totally happen for her. I mean, she's amazing. And footloose and single! I'm sort of jealous!" Kerri nuzzled her face against the baby's hair then spoke in baby voice. "Just kidding, sweetheart. I'm not jealous. Never never. Being single is . . . No. Fun. Are you married?"

Heather shook her head no, and Kerri rushed right ahead. "Well it'll totally happen for you too. Look at you! I mean, duh. Totally happening."

Nedra said nothing and didn't flick her eyes to Heather, but goodness, this was spiraling.

Thankfully, interruption came to their rescue.

"Hey, watch this," her son Tucker said. He bent over and put his head on the ground, as if he were about to do a somersault, but then quickly sat back on his haunches, pulled his head back up, and threw his hands into the air, the trick complete.

They all applauded.

"So you want to hear why you should vote for my mom?" Heather said, moving them forward much to Nedra's relief.

"I already read your website!" Kerri said to Nedra.

"Well thank you for taking a look at it," Nedra said. "I'd be happy to answer any questions or discuss any concerns you might have.

"I think knowing you all just makes it such an easy choice. But there's one thing Ryan wanted me to ask you about. So you know about the shooting range, up by the B?"

Almost every high school in Utah had a letter on the nearest mountain, a cement B or R or D or V, whatever the initial that went with the name of the school, set high up on the hillside. The students whitewashed them each fall and sometimes, enterprising class officers carried generators up and strung lights around them for Homecoming. Lanterns or torches would have been easier and more dramatic, of course, but the dry scrub was a wildfire waiting to happen, so no flames. The B, for Bountiful, was up past the paved streets at the end of a dirt road, but developments had been getting closer and closer for years.

"Sure," said Nedra.

"Well, then I'm sure you know there's been a petition circulating to close it. But that's just not fair. It's been there for ages. Ryan grew up shooting there. And just because some new people moved in who don't like it. I mean, isn't that what the second amendment is all about? Making sure gun owners are protected?"

"I'm pretty sure the shooting range issue will end up being resolved by the city council, not the state legislature," Nedra said evenly. "But that doesn't mean I can't talk to a few people about it."

"Would you?" Kerri said. "I know we'd really appreciate it."

"I'd be happy to."

When they took their leave, Kerri hugged them both at the door, as if they were the chummiest of friends. "Blow kisses to the pretty ladies, Tucker!" she said.

The little boy kissed his hand and grinned maniacally.

"Ha ha ha. He's my little goofball. I'll see you at the convention! Fingers crossed!" Kerri crossed her fingers on both hands, the baby in her arms grabbing for them.

Once they were in the car again, doors closed, engine on, Heather said, "Do you think they have more guns or more kids in that house?"

"I'm sure they lock them up carefully," Nedra said. "The guns, not the kids. Ha ha."

"Also, I wonder if she even knows what the second amendment says," Heather went on. "And by the way, people want that gun range moved because stray bullets fly into their yards. That's not exactly unreasonable."

"I didn't say I agreed with her. Just that I'd talk to people about it."

"How very politic of you."

Yes, exactly, Nedra wanted to say but didn't. Heather had behaved well enough. No reason to mount her usual lectures about judging not lest ye be judged.

"I'm sorry she went on and on about being single and all of that," Nedra said.

"Ha. Like I care," Heather said, though it was clear that she did. "But it was kind of aggressive, wasn't it?"

"I think the muffins were nice. I bet her little boy will like them."

"I think she's voting for you anyway, so who cares if she likes muffins," Heather said.

They drove a few blocks without conversation.

"Cute kids, though," said Heather, as if trying to redeem herself after great rudeness.

Yes, Nedra concurred. She didn't want her daughters to turn into Kerri Peterson exactly, but she still wanted grandchildren, even if she won this election.

"We're looking forward to meeting your boyfriend," Nedra said, hoping her chain of thought was not utterly apparent to Heather but suspecting it was.

"Yep," Heather said without enthusiasm, turning to look out the car window.

Chapter 11

After the opera, Heather had to ask herself what she'd really wanted from Ted. For him to act as if nothing had happened? (Because really nothing had, right?) For some new tension to enter their car rides to work? For Ted to start stammering like a teenager in the presence of her ethereal beauty? Maybe he'd declare his love for her, announce that he and Linda were planning to separate anyway, and then he'd reveal that he'd also decided to convert to Mormonism and that he now wanted children, and then he'd immediately propose and eternal happiness would be their lot. Sure.

Thankfully, there was a weekend between the opera and the return to carpooling. Enough time for her to calm down about it all, at least that's what she told herself.

Saturday morning, Heather's visiting teachers came over with a plate of blueberry muffins.

"They're still warm if you want to dig right in," Shadoe, the thin one said.

"You're so sweet. I just had breakfast, so I'll save them," Heather demurred, setting the plate on the table behind them. While she pushed the muffins aside she avoided eye contact with Kyra, the chubby one, though she'd given her a big hug at the door.

It had been how long, but Heather still remembered overhearing a boy in her A.P. Statistics class in high school flirting with a couple of girls, saying, "So it's true, the pretty girls really do hang out together." The girls had tittered away, pleased, and Heather had kept her gaze firmly diverted, prickly with discomfort. Flirtation is almost always embarrassing to overhear, there was that, but the exchange had burned a memory because of the truth of it—people did tend to group up in these ways, and she had feared the inverse all her heavy days. When you were fat you had enough notoriety all on your own, but join up with someone else overweight and you threatened others like a brigade. The fat girls.

Now, though, she could be friendly with Kyra without fear.

"So you and Devin are still going strong, I hear," Shadoe said.

Half of visiting teaching in a singles ward was just this sort of thing. A wheedling intimacy. A space for forced revelations and the sharing of news.

Heather looked to Kyra in hopes of some relief from the dating talk, but Kyra blushed a little and said, "I was hanging out with Kevin the other day, and he said Devin is, like, obsessed with you."

"Do I hear wedding bells?" Shadoe chirped, friendly enough, but not without the dangerous edge of a jeer.

The question was a jolt. *Did she hear wedding bells?* What good answer was there to that question? She hoped so? Too sincere, too vulnerable. Yes? Far too declarative. No? Who was to say that "no" said even as a laughing dismissal of the question wouldn't get back to Devin in some mutated form?

This was a moment where Caroline, a master deflector, would shine. To her chagrin, Heather found that she often answered questions merely because they were asked. In graduate school in a course on sexual health policies and programs one of her classmates had said, "So you're Mormon, that means you're a virgin, right?" a leering quality to the inquiry. And Heather had replied, "Well, yes I am," a shame descending upon her even as the words were leaving her mouth, not because of her virginity but because she was sharing such an intimacy for no reason other than a shocked unpreparedness to bat away the intrusion.

Channel Caroline!

"You and Kevin have been hanging out?" Heather said warmly to Kyra, as if Shadoe hadn't spoken at all.

"A little. I mean, it's not really anything, but he's fun. I mean, we'll see."

Kyra obviously felt more than she was declaring, and Heather moved them right along before Shadoe could set on her. She also decided she'd ask Devin if they could plan an evening out with Kyra and Kevin. Kyra was sweet, a touch lost, it seemed. She seemed like she might need a friend. And Heather wasn't exactly overwhelmed by friends herself. Maybe they could go to a concert in the park as soon as those started up again.

Once she was alone in her apartment again, Heather heard Shadoe and Kyra's words over and over, despite trying to put them from her mind. *Did she hear wedding bells?* She wanted to be the sort of girl who could hear wedding bells. She wanted to be married. Was that the same as wanting to marry Devin? Wanting him to want to marry her? She thought it was. And

Devin was, like, obsessed with her. Who wouldn't want to hear that? Maybe women who had long been objectified, adored, pursued. But Heather had never been those things, and they felt like a just and final reward for the incredible hard work of transforming her physical self.

In college, during one of the *theories of life and love* conversations that defined late-night dorm-room discourse, Heather remembered a friend saying, "In every relationship, there is the person who loves and the person who condescends to be loved." Heather had balked at the time. How horrible! But that had been because she had cast herself in the role of the person loving, the one whose adoration the other condescended to accept. But now, for the first time, she tested out how it felt in reverse. Herself as the adored. The object of obsession. The one who condescended to be loved. She felt a surge of power, both troubling and pleasing.

When her phone rang, Heather almost imagined her powers had leapt into the universe, eliciting an immediate call from Devin. But no. It was her brother Brian, finally calling her back.

"So, campaign manager?" Brian said with amusement.

"Yeah yeah," she answered. "But there's something else more urgent in this exact moment. I think I might be in love?"

She meant Devin, truly, but the words startled her, arrested her speech for a brief second with a singe of panic, a terrible fear that she had somehow said something about Ted. But no. She was fine.

Brian asked for details.

"A guy. In my ward. It's been a few months. He's smart and nice, a little bit younger than me. It seems like he's really into me?"

"You say it like it's some big surprise?" Brian said.

"Well, I mean, I'm not exactly used to this kind of thing."

"So have Mom and Dad met him yet?"

She had to admit they hadn't.

"Ha ha, well, you're in for a good time there. What's hilarious is they think they know how to play it cool, but they most definitely do not."

"Whatever you're imagining, it's going to be like ten times worse, since they've literally never met anyone I've dated."

Brian laughed and wished her good luck.

"How's your teenage girlfriend?" she said.

"Wow, super-jerky, Heather. And she was 22, by the way. But yeah, it didn't work out."

"Sorry," Heather said.

"I hear your sincerity oozing through the phone," Brian said, though it was clear she hadn't actually hurt his feelings.

"How about you?" Heather asked. "Anyone new?"

"Yeah, not so much. I'm taking a break again," Brian said.

Heather didn't like the sound of that. Truthfully, Brian's list of significant others was not much longer than Heather's. Of course he'd been married to Danica for seven years, but before that there had been years and years of blank.

"Don't make it too long," she said. "I worry about you."

"Wow, you get one boyfriend and just like that, you cross over to the smug couple side of things. I see how it is. *I worry about you,*" he said in a gently mocking voice.

"Uh huh, uh huh, laugh it off," she said.

"I always do," he said.

That night, Heather and Devin went out for what was now their standing Saturday night date, nothing big, just a little restaurant over near the State Capitol Building that had become one of their favorites. Without really noticing, Heather ate almost her entire plate of pasta. Looking down at the last few bites she almost panicked—how had she eaten so much! But then she looked across the candle lit table at Devin with his freckles, his mop of hair, his warm eyes smiling easily at her. This boy, he loved her. At the thought she felt a wave of warmth, a little firework in her heart, almost like the Holy Ghost—was it the Holy Ghost? She took a slow, deep breath. She could do this.

"So my mom's birthday is coming up," she said.

Although Heather hadn't heard anything about it yet, she assumed Caroline was planning a birthday party for their mother, birthday parties being a staple of DinnerForEight.

"Yes?" Devin said, with a sing-song sneaking smile.

"Well, I was thinking you should come to her birthday party."

"Showing me off to the parents!" he crowed.

"Haha, yeah, well."

"I'd love to," he said, reaching across the table for her hand.

"So have I mentioned that my sister has an entertaining blog?"

"You haven't," he said. "But other people have. She's kind of famous."

Heather shrugged. "Yeah, well, I'm just mentioning it because if you show up for this dinner you're going to end up on the internet, so like, wear your favorite shirt or whatever."

"This gets better and better," he said.

The next morning at church, Devin sent her a text during Sacrament Meeting. They often sat together at church these days, though Heather certainly didn't swirl her nails around Devin's back during the service. But she'd arrived on time, and Devin must have come in late. When her phone buzzed and she read the words "Dinner tonight with my fam at my parents' house?" she swiveled her head around to find him.

When her eyes landed on him he arced one eyebrow flirtatiously.

She made an owl face and punched letters into her phone. "Tonight?! You're trying to beat me to the punch?!"

"Pow. Yes. You in?"

"Um . . . okay!" she wrote back.

After the closing prayer he waited for her by the chapel door, then genially bumped her shoulder.

"Pick you up at 3?"

Mormon Sunday dinner, an early affair.

"See you then," she said, full of nerves, happy and anxious all at once.

Devin said family, but with seven siblings it was hard to get a real quorum in place, and when they arrived it was just Devin's parents and younger brother who had arrived home from BYU for the weekend with a trunkload of dirty laundry. Still it was clear Devin's parents had made an occasion of it. The table was set with china and his mother had roasted a chicken and baked a bundt cake.

Devin's brother was from some other part of the family's gene pool, shorter than Devin, more muscled, a sort of military air to him that was wholly absent in Devin's permanent slouch. Devin's parents were a few years older than her parents, and yet they seemed far beyond that. Devin's mother had the sort of permed and poufed haircut old ladies everywhere adopted, a style she could never imagine her mother going for, and Devin's father had a round belly and grandfatherly wire-rimmed glasses, as well as a shuffle that seemed to speak of unspecified joint pain. They cooed and clucked over Heather.

"So nice to meet you!" his mother said, patting her hand. "You are just as beautiful as Devin told us you'd be!"

Heather blushed.

Devin's father hugged her, with stiff sincerity. "We're so happy to welcome you to our home," he said.

At the table, they all bowed their heads for a blessing on the food, and Heather peeked up through her eyelashes at Devin. His eyes were closed, but when they opened at Amen he looked straight to her and squinted with a wonderful affection. Her imagination opened like a vision—a sudden glimpse of years of dinners to come at this very table. She could see Christmas sweaters, a line of children. She looked away from her conjuring quickly, knowing how exactly unwise it was to dwell in projections, and yet she couldn't deny the spot of happiness, like a little triangle ping.

Devin's mother wanted to hear all about Heather's job, with a focused questioning that went on for much longer than most polite "what do you do" inquiries. She asked question after question about identifying cancer clusters.

"Well, the two most important things are getting enough of the right data and controlling for variables," Heather explained. "Cancer is a reportable disease. What I mean is, anytime there is a case of cancer, the doctors always report it. In Utah they report it to the Utah Cancer Registry, which flows into some national registries, but anyway."

Devin's mother's eyes grew wide, and Heather, trying to read her expression, said, "I mean, it's not a public database or anything. It's only for research and it's tightly controlled. It's really hard to get access to it, actually. And it's not like it has your name right there. It's all cleaned and just information about the type of cancer and things like that."

"So you look at this registry and see if it shows areas where there's lots of cancer?" Devin's mother said.

"Sort of. It's more complicated than that. You need to look at the types of cancer and people's residential tenure, you know, how long they've lived where they live. You need to compare data to surrounding areas. And you need to look for causes and rule out other possible factors. You do a lot of stuff with census microdata and mapping software and there's a lot of follow-up investigation. It takes a lot to really find a genuine cancer cluster."

Devin's mother's eyes eagerly attended Heather's every word, her head bobbing with attentive nods. Heather wondered if perhaps there had been some cancer in the family, even if Devin's mother might have had cancer herself, but she seemed too delighted listening to Heather for that to be the case.

After they'd helped clean up, there were hugs all around and then a wave from the front porch as she and Devin pulled out of the driveway.

Devin said, "So yeah, I'm pretty sure if it came down to it my parents would pick you over me at this point."

They both laughed. But it was true, it had gone well. Heather had felt unmitigated warmth directed at her all evening. "They're so nice," she said.

"You know my dad texted me to ask me what he should wear," Devin said.

Heather smiled and laughed again. "That's so sweet. Seriously, they're so lovely. Your brother was nice too," Heather added, although he'd been a mostly silent participant in the evening.

"Craig, yeah, he's a good kid. But the rest of them are sharks. Just wait."

He was kidding, and yet Heather knew what he meant. Large families often had a mercilessness to them, competition for resources built in from the get-go, and strong identities that didn't always readily admit outsiders. Parents were usually immune, a bit oblivious to the militias they'd created, but the more siblings the fiercer the border patrols.

"Oh, the Walkers have a serious hazing process too," Heather said. "I mean, they're still hazing me, and I joined thirty years ago."

He took her hand, affectionately.

"Brian and Audrey used to tell me every year before my birthday that I was finally going to be one of the big kids. And then every year they said they were just kidding. I'm still waiting for the promotion."

He laughed and told her a story about his older brother giving him a swirlie—as in head in toilet and flush. She told a story about Audrey shutting her in a closet once and tying the door closed, not letting her out until after she'd wet her pants. And in all of this there was a clear subtext, the stories a sort of terrible boasting. They liked their boisterous families. They were proud of them. They wanted to recreate them. They looked at each other eagerly, and Heather knew Devin was feeling what she was feeling, both of them animated with pleasure at the thought of their possible future together.

After a while Heather said, "Your mom seemed very interested in cancer clusters."

"Oh, well," Devin laughed again. "I think it was more that she was excited to hear you sounding so smart. Let's just say she has sometimes thought my standards in that department have been a little low."

So Devin's mother shared Heather's own opinion of Devin's previous "standards"? This was amusing.

"I noticed the poetry on the walls of the laundry room," Heather said. At his parents' house you passed through a sort of laundry hall to get to the bathroom, and the laundry area was conspicuously tidy, with rows of gold frames hung perfectly square just above the washer and dryer, each one containing a handwritten poem on creamy white paper. She thought she recognized the ones she'd looked at closely—a Dickinson and a Robert Frost.

"That's my mom too," Devin said. "She's always loved art and poetry, and I think that's one of the things I really admire about her. She just finds ways to work it in."

"That's really great," Heather said.

"She memorizes them," he went on, proudly. "She swaps them out once she's learned them. It's what she does while she folds clothes and whatever else you do in a laundry room." He laughed at his own dimness on the subject of laundry room duties.

"Um, do you still bring your laundry home for your mom to do?" Heather said, a sort of indignant amusement in her voice.

"Uh, well, uh . . . I plead the fifth?" he smiled over at her, and she punched him in the arm.

"That's bonkers," she said. "Aren't you like thirty years old?"

"She likes doing it! It's how she shows me she loves me!"

Heather rolled her eyes, and when they arrived back at her house he came in and they kissed and kissed, and she almost made a joke about liking the smell of his mom's fabric softener, but it was a half-formed joke and quickly pushed aside by the urgency of lips and limbs.

But later that night, alone in bed, before sleep had claimed her, in that in-between-time when it seems sleep might in fact never come, she found herself returning to the thought of that laundry room. To the poetry. How was it that the poems seemed sadder and sadder to her the more she thought about them? A doomed effort to keep beauty alive in your heart while the drudgery of stain removal was the real occupation of your days.

That was unfair and overly dramatic, but something about those poems tugged at her. If they were married, would Devin expect her to find meaning in laundry room poetry? Devin's mother had never worked outside the home as far as Heather knew, and not that it seemed she wanted to, but she had been so hungry to hear about Heather's work—didn't that reveal an eagerness that was perhaps unmet by ironing? Then again, what did Heather imagine—that her career would get her out of laundry for the rest of her life? Laundry was a fact of life, as necessary as showering. What did she want, the staff of Downton Abbey to attend her needs so her fancy mind need not be troubled? Then again, wasn't it grating that worries about future chores could keep her up at night? Because she could guarantee this was not troubling Devin. She wondered who did the laundry at Linda and Ted's house. Surely Ted knew how to use a washing machine.

Chapter 12

Nedra was getting ready to go down to her dad's house for her usual morning visit when the phone rang.

"Are you ready for your first meet-the-candidate event?" Verna Smith asked with her usual creaky enthusiasm. "This Saturday. It's at Oak Haven apartments. Do you know them?"

This was the assisted living complex she'd called after her dad's fall.

"So soon?" Nedra asked, surprised. "I thought events like this would be after the County Convention." She had been focusing all her energy on winning over the 37 delegates. A big public forum? No, she was not ready for that in the slightest.

"Yes, people like to have these things nice and early in the election cycle," Verna answered. "Gives them a chance to tell their delegates who they should vote for, if they're so inclined." Verna went on to outline the format. The event was held at lunch so there was a built-in crowd of Oak Haven residents, though people from outside were obviously invited too. Each candidate was given five minutes, and then the floor was opened to questions from the audience.

"If you have particular questions you'd like to be asked, it's smart to have plants," Verna said. "You know, a friend or family member in the audience who will raise their hand and bring up the issue."

"I can't wait," Nedra said, masking her dread with enthusiasm. Because here it was. Holly Rasmussen. Face to face. No way out of it.

What was it Heather had complained about—that no one cared about her actual positions on issues? Nedra felt certain that was about to change. In the days that followed she set herself up the way she would have if she were giving a sacrament meeting talk or prepping to teach a Sunday School lesson. At the dining room table, notebook, pen, and bright yellow highlighter pencil. Instead of the scriptures or a church lesson manual in front of her, she opened her laptop to the Utah State Legislature's website and began reading all the bills proposed in the previous year's session.

Her eyes quickly began to blur. Appropriations, minutiae related to permitting, reporting, redefinitions of terms from previous bills, shifts in language that she was sure had meaning and clear implications for people in the know but that were opaque to her. But every once in a while there was a bill that was clear, that grabbed her interest. A bill to require divorcing parents to participate in a parenting class focused on the needs of children during and after divorce. A bill loosening restrictions on beekeeping. When her mind focused, it reverberated through her whole body. She remembered this feeling from school, the way that sharp pencils on clean paper had once put the sort of excitement into her that dance music put into other people.

She wrote a short speech. She practiced it repeatedly in the bathroom mirror. You could rely on the Spirit to guide and support you, but you also had to do the work. By the time the day of the event at Oak Haven came, she felt sure she'd held up her end of the bargain.

She hadn't bothered to mention the event to her father. If he wanted to silently disapprove of her campaign, so be it. But when she'd told Heather about the event, Heather had asked who was picking Grandpa up for it.

"Oh, I don't think Grandpa really wants to come," Nedra said, aware of the petulance in her voice.

"I'm sure that's not true!" Heather said. "I think he just didn't come to the neighborhood caucus stuff because it was at night. I'm sure he was just tired."

"Hm, maybe. But if he's not interested in politics these days he's not interested in politics these days." Nedra let out a long sigh. "Look, he has a limited amount of time left. He's allowed to focus on whatever he wants to focus on."

"Oh wow, you're so mad that you're counting down to his demise!" Heather said, as if it were one big joke.

"Good grief! I am not!" Nedra gave an exasperated huff. "Listen, why don't you just call him and ask him yourself if you really think he ought to be there," Nedra said.

"I will!" Heather said.

And who knows what Heather had said, but apparently they'd made a plan and Heather was picking him up and bringing him along. Fine. Nedra had herself to focus on. She said a long prayer the morning of the event, and at the appointed hour, she and Doug drove down to Oak Haven together.

They spotted Barbara and her mother right away among the tables filling up with residents preparing for lunch. They made their way to their table and Nedra gave hugs all around, all the while keeping a wary eye on the entrance, scanning for Holly Rasmussen at the door.

As the minutes passed, the woman she was looking for didn't come through the door, but Verna and Albert Smith did, so too did a handful of other acquaintances and faces she recognized from around town. Finally, as Nedra was making her way to the platform, Heather and Caroline and her father walked through the door. He looked well enough. She waved as they found a table near the back.

A number of the people Nedra had presumed were audience members proceeded to edge closer to the platform, just as she did, and soon it became obvious that they were candidates themselves. No one who could plausibly be Holly Rasmussen was among them. But Len Hemmings, the owner of Hemmings Hardware and Lighting on Main Street, stepped slowly along next to Nedra.

Len was an old-time Bountiful resident, though probably only ten or fifteen years older than she was, so Nedra knew she was old-time herself. Hemmings Hardware had stayed open even after the Lowes opened down by the freeway in large part due to customer loyalty engendered by Len himself. He was in the store almost every day. He greeted almost everyone who came in by name. But more than the hardware store, everyone knew Len Hemmings because he had been President of the Bountiful Stake for almost a decade, back when Nedra's children were young, before Bountiful had grown and divided into four, then five, then six stakes. During those years, he'd signed all of her and Doug's temple recommends. He'd interviewed Brian for his missionary paperwork and set him apart as a missionary after he got his call to Taiwan. Even years after Len Hemmings had been released as Stake President, when it was far from an obligation, he'd come to her mother's funeral.

Over the years, Len had lost almost all of his hair, but the remaining ring around the sides was pure white. This, plus his wire-rimmed glasses, a perfectly round pot belly, and a general demeanor of jolly good cheer made him look like a beardless Santa Claus.

"President Hemmings, I didn't know you were running for anything," Nedra said, as he followed her up the step.

"I'm almost as surprised as you are," he said, smiling.

She took a seat, and he sat down next to her.

"Are you running for state senate?" Nedra asked, still not quite understanding.

"I'm afraid I'm your Democratic opponent for the house," he said, his manner as cheerful and steady as ever. "Not that the Democrats ever put up much of an opposition," he laughed gently.

Nedra smiled back automatically, but she felt a lurch in her stomach and began immediately grasping at calculations. How many people would vote for Len Hemmings, regardless of his party? Maybe quite a few.

Before Nedra's worry could truly begin to whirlpool, a woman appeared at the back of the room. Holly Rasmussen, she was sure of it. The woman pushed a child in a wheelchair toward the podium, a handful of smaller children trailing behind. All the children were so close in age and grouped in such an untidy clutch of uncombed hair and ill-fitting clothing that it was hard at first to get a good count. Nedra wanted to stare, to assess, to get a handle on the woman steadily making her way toward the platform, but the son in the wheelchair made looking feel like gawking, a rudeness she could not indulge. She tried to take in Holly in glances. The boy in the chair looked like he was ten or twelve, maybe? And the chair was not quite a chair, more of a reclining platform that supported the boy's legs and arms, all bent at seemingly unusable angles, his neck turned, a tube near his mouth. For speaking? Breathing? Drinking? Nedra wasn't sure.

Was this the woman from the PTA meeting all those years ago? No. But she had a similar look. Vaguely chapped, limp, and yet with a sort of unnerving energy, like a flickering bulb that just might blow. She wore a calico print shirt with a long denim skirt and hiking boots. She had terrifically spartan eyebrows and eyelashes that read as no eyebrows and eyelashes at all, and not even a touch of makeup on her unsmiling lips. Her hair was a dishwater blonde, pulled back in two clips, one on each side, a jarringly youthful hairdo for a woman whose mouth was flanked by deep frown lines. Polygamists favored this exact barretted hairstyle. Not that Nedra thought Holly Rasmussen was a polygamist. As far as she knew there weren't any in Bountiful. They tended to live in small outpost towns, and it was more than just hair that set them apart. Sneakers with homemade dresses. Braids. A whole look. Unmistakable. But this woman had something of that same frayed and homespun aspect, a quality that broadcast: fringe.

Seeing Holly Rasmussen—because it had to be her, didn't it?—a war of impulses broke out in Nedra. Her caring Mormon woman instincts urged her to immediately tend to the children. Tie their shoes, wipe their faces, ply them with fruit snacks.

And yet one look at the flinty mother in charge of this group and you knew you were not welcome to intrude. Anger, pity, embarrassment, sympathy, anxiety—they all continued their confused swirl in Nedra as the woman pushed right up to the platform. She left the boy in the wheelchair beside the stairs, an act of abandonment that alarmed Nedra, and the little kids piled onto the floor in front of the first row of seats, a jumble of shoving and settling. Five of them. That was the final count. A set of twins in there? Nedra couldn't tell.

Without a word to anyone, the woman walked on stage and took the open seat on the other side of Nedra. Nedra waited a moment for her to say something, for acknowledgement of any sort, but nothing. The woman looked straight ahead, emanating the scalpy smell of hair a day or two past fresh.

At last, Nedra adopted a friendly *sotto voce* and said,"Hi there. I'm Nedra Walker."

The woman nodded and gave Nedra a sidelong glance. "I'm Holly Rasmussen."

So there it was, officially confirmed.

"Nice to meet you," Nedra said.

Holly Rasmussen nodded but did not say likewise.

A gawky, red-headed young man in a teal Oak Haven polo shirt, his neck broken out in a shaving rash, approached the platform. He looked like he'd been back from his mission for about two days.

"Thank you all so much for coming to Oak Haven today," the young man said to the candidates. "I'm the shift manager, Randy, and I'll be starting the session and introducing you all."

Shift Manager Randy took to the microphone, tapped it awkwardly, and began his general greetings. "Welcome everyone!"

he said, pronouncing his words slowly, as if everyone in the audience had failing hearing aids and might need to rely on lip reading. "We're glad to have you here today for this exciting political event! The bathrooms are at the back of the room, to the left. I'll leave it to the candidates to introduce themselves," he said, waving his arm at the row of men and women on the stage. So that was it, their introduction.

One by one candidates for other offices—county commissioner, state senator—began to make their way to the mic. Nedra paid about as much attention to them as the lunching seniors did. Her mind was too busy rehearsing and fighting off the gravitational pulls on either side of her—Len Hemmings one pole, Holly Rasmussen the other.

Down the line, and Holly Rasmussen's turn came before Nedra's.

Holly Rasmussen rose quickly and turned abruptly to face the microphone, an unexpected marshal force to her movements. And then her speech unfurled, a banner gusting erratically, first this way, then that.

"My name is Holly Rasmussen, and I am running for the Utah State House of Representatives. Why am I running? I am running because our families are under attack!" She swooped her hand down in a vigorous chopping motion. "Schools are being taken over by the federal government. They test and test and test. They put fluoride in water!" She paused, as if to let this great horror set in. "They have curriculum! They put forward whatever they want. About morality and America, and we are just supposed to roll over! But freedom and liberty mean something! Who is the government to come into our pockets and take everything! And bottom line poisoning children. Minds, hearts and bodies. The medical establishment, the government, people who say anything goes and who forget what makes America great. I promise you right here today that I will stand up and say not here!"

She turned abruptly from the microphone, her flag instantly falling, as if she'd expended every bit of energy in her bluster of words. Her face was utterly affectless as she returned to her seat amidst polite applause, a bizarre and eerie contrast to her ardor of moments prior.

Nedra's turn. Part of her was flummoxed—should she try to refute Holly Rasmussen? Calmly explain that nothing even remotely resembling what Holly Rasmussen was railing against was part of the regular business of the legislative session? There simply was no *Should We Poison Children Yay or Nay* bill. But no, this was why preparation counted. She couldn't be distracted. She needed to move right on ahead as if nothing had happened.

Nedra stood, shoulders back. She reminded herself not to idly touch her hair or face, not to fidget, to project calm authority, to forget every bit of Holly Rasmussen's speech, to focus on what she had to say, not another thought in the world. She smiled peacefully.

"I'm Nedra Walker and I'm also a Republican running for the State House of Representatives. I was born and raised in Bountiful. A number of you here may know my father, Ronald Peterson—he's here today!" She waved to her dad. "And you might have known my late mother, Ann-Marie Peterson, as well." She detected some murmurs of assent and some glimmers of new attention among the lunching Oak Haven residents. She went on to talk about how she'd volunteered in schools, worked on campaigns, served as a precinct chair in the Republican party and as a voting judge. She knew the big issues facing the state— tight budgets and increasing demands for fewer resources. She had the right priorities to help navigate these challenging times.

She sat down to the same polite applause Holly Rasmussen had received. For a moment Nedra was certain she'd received more applause. But then a moment later she wondered if in fact she'd heard less? How could that be? Holly Rasmussen hadn't made any sense. She'd ricocheted all over the place. But hadn't there also been something about her that gripped your attention? Maybe it was just how erratic she was. You couldn't look away, while Nedra felt a certain distraction in the crowd during her remarks. Was that what speaking rationally led to? Boredom? She was under five minutes, she was sure of it, but still, she felt like she'd gone on and on for ages. At the same time, the words had all come out so quickly. Not that she'd spoken too fast, just that she'd rehearsed and rehearsed her phrases, and then, poof, she said them, and they disappeared into the air. One instant, then gone.

Both Heather and Caroline gave her nods and thumbs up. She tried to take in their approval and buck herself up.

Len Hemmings rose and approached the mic stand, but then he withdrew the microphone and stepped down from the podium.

"This feels a little more natural, don't you think?" he said, and he began walking back and forth across the floor as he spoke.

His ownership of the space irked Nedra, but she kept the corners of her mouth pinned up pleasantly. He didn't say anything too different from what Nedra had said, but she watched as residents turned and craned their heads to listen to him. She watched as heads all around the room nodded at his words. She folded her hands in her lap and firmly avoided shooting beseeching looks to Barbara.

After he was done, he put the microphone back in the stand and returned to his seat. He reached over and gave Nedra's hand a gentle pat. It was a gesture meant to be friendly, reassuring. She knew that, and yet she couldn't help but feel condescended to. She maintained her polite smile.

Randy the shift supervisor jogged back to the center of the room.

"Any questions for the candidates?" he asked enthusiastically, his voice spiking through the speakers.

There was no stirring. The candidates themselves looked up and down their row at each other and shared bemused smiles. Finally, a thin, elderly man rose unsteadily from his seat at one of the tables, gripping the back of his chair with one hand and raising the other.

Randy ran to him with the microphone. "This is a question for President Hemmings," the man said hoarsely, clearing his throat. "President Hemmings, as a Democrat, do you agree with the president and all the other liberals in their pro-abortion position?" The elderly man nodded, a gesture meant to politely close out his time with the microphone, and then stiffly sat himself back down.

Straight to abortion. That was a bit surprising.

"I'm glad you brought that up, Richard," Len Hemmings said. Of course he knew the man's name. "Some of you might know that I served in a position of ecclesiastical leadership for a number of years, and in that position I counseled a lot of families who found their teenagers in unexpected and challenging situations, especially when it came to pregnancy out of wedlock.

I could talk about the counsel I gave them. I'll tell you that it was in keeping with my personal beliefs and the teachings of my church. But as far as what I think the government position should be, I'll tell you that I worry a lot about government overreach. I don't know about you, but as much as possible, I don't want the government involved in my personal life. Especially when it comes to sensitive, personal and moral matters. So as far as my position goes, I would say I believe in personal agency, not government control."

Nedra felt hotly restless, twitchy even. Surprisingly, a stronger reaction than she'd had to crazy Holly Rasmussen. He didn't believe in government intrusion in personal lives? What did he think Obamacare was? And banning abortion was the same kind of overreach as banning murder or child abuse. Did he want to do away with those laws as well? And "personal agency"? That was coded church language, personal agency being the official church term for what Satan tried to take away in the premortal existence, the whole point of life on earth, a term that came up in Sunday School all the time. Personal agency! What a gross misappropriation. Was he saying that laws took away personal agency? Hardly. If he thought that, he had to be some kind of anarchist.

All this shot up her throat in half a second, but she kept her jaw firmly clenched. Maybe in debates on TV or in rude states like New Jersey sniping back was exactly the thing to do, but Nedra knew how that would come across here in Bountiful: aggressive, in a bad way. It would be true if she were a man. It was doubly true because she was a woman. People in Utah, and Mormons in particular, refrained whenever possible from public confrontations.

Every time anyone was given a new calling at church, it was always put to a vote in sacrament meeting. Primary teacher, bishop, ward chorister, whatever it was, the bishop or the member of the bishopric who was presiding at the meeting got up and asked all who could sustain so and so in their calling to please do show by a show of hands. Everyone put up their right hand. Any opposed by the same sign. Not once in her life had Nedra seen anyone raise their hand in opposition. Brian told them it had happened once in his singles ward in L.A., years and years ago, but it was notable enough to be a story he saved up and shared with the family.

There had been a young man called to some leadership position, and a pale young woman had raised a quiet, determined hand in opposition. A notably surprised and flustered bishop said he would speak with her in his office at the close of the meeting. Brian said the rest of the service was charged with nerves, everyone trying to pretend they weren't distracted, that they were focused on the talks and the hymns when they were actually sparking with staticky curiosity. After the benediction, the young woman hurried off, presumably to the bishop's office. The young man slipped off somewhere. His calling was not mentioned in sacrament meeting again, and a few weeks later, someone else was called and unanimously sustained to the position. No one ever knew what the objection had been. Of course there was some quiet gossip, theories privately floated—maybe the young woman knew of some moral indiscretion, most likely because she'd been his partner in it—but no one ever said a word about it again at church.

You resolved conflicts privately. That was all there was to it.

Right now, the most Nedra could hope for was someone asking her a direct question that would allow her to gently but clearly highlight her difference of opinion.

Holly Rasmussen apparently felt no such strictures. She grabbed for the mic. "Think of the pain a baby experiences when its body is destroyed. The physical pain! You have people protesting chickens, but not human infants? I happen to know that some of the candidates here, not just Len Hemmings, whole-heartedly support abortion."

She sat down hard, once again not so much as glancing at Nedra, but she was close enough for Nedra to see the sweat beading on her upper lip, for Nedra to hear her nostrils rattling. What on earth did she mean? Nedra supported abortion? Was that what Holly Rasmussen was implying? She felt herself bursting with protest.

Of course she wasn't a person who lined up outside abortion clinics with gruesome posters. Mormons were not shouters and picketers. If they were ever going to have anything to do with abortion clinics, the most Nedra could think she or anyone she knew would muster would be plates of cookies and copies of the Book of Mormon, given out with smiles and handshakes. But that wasn't something you did either. She had no idea if there were even any abortion clinics in the state, though she supposed there probably were. That didn't mean it wasn't an issue. That didn't mean it wasn't a matter of concern. That didn't mean every woman who ever fell pregnant out of wedlock wasn't counseled to carry the baby to term. That didn't mean that abortion was a real possibility for a faithful couple under any but the direst circumstances. What Mormons favored was faith. The Lord was in charge of life. You trusted in Him. That was what

Nedra believed. That was what she thought everyone in the room believed. What was Holly Rasmussen trying to say about her?

Stricken, Nedra looked to her father and Doug and her daughters, and then at Barbara. She needed a question. She needed help getting as much distance between herself and this craziness as possible. Doug couldn't ask, that would be too obvious. Her daughters looked back with empty, encouraging expressions. Barbara, however, got the message. She raised her hand, looked around to make sure she wasn't cutting in before anyone else, and then, waving away Randy and his microphone, raised her clear, carrying teacher's voice.

"This is a question for Nedra Walker. Can you talk a little bit about some of your positions on big issues like abortion, immigration, and the national debt?"

Dear Barbara, a little overly broad, but still. Nedra was grateful.

"Well, thank you for that question!" she said, trying to steady herself. Posture but with ease, she reminded herself. Breathe."I think families are the cornerstone of any society, and I believe as many decisions as possible should be left up to families. That's why I believe in low taxes—families know better what to do with their money than the government does. But I believe absolutely in the sanctity of life, so that would be a difference between me and some of the other candidates. I think freedom of speech and freedom of religion are very important, and I think it's wrong for the government to tell people of faith they can't practice their beliefs, for instance when it comes to traditional marriage and families. Did I mention the debt? I think it's absolutely critical to live within our means. That's a value my parents taught me, and it's a value I've taught my children, and I think it's a value we as a society should live by." She felt herself growing increasingly breathless. Was she rambling?

After Randy the shift manager asked everyone to give all the candidates a round of applause, Nedra shook hands with Len and then turned to extend her hand to Holly Rasmussen, but Holly Rasmussen was already gone, already down the stairs and reaching for the handles of her son's wheelchair. The crowd of messy children coalesced around her. Without a further word to anyone, she pushed swiftly to the exit with the horde of them trailing behind.

Nedra should have followed Len Hemmings' lead, circulating around the room, meeting voters. But she felt all used up, as if she were about to turn into one of those runners whose legs collapse at the finish line, all tragic tumbling matchsticks. She quickly made her way to Doug and her father. Barbara and her mother and Heather and Caroline joined the circle.

"You were great, honey." Doug said.

"I thought you did very well," Barbara said.

"You looked just lovely up there," Barbara's mother said.

"You came across as very self-possessed," Heather said.

"Holy crap, Holly Rasmussen is crazy," Caroline whispered.

Nedra looked to her father.

He cleared his throat. "Len Hemmings made some interesting points, I thought."

Nedra acknowledges this remark with the barest of hms.

Back at home, after Heather had dropped her father off and they were all gathered in the kitchen, Heather said jokily to everyone, "Did you guys see the look Mom gave Grandpa after he said Len Hemmings was great. It was like 'how about we start packing your bags for Oak Haven *right now*."

"I did not!" Nedra said. Though Heather had correctly identified her outrage. Her own father was probably going to vote for Len Hemmings. Why? Because he was a figure of priesthood authority? And if he felt that way, how many other people did too?

"Well, let's be real," Caroline said, moving right along. "I think Mom is probably safe in the primary. Did you listen to that crazy lady? The real worry is Len Hemmings. Who cares if he's a Democrat? You know who's going to vote for him? Old people. He's old, and then he has the whole authority figure thing going for him. So we need to get young people to vote. Heather, I think that's our job today. Mobilize the young. I think we should get out the high school yearbooks and look up every single person we ever knew on Facebook and send them all personal messages asking them to like Mom's page. And then send the same message to, like, everyone in their family. Everyone and their brother. That's the motto for the day."

"That's not a bad plan, actually," Heather said.

"Don't act so surprised," Caroline said. "I'll fix us both Diet Cokes. You go get the yearbooks."

"Mom, you should go take a piano break or something," Heather said.

So they were dismissing her. They were right enough. She had yet to come down from her fluster. A full sense of internal disarray refused to release her. It was as if a rash had spread on the underside of her skin, all of her aflame with an itchy unease. Some Bach, an orderly counterpoint, might soothe and restore her. At least she hoped so. So fine, her daughters were right about that. But she feared they were very wrong about Holly Rasmussen. Safe in the primary? She didn't think so.

Chapter 13

DinnerForEight was all birthday all week. Caroline posted photos of cute invitations, hand-crafted with mint green and gold rickrack around the edges of the cards, with metallic confetti that spilled out of the matching envelopes.

"Do you want an invitation to give to Devin?" Caroline asked Heather. "I could totally customize it. Come meet your future in-laws!"

"Oh my gosh, please do not make jokes like that when he's here," Heather said, feeling a panic even though she knew Caroline was kidding.

"Seriously, though. I think you guys should get married. A wedding would be really good for my blog."

"So selfless! I'll be sure to let Devin know," Heather said, as if she were put out. But in reality, wasn't there something deeply gratifying in her sister's presumption? Heather imagined her wedding pictures on DinnerForEight, her bridal shots generating a rain shower of likes. Was it so ridiculous to imagine that she, Heather Walker, might be thought a charming bride? Caroline apparently didn't think so.

The next day Caroline posted photos of two different practice birthday cakes and let her readers vote for which one would be recreated for her mom's big night. She wrote a long post about the birthday parties Nedra had thrown for her over the years, complete with a good dozen old birthday photos of herself, naturally looking adorable through all ages. Heather made an appearance in a few of them, thankfully none in the teenage years. She hadn't remembered her favorite one until she saw it online. It was Caroline's third birthday, candles lit, Caroline's adorable face aglow, her cheeks puffed out mid-candle-blow, and Heather off to the side, eight-years-old, a hand on the back of Caroline's chair, leaning in, eyes excited, and her lips pressed into a perfect sympathetic half-blow, as if prompting Caroline. Not blowing from that distance, clearly not actually blowing, but sweetly, childishly, unable to keep from joining in in some small way.

She sent a link to the photo to Devin. "**Am I not adorable?**" she wrote.

"**Totes adorbs,**" he wrote back.

She wondered if Ted would see the photo. Somehow she imagined his reaction would be more sincere than "totes adorbs." She conjured him pulling up the photo in his office at work. Typing in the address again on his laptop at home, her picture drawing him in again and again. Not adorbs. Adored.

The night of the birthday she was planning to swing by Devin's place and pick him up so they'd arrive together, but Devin texted. "**Sorry. Stuck at hospital for a bit longer. Meet you there?**"

Heather texted him Caroline's address and drove up alone, a sense of exposure at his absence by her side and an irrational worry that perhaps he wouldn't materialize at all that evening.

Naturally, since Caroline was Caroline, she lived in the guesthouse of a mansion on a hill high above the state capitol, the whole gated community granted hundred-mile views to the south and west. The couple who lived in the mansion (that truly was the only word for the massive house) were on a mission in Argentina, and while they were away Caroline and her roommate, the couple's niece, kept an eye on the property in exchange for free rent, a shockingly minimal duty since a housekeeper still cleaned the big house once a week and a gardener stopped by at least twice a week to keep up the exterior. Fortunately for the gardener, the walks and the driveway were laid with heaters built into the concrete, which meant no matter how heavy the snowfall he never had to shovel. Heather had been at Caroline's when it snowed once and had watched, bewitched, as steam rose off the clear sidewalks while mounds of white piled higher and higher on the ground around them.

To be fair, Caroline's accommodations amidst all this luxury were modest. The guest house was a reasonable two-bedroom affair, albeit with beautiful finishes and a short walk to the pool. In the warm months, Caroline had most of her dinners outside, picturesque picnics in meadows or parks or cozy barbecues over campfires, but this time of year almost every blog post featured the guest house's dining room, which Caroline had painted a deep purple. Heather had no idea if she'd gotten permission first. It wouldn't surprise her if she hadn't.

Heather's parents' car was already in the driveway when she pulled up, and her mother answered the door.

"Sweetie, you look so nice! Are you wearing eyeliner?" she said.

Nedra had a way of complimenting that felt deeply unspontaneous, more like a concerted program of behavior-shaping positive reinforcement.

Heather shrugged.

"I thought you were bringing Devin," her mother said next, as if she had just now noticed his absence.

"He's coming from the hospital—just running a little late."

"Fantastic," her mother said.

His being late was fantastic? His being a medical student was fantastic? How irritating her mother's faux-nonchalance could be. Yes, it was a big deal. She had invited a man to dinner. A suitor. Did they really all have to pretend it was nothing? And yet she didn't actually want them to get worked into a tizzy either, so what was she hoping for? Somehow it seemed to Heather that everything about dating was embarrassing. It wouldn't have been had she been down this road many a time, everyone's reactions blunted by repeated exposure to "Heather and a boy," but "Heather and a boy" was indeed the new and exciting show in town, and they were all flubbing their way through the awful script before them.

Her dad, handsome in a grey suit, crossed the dining room to give her a hug. Caroline said hello without fully disengaging from the tableau of birthday cake, flowers, and fabric banner she was photographing on the dining buffet. Her mother's best friend Barbara emerged a few moments later from behind the hall's bathroom door. Her grandfather was nowhere to be seen.

"Is Grandpa not coming?" Heather said.

"He said he was feeling a bit under the weather," Nedra said. "Don't worry. We'll stop and check on him on our way home."

She had imagined him there, solidly by her side, diffusing her parents' manic energy. Her sense of exposure inched outward that much more.

Heather found her place card, Devin's beside hers. Please, let Caroline not do anything mortifying like ask them to intertwine fingers while she stood on the table for aerial hand-holding shots. That was something Caroline would actually totally do. You wanted to be a good sport, but there were limits.

By the time the doorbell rang again Caroline and Heather were ferrying food from the kitchen.

"I'll get it," Nedra's voice sang out.

Heather had an impulse to rush to the door before her mother. Why? To intercept and spirit Devin away from this whole meet-the-family event? Surely not. She wisely carried on as if her nerves hadn't spiked, and at the sound of Devin's voice entering the house she felt a plink of relief and happiness.

Devin quickly apologized for being late. He wished Nedra a happy birthday, and she crooned a thank you, as if he'd said the most charming thing in the world. Heather joined them at the door, and she thought Devin might give her a kiss on the cheek or some other affectionate greeting, but he made no move toward her. She blushed her hello to him, a glowing threat of sweat rising in her despite the chilly evening. While Devin was busy not touching her, her father shook Devin's hand and patted him vigorously on the back, an overacted manly gesture of welcome. Heather made introductions to Barbara and Caroline, and after a short bit of milling they all took their seats.

As they bowed their heads for the blessing on the food, Devin at last reached for her hand. It was just the sort of subtle gesture of companionability and romantic affection that she had been looking for, and yet now that it had materialized Heather felt twitchy. This picture—her family, her significant other—was one she'd so often tortured herself conjuring, so desirable and yet seemingly so impossible. And here it was. And maybe it was simply that the scene was overworked from all that imagination, but now that it was upon her she couldn't shake off a certain skittishness, like a nervous horse, just sure something is right there on the other side of the blinders.

After the prayer, Caroline brought in the salad plates and served them all around.

"Please don't mind if I snap a few more photos," Caroline said, mostly to Devin. "I hope Heather warned you that I'd be obnoxiously photographing the whole evening. If I don't post my every meal my Instagram followers become concerned that I'm starving."

Devin laughed but did not seem overly charmed. Good.

"Sister Walker," Devin said, turning to her mother. "Heather's been telling me all about the campaign, but I'm sure it's a whole different experience being the actual candidate."

"Please, call me Nedra," her mother said warmly.

Devin seemed pleased by this. "Heather said you had your first meet-the-candidate event the other day?" he continued.

"Did she tell you I have a crazy opponent?" Nedra guffawed, the words roaring out like a bray. It was a strange, jolting moment.

Devin glanced to Heather, a quick check for approval before proceeding. She was happy with the way it connected them, a team. She gave a little eyebrow flicker, and Devin forged ahead.

"She mentioned there's a woman who is perhaps a bit to the right of you?" he said, the words pronounced with an amusing staccato pluck.

"Oh, she's pretty much off the spectrum," Doug jumped in.

"Well, she's a little bit of a cipher," Nedra said. "You know, just seems to have come out of nowhere."

"I don't think she's a real threat," Doug said. "The party is supporting Nedra, and all you have to do is listen to this other woman for two seconds to know she's off her rocker."

"I just think it's weird that she's running. She has all these little children," Nedra said, with a bit of tutting chagrin.

"What do you mean?" Heather said.

She felt all the eyes on the table turn to her. She hadn't meant to sound so sharp. She should have let the conversation proceed without her. Was it Devin and nerves that had made her tongue spring ahead?

She watched as a starchy defensiveness crept into her mother.

"You were there, Heather," Nedra said. "You saw. She has quite a few children, and she seems to be their primary caretaker. I guess what I'm saying is I wonder how she's finding the time."

Holly Rasmussen was hardly the test case for a feminist stand on the rights of mothers of young children to work outside the home. She had one million kids, and they didn't necessarily seem perfectly cared for, and Heather wouldn't vote for her in a million years regardless, for reasons that had nothing to do with the kids and everything to do with her being bonkers. But in spite of all this it was suddenly like a reenactment of the Christmas fight fiasco. Heather knew better, and yet the words were spurting from her almost involuntarily.

"Having kids means you shouldn't run for office?" she said hotly. "You'd never say that for a man. I mean, right?"

But clearly the confirmation she was seeking was not forthcoming. Around this and virtually any other Mormon table, the consensus was that having children was indeed a very good reason for a woman not to run for office or do anything other than diligently care for them, and maybe blog about it.

"I mean, clearly the kids have a father," Heather said into the silence. Not like this mattered. Even if they had a doting father, in Mormon circles parenting by fathers was typically seen as babysitting, a brief bit of help for the true caregiver.

"Do they?" Nedra said. "I didn't see anyone else there at Oak Haven."

Caroline sashayed into the conversation. "Based on her Facebook page, I think she might be a polygamist, so like, sisterwives could totally help out with all those kiddos."

"Oh, she is not!" Nedra laughed, the mood instantly lightening.

"No, for real," Caroline said, clicking away on her phone and then holding up a picture of Holly Rasmussen for all to see. "That hair does not lie."

They all laughed now.

This was how Caroline thrived on the internet. She was like a politician—you could ask any question you wanted and she replied, but with whatever sort of answer she wanted, an illusion of transparency that was instead a bit of magical misdirection. She chose all sorts of tantalizing fine details to share with her readers, the way the peach pie she was baking reminded her of her grandmother, the foot stomping fury she'd gotten into during a backyard photoshoot when a deer ate the quinoa salad. It was easy to feel close to her with all these details. But they were also masterfully obscuring. A few years ago, when their grandmother died, Caroline had been sad and then sadder still until she had finally started seeing a therapist (whom she still saw every week) and had gone on medication. The internet certainly didn't know, and Heather also thought she might be the only one in the family Caroline had told. This was how Caroline kept a dinner party fun. No yelling and crying for her. Just deft steering. Heather admired her immensely. She'd have to thank her later for the rescue.

An embarrassed muteness came over Heather for much of the rest of the meal. Devin got her dad talking about his latest bit of reading on the Civil War, a favorite topic of his, and then her mom quizzed Devin on all the ins and out of medical school, and as all this unfolded Heather resigned herself to focusing on mindful eating, hoping that with a tortoise's determined pace she could leave fully half her meal on her plate by the time the dishes were cleared.

When Caroline determined it was time for cake, she directed Heather to fetch it from the buffet and asked Doug to light the candles while she snapped photo after photo. As Heather ferried the glowing birthday cake to its place in front of her mother, for the first time since her outburst about Holly Rasmussen she finally turned her eyes fully to Devin. He at last returned his full attention to her as well, and when their eyes locked he gave her a chin salute, the sort of tossing of the head, chin first, that you'd give a passing fraternity brother. It was not the reassurance of intimacy she might have hoped for.

Finally, after lingering over cake and ice cream (Heather pretended to eat hers but didn't, the ice cream puddling around the islands of forked-over cake), she found herself briefly alone in the kitchen with her mother, the two of them packing leftovers into the fridge, scraping plates and loading them in the dishwasher.

"Devin is very nice," Nedra said.

Heather nodded, noncommittally. Her mother was clearly gathering herself up for some further statement.

"I know you're going to roll your eyes at me, but I will say it anyway. You might want to watch the political talk around Devin."

"This from a woman running for office?" Heather said with a laugh.

"You know what I mean," her mother said seriously.

Heather didn't roll her eyes. Instead, she went stiff. She knew exactly what her mother meant. "Political talk" meant things like her outburst about women working. She'd been too flustered to stop and read Devin during her moment of defense for Holly Rasmussen. Surely a little righteous indignation on her part wasn't enough to put him off. He was a Diet Coke Mormon! And yet it seemed her mother had observed otherwise.

After a few more minutes of tidying, Nedra rejoined the rest of the family in the living room, but Heather hung back. She stood in front of the leftover cake, freshly wrapped under plastic film. Vanilla buttercream with lemon curd filling. She imagined uncovering it. She imagined lifting one forkful and then another into her mouth. She imagined the rush of excitement, the pinching surge of the glands in the corners of her jaw at the first hit of the sweet-tart citrus. She imagined licking frosting from her fingers. The rich creaminess of it. She pictured herself devouring it, the whole thing. She would start slow, savoring every sensation and by the end she would hardly taste it anymore; she'd only experience the frenzied headlong mouthfeel of unstoppable regret and distress.

She stood and looked at it for one further second and then turned calmly away. Maybe this should have felt like a moment of triumph, a hoorah of willpower, but instead Heather felt desolate, halfway to lonely tears. There were people in this world who ate cake, for whom consuming calories was a thoughtless endeavor, easy and unremarkable. There were people who never stood in a kitchen and pictured their ruin. She'd just had dinner with a whole roomful of them, and she would never be one of them. There was her fat self, forever pushing to return.

It felt like the exact same thing with the church. There were people for whom Mormonism was easy, people who had never felt the least bit of discomfort, people who had never imagined leaving. Heather couldn't say she didn't understand such people. Her whole life was full of them. It was just that she wasn't one of them either. Her whole experience in the church was a see-saw between a deep sense of belonging and alienation.

There was a person for whom Mormonism was perfect, and that was a straight married man at pretty much any time in his life and a straight married woman during the years of her child-rearing. As a man, the priesthood gave you a path to meaningful service, but also to prestige, authority, and respect. In any church leadership position, people looked up to you. Heather had watched her father in all his years of church leadership—sure, it was a ton of work, but there was camaraderie and deference and a deep sense of purpose. Such benefits!

As a woman, you didn't have priesthood callings to sustain you, but you had auxiliary callings to keep you busy and if you had children the church and its people thoroughly recognized the holiness and importance of your endeavor. Motherhood! The calling of women! And it wasn't just lip-service. Non-Mormons might always discount the worth of the stay-at-home half of a couple, but Mormon mothers got real cred. Families were the essence of the most important Mormon doctrines. Eternity was a chain of family, stretching forward and back, women every bit as central to that as men. Separate spheres were always problematic, but still it was easy for Heather to see how a married woman with children could feel powerful in the church.

But she was not a married man or a married woman with children. She was single and childless, a disempowered, unconnected misfit. Maybe if she'd sailed right into marriage in college rather than being marooned in singles wards for a decade, maybe if her body had never made her feel like an oddball, maybe then she'd have felt so straightforwardly secure and validated that she wouldn't ever have thought to be bothered. But when you didn't fit, boy, that could certainly spur some thinking. What about women like her? What about gay people? What about women whose children were grown? There was a reason her mother had gotten all civic all of the sudden, and maybe it had something to do with the church failing to utilize her now that her ovaries were retired. And once you went down the path of discomfort it was almost as if more discomfort sought you out. There were plenty of doctrines you could squirm over, historical events that could trouble you.

But what did she want? To leave? She wanted that just about as much as she wanted to be fat again. So what was there left to do? Step gingerly away from the internal conflict, refuse to pick up the fork, rejoin Devin and her family.

She heard them laughing happily on the other side of the door, some remark Devin made hitting its target. He fit so well with the people she loved. She took a deep breath, pinched her cheeks, and left the kitchen.

Chapter 14

Did you ever really like your children's significant others? They were such dangers to your children's happiness, jagged blades you watched them juggle. You tried not to wince. You tried not to jostle the situation until it sorted itself out. You politely masked your skepticism.

Nedra had liked Devin well enough. He could have stood to work on his posture, and he had a subtly smirking way about him that made Nedra nervous on Heather's behalf—he seemed the type who might be quietly, poisonously critical—but he'd made a clear effort to be polite and ingratiating, Nedra couldn't fault him there. And he seemed upstanding. He taught Elders Quorum, the class the men split off to during the third hour of church when the women went to Relief Society. He was pursuing a good career. He seemed bright. All positives. The fact that he was single at twenty-eight shouldn't have made Nedra suspicious—after all, Heather was single too. As were all her children currently except Audrey. But still, she had the thought: what was wrong with him, that he was still on the market? Added to all that, Nedra had not appreciated the way he put his hand on Heather's thigh late in the evening. She worried it was a sign he was the type of boy Heather would have fend off when they were alone together.

"Didn't you think Devin was awfully handsy?" Nedra had said to Doug in bed the night of the birthday party. "Maybe he should specialize in surgery. His hands need something to do."

"Maybe Heather needs someone younger and more timid," Doug had said, teasingly, kissing Nedra's neck. "Seems to have worked for her mother."

She laughed and arced her neck as he continued kissing her. She nuzzled him back.

"You probably don't remember," Nedra said, "but remember how Brian invited his whole baseball team for the party after his baptism, and Audrey invited all those little girls from school? When I told Heather to make a list of people to invite for her eighth birthday, she put like five people on it. Grandma and Grandpa. The Bagleys, you remember them? And then Sister Warburton, the old lady with the dogs. I couldn't convince her to invite a single kid."

"What does this have to do with anything?" Doug said with a half-chuckle, his mouth near her earlobe. "Are you saying she needs someone *older*?"

"No! Not all. I guess I'm saying I'm relieved she finally has a young-enough boyfriend, even if he is a bit touchy-feely. She's been carpooling with some old man neighbor who works in her office, and it's been making me nervous."

"Dr. Hands to the rescue," Doug had said, and they'd laughed and turned off their bedside lamps and reached for each other.

The most natural thing in the world after introducing people to your significant other was to solicit their thoughts. And of

231

course the most natural thing was to reply with kind thoughts. You could always find something. *She seemed sweet. He's tall.* Not that she'd have to stretch that far, but regardless, Nedra was all queued up with responses for Heather's inevitable inquiry when she dialed her daughter up the morning after the party.

"It was very nice finally meeting Devin!" Nedra said.

"Thanks for letting him come to your birthday," Heather replied, but she said it with a sort of clip, a curtness that signaled a clear desire to move along. Nedra opened her mouth to press ahead with a comment or two about him, but then she'd thought better of it. Maybe something had happened after the party, some sort of argument? Or maybe it was just that Heather wanted to make it clear she didn't care what anyone thought. That would be very Heather. Either way, no need to push it. Nedra moved them on to the real matter at hand: the upcoming County Convention.

Nedra had been a delegate herself enough times to know exactly how the County Convention would go. The gym at Ridgeview High School would open at five o'clock. Delegates would start arriving by six. They'd circulate among the tables she and her fellow candidates had set up earlier in the day. Some candidates would hand out basic brochures or flyers. Others would go for hats, t-shirts, candy, sodas. One year she'd even seen a candidate who rented a helium tank and printed his face on balloons so that spheroid versions of him floated all over the room.

The delegates would gather their goodies and circulate back and forth between the gym and the auditorium, where the candidates for county-wide office made their speeches. And then by 7 o'clock they'd divide into districts, each district in a classroom. In the District 17 classroom, Holly Rasmussen would say something, Nedra would say something, and then the delegates would mark their ballots and place them in a wooden box at the back of the room as they filed out. Once the room was clear, the judges would tally the votes right then and there. Nedra would know the outcome by 8 o'clock. If she got twenty-five votes, that was it, no open primary, no more Holly Rasmussen. If she didn't get that many votes, Holly would plague her till the primary in June. Or, unthinkable, if Holly Rasmussen got the twenty-five votes that would be it for Nedra. But that wasn't a possibility, surely it wasn't.

Thinking back to Brian and Aaron's student government elections made Nedra laugh now. What was funny was that they were set up to teach kids about civics, to run a small-scale version of the real political process. And yet in many ways the school version of an election was exactly like the real thing, if not, in fact, bigger and more intensive. Four-hundred-odd students had voted in Brian's eighth grade class election. Thirty-seven delegates would vote at the county convention. She'd get up in front of one single overfull classroom. Brian had had a whole cafeteria.

One difference, though: budget. She and Heather had spent a lot more than Airhead money on Nedra Walker tote bags, Nedra Walker buttons, and a big Nedra Walker banner with a velcro edge to attach to the front of her table.

"Where do you order stuff like that?" Nedra had asked Heather, as if her daughter might have some experience in this area she did not.

"I don't know, Etsy?" Heather had said.

And she'd been right. How strange to order campaign para-phernalia from the same place you outfitted birthday parties, but wonders never ceased.

On the phone with Heather now, Nedra said, "So does four o'clock work tomorrow?"

She wanted to be loaded up and ready to go well before the gym doors opened.

Heather hesitated.

"Is it a carpool issue?" Nedra asked. "I can drive down and pick you up if you don't want to drive yourself." She knew it wasn't a carpool issue, but somehow she couldn't help needling.

Heather gave an exasperated exhalation. "It's not a carpool issue, thanks. I was just looking at my calendar. I hadn't planned to leave that early, but you're right, I should be there to help you. I'm sure I can move some things around."

"Thank you, that'd be great," Nedra said, working hard to strip any sarcasm from her voice. Although last she checked knocking off early one afternoon from a government job was not that big a deal. It seemed instead that Heather wanted to make sure her mother noted her *sacrifice*.

"What time is Dad getting there?" Heather said, as if trying to highlight the fact that Nedra had not asked Doug to leave work early. As if it were some sort of valuing of men's work over women's work when in fact it was something far more straight-forward. Was Doug the campaign manager? No, he was not.

"He should be there at six on the dot," Nedra said, doing her best not to respond to Heather's provocation. "You can bring Devin if you want. He could help you man my booth if you're worried about being stuck alone."

"I'll be fine, I'm sure," Heather said, again with a sort of polite opacity that made Nedra want to read more into it.

When Nedra and Heather arrived at the Ridgeview High School gym with their rolling carts of supplies, a man with a clipboard scanned down his spreadsheet and directed them to table twenty-nine. Nedra glanced quickly at the sheet, hoping to see where Holly Rasmussen was stationed, but the font was too small and her moment of glimpsing too brief. She scanned the aisles as she walked to her booth, but didn't spot Holly Rasmussen then either.

As she and Heather began arranging the tablecloth, table skirt, and banner, Nedra kept peeking her head toward the door. She hesitated, and then finally said to Heather, "Would you mind . . . could you go ask the man at the door where Holly Rasmussen is stationed?" Nedra braced for a bit of ribbing, some scoff, but thankfully Heather spared her.

"Yeah, for sure," she said. "Be right back."

While Heather stepped away Nedra straightened her skirt and jacket. The red wool skirt suit had been an indulgence. She'd never had much need for suits. She wore dresses for church or slacks and a cardigan for anything casual fancy, like piano recitals. But Caroline had talked her into it. The suit had a '60s retro flair, with a slim fit and nubby weave, and she felt like she was playing dress-up in it. Nedra Walker, Business Lady. No. Nedra Walker, Politician. It wore like a corset for ambition, everything held just where it should be for proper presentation and confidence.

Heather returned in an instant. "Table sixteen," she said in a low voice.

They both looked furtively over a row to where table sixteen stood, empty, and then exchanged a wary look that told her that Heather shared her exact thought: Maybe Holly Rasmussen would be a no show. Was it too much to hope for?

As they laid out their bags, buttons, and brochures, the festival atmosphere began brewing. Booths were coming together. Eager-beaver delegates were already sneaking in. Soon enough, the clock hands clicked into place at six o'clock, and suddenly the gym felt just like the building at the state fair where people sold punched leather wallets and healing crystals, a clattering enthusiasm all about, everyone behind the tables exuding their best elect-me good cheer, everyone milling in front of them excited for their evening of burnished importance.

Doug arrived with hugs and kisses, and Barbara did too. Nedra and Heather loaded them both up with totes and buttons and sent them out to circulate around the gym floor.

Heather gave Nedra's hand a quick squeeze. "You got this, Mom," she said.

Nedra gave her an efficient but grateful head nod in return, feeling all bucked up and ready to go.

From there, it was an unending buzz of hearty handshakes and you-betchas. Nedra had a good memory for names. She didn't really believe people who said they didn't. What they meant was that they couldn't be bothered. But she'd put in effort, and now she stood in front of her table in her red suit next to the large banner with her name, greeting each delegate who passed by.

So good to see you, Brother Marsden!
How are you, Renee?
Hi Janet. Isn't this fun!

Although she kept an eye out for any action at Holly Rasmussen's table sixteen, no one ever materialized there. At five minutes to seven, a party official came over the PA system to tell everyone to make their way to their designated district classrooms. This was it. Truly, she might be spared.

The room filled quickly. Doug, Barbara, Heather, and desk after desk occupied by men and women whose living rooms she'd visited. Nedra smiled and chatted, trying to keep her eyes from flashing to the door in a constant check for Holly Rasmussen. Finally, the voting judges for their district called the room to order as she took a seat at one of the desks in the first row. No Holly Rasmussen. But rather than relieved, Nedra felt alarmed. Where was she? Was she going to burst in at any moment? Remarks and then voting, the judges instructed. The floor was Nedra's.

Breathe. Nedra stood and smoothed her skirt and smiled out at the crowd and smoothly delivered the brief speech she had prepared. *I love Bountiful. I grew up here. I raised my family here. I believe local businesses keep our community strong. I support eliminating excess taxes and undue bureaucracy that keep these employers from thriving. I believe neighbors helping neighbors and local communities coming together to support one another is a far more effective approach than any government program. I believe that working together, we can make our state stronger than ever.*

Nedra wrapped it up. Polite applause. Still no Holly Rasmussen.

The voting judge rose and explained that ordinarily the other candidate—he did not say Holly Rasmussen's name—would have a chance to speak at this point as well, but as she was unable to attend this evening, they'd move straight to voting, if the candidate could just step outside.

Nedra took a moment, gathering her purse, collecting herself, adopting a serene expression. Then she exited the classroom and closed the door behind her. She had spent a great deal of time imagining how it would go with Holly Rasmussen, waiting together in this hallway. She had imagined she would try some chit-chat with the woman, see how that went. She had imagined crouching down and saying hello to Holly Rasmussen's children. She was good at that, finding out names and playing coy games of surprise and peekaboo with even the shyest little ones. She had imagined some sort of breakthrough—you couldn't hate people who were nice to your kids. But no. "Unable to attend." How bizarre. Alone in the hallway, Nedra tapped her feet. She leaned back against a locker. She freshened her lipstick. She spotted a water fountain and walked down for a sip, just to have something to do. How long could this take?

At last a new bustle came from behind the door, voices breaking free from quiet, chairs scraping the floor, she straightened up and braced herself. The first delegate out the door gave her a smile. Then another few did the same. So that meant she'd won? She hoped. Congratulations, a voice said. And then another. She'd won, certainly that's what the congratulations meant. She felt elated tears rising, but she was still tensed with suspense. What was the count?

Heather reached her first and grabbed her hands and nodded vigorously in response to Nedra's inquiring face. "You won!" Heather said. She wrapped Nedra in a hug. "Twenty-seven votes," Heather said. "No primary. It's you!"

Doug and Barbara joined the squeezing, smiling jubilation. The voting judges offered handshakes and an official confirmation.

Twenty-seven votes.

Delegates waited to shake her hand. As she and Doug, Barbara, and Heather packed up her table in the gym, Verna Smith and a few other party figures swung by to offer applause. Nedra exuded enthusiasm and good cheer.

She and Doug and Heather drove home together, Heather all abuzz with plans for the general election. "We are going to organize door-knocking brigades!" she said with razzle-dazzle hands. Nedra kept her smile fresh.

Only after Heather was safely in her own car, only after she and Doug had returned inside, only after she had taken off her jacket and heels and sunk into a chair in the family room, only then did she say what was truly on her mind. "Twenty-seven votes. That means she got ten votes. She wasn't even there and she got ten votes."

"You won!" Doug said. "It doesn't matter. You're it. No primary." He came over to Nedra's chair to squeeze her shoulder.

"I know, but which ten people voted for her? I know it shouldn't bother me, but it is just really . . . Oh, forget it," she said waving her hand as if that were enough to push the thought away.

"Don't you remember, you have an immoral agenda," Doug said, trying to make it a joke. "Can you really blame them?"

Nedra smiled, acknowledging the joke, but she couldn't bring herself to laugh. She roused herself and told Doug she was heading up to the shower.

"I have to wash my hair out. Heather sprayed it within an inch of its life," she said, with all the good humor she could muster. But the real reason she wanted a shower was that she felt like crying and hoped the heat and steam would bring out the tears. What a ridiculous reaction to a victory, and yet that was the truth of it.

Nedra stayed under the water, flushing her skin pink till the steam was almost too thick to see through. She turned the water a touch hotter, till it stung almost uncomfortably. She waited and sighed and still nothing gave.

Enough of that. Moving on. In her pajamas with a towel wrapped around her head, Nedra opened her laptop to update her campaign Facebook page. She'd constructed the post in her head already. Something like, "Thank you to all the delegates who voted for me at tonight's Republican County Convention. I'm so honored to have won. Now on to November!" She should probably post a picture with it, but what?

But before she could bother with any of that, her eye caught on the newest post in her feed. A post by Holly Rasmussen.

"**The POWERS THAT BE do not want change. But change is COMING! I hereby announce my candidacy in the CONSTITUTION PARTY for Utah State House of Representatives.**"

Nedra snapped the laptop closed, as if that could contain the insanity.

"Doug?" she called softly.

No answer. She put her hand silently to her mouth, astonished.

Chapter 15

Nedra wished she had answered the phone. But of course she hadn't. She always switched her cell phone to silent during piano lessons, and the phone in the kitchen would have to have rung a dozen times before she'd have gone for it. When it got one call and then another immediately following toward the end of her 4 o'clock lesson, she thought nothing of it. Until later, of course.

By the time of the calls she was sinking into the day, to the pleasure of teaching, a welcome relief after the internal turmoil of the County Convention. Nedra's favorite piano lessons were always the first ones of the afternoon. It was always older students first, the high school out before elementary or middle school. With them there was a chance of real musicality, and at that hour low rays of sun beamed through the windows. The piano room took on a golden cast. Dust motes twirled prettily, suspended in the glow.

All that was over and the day had relinquished itself to a gray half-darkness and the plunking of an unpracticed 8th grader by the time a black pick-up truck pulled up in front of the house. Not a parent—this was the middle of a lesson—so who? Nedra watched through the window as a man she slowly recognized as one of her father's home teachers walked toward her door. He didn't walk quickly—this was not an emergency walk—but there was a mirthless purpose in his stride, a reluctance overcome. It flattened Nedra before the doorbell even rang.

"Excuse me for just a moment," she said to the student on the bench.

The pleasantries were brief, non-existent actually.

"Sister Walker, I'm your father's home teacher, Brother Bennington. We met earlier this year?"

"Of course," she said. She would have invited him in, but the way he hung back made it clear he wouldn't be coming in.

"I'm afraid your father has had a stroke," he said.

She stepped back toward the piano room and told the student they'd have to end it there for the day. He could use the house phone to call his mother. Brother Bennington waited outside the door.

"Your husband is with your father. We reached him at work. They're at the hospital."

She didn't get her coat, just followed him out to the truck. They were halfway to the hospital before Nedra spoke.

"How did you know?" she finally asked. "That my father had a stroke?"

"We were with him. Brother Rankin and I. Just a regular home teaching appointment. Your father always likes to do them early in the evening. He had a sort of . . ." here he paused, clearly considering his words. "It was clearly something, he wasn't quite himself. We called 911 and stayed with him all the way. I'm sorry we couldn't reach you earlier."

The way he said *we stayed with him all the way*. The way he apologized for not reaching her. All of it kept her from asking the obvious—was he alive? Because it seemed there was an inference to be made.

She thought *my father has died* and tried to see what that felt like. Her cheeks trembled and the rims of her eyes burned. But this was playacting. This was manufactured. She did not know yet. She pushed the feeling aside and waited.

She climbed out of the truck at the emergency room doors, and when they whooshed open she found her father's other home teacher waiting just inside. He shook her hand. "Sister Walker," he said with a solemn nod.

She followed him back to a curtained area where Doug sat beside a wheeled bed, and on the bed, and on top of the covers in his street clothes lay her father. He was still wearing his shoes. The shoes in bed—it should have been what struck her, but it was. She didn't have to look further to know. But of course she looked. Her father was pale. Not waxy, the way he would be later, but drained, inert, someplace else. She touched his hand. Not cold, but no longer warm. Soft though, still his skin, still his veins, still the sparse hair and age spots on the back of his hands, still his fingernails. He hadn't cut them in a little too long. But they were clean, and her eyes focused on the ridges, the extra texture they'd take on year after year. How well she knew those hands—the long fingers, the slight curve to his ring fingers, the writing callus on the side of his right middle finger. How almost exactly her own hands mirrored his, just smaller, and younger.

Doug stood and put his arm around her, and when she released her father's hand, Doug took all of her in his arms. She cried, but not as much as it seemed she might when she was back in the truck.

"We'll need to call everyone," she said.

"Soon enough," Doug said.

When her mother died, Nedra had texted all the children. This has been roundly reviewed as a morbid breach of protocol.

"Can we agree—no more death texts?" Caroline had said after the funeral, all of them gathered about in the kitchen eating the leftover rolls and creamed green beans.

It was clear Caroline was probably speaking for everyone and trying to be light. She'd said it as if it were a joke, and yet Nedra had bristled.

"I thought you'd want to know as soon as possible," she'd replied.

"Yes, just not like that," Caroline had tried to mollify her with a pat.

It still pricked Nedra to think of it.

So fine, no texts. Phone calls. Oldest first. Caroline would get the news when she got it.

Nedra did not understand people who leaned into sorrow. It was like putting all your weight purposefully on a turned ankle. You healed by limping away, gingerly on the move. People who cried *denial, repression!* were kidding themselves. You could never really ignore pain. No matter what you did, it claimed you. But worming around in your wounds was a kind of immature indulgence, the sort of thing you slapped children's hands to keep them from doing. And so Nedra embraced the days of gently releasing herself into action and finding what solace there was to be found in carrying out the duties that came with death, not ignoring her grief but saving herself with motion. Phone calls, funeral programs, obituaries. She forgot the campaign as far as she could, no checking Holly Rasmussen's Facebook feed, no worrying about Len Hemmings. She cancelled piano lessons. She refused to skip her walks with Barbara.

"You know, the thing is, I'm just mostly grateful," she said to her friend, the two of them walking uphill, a brisk pace, both of them breathing heavily, a hint of green dawn behind the mountains.

"Things can be so hard and long and there can be all sorts of horrible decisions," Nedra went on. "I know you know."

"Yes, I do. I know exactly what you mean," Barbara said.

Horrible images were easy to conjure—feeding tubes and breathing machines and agonized half-lives that went on and on, and Nedra's father had been spared that. Nedra had been spared that.

"I mean, I'm in a little bit of shock, I guess. And still a little lost in adjusting. But I'm grateful," Nedra said again. She knew there were people who'd hear a fraudulent gloss to her supposed gratitude, and yet she was not manufacturing the sentiment. Her mother's long decline had been much harder on her heart. At least as far as she could tell so far.

"Is everyone coming for the funeral?" Barbara asked.

"They're trying to," Nedra said. She talked Barbara through the program. They'd discussed it all already with her father's bishop. She was speaking, her brother Roger was speaking. The bishop would say a few words. Brian was offering the opening prayer. Her brother's oldest was offering the closing prayer. Audrey was playing the piano for the hymns. Aaron was going to play for a family musical number, all of the girl cousins singing a women's arrangement of "Lead Kindly Light," her father's favorite hymn.

Two days later, it all went just as planned, and the activity of it, one event after the next, washed over her, a wave that pushed her along without requiring any real volition, a tumbling that continued to preclude real thought, too much movement for grief to pool. They held the viewing the night before the funeral at the mortuary and then the next morning the family gathered for a final family prayer around the casket in the Relief Society room at the church. At the end of the prayer, the attendant from the mortuary closed the casket, and Nedra flooded briefly with tears. All her daughters wiped at their eyes. Aaron looked stricken, but in possession of himself. Brian's cheeks trembled and he joined his mother and sisters in tears. But after the welling up was granted its moment, they blew their noses and blotted their eyes, shared squeezes and pats, and then together they walked to their seats at the front of the chapel, the attendants wheeling the casket to its place in front of the stand.

The chapel was gratifyingly full. People from her ward and her father's ward, family friends, cousins and second cousins, and of course the children, all her beautiful children. Audrey's Mike hadn't been able to get away, but Audrey was there, nestled between her sisters. Brian sat next to Aaron and Aaron's new girlfriend (Brian's own new girlfriend seemed to have vanished, no real mention of how and when). Heather's new boyfriend wasn't able to make it, but it was a Thursday morning, and Nedra understood. She hoped Heather did too. Heather's carpool friend and his wife attended. Thoughtful of them, and the fact that they came together, husband and wife, mollified Nedra. She saw Len Hemmings and his wife in the pews. Verna Smith and her husband came too. She hadn't invited any of them, but they must have seen the funeral announcement in the Davis

County Clipper. Generous of them to take the time, all around. She gave them credit.

At the end of the service, the family drove to Lakeview Cemetery, up on the hill near the Bountiful Temple, where her mother was buried, where Caroline had taken her campaign photos. The sun was out and the day was mild. At last, the first hint of summer to come, bright and true. At the graveside, the bishop of her father's ward spoke again briefly. They might have all cried again—she was sure each of them had their moments of rising emotion—but there was no great collective break of feeling as there had been when the casket closed, just quiet experiences for each of them, kept to themselves or shared with quick glances and sad half-smiles. Doug offered a final prayer and they returned to their cars and drove back to the church, the body to be lowered after they left.

As always, the Relief Society had laid out a meal in the cultural hall (the fancy name for the church gym), round tables and folding chairs wheeled out from storage under the stage, set up, and covered with pretty white lace tablecloths. A buffet of homemade rolls and baked ham for sandwiches, cheesy funeral potatoes with corn flakes on top, green bean casserole and fruit salad with marshmallows, Jell-O, and sheets of brownies with mint green icing. All as familiar as it was plentiful.

Little kids, the children of Nedra's nieces and nephews and cousins, ran around the gym in their dresses and white shirts. Neighbors and cousins chatted amiably. As people started leaving they came by to hug Nedra and her brother. Len Hemmings and his wife hadn't stayed, but Verna Smith and her husband had, and they came by with condolences.

Barbara was among the Relief Society sisters managing the lunch, and as the gym began emptying she came and crouched near Nedra.

"We'll pack up all this food and bring it by your house."

They squeezed one another's hands.

All throughout the morning Nedra had felt a headache gathering force. Nedra's headaches were like the weather in Utah. In the vast western landscape you could see a storm coming from fifty miles away. Masses of dark clouds, ominously majestic, advancing toward you. A curtain of rain in another part of the valley, sweeping forward. In Bountiful you could always smell a storm coming too. Wind from the east brought the brisk smell of the canyons. From the west you got the sulfurous odor of the Great Salt Lake, something soft and almost comforting in the ripeness, like the pleasingly foul scent of silage from a distance on a summer night. Nedra's headaches were the same—the awareness of their inevitability long before they arrived, the susurrations, the scent of them in the offing, their mounting force, and the odd satisfaction in surrender to the blunt pain of their final arrival. She had her first headaches after Brian was born. The doctor had asked the perfunctory questions, always a little amusing and smugly satisfying for a Mormon to answer. Do you drink? No. Smoke? No. Caffeine? No. She'd briefly worried that she might have a brain tumor. But no. Just migraines. *Just.* In the end, they concluded that lack of sleep and stress were her triggers. Stress less, sleep more, the doctor suggested. *How helpful. Why thank you. I will inform my infant, and together we'll get right on that.*

The headaches had come to her ever since, sometimes with months between them, sometimes in agonizing strings, sometimes at times of obvious stress, and sometimes when she was unaware of discord in her life but had to go searching for the source because weren't the headaches a sign that it was lurking somewhere? She had woken with the first whispers of pain that morning, before the funeral, and now a line just to the right of the middle of her forehead burned with a throbbing pressure.

At home, Nedra told everyone she was going to lie down. She retreated to her room with an ice pack and a soft cloth, turned her face down into a pillow, and waited for time to pass, the pain in its way almost as obliterating as sleep.

When she came down to the kitchen hours later, she found Aaron and Jennifer, the new girlfriend, mixing a box of gluten-free cupcakes. "Oh my dear, do you have Celiac's disease?" she said before she even said hello. She knew it sounded a little accusatory.

Jennifer seemed unfazed. "No, just trying to make healthy choices!" This should not have irritated Nedra, she knew, but really, making your own gluten-free cupcakes instead of eating the amplitude of leftover brownies and cookies was a little much. It made Nedra want to roll her eyes. Most special diets made her feel this way. Really, everyone in the world was now allergic to wheat and dairy? She did her best not to betray this attitude.

In addition to a picky eater, Jennifer was something else she hadn't expected either: Asian. Not that this was a problem, except that every time Nedra looked at Jennifer it yanked a archived memory to the very front of her brain. Back when Aaron was a teenager, Nedra, putting away laundry, had discovered a stray black tote tucked away in the bottom drawer of his dresser. Without pause, she'd looked inside and discovered what appeared to be a Japanese comic book. How unexpected.

Aaron had never shown any interest in comic books or graphic novels before, so far as she knew, and he'd never been one of those kids who'd gone in for martial arts and nunchucks either. She leafed through it curiously, and it fell open to a drawing of a girl, shapely cartoon thighs splayed page-wide to reveal explicitly rendered genitalia. The book was full of plenty more where that came from.

She knew most people, the non-Mormons of the world, thought porn was nothing—slightly tawdry maybe, but not soul darkening and corrosive. But they were wrong. The world was full of such casual sin. Young people throwing their sacred bodies at each other as if they were trash. Married couples breaking their vows. Sex, this sacred, powerful, godly force, trotted out for commerce and the basest of entertainment. People exploited, irrevocably damaged. Nedra had never really understood how it happened over the years that all the other religious people of the world now just skipped over those verses in the scriptures, how fornication and lust had become non-issues. As far as she knew, premarital sex wasn't something that would get you kicked out of the Lutheran church or the Catholic church or Judaism or whatever else. It was something that any of those people would simply shrug about nowadays.

But for Mormons there were real consequences. You didn't get to go to the temple anymore. You had to wait a year before you could go on your mission. If you were a married person who'd made and broken temple covenants, you were likely to be excommunicated, disfellowshipped at the very least. And the line came far before sex. Your body was sacred. You protected it. You respected the bodies of others. Even thinking impure thoughts was a sin to be carefully guarded against. The New

Testament was pretty darn clear about that one. You dressed modestly. You trained your mind to push unclean thoughts away.

Of course there were occasional mistakes. Teenagers who wound up pregnant, wayward young people who stepped away from the church and into depravity, shocking instances here and there of married couples betraying each other, a missionary who was found with pornography and sent home. But that was the thing. These instances were rare enough to be shocking. They had consequences. None of it was a shrugging situation.

All those years ago, she'd taken the comic book to the back-yard, set it on the grass, and lit it on fire. She'd hoped for a swift conflagration, but she'd had to light it several times. Finally, she swept up the ashes and felt a grim satisfaction in the damage to the lawn, as if it were an appropriate physical manifestation of the wrong contained in those images.

After her discovery, she'd looked at Aaron with cold, altered eyes. This son of hers, what darkness was he capable of? She'd waited till bedtime, she and Doug in their room with the door closed, and then in a harsh whisper she told him what she'd found. "It was pictures, a comic book. Japanese cartoons, like those ninja comics, but explicit. Where did he even get something like that?"

"Maybe someone at school was passing it around," Doug had said calmly.

Was that a *boys will be boys* attitude? "You're acting like this is not a huge deal!" she'd said, her voice quavering, the terrible betrayal of tears making her seem weak and sad when in fact she was furious.

"No, I'm not," Doug had answered, still smooth but with an edge of defensive ire, as if to say *calm down, woman,* a tone that only angered her further. "I know it's a big deal. I'll talk to him."

"Tonight?" she'd said, more a command than a question.

"Yes, sure. Right now."

Doug had pulled on his bathrobe and closed the door behind him.

She was glad that at least it was drawings, not photos, no actual women exploited for the images' production.

Doug had been gone twenty minutes, Nedra more wound up by the end of it than she'd been when he left the room.

"So?" she'd said sharply when he returned.

"It'll never happen again. I told him he needs to sit down with the bishop, too. He's going to call the ward clerk tomorrow to set up an appointment. I'll make sure he does it."

Nedra had nodded. "Good. Thank you."

And although that should have been it, case closed, she'd fumed for days, Aaron avoiding eye contact with her, Nedra clenched in a morose reticence that extended to the entire family. The tension had eventually passed, like a gusty rain finally clearing, but not without leaving some wreckage, little angry breaks she could ignore but that still burst into her attention from time to time for weeks.

In the end she noted that Aaron took several Sundays off from blessing the sacrament, the priesthood duty of teenage boys his age. She presumed this was a period of time away imposed by the bishop, and in the end that was what settled her heart. The time away from the sacrament was part of the repentance process. It meant Aaron had sought forgiveness. And because of the Atonement, the act was now erased, forgotten, as if it had never happened. She'd have to do her best to forget about the comic book too. She'd tried.

How unfair of her to remember it now, and yet she could not deny her deep discomfort seeing Jennifer.

"I just became your Twitter follower," Aaron said to Nedra now as he and Jennifer spooned batter into cupcake tins.

"Oh, have I been sending out tweets?" Nedra replied, stealing glances at Jennifer.

"Hah, is Caroline the one doing it?" Aaron said. "I thought it was a little peppy for you."

"I'm not peppy?" Nedra feigned offense.

He pulled out his phone. "Davis County Republican precinct meetings this week, double exclamation point. Find your meeting location here, exclamation point."

"Well, I agree with Caroline," Nedra said. "Those precinct meetings were very exciting."

Jennifer licked batter from her fingers and hopped up onto the countertop, taking a seat there as she might have in her own childhood kitchen. She took her phone from her pocket and tapped away. "Okay, now I'm following you too!" she announced with delight.

Every time Jennifer moved her fingers, ropey bundles in her forearms twitched and jumped. Below her long hiking shorts, worn despite the cold, the muscles in her calves bulged with definition. She seemed as though she could never be anything but at ease. Presumptuously so. Just then she started to whistle, a good strong whistle, full of musicality and vibrato. Lucy in the Sky With Diamonds? Yes, that's what she was whistling.

Too much for Nedra. She returned to her bedroom. The aftermath of a headache for Nedra was not some scrubbed clean window, shiny and clear. She always felt more burned-over than that, as if the insides of her were a field of blackened stubble, everything raw and requiring delicacy. She lay very still for a very long time. Eventually, unawares, she passed over into sleep.

Doug was asleep beside her when she opened her eyes and decided to gingerly pick her way back down to the kitchen in the dark. She needed something. Toast, maybe juice. The house was silent save for the humming of appliances, but a weak light reached the stairs, and when she rounded the corner she found Heather, sitting at the kitchen table, the light above the stove the only illumination.

"Heather Honey," Nedra said in a low voice. "I didn't know you were staying over."

Heather shrugged, and then she tried to smile but couldn't keep her face from crumpling. She wiped her eyes quickly. "I'm sorry," her voice caught. "I'm just so sad."

Nedra grabbed her hand and held it tight. "Me too, honey. Me too."

"Did you know Grandpa sent me a card with two hundred dollars in it when I graduated from my MPH program?" Heather said. "It said, now go out and be successful and I will pretend to be surprised."

"You never told me that," Nedra said.

"I think it was one of the only intentionally funny things Grandpa ever said," Heather said with a half-laugh. She then lost the hint of levity. "He always believed in me," she said welling up again.

Nedra squeezed her daughter's hands again and tried to ignore the sting she felt. Maybe Heather didn't mean it, but it seemed as if the implication behind *Grandpa always believed in me* was an unspoken *and he was the only one*. And also this: Nedra couldn't think of a single occasion where her father had ever said anything half that encouraging to her. Maybe she'd been sure her father loved her. But believed in her? Wouldn't that have been nice.

Chapter 16

Ted and Linda came to the funeral. They wore navy not black, and it warmed Heather's heart that Ted had remembered. After the service, she was surrounded by family and shared only the briefest of greetings with them, but when she finally returned to her apartment she found a note slipped under her door. "The service today was beautiful. Just wanted you to know you are in our thoughts. We're always here if you could use some company." The signature was "Ted and Linda" but she could tell it was Ted's handwriting. Or at least she thought she could. She wasn't sure she'd ever actually seen Ted or Linda's handwriting. It was amazing how long you could go in the world today without knowing something as fundamental about a person as their penmanship. But seeing it at last touched her.

"Thank you for your note," she said to Ted the next morning in the car, her first day back in the office.

He put his hand on top of hers. He squeezed. He reached his other hand over to her shoulder and gave that a squeeze as well. Comforting, and yet here they were alone in the car together, his hands on her body. The moment went on and on. No gamesmanship, just connection.

In the days after the death Devin was also solicitous. He sent extra text messages. He brought her flowers. He planned dates. Heather appreciated it all, but in a dampened way, more of an awareness that she should appreciate his overtures rather than actual appreciation.

"Remember how you said it would be fun to go out with Kevin and Kyra sometime?" Devin asked. "I checked with them, and they can do Friday. Are you feeling up for it?"

She wanted to say no. She was still the sort of sad that had trouble making eye contact. There was nothing shocking about her grandfather's death. He was ninety-one! Clearly, it was coming. And yet it seemed that with him missing the world had fundamentally re-formed itself for the worse. How many times had he said to her "that's my girl." No one else had ever claimed her with quite as much affection. But what good did it do her to shut herself up in her apartment and fester? This was how a person got back into the world again.

"Sure," she said to Devin. "Let's do Friday night."

The night seemed doomed from the start. Kevin picked the restaurant. "The Melting Pot." Everything on the menu was meant to be dipped in cheese or chocolate. Heather decided she could order a salad and then agree to share a fondue pot but not really eat anything. Hardly the recipe for a good time, though. Even worse, the second they sat down, Kevin lurched the conversation to the touchiest of subjects.

"So you guys saw the excommunication news today?" he said.

There was a group of Mormon women who had created a website that called on church leaders to grant women the priesthood (or more accurately, they had called on church leaders to seek out divine guidance on the matter and see if Heavenly Father was perhaps ready to make this change). They'd gone even further and put together gatherings outside the church's priesthood-only general conference session to physically voice their request. The main organizer had been asked to cease and desist and when she indicated that her conscience would not allow her to do so she had been called before a church disciplinary council for apostasy, excommunication the almost-certain outcome. The news had run in the Utah newspapers that day, and if you were Mormon it was all you saw on Facebook all day no matter where you lived. Repostings of the articles with comments like, "You either believe in the prophet or you don't," or "Asking for change is one thing, demanding it is something else." A few posts here and there echoed Heather's own feelings. "Saddened by this," or more ambiguous but no less accurate, "I feared this day would come." Heather had scrolled but commented not once.

"Seems pretty overdue to me," Kevin said.

He was probably wearing a concealed weapon at that very moment, Heather thought.

"A disciplinary hearing doesn't always mean excommunication, though, right?" Kyra said with a bit of trembly hope.

Kyra and Kevin—they were the sort of couple you could mistake for brother and sister. They looked like cinnamon rolls, fresh out of the oven, both puffy and rounded, with pale skin and matching sprinkles of cinnamon across their pert noses. Some people found look-alike couples creepy. Heather always thought it bespoke a healthy self-regard—if you picked someone just like you it meant you liked yourself enough to find your reflection appealing. Good for you, then. Did she and Devin match? A general blondish-ness, perhaps a certain shared lankiness now that she could potentially be described that way. Ted seemed the truer match to her real self, the solid mass of him, the burly warmth. Not that her real self was her fat self. What a revolting thought, what a failure of positive regard! But Kyra and Kevin: they matched, at least physically. Where they clearly differed was in Kevin's blustery opinions and Kyra's tentative ones, in his seeming sense that he deserved any and all attention that came his way and Kyra's obvious gratitude for every morsel of affection that fell hers.

"I mean, that's true" Kevin said. "It doesn't have to end in excommunication, but that's totally what's going to happen. I mean, that's what she wants to happen. That's all part of her big PR point."

"I just think it's sad," Heather said at last. Sad was only half of what she thought about it. Outrageous. Terrible. Tragic. A huge step backward for the church. If you wanted to get into it there was plenty else she could have said too. For instance, let's take a look at the historical record. Women gave what would now be called priesthood blessings all the time in the early days of the church. Not just early days. It wasn't until 1914 that women were told they should no longer lay their hands on the sick, anoint them with oil, and give them blessings. For a woman to administer such a blessing now would be sacrilege, cause for a disciplinary hearing of its own, but back then it was an ordinary duty of the Relief Society. She could have argued that. She could have argued about what Joseph Smith actually meant when he said the Relief Society would be a "Kingdom of Priests." Because he said that, he really did, and you could read it in the minutes from the founding meeting, right in the Church History

Archives. And then there were all the arguments about fundamental inequity, about the warping that took place when one gender always "presided over" another. All this she could have said aloud to Kevin and Kyra and Devin, but she didn't. Because what was there to gain? And goodness, everything to lose. At the top of the list of what she'd lose if she opened her mouth: her composure. If it hadn't been for her grandfather, some small part of her might even have enjoyed getting into it, but now she knew she would cry.

"The real thing I wonder," Kevin continued his bluster, "is if they're so 'offended' and 'hurt' by something as fundamental as priesthood doctrine, why are they even sticking around?" He air quoted the words offended and hurt.

This was Heather's least favorite line of argument, that anyone who disagreed with anything should up and leave the church. If you were Jewish, no one ever told you you weren't Jewish anymore, even if you ate bacon for breakfast, lunch, and dinner or hadn't been to a synagogue in years. And Don Corleone killed a whole lot of people right in the middle of his child's christening, and no one was starting Catholic excommunication proceedings (real or fictional!) for him either. But Mormonism was different. Start drinking coffee and skip services for any sort of duration, and you crossed over. People would say you'd left the church. You'd feel obliged to say so yourself. That was unofficial, though. Officially, there were also mechanisms at the ready to eject you. Cross certain lines—extra-marital sexual relations, public questioning of church doctrines, or insanely unimaginable things like murder—and a church disciplinary council would immediately convene to consider your membership status.

You could trace it back to the early history of the church, an *us versus them* that emerged when mobs tormented Mormons and apostates not infrequently joined up with the enemy. Or you could say that a different sort of policing was unavoidable in a faith with living prophets, where ongoing revelation guided the doctrine and, historically, the mass migration of people. In that kind of church you had to make it clear who was authorized to lead, what proper following looked like, and where the boundaries of membership stood.

But whatever the reasons, the attitude of "if you don't like it, leave," still pervaded. As if faith required an end to questioning. As if a person could not love the church, wish to be one with the body of the saints, and still hope for changes of policy or attitude.

Again, Heather could have said all this, but didn't. She imagined her voice cracking. She imagined her tears dripping into the cheese pot. It didn't matter anyway—Kevin was already moving right along with his monologue.

"I mean, just because men and women have different roles doesn't mean they're not equal." Kevin said.

This was just too much. "You sure about that?" Heather at last shot back. "You're going with *separate but equal?*"

Devin had been silent during all of this as well, but Heather felt him beside her like dark matter, the gravity of him pulling at her uncertainly.

"Don't even try to act like this is the same as a race thing," Kevin said with a further frothing.

At that Heather excused herself to the ladies room and latched a stall door behind herself just in case Kyra decided to follow. She covered her face with her hands and waited for the pink splotches and wet eyes to recede.

By the time she returned, someone, probably Devin, had moved the conversation along to a detailed discussion of some TV show Heather had never seen. And yet there was clearly a lingering tension. But oddly, not between her and Kevin. Between her and Devin. Heather put her hand on Devin's knee under the table, but he didn't relax into her. She eventually took it away. She hadn't said anything terrible. She had in fact performed miracles of personal suppression! How could he possibly be mad at her?

When dessert came Heather dipped a cube of sponge cake in the chocolate pot and ate it, a gesture of extreme accommodation that she doubted anyone but her recognized as such, and yet she made it anyway.

She and Devin walked to the car holding hands but not speaking. It seemed clear that Devin was preparing something. Heather did her best to steel herself for it. And she was right. As soon as they closed the car doors, Devin began.

"Listen, you act like you think I don't know how you feel about all this Ordain Women stuff, but obviously I do. And I'm not against women having the priesthood at all. If there were a revelation tomorrow giving women the priesthood that would be totally cool with me. Seriously." He said all this in a rush, thoughts he had clearly been rehearsing. But she could tell he wasn't done yet. This was a wind up.

"Okay . . .," she said.

"But I'm not trying to marry someone who's going to get excommunicated," he said.

Marry? He was trying to marry her, but not if she was going to get excommunicated? What a terrible declaration, intention and rejection all rolled into one. It sent a lurch careening from her gut to her every extremity.

"Wow. What does that even mean?" she said.

He exhaled dramatically. "I'm not trying to tell you how to feel about this. Like I said, I wouldn't have a problem if women got the priesthood. It's just . . . in the meantime . . ."

"I'm not going to get excommunicated!" Heather said. "It takes a lot more than sympathy to get excommunicated."

"But that's not even the point," Devin said. "I just feel like in all of this, I don't know, I just feel like there's this person underneath, and like, there's this bitterness and cynicism there."

How was this conversation happening today, when every receptor in her brain was all full up with grief? And now, what, he wanted her to justify herself? To prove that she was a nice girl and not a misanthropic non-believer? Didn't he know her by now? How could a person even begin to deny a lurking secret self? The whole thing was crushing and infuriating at the same time. *Yeah, I'm an apostate. And I'm fat too.* That was what was hiding inside her. Is that what she should tell him?

"I don't mean you shouldn't hope for the church to be a better place for women or a better place for gay people or more welcoming in general," Devin said. "I don't mean that. I just mean, I just mean I'm not trying to leave the church. Just to be clear. I'm all for picking a fight in Sunday School if someone says something dumb, and I'm not moving to Provo or trying to work on a Mitt Romney campaign or anything. But I want to go to the temple with you. I want to sit beside you in church. I want to baptize our kids and raise them in the church. I don't want to wake up with you in ten years with three kids and have you say *I'm done*."

The temple. Their kids! Again with the declarations. Her cheeks began their terrible tremble. "I want all those things too!" she half-wept. "I mean, isn't it obvious? If I were trying to leave, I'd leave. I'm not leaving."

"Sometimes it feels like you might," he said. "Like I don't quite know where you'll end up."

"I'm thirty-years-old. I've been to church like every week of my life except when I got my tonsils out. I don't know what else to tell you." And here she turned acid. "What, do you want me to bear my testimony or something?"

"Why haven't you ever gone through the temple?" he said suddenly, accusation undeniable in his tone.

A knife point. She inhaled slowly, trying to regain her composure, but Devin had pierced something awful and true with that question. She could have gone through the temple by now, and she hadn't. Why?

The Temple. What went on inside Mormon church buildings was recognizably a version of what went on in just about any Christian house of worship. Sunday services and youth groups, singing and praying and basketball and Sunday School. What went on in Mormon temples, on the other hand, were something else entirely. They weren't for church services. They were for special rituals, in particular a ceremony called the endowment.

Before your endowments you didn't wear garments, just regular old underwear like every other kid in America. After your endowments, it was silky white underclothing forevermore, a top that covered your shoulders and scooped modestly in front and back, undershorts that draped all the way down to your knees. But there was much more to it than garments. The ceremony was a little like baptism plus, an ordinance with the promise of spiritual gifts. Endowments were a marker: committed Mormon adult. Once you'd gone through the endowment ceremony for the first time, you could go to the temple again and again as often as you wanted, and endowed Mormons did just that. Sometimes every week. Usually at least once a month. For endowed Mormon adults the temple was a place of retreat and spiritual uplift, revelation even. Take her mother. When Nedra wanted to commune with the Lord, she'd go to a temple session. Two hours, a change into all white temple clothes, a ceremony in a building of many spires (boy, did Mormon architects love spires). Heather, on the other hand—what were her options for communion? PJs and a spot on her knees next to the dust bunnies under her bed? Before you were endowed you were JV at best.

Mormon men went through the temple for the first time just before their missions. Mormon women did the same, or they went before their weddings, whichever came first. But what if you were like Heather and you'd skipped your optional sister missionary experience and meanwhile no mate had ever materialized? In that scenario there was no clear answer. At some point you just decided you were spiritually ready.

It wasn't weird if you were a single woman who hadn't been through the temple by age 24 or 25, or maybe even 26. But somewhere in there, somewhere a little before where Heather now stood, the balance tipped. Part of the barb of Devin's question was a mutton-dressed-as-lamb side-eye. Didn't she know that she wasn't an ingenue anymore? But that was only a tiny ping. The real hurt was this: if she was honest, wasn't there maybe, possibly a reason she'd never decided she was ready to wear garments, ready for her endowment, ready to become a full-fledged committed, adult Mormon woman? It wasn't that she was patiently waiting for a man to assist her (cue feminist barfing). It was that she was maybe, possibly, keeping a tiny escape hatch open.

If she left someday, if she ever just grew too weary, it would be better if she hadn't been to the temple first. She'd be breaking a lesser promise, a baptism from when she was eight, not a just-yesterday solemn commitment. Not that she was thinking about leaving! Not that she ever wanted that to happen. But did part of her think it was a possibility? No! And maybe, hear the whisper, yes. A fearful future possibility, not unlike the scenarios she imagined for her body, her old self layering once again over this thin stranger, returning her to form. Leaving the church. Getting fat again. Would she let either happen? No! But could she conjure it? Yes. Was it not perhaps her deepest fear that she might actually be lucky enough to marry, have children, and then find she couldn't keep it all together? That just as Devin said, she'd wake up in ten years and realize she just couldn't anymore? That the constant effort to accommodate would be too close to wearing her down to nothing?

"I don't know. I just . . . I don't know what to tell you," she said to Devin, angry tears dripping off her cheeks.

"We don't need to fight about this," he said. "I'm in love with you. I want to be with you." He took her hand and kissed it. "Don't be mad at me. I just . . . This is just stuff I've been thinking about. I just needed to get it off my chest."

Smooth it over. Back to normal. The Mormon way forward.

"It's okay," Heather said, trying to make it so. "It's important to talk about. If I were afraid you were going to join a bike gang and ride off or turn Catholic or something, I'd want to talk about it too." She was trying to be funny. He went along with the attempt.

"Bikers are always revving up alongside me and trying to recruit me. Catholics too."

They drove to her house and parked outside. They kissed, no passion in it. Just the quick hello-goodbye of the well-established couple. It wasn't a kiss that sought reassurance, and in that alone Heather found some reassurance. She squeezed Devin's hand and got out alone. At her front door, she turned the key and went into the empty apartment.

An empty, awful what-do-I-want night of personal reckoning unfurled before her. Be true to yourself. People who said that were idiots. As if *you* were some pure thing and not a bundle of conflicting urges and emotions. She wanted to be mad at Devin, she *was* mad at Devin—what kind of person said *I want to marry you, I don't want to marry you* in the same sentence? But he'd said he wanted to marry her! Part of her wanted to call him back and make a real proposal herself that very evening. But she also had the impulse to call Ted and examine the entire conversation with him. Gah! How exactly unhelpful that would be! What would her Grandpa have said? Obviously, she knew. It was high time she went to the temple. But who wanted to go when it felt like coercion?

Sleep was a stupid joke mirage that night. She limped more and more hopelessly toward it until she finally collapsed at dawn.

The next day, Saturday, the garage door across the street opened well before noon. Heather heard the sound of the table saw through her open living room window. And without a frenzy of assessment she followed the sound. By the time she'd put on her shoes and crossed over, the saw had gone quiet. She knocked on the Glenners' front door. She didn't know who would answer the door, Ted or Linda. Both cars were in the driveway. She didn't really know who she wanted to answer, either. She heard Hoover bark somewhere in the house. One sharp warning.

Ted opened the door. "Heather! What a pleasant surprise," he said.

"Is Linda home?" Heather said.

She looked around for Hoover. It seemed he might dart out at any moment.

"She's at a ceramics course. A friend picked her up," he said.

"Ceramics? I didn't know she was into ceramics."

"It's an experiment," he said with a dismissive pursing of his lips. "I was just about to have lunch. Would you like to join me?"

"I've already eaten, but I'll sit with you." She hadn't eaten, but it was a reflex now. She always claimed she'd eaten when offered food.

She followed him to the kitchen and leaned against the counter as he finished building his roast beef sandwich.

"You sure I can't tempt you?" he said. He said the word "tempt" slyly, flirtatiously.

"I'm fine," she said.

"How about a Diet Coke?"

One of his hands rested on the counter next to her as the other opened the fridge. His left hand. His wedding ring, right there on his finger. He was looking away, eyes in the fridge when she lifted her own hand to touch his. Just two fingers, her pinky and ring finger lightly overlapping his. Less contact than the little touches they exchanged regularly now. Less contact than a handshake. And yet there it was. The clarity of action. Be true to yourself?

Ted didn't draw back in alarm. He kept his hand just where it was beneath her fingers. He slowly closed the fridge door. He looked into her eyes. It was a long, meaningful look, soft but searching and eager. Maybe Devin now had mixed feelings, but it seemed clear that Ted wanted her. How utterly shallow of her to crave this confirmation, and yet how undeniably she craved it.

No one ever said, "You touched hands! Adulterer!" But she knew the moment for what it was. Permission. Invitation. Action. A moment of choice, of bad choice. And she made it deliberately anyway. No accident. No stumbling without really knowing what she was doing. She had lifted her hand. She had touched her fingers to his. And now she left her fingers there and didn't break away from the touch or the gaze.

Ted gently reached his other hand around to the back of her neck, under her ponytail, and traced his finger tips along her hairline. Her spine ran with waves of warmth, up into her brain and down into her body.

He leaned in and kissed her on the lips. She opened her mouth to his.

This was what crossing the street and knocking on the door led to. This was what touching her fingers to his led to. This is what a touch on the back of the neck led to. This was inexcusable. This was cheating. And she chose cheating and proceeded.

With Devin, their physical interaction had always been marked with urgency. A rush to get as much as could be gotten before the Mormon cut-off line. But this was not urgent. This was languid. This was enveloping.

Slowly, slowly, one hand gripping her lower back, the other hand traced down to her collarbone, then lower and lower, to the edge of her v-neck. He kissed and kissed her while his fingers descended.

She felt a low throbbing within herself. She felt her nostrils flaring. She felt her heart beating faster. And she pushed her body closer to his until there was no space between them so that she could feel all of it all the more.

In movies, it was as if one kiss led straightaway to rumpled sheets. But it wasn't like that really. You didn't become a zombie, frenzied with flesh. Your mind and will did not desert you. You decided yes and yes and yes, no always still available, still there for you to reach for, to claim.

But oh, momentum.

Ted's hand reached into her shirt and traced along the lacy edge of her bra. He moved his lips from her lips, down her neck, his beard softly tickling every bit of her skin, the smell of sawdust and scalp and clean spring sweat all about him.

Maybe it was the thought that next would come the lifting of her shirt. Of her body exposed. Or maybe it was that here her body surged with desire, a new level of extremity to the low aching whirl, the yearning for more. Or maybe it was the fact that she knew this was the confession line. You didn't have to confess minor sins to anyone other than the Lord. You went about repentance all on your own. But sexual sin and Word of Wisdom infractions, those you had to take to the bishop. And breasts got you over the line. They were about to go over the line. Whatever it was, this was the moment when she reached for a new word.

"Stop," she said. But she heard how it sounded. Breathy. Half-hearted. Hopelessly aroused.

"We need to stop," Heather said again, more in possession of herself.

If Ted had laughed at her then, or even so much as smirked at her, at her prudishness, at the Mormon girl retreating from a little breast fondling, she was sure she would have turned and walked away and never spoken to him again. But he didn't laugh. He looked at her again with his wonderful, searching, tentative, desirous eyes.

"I should go," she said, but longingly, with reluctance.

And he leaned in and kissed her again, and her hormones surged again at the pleasure of his lips on hers.

Ted finally pulled away, and Heather arranged her clothing. She looked at his rosy face, his wet lips.

"We shouldn't have done that," she said. "I shouldn't have done that."

He didn't argue. He stepped back.

"I'm going," she said.

As she walked away into the hallway, toward the door, she half expected Hoover to lunge at her. Some sort of just rewards. Wherever the Doberman was, he didn't make a peep. She walked across the street, into her own apartment and locked the door behind herself.

After church on Sunday, she rode with Devin back to his place and they cooked lunch together. They didn't say a thing about the temple or excommunication. It was as if now that he'd said his piece he felt free and easy, all the relief that came with a good strong airing. They chopped onions and browned sausage and boiled pasta and mixed salad in companionable peace. They nuzzled. Devin's abrupt return to good cheer didn't shock her— her parents' arguments had always had a remarkable similarity, patched up with a thick, sweet frosting. But she was surprised by how easy she found it to share in the peace with him. No canker of guilt. No Edgar Allen Poe tell-tale heart threatening to explode from beneath the floorboards. She knew there would be a reckoning, and yet it felt far away, theoretical, as distant as Judgment Day. For now, she felt surprisingly affectionate, cheerful, calm. As if she too had clarified something rather than further confused it.

On Monday, she walked over to Ted's and got into the passenger seat as always. They drove to work with the radio on. Neither of them said anything about the kitchen episode. And yet there was a coursing current, pulling them together. The pretense that nothing had happened was not maddening but somehow terribly arousing.

Mid-morning Ted sent her an email. "Lunch? How about we go out for something?"

He came by her desk at the appointed hour, and she followed him to the parking lot. They'd been eating in the conference room for long enough that she doubted anyone thought anything of it. They were a half-mile from work before she bothered to ask where they were going. "I'm not sure," he said. But a few moments later he put on his turn signal and pulled into the parking lot of a Laundromat. He parked the car at the far edge of the lot, in the shade of some trees up against a fence.

He turned to her, but it was she who leaned in to kiss him. Her choice, her action.

"What are we doing?" she said after a few minutes.

"We're having lunch," he said with a smile, leaning back toward her for more.

They had lunch every day that week. It never went further than kissing. It was daylight after all. The car had windows. She knew it was not good decision making, and yet she made the decision again and again.

When Heather was fat, she used to binge. She would never let anyone see her do it, but there were times when she would go to the grocery store and buy a pan of frozen Rhodes orange rolls, drive straight home and bake them and frost them and then eat one after the next until the whole tin was gone. Deliberate, level-headed the whole time. No illusions about what she was buying the orange rolls for. No denial about how many she intended to eat. Fully aware of the way she'd feel afterward, distended, ashamed. But while she was preparing to eat them, while she was eating them, she felt satisfied, purposeful, willfully in charge. It was not a surrender. It was not a lapse. It was a choice.

She had always had clear lines. She binged, but she never purged. That put you over into the category of disorder. That was the sort of thing that meant therapy and interventions. But binging all on its own? Well, didn't half of America do that? Kissing Ted would be like that. Bad. Under any sort of examination obviously something she needed to stop doing. Obviously, clearly, something she should stop doing. But not as bad as it could be.

Chapter 17

Nedra kept her laptop closed for a few days after the funeral, but when she opened it she found that Holly Rasmussen had once again been busy. She'd posted something new every day. A picture of herself holding a machine gun, seemingly snapped not at a shooting range or gun show but in her backyard, a swing set in the background that made it all the more alarming. She posted quotes about liberty and tyranny with pictures of flags. And then this:

"Abortion = Murder. Where are the Walker babies?"

No photo, just the words. A few comments followed.

"I know the Walker family personally. They are good people and attacks like this are completely inappropriate. In addition, whatever you are implying has no basis in fact."

"??"

"Ugly personal attacks = desperation."

But the post also had seventeen thumbs up.

Nedra was almost too flummoxed to process it. She felt tingly, like she'd stood up too fast and couldn't see what was before her eyes. She immediately called Heather.

"What!?" Heather said on the other end of the line. "Are you kidding me? I don't even know what she's saying. Like, five kids isn't enough, you must have had a bunch of abortions? Or like, clearly because your kids don't have kids we must have all been having abortions?"

"I know. I don't know," Nedra said, "It's crazy and nuts and so weird, but it's making me feel totally sick."

Heather made reassuring sounds, offered a few sorrys and and it'll-be-okays. Finally, she said, "Before we freak out anymore we need to get on a call with Verna Smith or whoever and see if there's even a legit way that Holly Rasmussen can get on the ballot. I mean, I don't think you can just declare some new party and get a spot. Right?"

Nedra agreed and hung up and called Verna. The news was bad: Holly had to get some signatures, but then, unfortunately, yes, she could be on the ballot.

She texted Heather the news. Setting down her phone and turning back to the kitchen Nedra knocked a glass off the counter with her elbow, and although she was not one to curse she said, "Ah, frick!"

The glass broke into large pieces, easy enough to clean up, and yet she grumbled throughout the sweeping. "Jeez Frickin Louise. Just perfect."

The thing was, it wasn't just Holly Rasmussen. In the days since her father's funeral Nedra had begun substitute-cursing in her head. *Shoot* and *good gosh* and *darn it* and *frickin fracking frick,* all said internally with as much anger as if she were unleashing true strings of expletives. It was as if the further she got from her father's death, the more upset she was getting. But that made no sense to her. She should be feeling more ship-shape by the day. These words in her head were creating an inhospitable internal environment. She was putting distance between herself and The Spirit. You couldn't walk around with vitriol brewing and expect the Holy Ghost to stay cozy. She needed to put a stop to it, and yet day after day it only got worse, Nedra thinking and mumbling and half-shouting expletives.

But angry words weren't all. She'd had a rolling string of headaches. Low grade, then building, and they just didn't seem to be stopping. And Nedra had noticed a distinctive change in her body odor too. Even though she scrupulously applied deodorant, in the last few days a sweet sharp odor had begun to escape from beneath the powder-scent by two or three o'clock every afternoon. She had to launder her shirts after just one wearing—usually she could get two or even three wearings. After all, she wore garments under everything, so her shirts weren't even in direct contact with her skin. Grief was one thing, but this strange agitation? Now, as she emptied the broken glass from the dustpan into the garbage, she turned her head and sniffed at her armpits. Too early for the smell, and yet there it was.

She needed something soothing. The piano. She made her way to the bench and began fumbling, trying to remember a bit of Schubert before finally locking into her muscle memory of the notes.

Proficiency feels good. This was a lesson Nedra tried to pass on to her children and her students. Knowing you are good at something, receiving regular objective evidence of it—hymns played without error, accompaniment carried out with precision and artistry that both followed and buoyed the other musicians—these were assurances that could give you a sense of sturdiness in the world. Minor failures in other aspects of life were always discounted by your area of certain competence. It was a balm worth pursuing. And yet in that moment the piano was not setting her right. She finished the phrase and tried another piece. A hymn. "How Great Thou Art." She improvised a supplement to the simple chords. But no. She stopped after two lines, the agitation right there, not budging.

How could Holly Rasmussen dream up something that awful, deliberately spell out those words, and then choose to click "post"? It was one thing to spark inappropriately in the moment, the stress of public speaking or in-person interaction fraying your personal wires. But sitting at home alone and typing that onto a cold computer screen?

She had to stop thinking about it! Work. Real work. That's what would help. She should get back to teaching piano, but after the funeral she'd foolishly given herself two weeks off. So what was it going to be?

Her parents' house. It wouldn't be the first time she'd been back since her father's passing. She'd gone to the house to retrieve her father's temple clothes for his burial—white pants, white shoes, white shirt and tie, ceremonial green apron, the clothes he'd changed into at the temple every week when he'd gone to his regular Tuesday night temple session, the clothes that every faithful, endowed Mormon was buried in. She'd found his temple bag just where it always was in the corner of his closet, all packed and ready to go. She'd also swept the kitchen floor and taken out the trash, a maudlin moment where she'd thought *his last crumbs*! as if this were a tragedy. She'd gone through the house with her brother Ralph as well. They'd sell it and split the proceeds, they said. No urgency, but no need to wait either. Ralph took a few things, some small framed photos, a silver platter he'd always liked, but that was it. Furniture, clothes, dishes, sheets—he said he didn't want any of it. Nedra could clear it out any way that pleased her, he said. How terribly gracious of him to allow her this latitude in *taking care of everything*. But truly, what did she expect? He lived in Texas. She lived five minutes away. And clearing the house was just the kind of absorbing task she needed.

On the way there a car cut into her lane. "Signal, you idiot!" she snapped aloud.

When she unlocked the door the smell of the house came to her exactly like always. Home. This had been her home. She felt limp with grief. She plopped on the couch. Her eyes fell on a bookshelf she hadn't dusted since her father's passing, and there on the ledge she saw one of his strange scraps. After a long moment, she lifted herself up and walked over to find his shaky handwriting just as she'd expected. But the words were unexpected, startling and puzzling.

"Nedra—lamb."

He'd dreamed she was a lamb? He wanted her to bring him lamb for dinner? It was almost funny except she wasn't in the mood for laughter. She was a lost lamb? A lamb going to the slaughter? The lamb of God? She didn't know what to do with the paper. Throw it away? Save it? She thought of her father's relationship with Heather, the way she'd felt so supported by him, whereas he seemed to think Nedra's foray into politics was a folly at best. And maybe it was Holly Rasmussen, maybe it was simply the jangled emotions that had been rattling her for days, but suddenly every bit of melancholic nostalgia blew out of her, replaced by anger. She was not a lamb!

After her mother's passing, Nedra had cleaned out her mother's closet. Her mother had always been a lover of starch, and in the closet each time Nedra had flipped a hanger it had released a breath of starch from the perfectly ironed blouse or skirt, Nedra alone with the clothing but her mother alive in the air. It had done her in. Not what she needed today, so no, there would be no tender textiles.

Instead, she headed to the basement, the repository of all paper. File cabinets and shelves and boxes, boxes, boxes. Her parents had saved every receipt a store clerk had ever handed them and every manual for every appliance they'd ever owned, every holiday card they'd ever received. She would trash it all.

She texted Heather again. "I'm in the basement at Grandpa's, going through papers. Come keep me company? We can pick up salads for dinner?"

Normally she would have regretted mentioning salads as soon as she hit send. Heather could decide what she wanted to eat without maternal coaching. Was it insulting to offer salad? Would it have been better to say pizza and let Heather reject that all on her own? But today she didn't care.

Heather texted back immediately, seemingly un-offended. "Sure. Be there right after work."

By the time Heather arrived, Nedra was deep in paper piles, busy and lost, just as she had hoped to be. Heather looked rosy, her hair curled, her makeup fresh, her attire for the day of the snug variety. The dimness that had come over her since her grandfather's death seemed to be passing, the flush in her cheeks surely a good sign.

"Pick a shelf and knock yourself out," Nedra said.

The basement was an unfinished one, a cement floor dotted with unevenly sized carpet remnants, the two-by-fours framing the walls stuffed with puffy pink insulation. Heather pulled out a box and settled herself on a carpet square.

"So are we going to talk about Holly Rasmussen?" Heather said, not two minutes later.

"I don't know what else there is to say," Nedra replied.

"That she's awful."

"Well, I would not say I find her campaign behavior very upstanding, I'll say that."

"Are you going to post anything on your Facebook page in reply?" Heather asked. "I mean, I'm not suggesting you engage her in any direct way. But I'm just wondering if maybe you should do some postings that clarify your policy positions."

"I think everyone knows my policy would not be to encourage rampant abortion," Nedra answered tartly.

"Sure, no one is rah rah hooray abortion is fun. But seriously, have you looked at the bills that have been getting proposed in the Utah state legislature over the past few years? Like, say Audrey is pregnant and there's something wrong and she's going to die if she doesn't get an abortion. Do you think she should just go ahead and die?"

Why was Heather ambushing her in this way? Nedra frowned and shot her daughter a curt reply. "Do you know what? I have read the bills. Every last one of them. And nothing like that came up before the legislature last year."

"It could!" Heather said.

"You're as bad as Holly Rasmussen!" Nedra snapped. "Turning everything into this big apocalypse when do you know what the legislature actually spends all its time on? Incredibly boring appropriations. The school bus fund versus the state park fund. That's what I'm getting into. Not this nonsense," Nedra said. She knew she shouldn't engage and yet Heather had tripped her into an argument. "And what is the 100% you're-going-to-die pregnancy anyway? It seems to me there is always a lot more gray than that."

"There are plenty of things," Heather said, not backing down. "Cancer you have to treat. Things like that."

"Audrey doesn't have cancer!" Nedra said.

"That's not the point. Audrey is not the point. It's a generality."

"I know that," Nedra said, clenching her teeth. It was as if Heather wasn't even listening to her.

"Or say Audrey gets raped."

"I don't understand why you always have to push everything!" Nedra's voice broke. "Why are you picking a fight with me? I am the reasonable one here!"

Now that Nedra's emotion had broken through, Heather pulled back too, her face suddenly wounded, as if this spat were Nedra's doing, not her own.

"Listen, sweetheart," Nedra said, trying to soften things. "I don't think I should post any sort of Facebook response, okay? And as far as bills go, it's all in the details, isn't it? And I have to get elected first, and this," she said, waving her hand back and forth between them, "isn't helping."

Heather turned back to the papers, her face stony. Nedra knew she'd hurt her daughter's feelings. Heather, so ready to throw punches and so far from ready to take them. Still, Nedra was the mother, maturity her obvious responsibility. She shouldn't have snapped. It was like her swearing, all this anger suddenly so at the ready. She wanted to bring them back to a place of peace. She sighed and decided to share a story.

"Have I ever told you about my miscarriage?" Nedra said, everything about her manner changed, turned suddenly gentle. "I don't think I have. Did you know I had one? Between you and Audrey."

Heather looked at her with surprise. "No, I didn't know. I'm sorry."

Nedra was well aware that she'd never shared the story. It had been a private matter, something she'd shared only with Doug and her own mother.

"It was really scary, the physical experience of it," Nedra said, "and then just awful when the doctor said there was nothing they could do. Anyway, about a week after it was all over I went to the temple by myself, and after the session I was just sitting there quietly in the Celestial Room, and I had a vision. I know that sounds like a grandiose word, but it's exactly what it was."

Heather didn't look at her skeptically. Her eyes were wide, receptive. Nedra took a breath and went on.

"I saw a boy. He was seven or eight, older than Brian and Audrey were at the time. And he had sandy hair and freckles, which was different from Brian and Audrey too. And I could literally feel him sitting next to me on the sofa, swinging his feet. He reached out and put his hand in mine, and I swear I could feel that too, that little hand, and every part of me just felt full of light and warmth and reassurance." Nedra's eyes turned teary, an echo of the experience called up again in her body even now.

Often the Holy Ghost spoke to you with words, but what had come to Nedra in the temple all those years ago had come to her with wordless certainty. The boy was her son, and she would have the chance to raise him, to love him, and to be with him in the eternities. He already loved her. She already loved him. Slowly, very slowly, that day in the temple, the Celestial Room had returned to itself and she had returned to herself. She'd wiped her tears, and then she'd made her way to the women's dressing room and changed out of her all white temple clothes and back into her regular dress and driven home to her husband and children, but it had been one of the most spiritual experiences of her life.

"So I guess what I'm saying is that none of this is a debate topic for me," Nedra said, trying to keep her tone mild. "It's very close to my heart."

Heather gave her a look of crumpled sympathy and started to say something, then stopped herself. She gazed off for a moment. Nedra thought an apology might be forthcoming, but instead Heather said, "Mom, do you think it's strange that I haven't been through the temple yet?"

This was not where she had expected this conversation to go. Nedra had waited until just before her own wedding to take out her endowments, and pushing Heather earlier had felt insulting, particularly back when she was fat. As if to say she wouldn't get married. As if to say *no use waiting*. Over the years she'd thought Heather might come to it on her own, just as she now thought Caroline might, but it didn't seem the sort of thing where anyone, mother or otherwise, should be applying pressure.

"Are you thinking about it?" Nedra asked.

"I guess it's something that came up in conversation with Devin."

Well, wasn't that vague and yet full of implications. If the temple had come up it must mean they were talking about marriage. Nedra was pleased but also felt a tiny grain of worry. Not that she thought Devin was a poor choice, just that she had yet to be convinced.

"It might surprise you to hear me say this," Nedra said, "but I think it can be nice to go through the temple on your own. Sometimes right before a wedding it can be overwhelming."

The temple was the site of Nedra's greatest solace, a place of peace, a ritual that regularly replenished her spirit, but that didn't mean she was unaware of its quirks, an experience full of strange clothing and strange language, a lot to wrap your head around when you were new to it. Not that she thought Heather would have any trouble with it long term. She was a smart girl, and she could certainly make sense of the symbolism, but maybe the morning of her wedding wasn't the time to be confronted with all that for the first time.

"I mean, we're not getting married," Heather said. "Not that we're not serious or whatever. I'm just saying no one has proposed."

"Uh huh," Nedra replied with a little playful suspicion. "Listen, I have nothing to say about any of that. Sort it out in your own good time. But I will just say that if you're thinking about going to the temple, I think that's a great idea."

They worked together for hours after that, shuffling through papers, pulling out and sharing delightful snippets—old photos, ledgers of household expenses from the '60s, a collection of Jell-o salad recipes on index cards. The house faced west, toward the Great Salt Lake, and the whole sky glowed a vivid salmon as the sun dropped over the water. The rosy sunset reached the basement's half-windows for a few radiant minutes until at last the sky went gray, and the overhead light bulbs cast dreary shadows everywhere.

"Let's get out of here," Nedra said at last.

At the stairs she hugged Heather, her daughter softening into her and then softening more and then more again, the way she had as a little girl, falling asleep in Nedra's arms, a moment that comforted Nedra even more than she imagined it did Heather.

But the comfort didn't last long. Back at home Nedra decided to open her laptop for a quick check. A mistake. Holly Rasmussen had posted again. This time the post included a picture. Nedra's son Brian as a teenager, his sweet young face smiling, his lanky arms in his basketball jersey, one of them thrown over the shoulder of another basketball player, the two boys leaning into each other exultantly, and this comment:

"What does Nedra Walker Stand For? This is her son. He's 38 now and "single" Welcome to 'alternative lifestyles!'"

What a horrible invasion. Holly Rasmussen must have tracked down an old yearbook to get that photo. That took effort, real effort put into being this deranged and nasty. And what kind of terrible exclamation point was that? As if the post were some amusing lark. Seeing Brian's dear, dear teenage face in this sudden awful context gripped Nedra's heart, horrified her with its wrongness. It was as shocking as blasphemy. Anger billowed through her, a fan turned on a windsock, all of her at once rigid with outrage. But as the seconds ticked by she felt something else too. The abortion post had set her off, but this one was different. The words were like a note that shook chandeliers, a reverberation that just wouldn't leave her alone. The photo of those two lovely boys. Her son. Single, 38. Alternative lifestyles. Was there not something there that Nedra had quietly wondered about herself?

Chapter 18

Heather didn't tell Devin about her abortion tiff with her mother. It would hardly have reflected well on her in the retelling. Why had she been foolish enough to think she'd hit upon a "teachable moment"? As if the right words at the right time, a magic political incantation, would bring her mother around to being a centrist Democrat. She didn't tell Devin about her mother's story about the miscarriage or their conversation about the temple either. Both felt private. Telling Devin she was thinking of going to the temple would have the sting of acquiescence, as if she were admitting that he had been right rather than that she was reaching her own conclusions. And how was it that she was considering going to the temple even as she was carrying on whatever it was she was carrying on with Ted? It was the grossest hypocrisy, the most obvious cognitive dissonance, and yet both tracks carried on in parallel, seeming somehow to have nothing to do with each other. And if she wasn't going to talk about the temple track she certainly wasn't going to talk about the other track either! She'd been worried at first that she'd be overcome with a compulsion to tell Devin about Ted. Wasn't that the human impulse, to blurt secrets? But there was nothing but harm to be had in that impulse, and if it arose in Heather it was so deeply buried that she barely registered it at all.

So what exactly was there for her and Devin to discuss at the moment? Holly Rasmussen, that was one answer.

"Wow, that photo of her with the machine gun?" he said. "She's staring at the camera with like, death eyes. And why does she have a gun next to a playground slide?"

"Right?" Heather said. "Like her kids are one inch out of the photo, or maybe taking the picture. Super psycho!"

This was in the kitchen of Devin's apartment. Gun-Defender Kevin gone to Jacksonville, Florida for a conference, the mood between them light, giggly, affectionate. Heather had kissed Ted that day at lunch, his hand moving up and up her thigh as she pressed her lips into his. But she had been wearing pants, not a skirt, and so she had felt safe in her arousal, safe in Ted's inability to push them too far. Perhaps this should have made her withdraw from Devin in the evening, a surly, guilty, tentative remove. But no. Instead she felt flirtatious. Sexy even—did she dare think such a word? As if Ted were not a betrayal but a warm up.

"And who the heck are the people giving that abortion post a thumbs up?" Devin said with a scornful laugh.

"I know!" Heather said, shaking her head. "It's insane."

"And the latest one about Brian being gay?" Devin said.

The truth was she'd been deeply unsettled by that post, strange what-ifs that felt both implausible and also impossible to totally dismiss, but she was hardly going to say that to Devin right now.

Instead, she replied snappily, "Right? I'm like, lady, his 'lifestyle' is being a 38-year-old man trying to date 20-year-olds, which is lame but I am sad to say not that alternative."

Devin gave her a look, and she said, "Oh, haha! I forgot who I was talking to. Sorry!"

He narrowed his eyes further, a flirtatious squint. He took her hand. "You know, I've been thinking a lot about the other night," he said.

She arched her eyebrows at him, surprised by this turn of conversation.

"You know, molten cheese of horrors night?" he said with a half-laugh.

"Yes," she said, flickering a wary, half-smile. "I seem to recall it."

"I want to apologize," he said, not a trace of a smirk about him. His voice was low, a slight gravel of emotion to it. "I think I went too far, and it wasn't even really about what I said it was about."

She flushed, tears rising, but not happy tears, not some flood of relief. Instead it was a sting of anger called up again, barely faded. But the anger was all muddied by Devin's present tenderness. She wanted to be mad, she was mad, and yet she couldn't help mirroring him, a tenderness in her rising to meet him, the way people smile back at smilers. She didn't say anything. She hoped her cheeks wouldn't start shaking. She waited.

Devin held her eyes. "I think it's just that I've never really dated someone with a critical streak, but I actually mean that in a good way." He shifted his shoulders, tossed his hair. "I mean, I guess I feel like you call my B.S., and that's kind of scary but also really good. And I think if I'm honest, I'm critical of a lot of the same stuff you're critical of, in the church and the world, and I guess part of me has been worried that, like, we'd amplify each other in bad ways, rather than good ways. But I don't think it has to be that way. I think we can make each other better. I mean, at least you can make me better."

He gave her a look of supplication, of entreaty. It was all vague and yet she imagined she knew what he meant. It seemed he had decided to believe he could trust her, maybe not to guarantee a perfect future, but to try, to share a hope for who they could be together, to make choices together.

She squeezed his hand. "So, I . . .," she shook her head, a sort of confused tossing. "I mean, what happened between last week and today?"

It was not a question for herself. It was a question for him. But she heard it outside herself and crumpled inside, imagining it turned on her. She saw herself in the kitchen with Ted. She watched it play out like a movie.

Devin laughed. "I talked to my dad. I mean, my mom is a pretty sharp cookie, so he has some experience."

She took her hand from his and wiped her wet eyes. "Whew," she said. "I, uh, wasn't expecting this." She half-laughed, meaning both her tears and the apology. She remembered exactly how Ted's hand had felt on her thigh that afternoon.

"I just really love you, Heather," Devin said. "I want this to work."

She covered her face with her hands. After a moment she lowered her face to his shoulder and burrowed into his neck. His clean-cut face, which of course made her think of Ted's bearded one.

She and Devin spent all day Saturday together, breakfast at a diner, a drive up to Park City for an early summer hike, the air in the mountains still with a bite of cool. Affection coursed through the hours, soothing her, putting the week of error behind her, or so it seemed.

Over dinner that night she said, "There's something I need to tell you." And for a second she felt a confession about Ted rising to her lips. But that was not what she said. "I used to be really heavy," she said. "I don't know if anyone told you. But I mean, heavy, and until pretty recently, actually. I don't know, it just seems like something you should know about me." She knew he probably wouldn't understand how much this confession meant to her, that for her it was as much about her soul as her body.

He reached across the table and took her hand. "So I may have been a little obsessive when we first started dating?" he laughed. "You're like a blank on Facebook, but I spent a fair bit of time and found a bunch of untagged pictures of you in other people's histories."

She felt the color drain from her face.

"No, no!" he squeezed her hand. "I think it's amazing. I mean, I was a little chubby in high school and I worked so hard to lose that weight, so I know what it's like. I mean, not all of what it's like, but I'm just saying, it's one of the things I admire about you."

Her throat thickened with a painful lump. She ducked her head and waited a moment for it to dissolve, then shrugged and batted her hand through the air. "Okay, enough of that," she said. "Let's, like, talk about novels or something."

After dinner, as he walked her to her door she did her best not to glance over at Ted and Linda's house.

"Do you want to come in?" she said.

"Indeed I do," he said with a sort of jokey seduction. "But it's late, and so I think I must demur for this evening." He paused and lifted his arm to the door jamb, arcing over her like James Dean leaning into a locker. "But what I'm hoping," he continued, "is that you'll agree to go out with me again on another date tomorrow night."

"Sunday night?" Heather said. "And how very formal you're being!" she added coyly. Most Mormons didn't spend money on Sundays if they could help it, a Sabbath observance that precluded restaurants and movies, which didn't mean you couldn't, say, picnic, but which did throw off your typical 'date night' agenda.

"Yes, very formal."

She said sure and he tilted her chin toward her face and kissed her softly. She felt a flip of nerves.

At church on Sunday morning Heather didn't sit by Devin. They exchanged flirtatious looks across the chapel. They maneuvered around each other in the halls between Sacrament Meeting and Sunday School like a pair of dancers briefly separated but still part of the same number, silent lopsided smiles. Devin found her after Relief Society and silently slipped a piece of paper into her hand, the feel of his fingers against her palm an intimate affection. "See you at seven," the folded scrap said.

Devin arrived at her house that evening at 7 p.m. on the dot, still wearing his Sunday suit and tie.

She'd stayed in her dress as well, the same one she'd worn to the opera with Ted. "Where are we going?" she said once they were in the car.

"You'll see," Devin said.

They made their way to the freeway and when they took the onramp to I-15 North she said, "Are we going on a date to my parents' house?"

"Not quite," he smirked.

They exited the freeway in Bountiful.

They drove up past Heather's parents' house.

"Phew! Saved!" Heather said.

They drove up and up. For a moment Heather thought perhaps they were driving to her grandfather's grave, but then they passed the cemetery and their destination became clear, and she felt a dread elation, the most confused anticipation of her life. The Bountiful Temple.

Temples were closed on Sundays—regular Sunday services all took place in ordinary churches, not temples, and so the parking lot was empty. Devin swooped the car into a spot right near the front portico. He walked around and took her hand as she climbed out of the car. She gave him a wide-eyed look of inquiry and he ducked his head and said nothing. He walked her across the grounds to the front of the temple. He led them to the stone steps, the whole valley down below them, the spire of the temple rising up and up above them.

"Sit," he said.

She knew exactly what was happening. This was a cleaving of before and after. This was as momentous as anything in her life would ever be. The vanishing point at last arrived at, passed over, life in its fullness on the other side. But this was too soon! Not that she had formed a clear plan, but she'd imagined that somehow she would sort out whatever it was she needed to sort out with Ted while she and Devin sorted out whatever they needed to sort out, and just a little bit of time would make it all clear. She hadn't dreamed that Devin would act so suddenly, that he'd swing from extremes and consider everything once and for all resolved.

It felt as if the seconds were sandbags, everything weighted and slow, the heat of the sun-warmed steps trying to seep into the back of her legs, like diffusion, to make her the same temperature as the stone. She could hear her own pulse clanging in her ears.

Devin took a small blue velvet box from his pocket.

Did she want him to propose? Did she love him? Yes, she thought yes. It was just that she'd been unprepared. He really loved her? She hadn't been sure. But it seemed yes. Yes, he did. She could be done with Ted. She could be done with everything that didn't make this work.

"Heather," he said, a gravelly scrape in his vocal chords.

His stooped shoulders were more stooped than ever, his whole body like a question mark, curving toward her. He, the supplicant. She, the wielder of power, of choice.

Everything seemed hyper-real, as if she could count his freckles, as if she could feel the circle of individual skin cells on her finger about to be covered by the ring. There were specks of yellow in the blue of his eyes right next to his pupils that she'd never noticed before.

He opened the box. He took her hand. He asked her to marry him.

And then all at once everything turned blurry, a tearful obscuring of the world. Disappointed? Liberated? Overjoyed? She couldn't tell, a red flush of feeling in her whole body, a ringing in her ears, a pixelation and fading, almost as if she were about to faint. Was she about to faint?

She pushed her face into his shoulder. She looked up and nodded. He put the ring on her finger. His grandmother's ring, he said.

They drove back down to her parents' house where her mom and dad and Caroline and Devin's parents were waiting for them, all apparently informed, secret keepers one and all. Caroline handed Heather a lipstick tube and some powder and held up a tiny compact mirror while Heather dabbed as instructed at her shiny forehead and her invisible lips, and then Caroline sliced a cake, handed Heather and Devin pieces and took one million photos of them. Devin and Doug shaking hands. Nedra hugging Heather. Heather kissing Devin. Devin's parents with their arms around their soon-to-be daughter-in-law, his mother a bosomy embrace of floral perfume, his father's knobby elbows knocking here and there like awkward chicken wings. They lit sparklers. Caroline put a flower crown on Heather's head. Caroline handed Doug the camera and posed for "sister shots," all smiles and duck faces. And throughout it all Heather floated, a puppet master who could flick a wrist and make the attached body hold hands and smile and squeal but who was ultimately removed, elsewhere, apart, above.

Her sleep that night was troubled, her brain rehearsing and rehearsing for her morning drive to work. She'd tell Ted right away, as soon as she sat down in the passenger seat. She'd say that obviously this meant they needed to step back. That was the phrase she would use. Step back. Not overblown, like saying *we have to end our affair* (could you really call kissing an affair?) and not embarrassing like saying *we have to stop kissing* (because how juvenile did that sound?) A reasonable phrase. Clear enough. He'd say he understood. He'd congratulate her. Everything would revert, the two of them back to being friendly neighbors and no more.

But as she crossed the street that morning, silver morning sun shining through the leafy trees, her shadow long and loping before her, she saw that Ted wasn't waiting in the car as usual.

He was standing outside it, leaning against it, waiting for her to appear. He locked eyes with her and gave her a long look, a look so long it became first alarming and then arousing and then alarming again. Just as her foot touched down on the Glenners' driveway, Linda bopped out of the front door.

"Heather! What delightful news!" she said, skipping across the lawn. When Linda reached her, she threw her spindly arms in the air, spangling her hands, and then brought them down around Heather in a quick, grabby hug.

"Oh, how did you know?" Heather said, flustered, blushing.

"Your sister's Instagram!" Linda trilled. "We're so happy for you! You two look adorable together!"

She hadn't realized Ted and Linda followed Caroline quite so closely.

She glanced quickly to Ted, but before she could get a read on him Linda grabbed for her hand.

"I want every detail of the engagement!" she said. "Let me see that ring!"

The ring was a pearl set on a simple gold band.

"Oh wow. I've never seen a ring quite like that," Linda said. "How unique!"

Unique was not perhaps the word every woman wanted to hear to describe her engagement ring. Heather knew girls who had been scoping out diamonds for years and who could tell you the exact type of cut and setting they hoped for, but she'd never allowed herself to dream up a ring, the whole subject of marriage so fraught with impossible longing that conjuring jewelry would have been a perverse and embarrassing self-torture. But now that she had a ring, this ring, she felt it suited her. His grandmother's. Unflashy. Not untoward. And the curves of the pearl reminded her of her former self, her rounded flesh, and maybe Devin didn't know that version of her, but he knew that she'd existed, he'd known all along, and somehow his choice of this ring led her to believe he might have loved her that way too, a reassurance whispered from the pearlescent glow.

"Can we have you over for a celebratory toast this evening?" Linda said.

"Oh, that's so sweet of you," Heather stammered.

Linda reached out and grabbed both of her hands. "Please, please? We won't keep you long! I promise! But this is just so exciting! I didn't even know you were dating anyone!"

Heather flashed her eyes to Ted, who was maintaining a pose of extreme serenity.

"I, uh, I don't know if I can tonight," Heather said.

"How about just ten minutes after work? We'll make it so quick," Linda said.

Ted gave a bit of a shrug and the slightest twitch of a smile, and Heather finally gave in, despite her overwhelming reluctance. "Okay, sure. A quick toast. Thank you."

"Good good!" Linda said, swarming Heather with more fluttery pats. "Okay, well, you two better be on your way before you're late. I can't wait for tonight!"

Heather's heart pounded as she made her way to the passenger seat. Linda waved and blew a kiss at the car as she and Ted silently pulled out into the street.

Where to start now? This was clearly not going as she had planned. "I'm sorry. I meant to tell you . . . um, not like this," she gave a sort of sad half laugh.

She braced for what he might say. She could imagine a half dozen unpleasant things. But Ted maintained an attitude of unruffled warmth. "It's great news," he said, nodding. Nodding for himself? For her? They drove for another block before Ted added, "He's a lucky fellow." He looked at her with a tender eye crinkle, a kind look, a look that conveyed that he wanted what was best for her. And also, attraction? Was it still there? She thought it was.

She waited for him to ask her questions. Or for her own need to jabber to take over. But instead they simply drove. She'd imagined this car ride full of spiky feelings. But he was going so easy on her. No blame, no accusations of dishonesty. She felt a huge swell of affection, of . . . love . . . no ban the word! But tenderness, warmth. If Ted had been cruel or crass her sentiments toward him would have shifted to exactly where they needed to be. But this gentlemanliness? This reserve? She wanted to kiss him. Yes, there it was. Desire, *her* desire, undiminished by her changed circumstances.

After another few moments of quiet Ted spoke. "Has Linda told you about Hoover?"

"No, she hasn't told me anything," Heather said. "What's going on?"

"She found a lump the other day, and it seems he has a fast spreading cancer. There's not much they can do. We're trying to keep him comfortable."

"Oh, I'm so sorry," Heather said.

"I'm okay," Ted said, "but Linda is taking it very hard."

There could have been something troubling in his suddenly casting himself in the role of sympathetic husband, concerned for his dear wife's pet-related grief, something manipulative even. *I'll see your engagement and raise you a full-fledged spouse!*

But Heather experienced this thought only glancingly. Her Relief Society impulses carried the day.

"Oh, that's so sad," she said. "Is there anything I can do to help?"

"It's nice that you're coming over tonight," Ted said. "She likes you a lot."

Heather winced a little. Linda liked her, which made the fact that Heather had been kissing Ted mere days ago that much worse.

Finally they arrived at work, and Ted went his way, she went hers.

All morning Heather's phone buzzed away on her desk. Heather's visiting teacher Kyra texted. "**Kevin told me the news. I'm so excited for you!**"

Caroline texted. "**Your engagement photos are blowing up the internet.**"

Devin texted. "**Thinking of you, hot stuff.**"

Heather sent him back an emoji with staring eyes and blushing cheeks.

Ted did not ask her for lunch. She spent the day attempting to immerse herself in census micro data but kept losing track of spreadsheet cells.

Ted came by her cubicle at 5:30.

"Shall we?" he said.

On the drive home it took all her restraint not to reach across the gear shift and touch his hand.

As they slowed to a stop in the Glenners' driveway Linda once again danced out of the front door. "Come in, come in, we must celebrate!" she sang, no indication of dreary dog sadness lurking about her.

When Heather came around the car Ted put his arm around her shoulder, a half hug he held firmly as he walked her up the front steps. The warmth of his body emanated into her, every bit that touched him alive with nerves. So this was to be it now? Public affection that looked but didn't feel platonic?

Linda had a little table set up on the porch, complete with an arrangement of pink garden roses, clear care taken in the presentation.

"We have some sparkling cider for you and some champagne for us!" she said.

"Though of course we're happy to pour you a little sip of champagne if you want," Ted said with an arch of one eyebrow.

Heather smiled but felt a slight twinge, the offer of champagne a sort of insinuation of disloyalty that didn't sit well. But of all the things to get worked up about—she was a newly engaged woman who'd been kissing this man behind her boyfriend's back two days ago. So did it really make sense to rear back in offense at an alcohol joke? Agh, she was so nervy!

Linda poured, and then she and Ted raised their glasses, and Heather watched and mimicked.

"This is my first toast," she said.

"Really? Ever? Or for your engagement?" Linda said.

"Kind of ever, I guess? Mormons don't toast?"

"Not even with water?" Linda gasped.

"You can't toast with water—bad luck," Ted said.

Linda jerked herself around in a strange comic shimmy. "So we better do this right! To your engagement! May it be a long and happy union," Linda said.

"To Heather, our bright, young, beautiful friend," Ted pronounced the words in a low and mapled tone, and did she hear an extra emphasis on beautiful? She thought she did.

"Hear, hear!" Linda said.

They all clinked glasses, and despite the clear strangeness of their trio and the moral panic at the edge of Heather's thoughts, the fizzy cider seemed remarkably elegant to her, part of a scene from some life not her own.

"So how did he ask?" Linda said after a few gulps. "And it was a short courtship, right? How romantic!"

Did Linda seem different already? Tipsy? How long did that take? Maybe it was just because Heather had spent so little time around alcohol in her life, but she couldn't help but scrutinize the Glenners every expression and movement even more than before. Had Caroline posted something about the number of months she and Devin had been dating? She shriveled, imagining Ted counting back to all the time she hadn't mentioned a boyfriend. Not that it mattered! He was married! But maybe it mattered.

Heather knew her engagement was quick in the grand scheme of things. She and Devin had been dating months, not years. And it felt very quick to her, of course. The sudden turnabout. But the timing wasn't all that unusual in the Mormon world. Weeks would get you an eyebrow raise. But months? Especially by the time you were Heather and Devin's age? You just got an "about time" pat on the back. Though Heather didn't really feel like explaining all that. She also felt strange telling Linda and Ted about sitting on the steps of the temple. They wouldn't get it. It might seem odd, cultish, a weird mix of religion and romance, not the exactly appropriate, weighty yet unfussy gesture it had been. And having any conversation about Devin at all while Ted emanated heat next to her felt deeply uncomfortable. So instead Heather kept it simple. She said they'd driven up on the hillside in Bountiful so they could look down on the valley and he'd asked her there.

The whole "toasting" lasted only a few minutes. Linda clucked about how lovely Caroline's photos of the occasion were. She asked questions Heather couldn't yet answer about dates and venues. But then she suddenly faded.

"I'm sure you have so much to do!" Linda said, conjuring a last bit of energy. "We really shouldn't keep you!"

Heather said yes, of course, it's true, and set her barely-sipped glass back down next to the flowers, feeling relieved to be escaping but at the same time wondering if she shouldn't stop and say something about the dog. Was it too late? It seemed odd to bring it up without some more natural opening.

Ted walked her back down the porch steps. He squeezed her again, but this time a full hug, his chest against hers. As Linda stood and watched Ted leaned down and kissed Heather's cheek, his beard and lips soft on her skin. The moment pierced her, a shard. She could feel it—she didn't want Ted to stop wanting her. A character flaw in every fairy tale: vanity. Did she really need a hall of male mirrors to answer her feeble questions? *Am I still attractive? How about now?* Pathetic that imagining Ted turning away from her, rejecting her, actually pained her, a physical squeezing of her heart.

She waited till he stepped back and then hurried across the street, trying to make it seem as if she weren't running.

Unfortunately, after leaving the Glenners', Heather's evening was far from done. It was Monday night, the night

Mormons set aside for "Family Home Evening." When they were growing up, Nedra had assigned every child a different Family Home Evening job, each of their names written on a laminated farm animal that moved around a laminated barn to labeled locations: prayer, song, lesson, game, snack. Heather's name had been painted on a yellow duck. (Thankfully, Aaron was assigned the pig and Brian the cow). In a singles ward, since you had no little pigs and ducks of your own to tend to, you were assigned a Family Home Evening group of other singles. Just as in a family, there were coordinators who asked various people to bring treats or plan a lesson or game. It could all feel warm and caring or else cloying, depending on your mindset on any given week. On this week? Well, Heather would have skipped it if she hadn't been given an assignment, but she had been: treats. Which might have been an obligation you could shirk in some circles, but most definitely not in this one.

Devin was not in Heather's FHE group, but Kyra was, and when Heather arrived she was greeted by squeals and requests to see the ring. Clearly, for those who might not have seen the internet, Kyra had spread the word. The attention hit Heather like an allergic reaction, all of her almost instantly prickly and over-heated. She did her best to find a seat before her throat closed up.

Getting engaged in a singles ward turned you into an instant lame duck. You were on your way out, suddenly in a whole new category, envied perhaps but also dismissed. You briefly experienced something like notoriety. People who'd never really spoken to you knew your news without you having told them. You noticed eyes on you, taking you in, the person of interest. *Why her* (*and not me?*) the ever-hovering question. You could still show up for activities. In fact, you were very much still obliged to do so, but now you had the shadow of the chaperone about you. A married Mormon, or soon to be; adult life—partnership, children, sex, real leadership positions in the church, full temple participation—now open to you. How could the single and searching feel anything other than stymied by your presence? But how to explain Heather's own extreme reaction to the momentary thrum of interest in her? She practically had hives.

Still, she sat through the prayer, the song, and the lesson without much of note beyond her own fidgety discomfort. But then came time for the game—a series of relay races, the game planners explained, that would start with ferrying marshmallows balanced on plastic knives across the room and end with oranges passed from neck to neck. Heather felt eyes upon her again. She could imagine just how it would go. She was seated next to and would have to pass the orange to a handsome young accountant. They would take extreme care to avoid any bodily frisson, and yet her jaw would still probably catch on his stubble as they crooked their necks together. The innocent physical contact was half the point of games like this, in fact. But now she just could not stand another second of it, of this whole Mormon singles scene. The shenanigans. The perdition. She would go anaphylactic if she spent another moment here. She grabbed her coat and slipped out without explanation just as the game began.

The rashy feeling hadn't entirely abated by the time she knocked on Devin's door. When he opened the door, the sight of him sent a flush of tears to her eyes, a momentary surge, gone just as quickly, but he must have noticed it because he gave her a quizzical look.

"Just glad to see you," she said. Kevin was home, apparently no gun seminar this week, and so Devin joined her for a walk outside, crickets chirping, a breeze shaking the leaves above them like pom poms.

Devin held her hand, his thumb finding its way to the engagement ring, giving it a little twirl.

"My mom thinks we should get married like next week," Devin said with a laugh.

This made her stomach squeeze. She tried to cover it over with a good-humored reply. "Well, my sister already made like ten Pinterest boards devoted to our wedding and put up a poll on her website about blush vs. bashful."

"Blush versus bashful?" he said.

"You know, like Steel Magnolias?"

"Yeah, I am a man. So no."

She gave him an eye roll and a half-laugh and along they strolled, hand in hand. Easy enough, comfortable, really.

"My mom isn't totally crazy, you know," he said. "I'd marry you next week if you wanted." He wasn't trembling with sincerity. There was a wryness in his tone. But it wasn't exactly a throw-away comment either.

She felt her throat close off, alarm clutching at her chest, the FHE feeling doubled. Next week shouldn't be a problem, and yet her reluctance seemed to tell her it was.

"I think maybe a little more planning than next week would be ideal for me," she said trying to match his wryness. After another moment she let go of his hand and took his arm instead, her palms grown irredeemably sweaty.

Chapter 19

The news of Heather's engagement might have stirred Nedra's feelings. Was it too soon? Was it a great relief? She could have gone back and forth, weighing it all out with the sort of worry that was in its own way a satisfying maternal activity. But it turned out that the weekend Devin proposed, Nedra didn't have emotion to spare. Her thoughts were fixated firmly on another child.

If you asked her, Nedra thought it was far too easy to say someone was gay. He likes pocket squares, or he knows how to julienne vegetables, or he has so many male friends, or doesn't it seem suspicious that he has no male friends? And if you started protesting, well then wasn't that the greatest evidence of all?

Besides which, what did it mean to be gay anyway? People out in the world acted like it was some sort of condition that you had no control over. If you asked Heather, she'd say being gay was like being tall, nothing you could do to stop it save a lifetime of malnutrition. But Nedra didn't think so. People made choices! Sex outside marriage was a choice. People liked to act like celibacy was some great tragedy, but it wasn't. Look at Barbara. She'd been divorced for twenty years and celibate all the while, as any unmarried Mormon was obligated to be, and were people organizing protest marches for her? What if Heather never got married? Or Aaron? Or Caroline? They'd abstain during this lifetime. That was what you did. Did having an attraction to people of the same sex make singledom sadder or more eternal? Nedra didn't think so. If anything, maybe it made a single life more straightforward. You could put away the effort of romantic pursuit and focus, undistracted, on service. What a gift that could be, actually. Maybe that was a stretch, but still, this life was a test, with many mysteries and much confounding sorrow only to be resolved in the world to come. You turned to Christ for succor and support and did your best, whatever came your way.

But despite these protests within herself, she still went searching for clues in Brian's history and personality. And it didn't matter that she sparked with arguments about choices and gifts and trials, all backbone and admonition; she still rummaged with a flinching heartsickness, a *please don't let this be*.

There were all those girls who had been "just friends," hanging around for years before they drifted away, no tears on Brian's part. There were those intense friendships with teammates and roommates. The boy from freshman year. The other boy from his first apartment after college. There were his blue periods, the sad slog after his mission that she had always attributed to a come-down from the high of full-time service, but which may have been more than that; the lows that had accompanied his move to L.A.; and why had he moved so far away anyway? There was Brian's at-long-last choice of a woman like Danica, their clear lack of physical chemistry. But most of all, there was Brian's reserve, arrived at all at once during puberty, her sweet and darling chatterbox boy's voice dropping and then almost dropping out. Eventually, she'd come to think of it as a maturity, a caution that bespoke thoughtfulness, wisdom even. But maybe it had never been anything as innocuous as reserve, maybe it had been a frightened retreat, lonely and ashamed. And this plucked at her, made the strings of her sing out with ache. Because what that would mean was that Brian had not trusted her, had never trusted her and did not trust her still. That Brian, her precious oldest son had been hiding from her. She could cry, just thinking of it.

Did she know? But no! Wasn't that exactly what she'd been trying to say to herself, that it wasn't fair to project all this?

When Doug found her late Saturday evening, sitting hunched over her computer at the kitchen table, she turned the laptop to him and wordlessly showed him Holly Rasmussen's post.

He raised his eyebrows, a look of surprise that quickly shaded into something closer to disdain. Disdain that she couldn't help but feel extended to her. A little *see what you've brought to our family?* But Doug certainly didn't say anything of the sort. What he said with a shake of his head was, "Ignore her. What's the word the kids use? Unfollow her. There's no reason to ever read or listen to another word she says. She's gone. Out of our lives. Just cut it off."

Nedra wanted to say, *but what about the post, what about Brian?* But the set of Doug's jaw stopped her.

"She's still going to be on the ballot," Nedra finally said, her voice meek.

Doug frowned and his eyes locked onto hers with all the force of his full attention. "That doesn't matter. No one is voting for her. Forget about her."

It was a cold chastisement, no room for further engagement. She closed the laptop.

Nedra's mind was still lurching with thoughts of Brian on Sunday morning as she diced onions and chopped off carrot tops, peeled potatoes and minced herbs—prep for a roast and vegetables that would cook in the oven on low during the three hour block of church. But even though she was a well-practiced hand at all of it, the vegetable peeler flew just so as she swiped at a crooked carrot, shirring off a long strip of skin along the side of her index finger.

"Golly frickin' aaah!" she exclaimed, dropping the tool and the vegetable, clamping down on her bleeding finger. She ran the covered finger under cold water, and not until a good minute later did she finally dare to peek. A dead ribbon of white skin still attached at the base, plenty of blood, but not a deep cut; a bandage would be enough. What a ridiculous error. She was squeezing the whole thing with a wet paper towel, still stalled by the sting and the bleeding, when Doug walked in, chatting on his cellphone.

"Uh huh, sounds good," he said into his phone, all smiles. "Okay, we'll see you then. Good luck!"

Nedra gave him an inquiring look.

"That was Devin," Doug said, an unabashed thrill in his manner. "He's proposing to Heather tonight!" Doug gave her an excited run down. Devin had called to ask for Doug's blessing and then to inform them that he and Caroline had cooked up a little plan to bring Heather back to the house after the proposal for a family celebration, Devin's parents joining them for some cake, sparklers, and whatever else Caroline showed up with, all that evening around eight o'clock.

"Oh!" Nedra said, looking around the room warily.

"Don't worry, I'll help you tidy everything," Doug said.

"Okay," she said, and then she held up her bloody finger and retreated to the bathroom to collect herself. She had known this might be coming. But it was still exactly what she'd been worried about: thin-Heather latching on to the first man who came her way. Not that she felt certain Devin was the wrong match, just that it seemed fast. After all, Heather and Devin had been single all these years. Surely they could hold off a little longer. And yet the thought was momentary. Her mind was back to Brian before she knew it. She kept seeing him as a teenager, in his basketball jersey, hitting jump shots, in his suit at church, blessing the sacrament. How could she have failed that sweet boy?

In the car on the way to church Nedra spoke a stray thought aloud. "I don't know how this happened."

"Oh, come on! It's not that fast!" Doug said, with a breezy, dismissive shrug.

It took Nedra a moment to realize he was talking about Heather.

That evening Heather said yes to the proposal, and they all twirled around the backyard for photos, no mention of the Holly Rasmussen post, a smile on Nedra's face that betrayed nothing but delight.

In bed that night, after all the cleanup, and after prayers and scripture reading and just before turning off her lamp, Nedra turned to Doug.

"I really need to focus on my campaign!" she said, as if the thought had just occurred to her, as if this, the hour of pajamas, were the time to rally herself. But it felt somehow urgent to declare, to herself if not to him. She could see how worries about Brian and about Heather's wedding and her parents' house would overtake her. She could see how she would go along ignoring Holly Rasmussen and Len Hemmings and everything else, letting the election drift out there in the ether, as if it would all take care of itself. She couldn't let that happen.

"Okay," Doug said, seemingly amused by this outburst.

"I'm calling Heather to make some plans," Nedra said.

"Now?" Doug asked, amusement turning to disapproval.

"No, tomorrow."

"How about you give it a day? She might need a moment."

Doug, further relishing his role as the voice of reason. How irritating. Nedra exhaled loudly and flipped off her light.

"Fine," she said into her pillow.

Did Doug know or have his own suspicions about Brian? Was that why he'd been so stony in the face of Holly Rasmussen's post? Did Heather know? Maybe that was why Heather had been so interested in riling them all up with her gay ex-boyfriend.

Nedra considered airing every bit of this with Barbara on their walk the next morning, but she held back, waiting for Barbara to perhaps raise the subject. If her friend had seen the post, though, she said nothing of it. Their walk the next morning was all engagement chit chat.

Nedra thought of calling Heather to talk about it, but what did she want? For Heather to divulge a confidence if in fact Brian had shared one with her?

There was really only one person to talk to. It was an hour earlier in L.A., and so Nedra waited until 9 a.m. She was alone in the house, Doug long gone for work, and yet she took her cell phone to the piano room and closed the door behind her.

"Brian, sweetheart!" she said when he answered.

They exchanged hellos and surprised remarks on Heather's engagement.

"Not that I don't think Devin is great!" Nedra said.

"Why not get the show on the road, I guess," Brian said.

She told him about going through the basement, a few treasures she thought he'd want to see. Did he know his grandparents had saved every single letter he sent them while he was a missionary, all filed in perfect order? She promised to ship them to him ASAP. "You'll laugh. You were such a darling missionary," she said.

But then at last she came to the reason for her call. "Do you have a few more minutes?" she said. "I have something important I want to talk about."

"Uh oh," Brian said in a jokey voice. But then he adjusted to her serious tone. "Sure. I have a few minutes. What's up?"

What exactly was she going to say? "I've been worried about something," was what she finally stumbled out with. "I think I'm worried that I might have seemed too judgmental, and that maybe because of that you haven't always felt safe talking to me about things."

"Okay," he said warily.

She waited for a second. She exhaled slowly. "I guess I'm wondering if there's anything you want to talk about?"

"Uh . . ., not really?" Brian said with a half-laugh.

"Okay, sorry, I'm going to ask something that might upset you. I wonder if . . . have you ever had any feelings for people who . . . I guess I'm wondering if . . .," she was stumbling horribly. She couldn't find the words. She tried once more. She said the words quickly, "Do you know anyone who has ever struggled with same sex attraction?"

There, maybe it sounded like a campaign question, like she needed guidance on policy. Maybe he could hear it that way and wouldn't be offended. Maybe he would laugh. The whole thing some funny joke, his awkward mother trying to talk about gay people, ha ha.

But no laugh came through the phone. Instead, Brian replied with a crisp and icy exhalation, the mood utterly shifted.

Nedra couldn't abide the quiet, "I'm sorry," she said instantly. "I don't know what . . ."

Brian interrupted her. His voice wasn't exactly angry, but it was harsh enough, and she could hear the terrible tell-tale shake coming through the rigidly enforced evenness. "You know what, Mom? I don't want to talk about this," he said

"I'm sorry," she said again, but again Brian interrupted her.

"You don't need to apologize for anything," he said, but with the same strain, making it clear that her attempted conversation had deeply upset him. And then, suddenly, he said, "I think I'm going to go now."

"No, sweetheart, don't go," she said. She waited for him to say something else, but all she heard was the fuzz of the line.

"Brian, honey?" she said.

"Nope, this is over," he said sharply, abruptly. "Goodbye." And with that, he hung up.

Brian had broken the divorce news in person, Nedra's birthday weekend last year, Danica mysteriously absent. Nedra had been in the piano room alone, playing a Debussy Arabesque she knew from memory. Brian had come into the room and sat on the edge of the settee. She'd left off at the end of the phrase and looked at him meaningfully. She'd been waiting for an explanation since his solo arrival.

"We're getting a divorce," he'd said quietly.

She had imagined him saying this. She had practiced a speech for him. *You made eternal covenants. All relationships go through hard times.* Something along those lines. But then she'd looked at him, his pale cheeks shaking as he squeezed at his eyes, a preemptive move that didn't stop the fat droplets from spilling over his lower lids. Her grown son, crying. She came and sat next to him. She put her hand on top of his, and the words she'd planned felt misguided, doctrinaire. She just stayed on the settee with him, her hand on top of his, her shoulder leaning into his. He finally put his head on her shoulder and she wrapped her arms around him and held him. After a long minute they both wiped their eyes, and that was their conversation.

A tough moment, but one where they had come together.

Brian's hanging up on her felt like the opposite of that tenderness. It was like that awful PTA meeting with Holly Rasmussen's doppelgänger all those years ago, Nedra stunned and checking herself for injuries, wronged by someone else's outburst of feeling, and yet an ashamed sense that she too must somehow have erred, but how exactly? How could Brian have hung up on her like that! She was not some stranger, dialing him up to meddle. She was his mother. She had loved him his whole life!

Heather's Jerry. Married, quote unquote, with an adopted child, attending church but stripped of his temple blessings. She couldn't want that for her Brian. Heather and her ilk tried to pretend it was so easy. Just swap out a woman for a man, smile for the camera, and *voila*. But it didn't work like that. Family—a man, a woman, their progeny—that particular unit perhaps didn't matter that much to every faith, but that was the core of the Mormon gospel right there, the very point of eternity. Eternal procreation and eternal progression went hand in hand. Although Heavenly Mother didn't get discussed that much, Mormon doctrine held that She was every bit as essential to the creation of the souls of man as Heavenly Father. Gender was eternal. You progressed through the eternities together, a man, a woman, a family. A law couldn't change that.

Brian had told her nothing, and yet hadn't his response told her everything? The thought that he'd never confided in her! That he had been carrying this around for who knows how long and he had never trusted her enough to tell her! She would have held him, cried with him, tried to help him make sense of how he should move forward. Didn't he think he could trust her? Did he think she would ever have anything but love in her heart for him? She had half a mind to refuse his rebuff, to dial his number again immediately. But what if he didn't answer? How many times would she call? You faced this with children again and again, the limits of your control. Even at their smallest, you could pin them down and force them, but not without regret the very instant you clenched your teeth.

Finally, she broke down and did something she'd never done before. She called Barbara at school, during school hours. Of course she wouldn't be able to answer, but Nedra dialed anyway, listened to the ringing, and left a message. "Call me, will you? It's not an emergency, but I really need some advice."

Barbara must have checked her messages between classes. Within just a few minutes she called back.

"Is everything okay?" Barbara said, clear worry in her voice. Yes, Nedra supposed, it was indeed worrisome that she'd dialed her friend up during the school day.

"Yes, I'm okay," Nedra said. "It's just, well, something came up with Brian. He's having some personal issues. And I just panicked. I don't know what to do! I know he's not a kid like Shayna was when she was having trouble," Nedra said, referencing Barbara's daughter, who had been into much more than bleached hair and piercings in her long-ago wayward years. "But, well, maybe you could tell me again how you made it through that. I'm just a little at loose ends."

"Oh, Nedra, I'm so sorry he's having a hard time," Barbara said. Hearing Barbara's voice, which was still concerned but not longer anxious, Nedra knew she'd done right to call her friend and not her husband. "I'm sorry you're so worried about him. Listen, we'll talk all about it tonight or tomorrow morning. But just love 'em. And be there. That's all you can do. Is he okay?"

"I think he's pretty mad at me for meddling," Nedra said.

"Well, that's a tricky one. He's a grown-up, so you have to tread lightly. But you know, little gestures make a difference too."

Nedra sighed. "Yes, okay," she said.

"Okay dear, my time is up, but I'll call you back after school."

The line went quiet and Nedra returned to the lonely house, nothing but refrigerator buzz and air-conditioner blow, everything shallow, muted, woozy.

When the house phone rang later that afternoon, Nedra jumped for it, imagining it might be Brian.

"Sister Walker," said a chummy voice. "It's Len Hemmings. I hope I'm reaching you at a good time."

Nedra gave her body a little shake, trying to adjust. "Yes! Absolutely," she said with put-on good cheer.

"I just wanted to let you know I'm going to be at the Bountiful Rifle Club breakfast tomorrow. They haven't invited me to speak! I can't imagine they ever would," he chuckled. "But I'm a longtime member, so I just didn't want you to be surprised when you see me." The local clubs—The Lions, the Rotary, the Kiwanis—all had regular breakfast meetings, and they had all invited Nedra to make presentations, as had the Chamber of Commerce and the Bountiful Rifle Club. Not meet-the-candidate events with a whole line-up of speakers. Just her. She'd almost forgotten about the breakfast.

Maybe Len meant his remark about not being invited to speak as a bit of self-deprecation—very few of the Rifle Clubbers would consider voting for a Democrat, so what would be the point? But Nedra heard another undertone. Len Hemmings needed no presentation at all because he was one of them, their respected friend. She was the stranger, the courtesy invitation. She bristled.

Still, she said thank you, told him it was kind of him to call, told him she was looking forward to seeing him in the morning.

Despite her annoyance, Len Hemming's call at least served the purpose of momentarily nudging Nedra out of her spinning thoughts about Brian. She'd been planning to review the files she'd made on all the gun-related bills proposed to the legislature in the last session and to practice some brief remarks, but now she went even further, using her phone to record herself delivering her short speech. In the piano room, she recorded and re-recorded and read and highlighted until late in the evening when she heard Doug pull into the driveway.

She hadn't decided yet if she would say anything to Doug about her call with Brian. She went to the kitchen to greet him, half-gearing up and half-wincing at the thought of getting into it.

He bounced through the door.

"Hi," she said, kissing his cheek. "How was your day? Anything interesting?" After work he'd been at the Stake Center for an evening of Stake Presidency business.

"Interviews, interviews," he said, kissing her back and loosening his tie. "The Grangers' oldest kid is finally going on a mission. A little later than expected, but still good."

Late departures for missions were unusual. If young men failed to go on time, they usually failed to go at all, with who-knew what kind of unraveling from there.

"Oh, that's great," Nedra said. "His family must be so glad."

Doug opened the fridge and pulled out a Diet Coke.

"There's chicken enchilada casserole in the glass dish there," she said.

Doug closed the fridge, no casserole in hand. "I stopped and got a sandwich," he said. "Sorry. Hope you don't mind."

His buoyancy deterred her. Maybe he would be a counter-weight. Let him stay high, and perhaps he could lift her from the mess she was feeling?

"How was your day?" he finally asked her in return.

She answered without answering. "I've got my presentation to the Rifle Club in the morning. At Village Inn. 7:30."

"Pancakes for my lady! Do you want me to come?"

She wished he hadn't asked, that he had planned to attend all on his own, no prodding necessary.

"Oh, I don't think you should worry about it," she said.

"Are you sure?" he said.

She hesitated, then back-tracked. "Well, maybe you should come, at least long enough to take a picture so I can post it on Facebook. Though who even knows what good that online stuff does."

"I'll come," he said. "No problem. How much did they give you again?"

"Five hundred," she said.

"Have you ever even shot a gun?" he said with a laugh.

"One year at girls camp when I was Young Women's president. Brother Boylan came up with some rifles, and we shot clay pigeons." She paused for a moment. "It was very meaningful."

They both laughed.

"I'm not really sure who exactly is in this club," she said, "but Len Hemmings will apparently be there. Not speaking. Just as a member."

"Hm," Doug said with a slight frown.

Nedra waited for him to go on, but when he didn't she finally clapped her hands together and said, "Well, I have some more prep to do before tomorrow."

Doug nodded, and she returned to the piano room, closing the door behind herself. And without ever having really decided, it seemed clear to Nedra that the moment had passed for telling Doug, at least for now, about her conversation with Brian. Whatever was going on was between her and Brian alone.

In the morning when Nedra set out for her walk, birds sang at the edges of the cloudless pastel sky, everything fresh and delicately pink and yellow. She and Barbara pumped along for less than a block before Barbara said quietly, "So, Brian. Are you okay? Is he okay?"

"Oh, that," Nedra said, her voice equally quiet, a seeming hesitance in both of them to disturb the beauty of the morning. "I'm okay. He is . . . I don't know."

Barbara waited for Nedra to go on, and after another few steps Nedra finally said, "I think I'll get back to you on all of that. I just don't really know what to say yet."

On talk shows, people rushed to blurt their every feeling. In her life, Nedra found that much more often strong feelings made her want to refuse eye contact, to retreat inside, even with her husband, even with her best friend.

"Sure. You let me know," Barbara said.

Their feet and breath marked their togetherness for the rest of the walk, talk scant and marvelously unnecessary. Bless her friend.

Nedra dressed carefully after her shower, blue slacks, a lilac shell and cardigan that she knew flattered her. She and Doug drove separately, so he could go to work afterward and she could head home, but he trailed her the whole way, and they parked right next to each other in the Village Inn parking lot. They held hands as they crossed the asphalt to the restaurant's door.

A burly man with thick brown buzz-cut hair greeted them beside the hostess counter. "President Walker!" he said, shaking Doug's hand hardily. "And you must be Nedra," he said, turning to her and extending his hand with a much lighter grip. "Burt Glover," he said. "Very nice to meet you in person."

"This should be pretty straightforward," he went on, talking as much to Doug as to her. "Just a chance to say hello and for all of us to get to know you a little bit. We've got a table in the back, and folks are just filling up at the buffet. Come on back and I'll introduce you."

She and Doug followed him through the booths and four-tops, Doug placing a gentle hand on her lower back as they maneuvered. The club supposedly had more than a hundred members, but Nedra saw that at the long table there were only six or seven men, all retirement age. Who else had time to make it to a weekday breakfast, she supposed.

Burt Glover stopped just short of the assembled group and dropped his voice slightly. "Definitely nothing too serious today. We find the most important conversations usually happen when it's time for bills to actually be considered." He delivered this comment with an unsubtle, closed-lip smile, as if to make it clear that he believed their five hundred dollars had bought the Rifle Club her eternal agreement. A moment later he lit back up with a public-facing grin. "Here we are," he said, waving his arm at the assemblage of golf shirts.

Burt Glover hadn't said anything out and out for her to object to, and although she was most definitely put off by his chumminess with Doug, as if she were the tag-along, not Doug, she did her best to dismiss that too. After all, what other course was there really but to move along? She smoothed her expression and thanked Burt again for inviting her.

Len Hemmings wasn't at the table and Nedra glanced to the buffet and spotted him at a distance, scooping pineapple onto cottage cheese.

"Do you want to grab a plate?" Burt Glover asked her.

"Oh, no," she said. "We're fine. Thank you."

Doug took a seat at the table, nodding at a few faces he recognized at the table and around the room. Nedra glanced back to see how Len Hemmings was coming along, but before she found him her eyes landed elsewhere, and her heart lurched—at the

320

drink station a face she hadn't expected to see: Holly Rasmussen. Was she a member of the club? Or was she just there to harass Nedra?

Holly stood in profile, barrettes as usual, pressing a glass against the lever of the orange juice machine. Nedra shot her eyes around the dining room, looking for the children, but they were nowhere in sight. Glass at last full, Holly Rasmussen turned toward Nedra, and for a moment they locked eyes. Nedra felt a zap, but Holly Rasmussen, who had obviously known she would be seeing Nedra, showed no emotion at all. Her gaze slid right past, as if Nedra were a stranger. She picked up her plate and moved toward the long table, but at the last moment she didn't join the Rifle Club men. Instead, she turned and sat in a booth beside the table, alone, right in Nedra's line of sight but apart from the group.

Nedra looked to Doug—had he seen Holly Rasmussen?—but he was chatting away with a couple of the fellows at his end of the table and clearly hadn't noticed anything. She glanced back to Holly Rasmussen who was quietly pouring syrup over her plate of french toast. Without her children she seemed diminished, as if, rather than making her vulnerable, they formed a force field around her. She looked so normal. Limp hair, unfriendly face, but nothing truly remarkable about her. Still, Nedra wondered what her plan was. As harmless as she looked, her presence seemed vaguely threatening, the shadow of a stalker to it.

After another few moments Len Hemmings took his seat, another couple of men filled in the other seats around the table, and Burt Glover clapped his hands and began his welcome. He thanked everyone for coming and said it was his pleasure to introduce Nedra Walker, the Republican Candidate for Bountiful's Representative in the State Legislature. She would say a few brief words, and then they'd open it up for questions.

Nedra did her best to carry on as if Holly Rasmussen weren't a poltergeist in the corner. She said hello, what a pleasure to be there. Silverware clinked. The table quieted, but the chatter of the dining room around them stayed at full volume. They were blessed to live in a state where personal responsibility was a part of their way of life, Nedra said. Utah did a good job of making it so people didn't have to go through a whole rigamarole to enjoy their liberties related to gun ownership, but that worked in communities like Bountiful because of gun-owners like everyone at the table who regularly stepped up and did what was necessary with education and reasonable precautions to keep people and especially children safe. She hoped, if elected, to move forward with the same terrific balance. Aside from Doug, who watched her intently, everyone else at the table directed at least half their attention to their eggs. As she wrapped up, they offered light applause. Burt Glover jumped up again. Time for questions.

What did she think of the gun range up by the B? asked a man with wire-brush eyebrows and a walrus-fringe mustache.

She thought this was more a municipal issue than a state one, but in general she thought there might need to be some changes, both in relocation of the range and in zoning for future development. She'd be happy to talk with them more about it. No applause for her response there.

The next question came from a man with ruddy cheeks and a double chin, sporting the same style buzz cut as Burt Glover (the official haircut of the Rifle Club?) He wiped a napkin across his lips and said, "Given that Utah is an open carry state, do you think it makes sense to require permits for concealed weapons? Isn't that really just a permit to wear a jacket?" Light chuckles all around.

She took a breath and flicked her eyes to Len Hemmings. His face was lit with interest, his forkful of pancakes hovering in mid-air. This was why she had been reading all those bills. This was the moment she had known would come eventually. Issues like this were the reason she was running, weren't they? She tried to come alive with a sort of impassioned fervor, but couldn't quite muster it. She managed to stand up straight, but when she spoke her voice wavered with a hint of emotion, not at all what she wanted to hear.

"If I'm being honest," Nedra said, "I think we should probably be pushing the other way. I would likely be in favor of permits for both open carry and concealed weapons." She didn't sound bold. She sounded nervous. But there they had it. She knew this was likely heresy among this group, but she'd said what she believed.

The tinkling of silverware stopped, everyone at the table at last paying attention to her. She took in their expression, mostly bemused, with one or two men overtly frowning their displeasure. Burt Glover moseyed to her side.

"Well, I know you'll have some folks who'll want to follow up with you on that last one there!" he said to laughs.

He patted her on the back gingerly. "I think that ought to do it for today. Thank you again for taking the time to meet with us this morning." Then, more loudly, directing himself outward to the group, he said, "Everyone, let's have a hand for Ms. Walker."

He thoroughly buzzed the "z" in Ms., drawing it out comically, making a joke of it, a joke at her expense. No one called her

Ms. Walker. It was Sister Walker or Nedra, Mrs. Walker perhaps in a strained circumstance. She'd be Representative Walker if she won the election. She certainly hadn't asked to be called Ms. Walker. It seemed clear that the buzz of Ms. contained a barb of rebuke. Really, one comment about permits and they were going to treat her like a liberal kook? She looked to Doug, but he nodded back obliviously, as if he thought the moment had contained nothing.

Nedra had kept her attention away from Holly Rasmussen's booth for the entire duration of breakfast, a feat of self-control she applauded herself for, but at last she let her eyes dart in that direction. Holly Rasmussen didn't look away this time when their eyes locked. She arched her eyebrows, a look that Nedra knew could mean almost anything, but which seemed to Nedra to signal a moment of recognition passing between them. The two of them, women, both on the outskirts of this gathering in their own ways. Holly Rasmussen didn't look away, and it was Nedra who finally broke their connection when Doug rose from his seat.

A handful of the men at the table shook Doug's hand. Only Len Hemmings came around the table to shake Nedra's. Holly Rasmussen stayed immobile in her booth.

Burt Glover hovered at her side. "Let me walk you out," he said finally. At the door he shook her hand. "You know, we've always had a great relationship with our representative, and I'm sure if you're our gal we'll be able to keep that going." Another smile and another pat.

Our gal. It wouldn't have bothered Nedra coming from someone else, but from Burt Glover the words felt frosted with condescension.

Once they were safely in the parking lot Nedra turned to Doug. "Well, that was something," she said with a snap.

"I thought you did great," he said, not slowing his pace to their cars.

"Did you not notice?" she said.

"What?" Doug said. "I thought you spoke very well. And that was what, eight guys? Hon, I hate to be the one to break this to you, but you're winning this election with or without the gun club." He leaned in and kissed her quickly. "Listen, we'll talk more tonight. Sorry, I have to run. I've got a nine o'clock call." And just like that he was climbing into his car.

Displeased but unable to speak her displeasure, Nedra waved as Doug drove away, and just like that, whatever calm she had mustered in the restaurant scattered like startled birds. Really, Doug hadn't noticed anything amiss? Nedra's hands fished in her purse, pushing aside stupid receipts and old lipstick tubes and stray earrings in a search for keys. She fake swore under breath as she turned her hands through the mess. There, she had them. She turned the ignition, and barely looked before backing up. A loud horn honked, jolting her. Really? Had she just almost backed into another car? At the stop sign to leave the parking lot she banged the steering wheel with her palm.

What was it she'd said to Heather? She wasn't a feminist because she wasn't angry about anything? She pulled into traffic. *Nedra—lamb.* How timid she'd been in there, bleating for votes. How infuriating that she hadn't had the presence of mind to stride around, shaking everyone's hands. Was it really their fault for not respecting her if she didn't confidently stake her claim? And yet, hadn't she said what she believed? Wasn't that the moment when Burt Glover had decided to put her in her place? She wasn't paying attention yet again and tuned in just in time to slam the brakes, barely avoiding the bumper in front of her at a red light.

"Fuck."

She said the real word, not a substitute, the actual curse.

She could hardly believe it. She tried to breathe slowly. The ticking of her watch on her wrist sounded monstrously loud.

Not angry? Well, that was hardly something she could claim anymore, now could she?

Chapter 20

Heather avoided Ted and Linda for days. She claimed appointments that required her to drive herself to and from the office. She made sure not to be out and about in the neighborhood after work. She spent an evening watching a movie at Caroline's house while her sister edited and uploaded photos. She spent another evening over at Devin's apartment, helping him place ant traps in corners around the apartment to fight a sudden summer infestation. But finally, there was a morning when she strolled back across the street for carpool. It seemed to her that it would seem stranger if she didn't. That Linda might wonder. At least that's what she told herself.

They'd texted so Ted was expecting her. No surprise. But once they were seated in the car together and on their way he said, "I wasn't sure we'd be driving to work together anymore. But I'm glad we are."

Her heart surged.

"Oh, me too," she said.

The radio was back on as it had been on most of their drives, and for a few blocks they drove peaceably forward. But then she did something. She placed her hand on the console between them. Not palm up, asking for Ted's hand. But not in her lap either. People rested their hands on consoles in cars all the time. It didn't necessarily mean anything. And they drove on for another minute without this movement on her part altering anything. But then Ted did something too. At a stoplight he looked down at her hand. He looked up at her eyes. And then he took his hand and rested it very lightly on top of hers. She did not take her hand away.

He gave her a look of squinty-eyed inquiry, and all of her turned liquid with warmth and nerves. The light changed and he put both his hands on the wheel again. They listened to further news updates and said nothing. And then when they pulled into the parking lot at work, he reached over, took her hand, and brought it quickly to his lips, then just as quickly let it go and got out of the car.

They walked into the office and went their separate ways. Nothing. It was nothing. A gesture of affection. A recognition of their connection. Nothing more. Heather wasn't going to spend the whole day thinking about it, she told herself every time she found herself thinking about it.

Then at 4:30 that afternoon, just as the office began to clear out as government offices will do that time of day, Ted sent her an email.

"Can you come up to my office?"

She stared at the message for a full minute. And then she tucked in her chair and went up to his office. She carried a notebook, folder, and pen, as if they had a scheduled meeting. His office faced west, the shades drawn against the afternoon sun. He stood up from his desk when she appeared.

"Come in," he said in a friendly, carrying manner, a collegial voice for anyone and everyone to hear. She stepped inside, and he walked toward her and closed the door behind them.

And then there they were, standing two feet apart from each other. It was the first time they had had actual non-car privacy since the first day they'd kissed in the kitchen. Were they about to talk? Were they about to kiss? Heather knew she should want one and not the other, and yet what she wanted was lost in the thrum of heat. She felt her ears turn red. She felt her nostrils flare. All of it so animal.

Ted's jacket hung over the back of his desk chair, and he'd rolled up his shirt sleeves. Somehow the dark hair on his forearms was so intimate it arrested her.

He raised a hand to her cheek and rather than flinch she tilted her face into his palm. Oh, the feel of his hand on her face. Every bit of her tingled with life. And from there everything languid and slow-moving about his touch vanished. He pulled her close and kissed her feverishly, and she kissed him back, hesitant for one brief moment and then with energy that matched his exactly. He moved briskly to her neck. She took two steps backward toward the desk, and he followed her. She leaned her body back against the surface, a stretch that invited him to her, and he rushed into the opening, quickly kissing his way from her neck to the edge of her shirt.

He undid the top buttons of her shirt, and her skin goosebumped in the air-conditioning. He kissed her lips again and pushed his hand into her bra cup, cradling her breast. So there they were: all of a sudden across the line. She shuddered an exhalation. She could have said stop, no, stop, and part of her wanted to yell it, part of her felt sick with instant grief, but another part of her wanted to moan, wanted his hands to go much further, and so what she actually said was nothing. She gripped his shoulder, and he took off his glasses and kissed down her chest until his lips reached her nipple, and then he gently sucked and bit at it. She couldn't help it—she gasped at the pleasure of it. Nothing with Devin had ever felt this way. The surge of it all, the urgent low rush of hormones and energy and lust was almost obliterating.

But not entirely obliterating, and so she said in a hushed voice, "does your office door have a lock?"

Ted looked up at her with blurry eyes and whispered back, "no."

She shook her head, a quick panicked no, and then immediately hunched her shoulders and pulled her clothing back around her body.

Ted straightened up. He put his hand out to caress her cheek. "Let's go home," he said quietly. To his home? To hers? To their separate homes?

She felt so suddenly exposed now that they'd separated, and she reached up and put her hand behind his neck and pulled him down to her for another kiss. She meant for it to be quick, but then her mouth lingered, and she felt herself eager for him to keep covering her, for his body to enfold her. But she finally pulled away and straightened up. "Just give me a minute," she said, straightening her shirt, running her hands through her hair, wiping her fingers under her eyes.

"You're so beautiful," Ted said. "Come home with me. Come home with me right now."

But "home" came at her with a jab. "What about Linda?" Heather whispered.

So here she was, discussing the logistics of adultery.

"She's not home. She won't be home. She's with Hoover."

Heather looked at him not understanding, a clear further questioning on her face.

"She's putting him down this afternoon."

All the vigor rushed out of Heather's body at these words. So his wife would spend the day mourning their dog, and he would spend the day what? Frolicking with his mistress? And that was her? She was the mistress? This was not a story she wanted any part of.

"Ugh," she said aloud, quietly but with real drama. "I . . . I just . . .," she trailed off and plunked down on one of the office chairs. He came and sat in the chair opposite her.

"No, it's okay. I get it," he said. "Another day."

But this moment had happened because she was ignoring the future. She could not make *plans* for this to happen again. Calendar appointment: cheating, penciled in! She made another displeased vocalization.

Ted reached for her hand, and she gave it to him.

"There's something I have to say, something I've been wanting to say to you for a long time, Heather," Ted said, his voice tender yet urgent. "You don't have to marry him. Not just that, you don't have to do any of this," he waved his arm at the air, at the whole of the Salt Lake Valley. "There is such a big world out there. You have so much potential. Here everything is Mormon or not Mormon, but there are places where you could live your whole life without the word Mormon ever even coming up."

She took her hand from his and wiped her face. She wasn't crying yet, but she could feel a familiar tremble coming on.

"You should stop," she said.

"No, listen. I see you, and I hear your struggle, and I care about you, and I want you to know you don't have to have the same arguments over and over for the rest of your life. You don't have to be stuck here. There are a lot of people out there who aren't Devin and who aren't me."

He looked at her softly, casting himself in the role of sage advisor, gentle therapist, kind and wise, and she hated him for it. *People who aren't Devin and who aren't me?* It would have been one thing had he begged for her love, for her to sacrifice for him, but no, not that, instead he simply wanted her to waste herself on him and then go free into the wilderness. As if he knew, as if he could imagine what he was actually suggesting for her.

"It's very nice that you care about me," Heather said, with a quiet sarcastic edge.

He let out an exasperated exhalation, and that's when she began to actually cry.

But her tears didn't seem to bring out any comforting impulses in him. She felt him grow stony.

"I'm sorry," she said. And after a moment when he said nothing, she said. "I just . . . can't," gesturing her hand between the two of them.

He might have hugged her. He might even have kissed her again. But his shift in manner went from slightly cold to something else, all traces of the kindly therapist vanished.

"I suppose I knew you would say that eventually." He paused, and then spoke with a mocking edge. "The virgin bride must make her way to the altar."

It was the first truly distasteful thing he'd said to her, and her anger curdled into disgust.

"I mean, you're married," she said.

"My dear, what did you think this was? You've known I was married since the day we met." He said this with a treacly calm, as if he were kindly pointing out the flaws in a troubled patient's logic. It only further infuriated her.

"What did *you* think this was?" she said, firing the words back at him. "Don't you care that you're married?"

"I believe we're enjoying the moment," he said. "And Linda and I have been married for twenty-two years, and we understand each other perfectly. So if I were you I wouldn't be worrying about *my* marriage."

Enjoying the moment? The supposedly enlightened excuse of careless and revolting people everywhere. And what was he saying, that Linda *knew*? Or that if she didn't, she wouldn't care even if she did? It seemed untrue, and yet not entirely implausible, and it made Heather flare with anger.

"Maybe it doesn't matter to you, but it matters to me," Heather said, her cheeks shaking, tears rising in her eyes. How maddening it was that she couldn't even properly rage! That she always trembled like this, a rabbit when she felt like a bear.

"Oh yes, I can tell. Devin matters so much to you," Ted said sarcastically. "How about this? You call me in about five years when you can't handle the repression anymore."

She stood up, opened the door, and walked out of the room without a further look back at him. And then she walked as quickly as she could to the bathroom and locked herself in a stall where she cried as silently as she could, without much success.

Mid-tears she took out her phone and started a text.

"Fuck you, never talk to me again," she typed. But as she looked at it the words seemed so . . . exposed, dramatic, as if Ted deserved more emotion from her when in fact he deserved nothing. Perhaps she should start never talking to him again by just never talking to him again. She hit delete and instead wrote a text to her mother.

"Can you come pick me up at work?" she typed. "I really need you."

Her mother's reply was instant. "I'll cancel lessons. Be there in 20."

As dramatic a gesture as Heather could ever imagine. And one that she fully appreciated.

Chapter 21

Nedra pulled up right outside Heather's office. She rolled the windows down and hoped the shade would keep her from sweating for at least a few minutes. She could have scrolled through her phone while she waited, but instead she kept her eyes trained through the glass doors, alert for Heather. And then she saw her daughter, hurrying through the lobby. In a yellow pencil skirt and slim fitting white shirt she looked like she had dressed for good cheer, but her shoulders were tensed, and in her haste she wobbled in her heels and almost fell.

Nedra waved, and Heather lifted her hand in the barest of acknowledgements, as if the flutter of fingers were almost too much for her. The pinch of her face as she came through the doors and climbed into the car made it clear she was near tears.

"Hi, sweetheart," Nedra said carefully.

Heather arranged her face into a vast smile that quivered and fell a nanosecond later, her face flushing red, her eyes filling.

"What's going on?" Nedra said, reaching for her.

"Let's just go. Please. Just drive," Heather said urgently, shaking her head.

Nedra pulled out of the parking lot and onto North Temple, pretending she was not alarmed. "So are we going to my house or yours?" she said.

"Yours, please," Heather said.

"I'm going to take Legacy Highway, okay?" Nedra said. The new road swung out to the west, cutting up to Davis County through empty brush and salt marshland, past black asphalt bike trails and hopeful starts of new subdivisions, more mileage, less traffic, a view of sky and land far more soothing than the strip malls lining the exits of I-15 North.

Heather made no objections. They drove silently up to the I-215 interchange and from there out to the Legacy Highway, long quiet minutes that she hoped would help Heather settle a bit.

Once they hit the onramp, Nedra ventured in. "Okay, what's going on?"

Heather made a sound like a child, a shaky whimper. "I made a huge mistake," she said, chin quivering, cheeks instantly wet.

"Is this the carpool man?" Nedra said. If she were wrong Heather would snap at her, roll her eyes, dismiss her, but somehow she couldn't help but jump to him. She tried to keep the bite out of her voice, fearing that Heather would think the clip of anger was for her, when in fact it was all for him.

But instead of rebuke Heather dropped her head and nodded.

"Did he hurt you?" Nedra said, with alarm.

"No. I mean, he said awful things. But no. I just feel so stupid."

Nedra was quiet, waiting for Heather to go on. She was grateful for the car, the road, the forward movement and shared space, the windows to look out, the freedom and enclosure. You could have hard conversations in a car.

"I guess we had an affair?" Heather said. "No, we didn't! I mean, we didn't! I didn't sleep with him or anything. But we kissed, and some other things."

And *some other things?* Nedra knew that a screeching display of judgment would hardly serve her well, and yet how hard it was to tamp that down! How could Heather have been so foolish! Hadn't Nedra warned her of exactly this? And that man! Hate was not a healthy emotion, and yet how could you keep from hating the people who hurt your children?

"Did you end it?" Nedra asked in as straight-forward a tone as she could muster.

"Yes, it's over," Heather said evenly, mirroring Nedra's manner.

"Does Devin know?" Nedra asked, again maintaining calm.

"No," Heather said, starting to cry again, shaking and wiping her face.

"It's okay, sweetheart," Nedra said. "It's okay." She reached for Heather's arm. She squeezed. "Now listen to me. It's okay. Whatever happened, it's done. You ended it. It's done." She wasn't just saying it. This was important. Moving on, and fast.

Heather nodded, and then she dropped her face into her hands. "I'm such an idiot," she said.

Legacy Highway was sprinkled with stoplights, and when they pulled up to a red light, Nedra made a snap decision, turning abruptly left the second it turned green, off the highway and onto an empty road, nothing but barbed wire and a shed off in the distance with a few cows grazing the brush. Heather said nothing, apparently relinquishing all control to her mother for the moment. A little further down they came to a patch of silvery Russian olive trees alongside a wash, no rain for weeks now and the dry bottom nothing but white silt and tumbled rock. They pulled into the spartan shade of the trees, and the smell of dust and silage rushed into the car as Nedra lowered the windows.

"You're not an idiot, sweetheart. You made a bad choice. Sometimes that's how we learn."

Heather leveled a look at her, as if she were about to object to this mini-lecture, but Nedra watched the fight within her flag, and Heather finally nodded her acceptance and wiped at her runny eyeliner.

After a few more quiet moments, Nedra gently raised another question. "Honey, are you sure you want to marry Devin? I'm not saying that you shouldn't or that whatever happened has anything to do with whether or not you should marry Devin, I'm just asking."

Heather started crying again. "Yes!" she said. "I want to marry him! I do. It's just . . .," she trailed off.

Nedra waited for her to go on, and when she didn't, Nedra said, "Do you love him?"

"I don't know!" Heather's face flushed again. "I mean, yes! But what does that even mean? I've never been in love before so how do I know?"

"Have you prayed about it?" Nedra said.

"Not really, I mean, sort of," Heather said.

"What does that mean?"

"It means I've felt good about it, but I haven't had some big moment," Heather said.

"Well you might want that," Nedra said.

"It's just that . . ." Heather trailed off, turned her head toward the window, and then collected herself again. "It's just that this stupid thing," she twisted her hands in front of her face, conjuring and dismissing all at once, "happened because . . . I mean, it was about something. And I think it was because I'm afraid that Devin and I are going to get married and have three kids and then one day I'm going to wake up and have to tell him I just can't do this anymore." Heather's tremble returned. "I mean, like all of this. Like, nice Mormon woman, this whole thing. It just makes me crazy sometimes." She looked up at Nedra as if she expected a fierce scolding.

Ah, so here was the crux of it. It wasn't that Heather doubted Devin. It was that she doubted herself.

Nedra nodded and covered her own face with her hands for a moment, trying to gather her thoughts. She prayed a silent half-wisp of a prayer for guidance.

"Listen, sweetheart," Nedra said, taking Heather's hand and squeezing it. "It's not like that." She drew in a long breath. "I know you think I don't even know the word patriarchy, but I do."

Heather's eyes narrowed. Nedra went on. "But when you're married it's not like that anymore. It's not you versus some system. It's just you and your husband, one person, and it's the two of you, together, figuring things out. And you're not going to wake up one day a different person. Things don't just happen. You make decisions, and you're in charge of those decisions."

Heather looked at her with assessment, with surprise. Finally, her daughter nodded. "You think I should marry him, right?" she asked.

"I think you need to pray about it, for real. Not a sort of vague good feeling," Nedra said. "That's all that matters to me."

Heather chewed on this, as if testing it for satisfaction. Nedra knew it was not an emphatic endorsement, some *of course I do! We all love him!* But who cared if they loved him. They would, with time. What mattered, truly, was whether or not the Holy Ghost confirmed Heather's choice.

"I think I have to tell him," Heather said at last.

"No!" Nedra said sharply. "No, absolutely not." She tried to even her tone, but on this matter her feelings were utterly clear. "Listen to me, there is nothing good that is going to come of telling him. Maybe if you'd slept with that other man, but you didn't." She saw Heather recoil a tiny bit at the mention of physical intimacy, and Nedra rushed past it. "And it's over. You chose Devin. That's what matters. Talking about everything does not make it better." She could see Heather still not acquiescing.

"Listen," Nedra said again. "This is one of those things that may mean one thing to you and something very different to him. If you tell him . . . If you want to marry him . . ." She exhaled loudly and pushed her hands at the air, as if rattling a locked door. How exactly to say this? "If you tell him, he will not marry you," she finally pronounced.

She could see this offended Heather, riled up her noble, youthful sense of truth-telling. "If you have something to confess, that's between you and the bishop or you and the Lord," Nedra went on, trying to satisfy her. "You're not married to Devin yet. You haven't broken any covenants with him. What happened is about you. Not about him. Keep him out of it."

They sat quietly, Heather neither accepting nor debating Nedra's advice. Heather turned and stared out at the gravel along the roadside, the scraggle of weeds. Then at last, Heather nodded, a tiny gesture, almost missable, but there it was, agreement.

Nedra was surprised by the relief she felt. Apparently she was rooting for Devin after all.

"Don't tell Dad, okay?" Heather said.

"I won't. I promise." Nedra said, absolutely untroubled by this. If it wasn't Devin's business, it certainly wasn't Doug's.

"Do you think I could maybe move into Grandma and Grandpa's or something?" Heather said. "I don't want to be across the street from carpool anymore."

Nedra turned the car back on, and even though there was not a soul on the road she still flipped her blinker before pulling away from the shoulder. "I think that's a great idea," she said to Heather. "We can move your things this weekend, and you can stay at Grandma and Grandpa's or at our house till then. We'll tell Dad we're on an immediate campaign intensive, and then we'll say you're moving into Grandma and Grandpa's before the wedding to save money. Which you are. And besides, it's not good to have a house sitting empty."

They drove the last few miles home without another word. Nedra prayed silently, incomplete thoughts circling over and over—*please help her, and Brian, and me, and forgive us.*

Finally, they pulled into their own driveway.

"Don't tell Barbara either, okay?" Heather said, as Nedra turned off the engine.

"I won't," Nedra said.

Heather nodded. "Thanks, Mom," she said, tucking her chin, making it clear it was a thank you for more than just the promise to keep this from Barbara.

"I love you," Nedra said. "You're going to be okay. This is all okay."

"I don't want you to think I'm a different person," Heather said.

It felt like hitting her funny bone, too true for its own good. Hadn't she already been reorganizing her understanding of her daughter to include this new information? Hadn't she also already begun to think of Brian not as independent but troubled? It was like an answer to her prayer, a check for her judging impulses.

"I know you're not, sweetie. You're still you." Now it was Nedra's turn to tear up. "I know who you are, and who you've always been and who you will always be. And I will always love you." That was the sort of mother Nedra needed to be, and maybe she wasn't quite there, but she'd work to make it so.

"I love you too," Heather whispered, emotion choking her voice.

After another moment, Heather lifted her sleeve to wipe her dripping nose, and they both laughed and gently patted away the mascara beneath their eyes.

That night after Heather was in bed in her old childhood bedroom, a solid thought formed into sense for Nedra. Downstairs at the kitchen counter, she opened her website. There she was in her red suit, standing up on the Bountiful hillside. She looked so pink-cheeked and hopeful in that photo, taken next to Lakeview Cemetery before her father was buried there, taken back when she thought the campaign would be fun and easy.

She logged in to the site, just the way Heather had shown her, little boxes and frames appearing around the words and images. Back when she'd written up her copy for the site she'd used the Utah State Republican Party Platform as a guide. She'd tweaked one of the party lines—"We recognize the traditional family as the fundamental unit of society" to sound a little bit more colloquial. Her own homepage said, "I believe the traditional family is the heart of a good society." She clicked on the sentence now, and brought the cursor to the word "traditional." Slowly, deliberately, she hit delete, delete, delete, erasing the word. I believe the family is the heart of a good society.

Who but her would notice the removal of "traditional"? Would Brian see it? Would Heather? She didn't plan to flag it for them. And what did she really mean, erasing the word? Certainly not a doubt about the divine institution of fathers, mothers, children, families, together forever. Certainly not that. So what was she erasing it for? She wasn't sure. She didn't know. But it felt like a gesture, a moment as tiny as wiping a child's face clean or matching a pair of socks out of the laundry, like all the million things she had done over the years for her family that no one remembered or maybe even noticed in the first place. Some people would say all those moments were pointless. But they mattered to her. This mattered to her. What else was love but an accumulation of gestures?

Chapter 22

Heather got into her bed without praying or reading her scriptures, and no matter how still she lay, there was no sleep to be had, her brain replaying the awful scene in Ted's office over and over. She could feign blamelessness, but she'd gone through the door and kissed him and invited every bit of it. If Devin was right and she was looking for an out she'd found a swift and vicious one. Just follow this through to its end, and there was all the destruction she could hope for.

Follow your heart! How she hated that supposed little nugget of wisdom. As if hearts gave clear directives. As if you should listen to erratic pulsing. What you got, if you listened to craven emotional compulsions, was all the Cheetos powder from the bottom of the bag and lunch time make-out sessions in the car with your old man neighbor. What you got was worse than that. It was betrayal, self-loathing, and wispy thoughts of never again that made you hate yourself all the more for how fraudulent you knew they were.

But still: Choices. You *could* make choices. And some clearly led to better outcomes than others, even if they didn't beckon to you in the moment. Choices that left you with dignity.

Choices that led somewhere better. What did she really want? A family. A life.

She pushed her face into her pillow and pretended to scream.

At last she opened her laptop and pulled up DinnerForEight. She clicked back and back until she came to the engagement post. Caroline had taken great pictures and edited them all into a state of relaxed perfection. Heather and Devin exchanging smiles, a close-up of her ring with a Caroline-provided bouquet of peonies in hand, a final photo with the glow of a sparkler brightening Devin's freckled face as he looked at Heather adoringly.

She scrolled and scrolled. Birthday parties, holiday parties, color-themed parties, breakfast parties. Eventually, Heather came to a mountain picnic post, Caroline in a green flannel shirt, a blue knit cap perfectly styled over her long honey waves. In one of the photos she sat on a boulder at the top of Mount Timpanogos, sipping hot soup from the cup of a Stanley Thermos. In the next one she stood facing away from the camera, her arms out as if she were embracing the world. You looked at the photo and wanted to be there. You looked at the photo and wanted to be her.

Heather knew it was just a picture, not the truth about Caroline, not the truth about how she'd feel if she were sitting in the exact same spot. And yet it felt like the mountains were calling to her. In the morning she called in sick, and then she took herself for a long, quiet hike.

Emigration Canyon—this was the route the pioneers took into the valley. There were no towering trees here, just scrub oaks, close in, dense, a forest that made you duck. The pioneers had averaged twenty miles a day before they hit the scrub oaks of the Wasatch Mountains, and then they slowed to a mile a day, fighting through thickets of branches before breaking free into the valley.

Sick with the fatigue of a sleepless night, Heather tried to focus on any other sensation as she walked along the trail. The sudden cool or shade patches, the dusty, barely-touched-by-green scent of life on a sunny day in the mountains of the west, the snapping grasshoppers, the chirping birds, the rustling leaves above.

At a crest in the trail she veered off the path, through the scrub oak, not to a clearing but to a closed-in spot in the trees, protected, away from view. She knelt down in the dust.

Not the temple, but good enough.

She prayed, moving her lips to pronounce the words.

How sorry she was. What foolish mistakes she'd made. She needed forgiveness. She needed help. She needed guidance. She hadn't prayed about it before and she should have—was Devin the right choice for her? Was she the right choice for him?

She covered her face with her hands.

There was not even the slightest hint of breeze to riffle her hair here under the trees, just still, dry air.

She waited.

Heather did not have a vision. She did not see her future children, lined up hand in hand between her and Devin. She did not see the temple altar, his form kneeling across from her for the temple sealing. But she began to feel a familiar warmth in her chest beneath her ribs, a wave of it, and then more and more, a warmth that overtook her, that tingled up to her face and down into her arms.

She was overcome with a flush of sobbing tears, a sort of throbbing relief, her heart truly burning, a slow and steady reassurance, a peace that settled into her, that spoke wordlessly and softened her fears. Yes, she thought. Devin is the right choice. The warmth in her heart reasserted itself.

What you could never fully explain to a non-Mormon was that it was more than family, more than community that kept you in the faith. Those were easy things to understand. But there was something much more private. A testimony was what Mormons always called it, but what it really was was a majesty of feeling. Heather had been experiencing it her whole life.

If you grew up Mormon, you started praying for a testimony when you were a little kid, and the feeling of it came to you again and again whenever you asked, a burning in your bosom, a joyous prickle in your limbs. Heather knew there were myriad explanations. Stimulus and response, priming, cultural expectation, on and on, arguments you could use to explain it away. But all those explanations didn't change the feeling. And as you grew up, another feeling added itself to the joyous prickle. A quieter sense of reassurance, a pure unembarrassed reverence you experienced at certain moments alone or in the company of your fellow believers. As annoying as you found them sometimes, they were the ones who knew this feeling too.

It was the very feeling Heather had as she rose from her knees and returned to the view on the mountainside, the entire valley spread out below, a clear view from peak to peak. The serenity was all the more powerful because of the effort of the climb.

And wasn't that just it? Mormonism was not without exertions. For Heather it was always going to come with arguments and irritation and repression and self-sacrifice, and yet for that feeling in your soul, that sense of goodness and truth vibrating around and through you—wasn't it worth it for that?

Put off the natural man. He's an enemy of God. She'd been doing it for years now. She could do it again in this new way. She could. She could. Could she? She thought she could.

She felt light-headed on the path back down the mountain, her skin tight with the salt of dried tears and sweat, all of her hollowed out but pure, the way she felt after a day of fasting.

Despite keeping her eyes on the trail, at a moment of steep descent one of her feet hit loose rock, and she slipped, thrusting an arm down to catch her fall but landing with a hard bump on her bottom anyway. Her impact sent up a cloud of dust and she breathed it in, the arid taste of Utah.

She could have gotten right back up, but she didn't. A white moth fluttered in the golden brush by the trailside. Everyone talked about how overjoyed the pioneers must have been to at last arrive in Zion. But Heather imagined that was probably only half-true. They were probably relieved to be done walking, starving, dying, but surely many of them looked out on the desert grassland and saw not abundance but desolation. This was the end of their journey?

Mormons always talked about the desert blossoming as a rose, and lo, the wonders of irrigation, but they had still dug every one of those ditches.

She wiped her stinging palm on her pants and raised it for inspection. Scratches down the whole thing with blooms of blood just below the surface, dirt ground into the skin. That seemed just about right. She finally set her other hand down and pushed herself back up.

Spiritual experiences could be so hard to hold on to. They happened inside you, and other things inside you—anxious thoughts, swells of shame—could crowd them out so quickly. Heather knew the time to act was now, before she could withdraw any further from that burning in her heart. She needed to see her bishop.

When Heather was young, she first encountered the concept of confession through movies, Catholic scenes of dark little booths with latches and screens, such marvelous apparatuses for contrition, and she'd been nothing but jealous. Wouldn't it be nice if Mormons confessed like that? Every little thing—I hit my brother, I lied about doing my homework, I wasn't really paying attention when I said my same-as-usual prayers last night—you could just go to a priest, express your sorrow, do a little penance (which somehow involved beads? Yet another bit of paraphernalia to admire) and *voila*, a priest clears you.

For Mormons, it was up to you alone to avail yourself of the atonement, to decide if you had been sorry enough, if you had truly left your sin behind, if you had made amends as best you could, if you had properly appealed to the Lord. No booth. No priest. As a child Heather had always fretted about sins slipping through the cracks, imagining that she would reach Judgment Day and find herself barred from glory for failing to repent for incidents she had entirely forgotten about.

But now, for the first time in her life, her sins weren't her own to absolve. Not much in Mormonism got you there, but sexual sin did. For that, you had to confess to the bishop.

She felt dread but also an odd subdued giddiness, like a person climbing a ladder toward a terrible high dive.

In a singles ward, the bishop and his counselors were shipped in from family wards, a panel of married men overseeing the whole operation rather than a panel of singles scanning the congregation for their future eternal companions from their positions of ecclesiastical authority. But the Executive Assistant, the one who set up all the appointments for the bishopric, that particular calling was always filled by a member of the singles ward, and the current Executive Assistant in Heather's ward was one Kevin Reese, roommate of Devin McIntyre.

He was on a gun trip at the moment, a hotel ballroom in Tucson, if Heather had it right. She wasn't sure, but she knew enough to know that he was out of town so that when she called, Kevin would not say "Heather, to what do I owe this pleasure?" within Devin's hearing.

She could have needed an appointment for anything. To talk about her calling, to talk about her upcoming wedding and secure the required paperwork, even to talk about her job. People met with the bishop for all sorts of things. But then there was the other obvious though never-to-be-spoken-of possibility: confession.

She left Kevin a voicemail. He called her back, his tone utterly professional, to say the bishop had a free appointment the very next evening. That worked for her. End of conversation.

Bishops came in all types, but her current bishop was a thin rubber band of a man, elongated and energetic, a balding, bespectacled lawyer and father of four. He bounced around the church building, shaking hands every time there was the least reason to stop. In one three-hour session of church, if you happened to be in the hallway at just the right moments, you might shake his hand two or three times. He seemed not to keep track.

There were always cars in the church parking lot, and the night of her confession was no exception. Multiple wards used the same building, and if her ward didn't have an activity that night, someone else's did. When she came through the doors she heard dribbling and the squeak of shoes from the gym, the soundtrack of light recreation to accompany her penitential walk.

The bishop's office door was open. As always he was dressed in a suit and tie. She'd put on a dress for the occasion herself. He saw her and rose from his desk in greeting.

"Sister Walker! I understand congratulations are in order!" he shook her hand vigorously. "I'm sorry I haven't had a chance to say anything to either of you yet. Very exciting news."

"Oh, thank you." Heather said.

"Come take a seat," he said. He closed the door behind them. "Have the two of you set a date yet? We need to get you in here for an interview to get your living ordinances recommend squared away, I think."

"Yes, we do." Heather said.

"You need to take out your endowments in addition to the sealing, isn't that right?"

"Yes, I do," Heather said. This would have been a good moment for her to segue, but she found her voice failed her.

The bishop smiled and settled into his chair. He swiveled it back and forth a little, like a kid testing out an office chair for the first time. "So what brings you here tonight?" he said, suddenly serious.

She felt her cheeks begin to quiver. "There's something I need to take care of before I can go to the temple." Her voice thinned as she spoke.

The bishop nodded slowly and looked at her with kind but assessing eyes. When Heather didn't immediately speak again, he lowered his voice and asked, "Are we talking about a Law of Chastity issue?"

Heather nodded.

"Sex or oral sex?" he asked.

The words shocked her, but she supposed frankness was more reasonable than vague terminology. She supposed he wasn't the bishop of a singles ward for nothing.

"No," she said.

"Heavy petting?"

Was it heavy petting, or light petting? She had no interest in parsing the particularities. "Yes?" she said, but her voice arced up, as if it were a question.

The bishop raised his eyebrows at her.

"I guess I'd say light to medium petting?" Heather continued with the same uncertain tone. She had absolutely no desire to recount exact details. Nipple. Teeth. She cringed with shame. Just let this be done.

The bishop nodded and looked somberly at his desk for a moment. She braced for a humiliating further inquiry. But no, he returned his gaze to her, nodded slightly and moved on. That categorization was enough for him. Her heart clenched with gratitude.

"Well, it's June now," he said, "and I think as we work through the steps of repentance we may be able to get you to the temple by August or September, but I'm afraid that may not be possible for Devin. As someone who has made and broken temple covenants, there are some more significant repercussions for him, potentially. I think the two of you may need to come in and talk to me about this together if you're going to be able to move on."

She had been prepared for this, and yet it still felt like a dropping elevator. "I'm afraid Devin isn't involved," Heather said, wincing inside but trying to project calm.

The bishop grew very still. "I see," he finally said.

Did he? Did it matter that Ted was married? Did she have to say that? This was the moment she had truly feared.

"And the other individual involved?" the bishop asked.

"A co-worker." That was all she could bring herself to say. The sin was the same for her either way, wasn't it?

"The first step is to leave the sin far behind you," the bishop said. "Is this someone you see at work everyday?

"I don't have to. We don't really work together directly."

"Well, then, my counsel would be to spend as little time as possible together. In some ways this is much easier since it's not a relationship that you otherwise want to continue."

She nodded.

She waited for him to say dreaded words. That she'd need to tell Devin. That they'd need to reconcile this together. Instead, the Bishop reached wordlessly for a drawer and pulled out a sheet of paper, green, a pre-made hand-out, all ready to go. "Here is a list of scriptures I want you to read and think about," he said as he handed it to her. "And I think we should meet every week or so for the next few weeks, just to make sure you are headed in the right direction, and to talk about these scriptures and the atonement and what you need to do to move on from this."

She nodded again. And then that seemed to be the end of it. He rose and came around the desk to shake her hand, no jollity this time but no unkindness either. She had imagined it would take longer, that something involving such shame would take more than eight minutes.

She shook his hand in return. He opened the door for her, a gentlemanliness in the gesture. She nodded and stepped into the basketball noise of the hallway. Did the same team still have the ball? How many points could possibly have been scored while she was inside? She walked quickly, hoping that if she knew any of the players now was not the time for their water break.

Outside the church, the sunset just turning yellow when she entered was now a salmon flame across the sky. The whole world glowed with a rosy hue, the grass greener, the scent of the roses and wood chips from the planting beds filling the air. The parking lot radiated captured heat, but you could feel the first evening cool in the gentle air above it. The stridulation of crickets echoed around her. A tingling numbness had overtaken her fingers and face in the bishop's office, but it began to dissipate now. It was a beautiful evening, as beautiful a summer evening as Utah ever gave you. She could hardly take it in.

Once she'd pushed past feelings of guilty just desserts, she had agreed with her mother. Devin didn't need to know. And yet she had feared the bishop would disagree. *You need to talk to Devin about this.* She'd imagined the words, braced for the words, but he hadn't said them. He hadn't said them! Relieved didn't capture the feeling. Happy? Not that either. Spared and almost blankly stunned was more like it. She stood in the parking lot with the pink of the sky lighting her skin and prayed—gratitude, penitence, a jumble of thoughts, but a prayer nonetheless.

She'd planned to head back home, to Bountiful, but instead she drove to Devin's apartment. The walk to his door felt meaningful, each step closer to her future. She knocked on his familiar door and it opened, the face from the DinnerForEight engagement photos appearing before her: smiling eyes, freckles, a swoop of sandy blonde hair.

"Hi!" she said with what must have seemed strange urgency.

"Hello yourself," he said. "Where have you been hiding?"

"Campaign emergency. My mom got a float approved for the Pioneer Day Parade in Bountiful, and she's like freaking out."

Not a lie. There was a float to work out. Nedra's mood regarding it was an embellishment, but fair enough.

"You are in luck, my dear!" Devin said, pulling her in for an embrace. "You are looking at a proud three-term member of the Fruit Heights Youth Council, and a bona fide Float Committee Specialist." He pantomimed a bow.

"Oh, if only I'd known!" she said.

They laughed.

"You want to go on a walk?" she said. "It's beautiful out here."

"Sure," he said. "You want a Diet Coke for the road?"

"Sure," she said, and she followed him into the apartment as he grabbed cold sodas from the fridge.

"You look fancy, by the way," he said, with an approving leer.

She looked down at the dress and almost said, *Oh, I had a church thing,* before she realized just how problematic that would be.

"Oh, this?" she said with a shrug.

"You can dress up for me anytime you want, doll!" he said.

"Doll?" she said.

"What? No? That doesn't work? Sweet cheeks?" he said.

She joke-scowled.

"Glamour butt?"

"Oh my gosh! No! Never! Can we just agree right now that there will never ever be a nickname with 'butt' in it?"

"Whatever you say, cutie buns."

"You're done!" she said. "Just get over here and give me my Diet Coke and let's get out of here."

He shrugged and smiled and she scowled again and then pulled him roughly out the door.

"So, floats," he said, as they began their stroll. "What are we talking here? Modern glitz and glamour? Covered wagon? Under the Sea?"

"Still in negotiations? Definitely not Mermaid themed. Caroline is coming over tomorrow night for a planning meeting. You want to come?"

"Family float planning? Oh, I'm in."

Salt Lake had once been a treeless desert, but here and now they walked past houses with vast trees arching over the streets, lush lawns, and flower beds sweetly scenting the night air.

Heather stopped Devin under the branches of a stately oak tree, thick branches stretched out over the sidewalk. She pulled him to her.

"Do you want to get married in September?" she said.

"September?" he said, eagerly. "Yeah, I say yes to September."

She kissed him and felt a deeply protective tenderness, a tug that hadn't been there before.

"Bountiful or Salt Lake Temple?" he said.

"Bountiful," she said. It felt like the right place for this, for them.

"I'll call tomorrow and make an appointment," he said with a happy jangle.

She kissed him again. Her heart ached with even more of that new, nurturing tenderness for him. As they interwove their fingers and walked down the sidewalk together into the darkening night, she didn't buzz with nerves or sniping worry. The calm from the mountainside quietly returned to her. There was a line of green at the horizon, where the mountains met the sky.

Chapter 23

The 24th of July, Pioneer Day, was almost as big a holiday in Utah as the 4th of July. Bigger, in some ways. There were parades, rodeos, picnics, and fireworks—repeats of Independence Day— but there was also a particularity to Pioneer Day that made it special. While a few people in Utah had family members who'd fought in the Revolutionary War, almost everyone had an ancestor who had crossed the plains. For weeks, talks and lessons at church overflowed with tales of pioneer hardship. At the festivals in parks around Utah on Pioneer Day you got the same carnival rides and bounce houses you got on the 4th of July, but you also got hatchet-throwing stations and log-sawing competitions. Dutch ovens came out for open fire cooking, too, and nothing beat Dutch oven cobbler.

This year, the Nedra Walker Campaign would be floating in the Bountiful Handcart Days Parade, which took place every year on the evening of the 23rd so as not to conflict with the Days of '47 Parade in Salt Lake the next morning. People lined the sides of Bountiful's Main Street with folding camp chairs, claiming places hours and hours before the parade began. Kids with faces pink from heat and play ran along the mow strip with balloons tied to their wrists and melted popsicle dripping from their chins. Parents and grandparents drank giant Big Gulps in the shade, the cups sweaty with icy condensation. Everyone carried buckets or bags with them to collect the massive amounts of candy that would be hurled their way.

Nedra's float would need work, a top-to-bottom vision, and she'd called a meeting. Caroline, Heather, and Devin occupied the floor of the family room, flipping pages in a 1970s photo album. Nedra sat on the couch, scrolling through parade photos from previous Pioneer Days.

"This is the one I was thinking of!" Heather said, tapping a page of the photo album for Caroline and Devin and then lifting it to show her mother.

Nedra took the album onto her lap. It was a photo of her, Brian, and Audrey dressed up for the Bountiful Handcart Days parade, thirty-some years ago. Audrey was about two, in Nedra's arms, wearing a pink pioneer sunbonnet and a pink and white gingham dress with an eyelet apron. You could see a few wisps of her dark brown hair around her chubby face, curling out of the sides of her bonnet. Brian, age six or so, wore a fringed vest and little cowboy boots, with a floppy, homemade stove pipe hat on his head. Both of them were cartoon versions of pioneers, but then there she was, Young Nedra, wearing a plain graze-the-top-of-your-shoes blue dress, with long sleeves and buttons from the waist up to the neck, a simple white apron tied around her waist. Her long brown hair fell over her shoulders and down her back, *Charlie's Angels* not *Wagon Train*, but the look on her face more than made up for the anachronism of her hot roller curls. Long-ago Nedra was gazing straight into the camera, and she wasn't smiling one bit. With her chin tilted up and her jaw squared, she looked beautiful. Beautiful and defiant, like she'd already crossed half the country on foot and wasn't afraid of the rest.

"I forgot that picture even existed," Nedra said. Dressing up as a pioneer and marching in a parade every year—something Nedra had done throughout her own childhood and clearly carried into her own children's experience—never struck her as silly. It made her feel tough. And loyal. That look on her young face was exactly it.

"So are we going to dress up for this float or what?" Heather said.

"Ooh, I'm doing pioneer food on my blog that whole week. If you agree to wear a bonnet and stir some beans over a fire, I will totally owe you. Devin, you could be in the background like you're a frontier blacksmith or something."

"Thank you," Devin said with sarcasm. "That sounds terrific."

"No, I meant, should Mom dress up?" Heather said, ignoring her sister.

Nedra could have been put out by the way her daughters talked past her, as if she were hardly in the room, but instead she was struck by the sweetness of the two of them, skipping along excitedly together, of Devin there with them, an easy companion.

"No, I think she should look more official. Right, Mom?" Caroline said, throwing a stray rhetorical request for approval her way. "Like wearing a blazer, sitting up on the back of a convertible that's pulling the float. It has to be red, of course. The blazer and the convertible. So I guess we need to add that to the list—borrow a red convertible! I bet one of the dealerships would sponsor us. Also, we need to borrow some babies. Our float isn't going to be nearly cute enough without them. Maybe Barbara's grandkids!"

"For the record," Devin said, "babies on a float is a terrible idea. They fall off. Or cry. Both of which are bad."

"Yeah, okay," Caroline said, barely pausing. "Fine. Let's think music. We should put Aaron and a piano on our float. He should play 'Come, Come Ye Saints, but like a Joplin-y version, all jazzed up. Or maybe not jazzy 'Come, Come Ye Saints,' because maybe that's like blasphemous or something, but some other fun and old-timey stuff. Like 'Old Susannah' or whatever."

"I think it's "O Susannah," Heather said. "Not Old Susannah."

"Whatever! She's old too!" Caroline laughed.

They all laughed, and then there was a momentary lull.

"We have a temple date, by the way," Heather said into the silence.

Caroline socked Devin. "What! Don't be all coy about it!"

"September 13th," Devin said, with a bit of pleased puff to his chest

"I'm planning to do my endowments that morning," Heather said. "And then we'll do the sealing that afternoon." She shot a look over to Nedra, as if she were seeking motherly approval for this. For the date? For the endowment timing? For Devin? It seemed possible for everything, and Nedra nodded, granting whatever approval was necessary.

"September 13th! I can work with that!" Caroline said.

"Have you told your brothers yet?" Nedra asked. She tried to sound casual, but the question made her a hollow drum, awaiting the thump of an answer. Had Heather told Brian? That was what Nedra was getting at. They hadn't spoken since their terrible phone call. Nedra had been waiting, hoping he might call her, and considering the occasion to reach out to him if he didn't. If he was joining his sister at the temple that was a different calibration for Nedra's next approach than if he wasn't, couldn't, in fact, because he wasn't worthy to enter the temple.

"I haven't told them yet," Heather said.

Nedra tried to skirt away from her own emotions. "Well," she said, "Very exciting! And just let me say that you shouldn't let Caroline bully you into making everything pink."

Caroline gasped with mock-outrage.

"Didn't you know?" Devin answered sardonically. "Caroline's blog fans voted. It's too late now. Pink, pink, pink."

"It's called blush," Caroline said with a wink and a kissy face, as if she were an emoji made real.

In the end, Devin was remarkably helpful with float design. His older brother had a truck with a hitch they could borrow, and his parents had a flatbed trailer they used a few times a year for hauling fruit from the orchard, which they were happy to lend for the float as well. He also had suggestions for large scale papier-mache curing and the best purveyors of shiny metal float fringe. Nedra hugged him at the door before Heather walked him out to his car. He stooped to hug her back, a sweet caution to his embrace. So this was the future, taking shape. Nedra was warming to him day by day, and she felt a maternal tenderness tonight, sending him off.

It had only been a week or so since Heather had taken leave of her apartment. Mormons were loath to hire movers—loading moving trucks for members of the ward was a regular activity of any Elders Quorum—but Nedra had insisted. She had conjured a frightful scenario of Devin the helpful fiancé, arms loaded with boxes, confronted by the angry neighbor. Or Heather, or Doug, or her, or any of them, somehow cornered into a terrible face-off. Perhaps unlikely, perhaps a stretch of the imagination, and yet was this not one of the reasons Nedra had taught piano lessons all these years, so that when there was an indulgence she deemed necessary it could be carried out without hand wringing. She'd hired the movers. Heather's furniture, meager and post-collegiate assemblage that it was, was safely stored down on the west side of the freeway in one of those Self-Storage garages. Her clothes were safely hanging in the guest bedroom at the grandparents' house.

When Heather returned from the driveway, her chin red and her lips puffy, Nedra could have teased her but knew better. She offered her a soda instead. "I have a case of sparkling water in the garage. Orange flavored, I think?" Heather said sure, and Nedra went to get their drinks.

Nedra believed in drinking beverages in glasses, not out of cans, and she poured Heather's sparkling water over ice.

"I'm proud of you, Mom," Heather said, sitting down at the table with her.

Nedra felt the echo of earlier exchanges between them, but instead of the rough grit of friction, all she felt from her daughter now was affection.

"I think you're exactly the right kind of tough," Heather said. "You're going to be great at this."

"I have to win first!" Nedra said with a laugh that covered the bloom of feelings her daughter's words caused in her.

"You will," Heather said, and then she reached across the table for her mother's hand.

"We'll see," Nedra said, squeezing her daughter's hand back. "But I'll tell you what. Win or lose, I've realized I need to find new ways to serve. There are always going to be ways to serve." The warmth in her heart spread up and out and her eyes grew wet and she shook her head and laughed a bit.

Nedra had been biding her time since the Rifle Club breakfast, pondering what to say to Doug, but Heather's declaration, and her declaration to herself, stayed with her all evening, like a song she couldn't get out of her head.

Just as in her first conversation with Doug about the campaign, he and Nedra were again on their knees at their bedside that night when she found her moment to speak.

"I need to talk to you about the campaign," Nedra said.

He exhaled and gave her a wary and amused looked. "Yes," he said, drawing out the word.

"That's it, right there, that tone. That's what we need to talk about."

He took her hand. "Nedra," he said, clucking.

"No," she said. "I'm serious. Are you with me on this or aren't you? I get the feeling that you think my running for office is cute or something."

"I'm with you," he said, but still there was a batting to his eyelashes, a patronizing air, a sense of a sweet little back pat and a *let's be on our way*.

She rose smoothly from her knees onto the bed, trying to contain any air of flouncing or drama. He rose too and sat beside her.

She took his hand and looked squarely into his eyes. "Saying that is not enough. I know this election, me running for office, all of this, is not what you bargained for. This is not how things have worked between us before. But I want this, Doug. I really want this. And I need you to be with me."

At last he spoke as soberly as she did. "I know," he said. "You're right." He gripped her hand and raised it to his lips, his eyes firmly holding hers the whole time. "I'm with you," he said.

She felt the wonderfully familiar flip of nerves, her husband for all these years, the energy between them still enough to pull her taut. He ought to love her, and he did.

"Okay," she said. "Thank you." She intertwined her fingers with his and said no more.

In the end, the parade went exactly as the girls dreamed. Aaron plunking away with flair and fervor on an electric piano hooked up to a loudspeaker. Caroline and Heather, all pioneered up, throwing what must have been a thousand full-size candy bars. Full-size had been Heather's idea. "A full-size candy bar is memorable," she'd said. And if there was a family member to be believed about the power of candy, it was Heather. Nedra herself waved like a beauty queen from the back of the convertible that pulled their float, Doug sitting right there beside her. She had to admit it had been a delight, return waves and cheers all the way along Main Street.

Len Hemmings' Handcart Days float featured a real-life log cabin. "Build your own! Blueprints and supplies available at Hemmings Hardware!" read the sign on the back. He sat outside the log cabin on a bale of hay with an ax at his side, a sort of manly, pioneer armrest, as if he'd felled the trees for the cabin himself that very afternoon. He had a good dozen grandchildren at his feet waving and smiling in their caps and bonnets. None of them fell off his float, but he didn't have music, and what was more pioneer-y than a good tune?

Holly Rasmussen didn't appear at all, though Nedra imagined she saw her all along the parade route, only to have the blur in the distance resolve into someone else again and again.

Nedra left Brian voicemail messages, trying to spread them out so she wasn't too harassing, chatty recordings she lobbed into the silence. Finally, after a long sing-song-y message about the parade he called her back. They talked about the weather, his work, the campaign. She left the other topic alone, until at last she ventured the question.

"So, September 13th! Are you going to be able to make it to town for Heather's wedding?" This was a feint, a stand-in for the real question, which was not if he'd be in town, but if he would be present for the temple ceremony itself.

"Yeah, she sent me the date," Brian said genially enough. "I haven't booked tickets yet, but I'll definitely be there."

"Well, I will definitely save a seat beside me for you," Nedra said, hoping her reference to the temple ceremony was clear. Not a question, a declaration, but one that she hoped opened the possibility for declarations of his own, should Brian choose to make them.

He sighed, exasperation fraying the sound. "Sounds good," he said flatly.

Nedra changed the subject to campaign yard signs.

Whatever was there, Brian had been dealing with it for years and years. He didn't want to discuss it. Fair enough, she told herself. After all, what did she think, that there was some conversation that would clear it all up? As if confrontation led to transformation, as if collisions led to healing instead of injury. Maybe there were loud people in the world who did indeed experience such miracles, but Nedra knew Brian better. She knew herself better, and who was he if not her son?

But he'd be there, in the temple. He'd be there beside her. She would loop her arm through his. She would catch sight of the same tremble in his cheeks that she felt in hers. She would rest her head on his shoulder, and he would lean into her, a physical conversation clearer than anything they could say aloud. Together, they would share in the peace of that holy place. She would pray for him, for herself, for understanding and love. And that would be enough—at least for the time being it was all she knew how to do.

Chapter 24

At the bridal shower that Caroline artfully organized and vigorously photographed, Nedra presented Heather with a big square
box wrapped in brown paper and tied up with a white grosgrain
ribbon.

Some showers were all about lingerie, or blenders. Not this
one. Inside the box was a small powder blue bag from approxi-
mately 1962. The perfect temple bag.

Nothing said you couldn't cart your temple clothes around in
a gym bag, but most people didn't. The bags Mormons typically
used to ferry their temple clothes looked like 1950s carry-on
luggage, petite, the size of bowling bags or old school camera
cases. Once your eyes were opened, you could always spot a
temple bag, just as your eyes became trained to spot garment
lines beneath clothing. The best temple bags came from D.I.,
vintage vinyl or 70s floral. Thou shalt not covet, of course, but
you always admired a good temple bag.

"From me and Audrey," Nedra said.

Heather texted a photo of the bag to Devin. He wrote back
immediately. "I've got a zip up one-piece. We're going to look
so good together." A joke about an old-fashioned type of mens'

temple attire, a sort of celestial leisure suit favored by no one under the age of seventy, a joke that no one but a Mormon would appreciate. Heather felt an aching gladness at this simple exchange.

Heather had been meeting with her bishop every week, and at last he signed off on her temple recommend. Nedra took her to Beehive Clothing that same week, Heather with her new recommend in hand to show to the store clerk, packages of garments soon-to-be-worn handed to her from behind the desk. Heather picked out a temple dress as well. Not the wedding dress she'd wear for the reception and photos, but the dress she would wear for her endowment ceremony, the dress she would wear again and again every time she went to the temple for years to come: high collar, long straight sleeves with delicate buttons at the end, a placard of lace and buttons in the front, a dress she knew would never qualify as beautiful in the world, but which made her feel like a heavenly Jane Austen. She packed the dress and the garments and the rest of her temple attire neatly in her new bag.

Heather would have to go to the temple again and again before she'd remember every blessing, but that first time in the temple, in the initiatory as she put the garment on, the phrase that stayed with her was the blessing for the nose. Everything else was given a godly purpose. Your ears that you may hear the word of the Lord. Your eyes that you may discern between truth and error. But not the nose. The blessing was just *your nose that you may smell*. Which seemed to Heather a pronouncement on the beauty of the world, the worth of the senses. Simple, and yet so full of marvelous implication.

Even the largest of temple sealing rooms held only thirty people, and when the time for the ceremony came immediate family filled every seat. Caroline, unendowed, waited outside the temple doors, but here were her parents, Brian next to her mother, her arm tucked through his, Audrey and her husband Michael, Aaron, Devin's parents, and all the siblings and spouses she was meeting for the first time that day. Heather and Devin took their places kneeling at the altar in the center of the room. The mirrors on both sides of the room reflected the two of them times infinity, smaller and smaller until they disappeared.

Heather's back was to her parents, but their faces appeared right next to hers in the mirror. She met her mother's eyes. Nedra nodded, almost imperceptibly, and that gesture, so small, such a nothing, went on and on, everlasting in the reflection. How perfectly that nod captured her mother, how thoroughly it bucked Heather up. She returned the nod, with minimalism exactly matching Nedra's.

After the wedding, after the reception, after the thousand handshakes with cousins and second cousins and parents of piano students and neighbors and friends, a receiving line of hundreds, she and Devin packed themselves into a rented red Mustang—a joke and not a joke, their sports car getaway—and alone, together, married, they drove up and out of the valley, toward Park City, a fancy ski resort hotel room theirs for the weekend, cheap in the off-season, a two-day honeymoon all that Devin could manage away from medical school.

In the car, Heather felt the newness of garments all over her body, the curve of lace trim on her upper back and chest, the touch of the cap sleeves on her shoulders, the slight bunching of the garments' seams beneath her bra, the silky polyester on her thighs. All of it slightly alarming. Uncomfortable. Too much stimulus. Nerves firing with awareness that set off an almost panic in her. But no, she wouldn't notice it forever, she couldn't notice it forever, she would get used to it. She said it over and over like a mantra.

Devin's hand reached over the gear shift to rest on her thigh, an echo of many another touch, but different, because this was her husband and because her thigh was now covered in garments. A covenant forever.

The moon rose over the mountains and then disappeared again as they entered Parley's Pass, the rock blasted from the mountains to make room for the highway. But as the road rose and curved toward the summit, the moon returned, silver-lighting the two of them together. Even at the altar she had feared Devin would waver. Or that she would. But yes had been their word. She took his hand and raised it to her lips. She would get used to this forever.

Chapter 25

After the wedding, Nedra began walking out with the brigades of door-knockers that she and Heather had organized. Barbara had promised extra credit for any manner of electoral participation, and a whole crew of Civics students signed on to walk neighborhoods and deliver campaign materials. Nedra took turns with Barbara, Caroline, Heather, Devin, and Doug, each of them pairing up with other volunteers for door-step conversations. Nedra hadn't served a mission—far fewer women did back then—but she imagined this was what it felt like, girding up your loins and marching out the door to share your message. Even after hours of it she found not that her feet hurt but that her face did, her cheeks at the end of the day quivering from smile muscles strained by overuse.

She said the same lines over and over until they felt perfectly shaped, as consistently marked as a well-practiced musical phrase. *I just wanted to introduce myself. I'm Nedra Walker and I'm a Republican running to be your representative in the state legislature. I'd love to answer any questions you might have.* If they had no questions, she made sure to tell them she was all about better supporting families and making sure the values that the people of Bountiful stood for were represented in the state legislature. She never once used the word traditional.

She sent weekly email updates to all her children, with photos from the campaign and little snippets of memorable conversations. "Sister Meacham told me I looked so pretty I could be first lady. Heather did a very good job and waited until we were off her porch to have a fit about the obsession we have with women's looks instead of their brains. Ha!" Audrey and Aaron replied occasionally, Heather and Caroline even less frequently, but Brian wrote back every time. "You're doing great, Mom!" Little messages that felt like so much more.

By the end of September, yard signs for Len Hemmings appeared all over Bountiful.

"You know that the signs mean nothing," Barbara insisted when Nedra began to fret about them. "It just means Len Hemmings asked them to put them up and they didn't want to say no. They'll still vote for you."

Nedra thought about what she would have done if an acquaintance were running and had asked her to display a yard sign, and yes, Barbara was right: you put up the sign and then voted for whoever you wanted anyway, because why ruffle feathers and strain a relationship? A sign was not a promise. It was just a sign. With Barbara that very Saturday, she marched right up to a dozen doors with Len Hemmings yard signs out front and got not so much as one unfriendly answer. Everyone graciously took her materials and politely listened to her pitch. And granted, that was also what she would have done if she'd been planning to vote Len Hemmings, but still, it gave her hope.

Holly Rasmussen went silent on Facebook, her shot at Brian there at the top of her page every time Nedra checked, until she couldn't be bothered to check anymore.

A few weeks after Heather's wedding, the family gathered again, this time for General Conference. Not everyone, but a sizable assembly: Heather, Devin, Caroline, Aaron, his girlfriend Jennifer, and of course herself and Doug.

Every April and October the entirety of the church convened. Once upon a time this General Conference was a literal coming together, but nowadays it was talks from general authorities broadcast out to the body of the saints. Regular Sunday services were cancelled for the affair, but it was hardly a break from church.

As with everything in Mormonism, General Conference was its own significant time commitment. There was a two-hour Saturday morning session, a two-hour Saturday afternoon session, a two-hour Sunday morning session, a two-hour Sunday afternoon session, a two-hour women's meeting, a two-hour priesthood meeting. In sum, a marathon of gospel inspiration. Outside Utah, you watched General Conference via satellite broadcast at your local ward house, or on the internet. In Utah, you could watch General Conference on TV or listen to it on the radio thanks to the local church-owned CBS affiliate, your family sprawled around on the sofa or the floor, mostly paying attention, but sometimes lapsing in and out of sleep, a dreamy pleasure and ease to the entire experience.

Nedra always saved all her mending for General Conference, a basket of buttons to reattach and rips to repair while the Mormon Tabernacle Choir sang and the familiar voices of church leaders filled the house. General authorities served for decades, and their cadences were as familiar and as soothing as those of relatives. President Monson with his sing-songy lilt and rhyming poetry and boyhood stories. Boyd K. Packer with his sandpapery tones and doctrinal lectures.

The bright, clear October morning of Saturday conference she came downstairs to find Caroline snapping photos of flour spread just so on a cutting board, a pretty little bowl full of orange zest, a batch of dough rising in a wooden bowl with a rustic tea towel draped artfully over it.

"You're up early," Nedra said.

"Best light for baking," Caroline said.

"You're a hard worker," Nedra said, giving Caroline a squeeze.

Caroline pursed her lips and half rolled her eyes.

"Mom, I know everything thinks blogging is like a conceited teenage hobby or something, but listen, you know I make, like, a lot of money, right? I mean, that's relative, but like, this is a real thing. I made more than Aaron last year, FYI."

Nedra stiffened at the chastisement, but in truth this was news to her. Caroline made more than Aaron? She put her hands up, a pantomime of harmlessness. "I wasn't implying anything!" she said. "I was really truly just saying that I admire how hard you work."

Caroline shrugged but not without some lingering suspicion.

"I'm glad to hear you're doing well, though," said Nedra. Truly, she meant it. Flighty Caroline, serious about orange zest, and apparently making a fine living because of it. Who would have thought?

"Or should I say I'm glad to hear you're 'making some dough,' haha," Nedra said.

And again, Caroline rolled her eyes, but this time with a real smile. "That was terrible," she said.

"Wait, are those gluten-free?" Nedra whispered, as if Jennifer, the girlfriend, still asleep upstairs, might be listening at the doorway.

"She's back on wheat!" Caroline whispered back. "But off dairy. So I guess these are rude of me to make either way?"

By the time the orange rolls were out of the oven, the delicious smell of hot bread warming the entire house, the TV was on and Doug had lined up all his shoes for polishing; Caroline had a laptop open before her for photo editing; Nedra had a needle threaded and ready for action; Heather and Devin cuddled on the couch, Aaron and Jennifer took to the floor. They all bowed their heads for the televised opening prayer.

The session rolled pleasantly along, as lulling as gentle waves. They broke for lunch. They returned to the family room for the afternoon session.

When that was done, the boys got ready for the Priesthood Session. Although it could have been broadcast like the rest of the sessions, it never was. All the men always gathered together at the local Stake Center for a satellite viewing. Until this year. Perhaps as a concession to Ordain Women, perhaps as a simple step of further modernization, this General Conference the church had decided to start streaming Priesthood Session online. For the Walker men, however, the tradition stood: they would dress in suits and attend the session in the chapel down the road together, and then they'd go to Sizzler.

"So what are we doing tonight?" Caroline asked Heather and Nedra, the three of them lingering around the kitchen, Jennifer already off and about, meeting up with friends for the evening.

"I was thinking it might be interesting to watch the Priesthood Session," Heather said.

Nedra raised her eyebrows. Was this the beginning of some feminist rant?

"Interesting or boring," Caroline said.

Heather shrugged.

"Fine, but I'm going to paint my nails while we watch," Caroline said, as if agreeing to watch the Priesthood Session meant nothing to her.

"Fine. Not stinkier than Dad's shoe polish, so whatever," Heather said, as if she didn't care either way.

They both looked to Nedra, perhaps expecting some sort of veto. It was an odd feeling. How could more conference be a bad thing? And yet wasn't there the unsettling scent of rebellion in this? But what exactly was the objection? She felt a strange prickled ambivalence. And then at last she shrugged too.

"Fine," Nedra said.

They all shrugged once more as if they didn't care. And yet she could feel it, they cared so much.

Despite the tingling sense of illicit viewing and despite the Diet Coke half-drunk resting in the crook of the arm chair beside her, Nedra fell asleep shortly after the Priesthood Session began, but she drifted back into consciousness in time for the final talk by President Monson, his crooning voice coming to her as if she were still in a dream.

"Every one of us has been foreordained for some work as God's chosen servant," he lilted.

He meant the priesthood brethren, not her, and yet Nedra's ears perked up.

Foreordained. God's chosen servant.

"Always remember that people are looking to you for leadership and you are influencing the lives of individuals either for good or for bad," he said, his voice picking up energy.

Leadership. Influence.

"The greatest force in the world today is the power of God as it works through man."

Force. Power. He wasn't talking to her. She knew it. He said man. He meant man. But even so, Nedra felt the spirit in her chest, a sparkler fizzing and spitting.

The power of God as it works through man.

She was foreordained to be a mother. And probably a grandmother. She was also foreordained to be a pianist—what else was talent but a calling to serve?—but maybe she was foreordained for even more. Not a priesthood leader. She was not joining those marchers anytime soon. But a civic leader. *Maybe, maybe not*, said her father's voice in her head. But *yes*, said her own voice in her heart.

When Doug and the boys returned home late that evening, Nedra and the girls made no mention of their viewing. Maybe Heather would tell Devin later, but she had no plans to raise it with Doug. What was there to say after all?

A few weeks later, the people of Bountiful lined up in school gyms around town and waited their turn to enter curtained voting booths. Nedra walked with Barbara as usual that morning, and she taught piano lessons as usual that afternoon. She and Doug and Barbara and Caroline and Heather and Devin gathered at the house that night to wait for the phone call. A cake and sparklers at the ready. For celebration or consolation, either way, Heather and Caroline said.

And then the call came. Vera Smith's warbling voice.

"Hello, Representative Walker."

Foreordained? Nedra couldn't say, but she whooped with delight.

Acknowledgments

I owe my first debt of gratitude to Kristyn Keene Benton, who has supported me as a writer from the very beginning and who loved and shepherded this manuscript along from its very earliest days. Thank you times infinity for all the many, *many* versions of this novel you read and for all the work you put into this project. You are unfailingly generous, always insightful, and a true friend. I am forever grateful.

At BCC Press, my particular thanks go to Lori Forsyth for her thoughtful, generous, and detailed editing, to Michael Austin for his work pushing the book forward, and to Steve Evans for giving Bountiful a publishing home.

During the eight years I worked on this book, I went from having zero children to having three children. I was able to continue writing only because of the wonderful individuals who have cared for my children in that time: Christopher Ninman, Mimi Hayes, and Ashlyn Paige. Thank you to each of you for the talent, energy, creativity, and patience you brought to caring for the boys every day. I am immensely grateful for the role you have played in our lives.

In the early days of envisioning this book, I spoke with Utah legislators Carol Moss, Ronda Menlove and the late Becky Lockhart. I am grateful to each of them for graciously answering my many questions about the ins and outs of running political campaigns in Utah. Earlier versions of this novel also contained extensive historical material, and although those chapters no longer appear, I am thankful to the staff of This Is The Place Heritage Park for trudging through many feet of fresh snow in January 2013 to give me a special tour of the Deseret Hospital.

My heartfelt thanks go to the friends and family members who read all or part of various versions of the manuscript and offered thoughts along the way: Julia, Levi, and Larry Shumway, Alexia Green, Shira Ginsburg, Kristin Solomon, Jess Kimball Leslie, Kate Jackson, Helen Thomas, Lisa Fraser, Priya Patel, Esther Farkas, Sarah Cantin, Jennifer Pariseau, and in particular Melissa Inouye, who offered important critiques and vital encouragement and without whom this novel would be sitting in a drawer. Thank you!

Thank you also to the dear friends who nurture my spirit and who have encouraged this novel in myriad ways over many years, especially Tiger, Erika, Helen, Desiree, Jac, Simi, Shira, Kate, Sandra, Shola, Scill, Morgan and Nadia. You heard so much about the ups and downs of this book for so long. Thank you for listening and walking along beside me.

And finally and most importantly, all my love and thanks go to my husband Greg Starner for his enduring support of this project as well as the project of our lives.

CHARITY SHUMWAY is the author of the novel *Ten Girls to Watch*. She grew up in St. George, Salina, and Centerville, Utah and graduated from Viewmont High School in Bountiful. She now lives in New York with her husband and children.

Made in the USA
Monee, IL
09 March 2021